MW00788707

## Raves for *Deadly Trespass:* A Mystery in Maine #1

"...an environmental murder mystery, where the stakes are high and a vanishing world inspires violence." *Mystery Writers of America, national Helen McCloy award*

"...exceptional, jaw-dropping TALENT..." *Women's Fiction Writers Association Rising Star finalist*

"...a rare talent in indie literary fiction, delving into women's issues in a way that rings so true...reminiscent of good contemporary American authors such as Joy Williams, Joanna Scott, and Cheryl Strayed" *SPR*

"...will propel you across the wildest of Maine's terrain and into its coldest waters--in search of whispered wolves, possible murderers, odd bedfellows, greedy sons of bitches, and reasons for it all." *FAPA award winning author Meredith Marple*

"...a beautiful book that brilliantly captures the battle to conserve Maine's mythical woods..." *Ron Joseph, wildlife biologist and Down East Magazine author*

"When wolves show up in Maine's north woods, landowners and others launch a major, but secretive, effort to kill them. Neily's novel has already won literary awards and is getting rave reviews. Add my review to that list; she's had a lifelong passion for conservation and our native wildlife..." *The Maine Sportsman Magazine: reviewed by George Smith*

*Deadly Turn*
Copyright 2020 by Sandra Neily

All rights reserved. No part of this work may be reprinted without the written permission of the author, except for small passages for the purpose of promotion or review
   This is a work of fiction. While some Maine place names are real locations, some are fictionalized. All characters, businesses, and incidents are products of the author's imagination and are used in a fictitious manner. Any resemblance to actual persons, living or dead, or actual events is purely coincidental.

ISBN: 978-1-950381-52-4


Piscataqua Press
32 Daniel St., Portsmouth NH 03801
www.ppressbooks.com

Cover: Wind turbines by Aerial Photo NH

Printed in the United States


www.authorsandraneily.com

# DEADLY TURN

## A MYSTERY IN MAINE #2

## SANDRA NEILY

This story is dedicated to Dr. Julia Moukharskaya and the entire Harold Alfond Center for Cancer Care team … because they also honor all precious life.

# ONE

Alone on Eagle Ridge, I clutched a dying bat. Against all rabies advice, I pulled off my gloves to find the animal's heart and my bare thumb stroked a tiny throb. At the last limp spasm, the bat's eyes filmed over. My eyes blurred, too. Then I bent and smelled her, hoping she was female and we had something in common.

I liked to think I could smell leaves on animal sides, pond weeds on moose noses, and wind in bird feathers. It helped that I worked odd jobs for biologists who let me get close to wildlife that could no longer run from me. I liked to smell my way back into animals' lives. I wasn't sure about wind on the bat, but tiny insect bits crinkled against my nose when it touched her fur. They smelled like ancient parchment.

I closed my eyes and saw her. Almost as dark as the nig around her, she turned toward a flying moth, chirping as closed in on her meal. Cupping her tail into a shovel shape, scooped the moth from the air, bent herself over, and sh it up into her mouth. Before she could land and eat, she double again and fell, panting for breath, feebly beatir wings against bushes that held her.

I shifted the bat so it was cupped carefully in my thought the only thing we might have in common knowing what caused us to falter and fall.

Time to admit the obvious. Collecting dead bats at Maine wind-power sites and getting paid essentia for doing it was a doubly depressing situation. I ha a dead eagle, but if our weird September heat wa birds found thermal currents rising over the rid

1

one. My boss had already warned me. "Eagles hunt with their heads down and don't see the turning blades. Dead on the ground, they look like an axe murderer celebrated something." If I got emotional over a dead bat, I couldn't imagine what a meat-cleavered eagle might do to me.

Holding the bat's tiny body in both hands, I used my thumbs to smooth its webbed wings and I tried to close its eyes. They were already dry, staring at a strange, bright world. I squinted down the long line of towers topped by spinning blades—all shimmering in heat that would make Miami proud. Thick transmission wires, strung between massive poles, commanded the treeless ridge, sending electricity south, way out of Maine. Hundreds of miles away, people in Boston were probably plugging in too many fans and air conditioners.

I bent my head back until every shoulder tendon screamed for help. Tower Sixteen loomed over me like an alien spaceship. At least forty stories over my hard hat, curved blades, like flower petals on steroids, slowly whomp-whomped in the wind, but that was an optical illusion. Up where eagles hunted, the blades' manic speed shattered Daytona's speed records.

Up close, each tower looked as if it had crash-landed into a concrete landing pad, perched on a ridge sucked free of trees. A gear box about the size of my Subaru hung under the blades—enough machinery to land on earth and return to a faraway planet.

Even without morning sun, the L.L. Bean thermometer tipped to my pack read eighty-five—a perfect day to lean against a cold wall with my shirt pulled up. Thin and very used, wasn't much of a shirt, but it had sleeves. After age fifty, when the gym failed to discipline the Silly-Putty skin under my arms, I'd sworn off sleeveless apparel. If I could have managed

the heat wave working naked, I would have, but instead I sought out thrift store shirts and hacked off half of each sleeve.

I picked the nearest tower and, using my gate keys, slid inside, lifted my shirt with a free hand, and sagged against chilly metal. Machinery throbbed behind other doors I couldn't open. My teeth vibrated against each other while my chest cooled. I leaned my back into what I was sure was going to be the best moment of the day. The tower had a cold pulse, reminding me that I held a bat without one. My work day was on.

Slamming the door and looking for Pock, I saw where he'd lifted his leg to yellow the walls that had swallowed me up. His whole body wagging, he leaned up to sniff the bat, muzzled nose nudging my fingers. I shoved stray hairs back into my pony tail. With one animal lifeless and one rubbing up against me, I thought about poor life choices. Pock often made poor choices about porcupines and skunks, but he had me to bail him out. The bat, hungry for insects teasing the darkness before her, had chosen a deadly route and paid for it.

Soon after I'd quit my full-time job, I found I couldn't rely on returnable beer cans to fill my gas tank even though nearby ATV trails offered up a generous supply of Bud Light refuse. I'd sworn to take any job that freed me from airless rooms—any job that put me near wild creatures. Maybe I should have looked for something that was outdoors and lucrative at the same time.

Pock whined and tried a back flip off my leg. "Of course not. No bat for you. It's family. Animal family. And save the betrayed face. You even look like a bat when you sleep. Ears out like wings. Snaggle tooth over your lips." I pulled a plastic bag from my pocket, slid the bat into it, and leashed Pock. "Let's get to it."

———

Three weeks ago, on my first day collecting animal debris, Anita Stockdale had handed me a hard hat and pointed to the port-a-potty whose door said, *Ladies. Unless There Aren't Any.* "Bring your own toilet paper though. Whatever I leave in there vanishes overnight." Then she'd squinted at Pock. "You and I are hired to complete research that this company can take to regulators to make them happy. I'm thinking your dog might screw that up. If he's like other Labs, a good romp with a carcass is too tempting."

I'd strapped a wire muzzle over Pock's nose and mouth and I held up his favorite toy. "This will work, Anita. He'll fry if I leave him in the car."

Pock shoved the white plastic mooring buoy around on the ground, unable to sink his teeth into it. "You made your point," Anita said. "Premier Power & Energy doesn't care what goes on here if I hand in a report that counts dead animals the way they tell us to count them, which is corporate-ass silly: searching a tight box of terrain when the blades throw out death in a wide zone. I know that game."

When she reached down and rubbed Pock's belly, he soft-growled his ecstasy. "A dog might find more carcasses. Just don't let him chew on what he finds."

Although it felt like sweaty summer, we were three weeks into September's fall migration, when bats and birds were on the move and Eagle Ridge's towers offered them different kinds of death. To birds in the air—and humans far away—the blades probably had a dreamy white quality—like slow-motion Ferris wheels. Up close they were navigation hazards taller than any Maine building. Blade-sliced birds looked like a food processor had run amok as it sliced tomatoes. Crumpled bats looked like limp dolls without stuffing.

Holding the bat with one hand, I watched Anita stop and park her truck in a dust cloud. Grunting as she swung her pack of bottles, baggies, and tools onto her back and marched away toward Tower Fifteen, she was so thin her load looked like it walked itself down the road. Her long, blond braid bounced over her pack and slapped her rear end on each stride.

She stopped and turned toward me in the road. "Still alright with fingers in critter muck?"

I straightened my hard hat and gave her an enthusiastic thumbs up, the way I would for something chocolate.

"I don't know," she said. "I kinda expect you to bail on me when you figure out what's really going on. I mean, it's healthy air up here miles from your stinky legislature job. Now that's genuine mayhem. Money and how it gets spent is so messy. Here it's simple. Death and decay. I can cash my paycheck knowing what I signed on to do and it's still somehow about science and biology. I suspect you're living low and rough because you have to, but from what I know of your past work, you're not going to feel good being owned by these boys." She waved her hand to take in the line of towers. "And on that subject, if you want to keep camping over here to save on the commute, remind me to lend you a tent that doesn't leak."

She shifted her pack. "I think you've got the hang of how I want the GPS location data. How about today you number and flag specimens uphill. I'll head downhill. We'll meet up and drive down to lower towers at break time. Bring me some fresh ones. I need to complete some field necropsies."

"Hang on," I said, unleashing Pock, trotting after her and holding out the bat. "If a bat's so sensitive it can find and snag mosquitos from the air, why can't it miss a chunk of metal?" I removed the bat from the bag and held it toward her. "And I really don't understand. It looks fine, but it's dead."

When Anita dropped her pack and felt around her pockets, I thought I could avoid another biology lecture by stepping up. "I don't need a complete replay," I said. "I get the echo thing—bats send sounds that echo off what they hunt so they can find dinner—but this makes no sense."

"Echolocation's not involved here." Frowning at my naked hands, she pulled gloves from her pocket and snapped them over her fingers. Then she lifted a scalpel from a case tucked into her shirt pocket. The cut bat slurped open like over-ripe fruit, its innards a bright red blood bomb.

"At two hundred miles an hour, rotating blades change air pressure," Anita said. "The dropping pressure explodes blood vessels next to the bat's lungs and the lungs fill with blood. Bats drown in their own blood. Kind of like scuba divers getting the bends when they don't take time to equalize pressure as they surface. They say the pain is something else." She pressed the bat's chest back together, slipped it into a bag at her waist, sheathed her scalpel, and walked downhill.

We only collected and catalogued on days Premier Power & Energy decided were auspicious days. I guessed that gave coyotes, foxes, eagles, and other carnivores time to drag carcasses away and lower the body count. The limited schedule of collection days made Anita crave each daylight hour, so it was going to be a long day, and because our side of the ridge had been mowed into a wide road, it was going to be a long day without shade.

From somewhere beyond roads and concrete, the aroma of

decomposing leaves was like a rich casserole cooling on a faraway window. I thought I might move my tent even deeper into the woods at the end of my shift. I shoved the stick end of an orange flag into the bush where I'd found the bat, numbered it, and then searched a careful grid around Tower Sixteen. I didn't miss Pock until I needed him to sniff out thick brush beyond the road. Eagle Ridge's low growth had been sprayed with herbicides, but it grew back like thick, mutant landscaping. I counted on his wagging tail to advertise carcasses.

I yelled his favorite invitation—the one that signaled ice cream or burger grease on the grill. "Yip, Yip! Zip, Zip." I called and waited. Waited and called. If I hadn't been facing uphill, I might have missed his blurred shape speeding across the road above me. Of course my dog was up to no good up on Eagle Ridge. "Texas," I panted. "Could use Texas right about now. Or Oklahoma." On a flat plain, I could have dashed from tower to tower, maybe dodging cows, but in Maine's north woods we all have to go up, up, up.

I dropped my pack and hard hat, tightened the band holding my ponytail, and tried to jog up the road. Nothing had changed since the last time I'd asked my knees to challenge elevations. Since I'd turned fifty, they just complained.

Stopping where Pock's dusty prints left the road for the trees, I held my breath and strained to hear real world sounds. Up over the last rise of ridge, machine noise grew loud and ugly. I didn't hear the familiar whomp, whomp swishing noise. What I heard sounded like a car commercial where inferior models get crushed into walls, and metal pieces fly off to clang away on concrete floors.

Hands on knees, bending almost double to breathe, I hoped for some dog information. A bark. A howl. Partridges flushed from cover. Deer bounding away. Hopefully not a repeat of last spring's cowardly move when he'd brought me an angry mother moose, her nose inches from his fleeing butt. I'd climbed a tree. Pock had to run for it.

I heard only my hoarse rasp and the calls of chickadees hopping into the nearest tree. They were the forest's perky bird investigation squad, a winged gang that didn't feel threatened as they clustered toward activity that promised cheap entertainment. Even when the occasion was a remote dirt road, they always looked dressed up with black hats, throats like black bow ties, and tuxedo-grey coloring over their shoulders.

I heard Pock's muzzle scrape on gravel before I saw him. Wagging, he nudged a brown tree limb out onto the road. It flopped awkwardly from side to side, one narrow part attached to something that looked like a lump of trunk.

"Quit clowning around," I said standing up. "We're working here."

Yipping with delight, he shoved his find toward me. Too late I realized it was a limb, but not from a tree. It was an arm attached to a shoulder—a chunk of shoulder wearing tattered, bloody clothing that did nothing to hide stringy tendons wound around splintered bone.

I fainted.

# TWO

I came to with Pock whining and nudging my head into road gravel. Dirt packed my nose. I'd swallowed gritty motor oil and thrown up breakfast, leaving my right fingers in a pool of vomit. Pock wedged the tip of his tongue through his muzzle trying to lick up what he thought was yummy. What are good friends for? I wiggled toes and fingers, testing for pain before I tried to stand. Everything worked. Up the road the blades sounded like an accelerating road race where manic drivers grinded gears toward the finish line. Even the chickadees were gone.

I slowly pushed myself up onto my hands and knees, swaying from the effort.

"What the hell are you doing in the road? Yoga?" Anita yelled from below. "Get out of there. A blade's probably gone missing! Grab the dog. Come down! Patton? Patton! Move it! Now!"

I risked a glance at the severed limb. Seeing someone dismembered was strange and surreal. The sweatshirt looked like what my daughter wore on cold nights next to the woodstove. Even more than bloody tendons, the shirt marked the shoulder as human. It wasn't right to see a person that way—in pieces, like a large animal cut up for the freezer.

Blue and bruised, the upper arm was pruned up as though it had been too long in a bath. If a piece of human could ask a human question, the attached shoulder asked it. Clothed but bunched and hunched at an odd angle, it said what we all say with raised shoulders. What gives? What's the deal here? Someone going to explain this shit to me?

"Cassandra Patton Conover," Anita called. "You hear me? Come down. I'm not coming up. Say something!"

The tower uphill shrieked as metal chewed metal. I lifted one arm and shoved a thumb into the air. All good, Anita. All good here. I pulled Pock under me and pushed myself off his body, wrapping my hand around the harness at his neck.

"Coming, coming. Don't come up," I panted. "We're coming down."

Uphill, something exploded and rained metal. We broke into a run. I could run downhill.


From the cab of Anita's truck, with Pock tucked low between my knees and his tongue treating my scratched hands, I watched the Eagle Ridge Wind Project's parking lot fill with vehicles. Anita's satellite phone crackled and beeped, but she ignored it after she'd made one emergency call. How could it be that sixty miles deep into the Maine woods—sixty miles from the nearest house, the nearest fresh milk, and the nearest laundromat—someone's body parts invited a big-boy vehicle convention?

Game warden trucks, a platoon of Premier Power & Energy bright green trucks, some loggers wearing hard hats and sweat stains from necks to groins, a state crime unit, state police, county sheriff, and the geeky curious who monitor scanners and show up where they're not wanted. All of that spilled from the lot down the access road. My battered Subaru was the only gas-efficient car in sight. Ridge Dumais, Great Nations Forests' crew boss, his red hat knocked sideways from peering in my parked Subaru windows, looked as though he hoped to find me.

"If you build it, they will come," said Anita. She swiped

blond wisps from her forehead, cobalt blue eyes lighting up her wind-chiseled face the way a lighthouse animates solid rock. Handing me slices of crystalized ginger and a can of juice, she said, "Blast a mountain smooth, scrape an interstate up it, and throw up towers that dwarf any building we've got. We just need a sign that explains how this is all good for us, and—oh, goody—there's one of those bolted to the gate. Eat the ginger first. Settles the stomach if you're done heaving."

"You're not big on PP&E," I said, hoping I wouldn't have to talk about anything. In the field Anita didn't talk much. Like slicing the bat to explain its death, she preferred hands-on education. In the truck she was like talk radio. Just what I needed. Distraction from thought just about summed up talk radio anyway.

Anita kept going. "Actually, the company's just doing what all the extraction folks do. Mine, log, dam, excavate, bulldoze, build. What rubs me rough is this. I'm hired by the New England Wildlife Consortium to conduct independent wildlife research, not help some corporation check a bureaucratic box so it can say it's done something it really hasn't done. I don't like doing my work dirty so I can facilitate my employer's questionnable contract arrangements."

I think I groaned, but she was wound up and didn't hear it. I liked to lecture as much as the next pissed-off person, but I was trying to reform and Anita was just getting started. "They're making me use a search grid designed for smaller turbines. The new tall ones throw wings and bones the length of a football field. And no engineer with his ass in a chair should limit the seasons and days I can and can't be here."

She pulled the tab on my juice and lifted my arm and the can. "Drink this. Replace some fluids. You aren't recording this, are you? I don't think I've chewed on the politics of this with you before. You don't say much, but you've got a reputation for setting people up so your fingers aren't on the trigger and people seem to shoot themselves. A reputation for being a very efficient spoiler."

Oh good. More reminders about why I was hibernating in the woods. I seem to have been a problem from birth, and even retiring to a cabin down a dirt road wasn't working. I looked at the parking lot and saw that I was trapped. I liked Anita, but I wasn't ready for therapy, even casual truck therapy. I mumbled something about being retired and moved my hand toward the door.

Anita wasn't done. "I know you're supposed to be Maine's most visible green do-gooder lobbyist. I know you spent two years lugging a briefcase of good intentions into the state house and fighting these corporate wind boys a while back. I know you lost that battle and they can build what they want, pretty much where they want." She reached between my legs and rubbed Pock's ears. "Unless you're doing your dog a favor by offering him a carcass-sniffing vacation, for the life of me I just don't know what the hell you're doing up here."

I put the entire slab of candied ginger into my mouth.

Anita nudged me. "Doesn't each dead bird and bat pour serious salt into your wounds?"

That made two of us who didn't know what I was doing up here. When I moved up to hibernate at my family's camp and embrace a stripped-down life, I'd made a solemn promise to take any and all jobs that put me close to woods and wildlife. I promised myself that I would not get picky, uppity, or weirded out by what I had to do. I bought a rugged wardrobe of men's pants and shirts at the Baptist Thrift Store so I could save my last two pairs of jeans from anything nasty. I couldn't figure out how nasty had come looking for me, so I sipped the warm juice and wished I had ice to use on my throat, and then on my knee, and then for sure I'd toss the ice down my bra.

Bursting from an overgrown logging road near tower two, a muddy ATV bristling with military-looking searchlights and ground-eating tires skidded to a stop inches from our bumper. A lean man in a dark helmet, green game warden uniform, and muddy black boots got out, stretched, and adjusted the gun on his hip. Everyone else in the parking lot had sweat stains that reached from their pits to their crotch but not this man. He looked crisp and pressed.

"Robert Akins," I said. My heart lifted and sank at the same time. "It's Moz."

"Abenaki word for moose," Anita said. "He's called moose?"

"Not many white folks would know that," I said. "Penobscot. He's Penobscot Nation though."

"I know more American Indian animal terms than Latin names I'm supposed to know." She chuckled. "That's how I break the biologist mold. And if he's Indian trying to be a warden, I'll bet there's no mold at all for that combination."

Moz pulled off his helmet and slid straight black hair under a warden-green baseball cap. He squinted through Anita's windshield, found me through the dust and bugs and nodded. I could have used a hug. Alone, I thought I'd get it, but not with Anita staring and other wardens crowding into the lot. Watching Moz part the milling crowd like smooth, swift water scattering bits of aimless driftwood, I slumped in my seat as if someone had sucked out my blood.

Moz adjusted multiple leather-covered implements at his waist and aimed for the dark-green Maine Department of Game and Wildlife truck. Official-looking Premier Power & Energy people in reflective vests and hard hats had a map spread on its hood. They'd already pulled the switch on the wind project. Above us in a line all the way up the ridge, blades hung silent and still like giant white petals on giant stems.

"No law enforcement buzz cut for the handsome Robert Atkins moose man?" Anita asked.

"It's complicated. He saves an inch or two in back to braid. For ceremonies and fitting in."

"But not with other wardens," she said.

I reached for another piece of ginger candy and sucked the rough sugar granules off it. "Moz runs the search and rescue team and always gets his man, woman, child, or lost dog. He earned that name navigating woods the way moose do—in a straight line, stopping for nothing no matter how tangled, wet, or vicious the terrain. His reputation pretty much obliterates personal hygiene chatter about hair."

"And you know him how?"

"He was Evan's best friend."

"Evan the ex-husband?"

I nodded.

"Moz is your friend now?"

"I think so," I said. "Sometimes it's complicated." I rolled up both pant legs to inspect scrapes and cuts that left dark stains on my jeans, dropping some tears down onto the dried blood. It was silly to mourn a pair of already patched pants, but then I lived a life where I dreaded price tags even on the dollar rack.

"Are you OK?" Anita asked. "I can drive you home if they'll let you leave."

"Thanks," I said, "but I'll see it through. We're stuck anyway. What's with the fire trucks?" Greenwood's ambulance and two fire trucks showered the lot with dust as they braked by the gate.

"PP&E donated over a hundred thousand to the town's emergency services. And as a real surprise, the town selectmen are probably going to support the company's next expansion—twenty-six more turbines up the other side of the ridge." She sighed, but one of her unearthly pale blue eyes winked at me. "This looks like a good time for the volunteers to show off new toys."

Moz unfolded black body bags and divided the firemen and wardens into search teams. They spread out up the road and into the woods, searching a methodical grid the way Anita and I did when we looked for smaller bodies.

Pock thumped his tail and whined inside his muzzle as Moz came to lean in my window. He smelled like fresh wood. My dog likes to chew wood, and I'd left my old job to hibernate in the woods. It made sense that Moz smelled good to us.

Blacker than his hair, his eyes gleamed like wet stones in a clean river. They sparked with light and meaning, but he could flip a switch and shrivel them to a flat stare. I thought the gleaming eyes might be the Penobscot, and the flat eyes might be the warden.

He reached down and scratched Pock behind his muzzle and dropped his other hand down to my knee. "Better keep Pock low and out of sight for now," he said, running his fingers over my knee, circling my dried wounds with a firm touch. Anita leaned closer to watch.

"Are you injured?" he asked.

"Nothing beyond Band-Aids," I said, a bit awed that his fingers felt strangely cool.

"And you, Anita?" he asked.

She nudged me.

*Yes, he already knows your name,* I thought.

"On what you found," he said, "were there recognizable

details that might help us identify the victim?"

"Recognizable details." I said. "Outside of my urge to throw up?" I gripped the juice can and slid the last drops onto my tongue. Apparently it didn't matter that for years I'd helped my father cut up and package his deer, because I was shivering and sweating at the same time. "Nothing . . . nothing could . . . could . . ."

Moz leaned into the truck. "It may not stay with you as long as you fear." He squeezed and released my knee and then stepped back from the truck. "When my team discovers how your dog has rearranged the scene, they will want him for possibly contaminating what they hope to understand. I would retain the muzzle for now. We may need to prove bite marks are not domestic dog."

"Bite marks?" I asked. "You've seen bite marks? Up there?"

Moz pulled off his ball cap and slicked his hair back under it. "Yes, I have."

Anita turned in her seat to face Moz. "And what brings you into PP&E's territory from the great woods beyond?" she asked. "Everyone else came from civilization."

I could have warned her not to spar with Moz, but I was stuck on bite marks.

Moz answered, but his eyes were all over the parking lot. "I was investigating camp burglaries at a lake below this site. Old logging roads are faster."

She pulled her truck keys from the ignition and tossed them up on the dash. "It used to be only moose could navigate woods up here. Now anyone can. Anyone with initiative can drive an ATV through here and now there's sixteen miles of new roads at their disposal. That should narrow your suspect list."

"Excuse me, folks," I said, twisting back and forth between

them. "Excuse me—but bite marks?"

When Moz pulled his thick brows together his forehead looked like a bank of black clouds pushed before a storm. He smoothed his face into a careful granite mask. "I found what you found and examined it closely. There is further evidence we will find more of the victim near the road."

Of course he'd also seen my vomit and the outlines of my struggle in the dust. No mention of how I'd contaminated the scene. And no mention of what bits and pieces might have been "further evidence."

Sounds of shouting at the gate snapped our heads toward the parking lot. Two cows trotted up the tower access road, followed by a state trooper waving his arms. Several sheep gathered in a bleating cluster in front of Anita's truck. Someone had spray painted "Wind Weasels" on the shorn side of one sheep. The entire side of a large cow read, "Stupids! It's a Wind Factory, Not a Farm."

Moz sighed and peeled away toward the front gate where a crowd gathered around a media truck, its satellite dish rotating for signals.

"Damn," said Anita. "We should have escaped when we had the chance. Now the entire circus has come to town, and it never comes unless it's expecting someone's bad behavior to make their day. We'd better settle in." She reached for her briefcase and thumped scientific papers on her lap. "I'd better read up. The feds are listing some bats as endangered species because there's a fungus killing millions." She dropped papers on my lap. "Here's something for that column you write. The one on the outdoors and money."

I glanced down. Somehow bats were worth twenty-two billion dollars to American farmers because they killed pests and pollinated crops. Somehow, it also seemed that tequila would vanish if bats didn't pollinate Agave plants. The words appeared to be melting off the page, so I pressed both hands over the top sheet. Anita gently pulled the pages away and opened a yellow highlighter, pointing it at the parking lot. "Your warden doesn't talk like a warden or an Indian."

I sighed. Moz didn't really belong to anyone. Not me. Not the warden service. Not even the Penobscot Nation he was born into. "He's probably better educated than both of us put together, even with all our degrees." I rolled my bloody jeans back over my shins. "I can't just sit here and marinate in your truck."

"You're going out there?" she said. "Someone's going to stick a microphone in your face. They'll ask you what you found, and because they already think someone's been executed by this company's screw-up, they'll ask you about wind power. They stuck microphones in your face lots before." She popped a CD into the truck's dash. "OK. Your show. But I'd rather listen to Springsteen chew his words in that sexy way he has. Any day."

I needed to escape Anita as much as I needed fresh air. She sounded like what I used to be.

A cow with a banner secured to its neck and belly deposited manure outside my door. The banner's message heaved in and out with each cow breath: "Mountains. Not Renewable."

"OK if I leave Pock here?" I asked. "Not a good time for him to learn about livestock. He's already got half his head squished out the window. Some good smell must be calling his name."

Anita was studying a photo spread of diseased bats that looked as though they'd been dipped in confectionary sugar, with their noses, mouths, and even their wings powdery white next to the rest of their brown bodies. "Good god," she said, reaching back to scratch the part of Pock's head she could reach. I opened the door and jumped a pile of cow poop.

I heard a familiar soft chuck-chuck call and saw Ken Douglas bobbing his head absurdly as he leaned on his green state truck outside the gate. The scene was so charged with activity that no one noticed his partridge imitation, but out in the field, that's how he'd called me when he wanted me. Ken hadn't fired me, and I don't think the Maine Department of Game and Wildlife had either. It just didn't rehire me when hunting season arrived. Somehow, I'd become a liability. Only Moz and I knew about my problem history with wolves. Ken's bosses just guessed.

"Of course you'd be here in the middle of some outdoor mess," he said. "I can't say you didn't warn me when you said the wind thing might turn ugly." When he wrapped me in a tight hug, his head barely touched my chin and his bushy eyebrows landed somewhere low between my breasts. I squeezed back and tried to think about his biologist expertise, not his sweat sticking to my shirt or his gender. It wasn't hard. His sparse hair looked like coyote-digested rabbit he'd once shown me—bits of gray, white, and tan woven into a tight mat. I hoped he wasn't inspecting me in some equally awkward way.

Ken leaned away but held onto my arms. "Didn't expect to see you working here for Anita Stockdale and the corporate folks, unless you're still having trouble affording dog food. Don't get me wrong. She's a top-flight biologist who's probably making gobs more money than I am, but you don't really buy the garbage her bosses signed off on. Do you?"

Ken was good at giving me a gift of simple chat when I was obviously sinking into something very unpleasant. He'd done that for me before.

"What are we talking about, Ken?" I asked.

"You know. Anita's employers? The New England Wildlife

Consortium? It dropped its bat lawsuit when PP&E agreed to reduce operations during bat migrations to save some of them." He waved his arms in large circles and chuckled. "Course it's a bit weird they settled on just trying to save bats and ignored the birds."

"Everyone bought the argument that tall buildings kill more birds than this stuff does," I said.

More game wardens talking on more radios arrived in the parking lot. They grabbed more body bags, but Ken plowed on, raising his voice to cover up the whine of ATVs headed back into the woods.

"Well, maybe big city buildings can kill, but not here. Imagine a giant letter S that starts up north in Canada and shoves its big curving belly right through Maine's north woods before it drops into the ocean. Spring and fall, along that curve millions and millions of birds are flying. From the Arctic. Canada. Maine. We got a feathered freeway here. Spinning metal stuck up in the birds' road during rush hour is a giant traffic accident."

"You are a backwoods poet,' I said. "Let me hide out with you for a while." We climbed into the open bed of his truck and settled into two lawn chairs welded to the floor. When I'd worked for him, we'd dropped a camouflage colored net over our elevated perch and turned his truck into an observation blind so we could watch animals go about their business.

"What's covered up?" I asked, reaching for a tarp covering a boxy shape.

Ken grabbed my arm. "Don't rile her up. She's thinks it's night time."

"She?"

"I have permission from the Maine Wildlife Park to release a female golden eagle they've rehabilitated. I was scouting

20

locations when the radio kind of exploded and I heard you might be part of the fireworks."

I nodded and slid lower in my chair.

Ken looked uphill. "I'll keep looking. Nuts to release her anywhere near here. Since they blasted the top off the ridge, any furry thing that's edible has to dash across lots of open terrain. We might as well put up bill boards advertising cheap, easy, dangerous dinners for eagles and hawks. I've kind of fallen a bit in love with her. She's a beauty, but she's getting very antsy. It's time."

About fifteen protestors were trying to shove livestock through the gate, argue with wardens, or swarm reporters. Moz was on his knees, looking sideways at a long-haired protester chained to the underside of a bulldozer.

"OK, let's get to it," Ken said. "How are you holding up?" I shrugged.

"It was all over our radios you found human parts. That's gotta be rough." He nudged me. "Prob'ly nothing I handed off to you tops that."

Last year I'd helped Ken's biologist crew investigate wildlife mysteries and crimes. My job involved labeling duct-taped garbage bags filled with animal evidence or mysteries Ken wanted to pursue. I also had the care and feeding of ancient refrigerators cranked up to arctic temperatures to freeze it all. But Ken was right. Nothing I'd seen came close to the shoulder in the road.

He nudged me again. "You can tell me. Maybe if you tell someone, you'd look better. Right now you look whiter than snow."

I put my feet up on the railing and bent forward into my knees. "Ken. I still can't take a shower alone in a motel room decades after watching the movie *Psycho*. Now this. I know you're curious, but I'm not sure sharing all this will fix me. It was more than rearranged roadkill. It was human. Who knew that only a part of a person was still so human? It even asked me a question."

"No shit," said Ken. He unwrapped a chocolate bar, split it into two, and slipped half under my hands. He knew about chocolate. "Lottsa blood?"

I didn't mind his question. It sounded like conversations we'd already had. I slouched low in my seat, letting chocolate melt in my fingers. "No, but Moz says there's bite marks."

Ken kind of bounced in his seat. "I'd like to get a good look at those. Not much opportunity to examine human mortality that involves critters. Maine's just too safe. No rattlesnakes, cougars, grizzlies. They'll probably put some forensic flunkies on it."

I sat up and turned toward him. "Could you tell a dog bite from some other canine bite?'

"You think it was dogs?"

"Don't know. But I don't want the wardens thinking it was my dog."

"You using the muzzle I gave you?"

"On the job? All the time."

"Well, they can use DNA to exclude your guy. Might mean some quarantine time, though."

"That's not going to go down well with Pock," I said, but there was more. I didn't want anyone official finding what I didn't want found. Pock had been on my bed for two years, each night turning at least three circles so he could land on my feet and interrupt circulation. He was the warmth in my life. Pretty much the only warmth in my life. But I couldn't prove he was legally mine if I had to.

Two Premier Power & Energy officials crossed to Anita's

truck carrying clipboards and files, their blue hard hats tipped into jaunty, useless attitudes. One had dirty L.L. Bean boots, while the other wore black loafers that looked as if they'd been shined with dust repellent.

Ken rocked left and right in his chair, untucking his shirt and trying to wipe his belly without calling attention to it. I thought I'd smelled every odor he could accumulate, but maybe not. I reached for a rag on the floor and wiped the melted candy into its wrinkles. It was even too hot for chocolate. "What are you up to, Ken? I can't place that smell."

He beamed, showing unusually white teeth for someone our age. I'd seen him loosen rope knots with them, bragging that his dental sins worked better than floss. "Oh, you like that?" he crowed. "Special carnivore bits from the Maine Wildlife Park. Even I don't want to know what critters they've fed this eagle, but she's healthy and ready to go."

The hard hats turned away from Anita and aimed for us.

Ken tucked in his shirt. "Not looking for me," he said.

# THREE

The black-shoes man pointed and raised his clipboard to wave me out of the back of the truck. A military buzz cut barely covered his scalp. It could have hidden gray hair, but I guessed him as early forties and very serious about ascending the corporate ladder.

"Attorney. Or muckety-muck management.," whispered Ken. "If the shoes don't give it away, there's always the first thing they do to remind you you're not much but they are. Watch out for this crew. It's slippery. Come to dinner when you get a chance so Millie and I can make up for whatever he might do to you."

I leaned over and kissed him on the cheek—first to accept his invitation and then to annoy black-shoes man who expected me to hop to attention. Ken climbed down and then ceremoniously reached up to lift me to the ground.

"Ms. Conover," Black Shoes said. "I sincerely hope you were not discussing any aspect of this situation with anyone at this time." He scowled at Ken, handed me a file, and waved his clipboard at a cow that wandered toward us. Where was cow poop when you really needed it?

"And this is?" I asked.

"The confidentiality agreement you signed when you agreed to work for us."

I took a deep breath— a breath I used for bureaucrats of all types and stripes. A breath that was supposed to allow my calmer self time to choose diplomatic words, but that might have been in my former life. "That's it?" I asked, leaning forward to read his name tag. "That's it, Matt Pruitt? You've got someone ripped apart up there. Someone who has a family or people who expect him . . . or her . . . home tonight, and you're trotting around down here with paper you expect me to care about?"

He pointed to the file I was slapping on my thigh. "Please review the agreement you signed when you agreed to work for us."

"I work for the New England Wildlife Consortium," I said.

"And they work for us. A copy of your contract is in the file."

I lifted a sheet from the folder just long enough to see that it was attorney-speak. "What are we keeping confidential?"

The L.L. Bean-boot man shuffled his feet and looked away. Black Shoes lifted his chin and barked at me. "Anything that happens on this property."

"Anything?"

"Anything. I will be present if and when you are interviewed by law enforcement officers. If I direct you not to reply, you are directed not to reply."

Ken squeezed my elbow, but I shook him off. "I'm confused. Didn't I sign up to conduct research that will be part of the public record some day? You know, reports of animal mortality associated with your operation?"

"The research we acquire is proprietary. It's ours. Our leases secure this land, our project, and our information."

Ken coughed and cracked his knuckles. That crisp come-to-attention sound made up for his small height. "Ah, yes," said Ken. "It might be your information unless you interfere with a listed species. Could be listed as threatened, or it could be listed endangered."

"And you are?" said Black Shoes.

"Your friendly regional wildlife biologist," Ken said. He

26

unbuttoned a shirt pocket and removed a wrinkled card.

Black Shoes lifted a gleaming pen from his shirt pocket and clicked it open. "And your supervisor is? You answer to . . . ?"

Ken winked at me and turned to walk away. "I like to think I answer to each wild animal in Maine, but today you can find the right boss-man at the Maine Department of Game and Wildlife. If he isn't fishing."

I didn't notice the group surrounding Anita's truck until it was too late. Two state troopers, legs wide apart, hands over their holsters, were deployed at the front and rear of the truck. Moz stood in front of the truck's side door, blocking a round, gesturing man who brandished a long pole with a loop hanging at its far end. In frustration the man with the pole raised his ball cap and thumped it down backwards so the front and logo faced me. *Animal Control.*

Over my dead body.

As I ran toward the truck yelling his name, Pock squeezed himself out the rear window, scraping the muzzle off his mouth so it hung at a crazy angle and bounced off his chest. Moz lunged for him and missed. The Animal Control officer whipped the pole's noose in Pock's direction, but caught only air. The troopers spread their arms trying to corner him between Anita's truck and the crime scene van, but he crawled under it and ran for the woods. I saw the tip of his brown tail thrash late-blooming flowers, and then he was gone.

The flower petals hadn't settled on the ground before I was surrounded by angry men. I couldn't understand their words. They came at me like waves. My stomach felt sea sick.

"Oh, here we go; here's the tears," one state trooper said.

I felt Moz against my back. Yes, he smelled like wood, but when everyone stopped talking and stepped back, I knew Moz really did have my back. The tears were a surprise. I swiped a

SANDRA NEILY

sleeve at my lids. The folks wearing crime scene T-shirts winced.

"Please nod if I have anticipated your requests," Moz said. To the techs carrying what looked like tackle boxes he said, "You want to process her and her clothes for scene evidence." They nodded. To the state police he said, "You want a statement." They didn't nod, but they didn't say anything either. To his search team he said, "You want to know exactly where she went and what she did there." The youngest one gave Moz a thumbs up. Moz nodded. And to the PP&E hard hats he said, "You want what you cannot have right now. Please wait outside the gate."

Black Shoes started to protest but Moz said, "Mr. Pruitt, you may wait inside the gate if you wish, but I expect you to be within two feet of it when I return to you." He put one hand on my shoulder. "Unlike what has already taken place at this scene, I am unwilling to cut Ms. Conover into pieces and feed her to you, so you will wait until I have assessed her readiness to cooperate. Each of you might try and recall the last time you fell within inches of a severed human shoulder and then behave accordingly."

The men fell back and walked away, all except the animal control officer, who thumped his pole angrily in the dirt. "For Christ's sake, Atkins," he said, "the dog's already wearing a muzzle. What's that tell you?"

"Jerry," Moz said," I know you want to collect the dog and process it for evidence. We will try and find him before he has altered evidence he may carry. I will radio if we locate him."

After Jerry stomped away, Moz bent toward me, small glittering lights in his coal-black eyes. "Of course we do know Pock will not be in an altered state when we find him."

I sat in the dirt because my legs melted and I couldn't

imagine my next move.

Moz crouched beside me. "Unfortunately, if I am to assist you, we must keep moving."

"Where?" I asked.

"To the crime scene van to change from your clothes to something—something more comfortable."

"I'm some kind of suspect?"

"No." He lifted his head toward the top of the ridge. "But you may help us. Pock may help us. You both interacted with possible evidence. He touched it. You fell near it."

As if I believed that line. That was Robert Atkins the warden. My friend Moz wouldn't look away when someone wanted truth.

Snap. There it was. The snap that came when my brain stepped outside my body and slapped myself on the head. People do not just go lopping themselves in half. Of course the assembled posse suspected murder. "There's privacy there?" I asked, pushing myself up off the dirt.

"I will clear the lot around you and stand guard," Moz said. He called over his shoulder, "Anita, Patton will need her pack."

Anita jumped from her truck. My pack looked lumpier than usual.

"I stuffed it with water and snacks," she said," just in case. I'll stay here until they're done with you no matter how long it takes." She started to hug me, but Moz raised his arm to stop contact. I felt like I might be the start of a pandemic.

"They're going to comb me for evidence," I said. "My phone's in there, too?"

She stepped back. "If you call that thing a phone," she said. "It's in there."

As we walked to the van, I developed a limp. Looking

helpless seemed like a good idea since everyone was watching me. Moz noticed, frowned and said nothing. "If they take me somewhere—if the troopers take me somewhere, what about my car?" I asked.

"My team will drive it to your camp," Moz said. "If you cooperate, we should be able to return you home tonight."

The van smelled like corn chips and disinfectant. One of the techs placed a massive garbage bag on the floor, opened it, and explained that I was to stand inside its folds and drop my clothes into it. "All of them, if you please," she said. "And your pack unopened. I left you a pair of hospital scrubs on the counter. When you're done, wave out the door and I'll come in to do the hair and DNA stuff. Then we'll see what's bothering your leg. OK?"

"I won't do this until folks back off," I said.

She jumped from the van and helped Moz herd people toward the gate. I sat and leaned against a side window trying to suck in fresh air as I looked around for anything helpful. Everything looked either helpful or useless except the iced coffee. I gulped the last drops and, holding my breath against what my surprised flesh might do, dumped the ice cubes down my bra. They melted so fast, rivulets of water reached my knees in seconds. Munching loose chips left on a seat, I stuffed duct tape and tweezers into my pack. When I found Pock, I expected there'd be grooming. Duct tape yanked hard or tweezers against his hide should cover most of the nasty possibilities.

I found an open topographical map with search coordinates drawn on it and stuffed it into my pocket. I picked up a compass and almost tossed it away. I was a licensed Maine Guide but that didn't mean anything. I usually navigated by rivers that ran downhill and mountains that climbed up. I put it in my pocket. The emergency flares were too tempting, so I took three and wrapped them in Anita's jacket. I grabbed wire cutters, raised a window that faced the woods, and slashed mesh and screen out of the way. I dropped two large bottles of disinfectant out the window, tossed my pack into the woods, and stared at the window.

Slow or fast?

I was generally a fast person. I raised arms over my head, clamped my palms together, closed my eyes, thought about swimming, and dove through the window. A mound of leaves broke my fall, but I had to spit dirt that tasted like old mushrooms. I wiggled into my pack, double-tied my hiking boots, grabbed the disinfectant, and slid into the trees behind the van. It took less than a minute to saturate the woods around the van with something that smelled like bleach.

I felt a twinge for the wardens' tracking dogs. Most of them were Labradors like Pock. I kicked leaves over what I'd spilled; I didn't want to blind them.

I could run if I had to. Arthritis paired with extra pounds isn't a terminal disease. I was in the move-it-or-lose-it time of life when butts grow into soft cushions that fit couches. It felt good to have an excuse to run. I aimed for where I'd seen Pock take flight and found a grove of birch thinned by fire. I jumped black stumps and twisted around white trunks. My passing lifted sheets of loose bark that waved like a scattered cheering section.

It was no accident that Moz put me into a vehicle shielded by trees, called for my pack, and arranged crowd control. I was sure he'd helped me escape. I had no idea why I ran, except it felt right. Maybe it was a gut reaction to Black Shoes and his wind empire. I certainly needed to find my dog before PP&E's crew did. I didn't trust them with Pock's safety or the safety of any wild thing that lived on or near the ridge. I felt a small, grim smile grow between gulps of air. I didn't trust them with anything I cared about.

I certainly didn't trust them with my family. Pock was family.

I'd been working for folks who could find an animal by hairs left on twigs, but Pock was my messy best friend. Water slurped from his bowl became rivers on the camp floor. He regularly overturned his dinner so he could chase kibble on linoleum. He rolled on surfaces that promised odor or endless joy. I slowed and studied the ground, wiping away sweat that poured into my eyes whenever I looked down.

A hastily scratched pile of leaves didn't really cover the remnants of his breakfast. Bits of orange carrot in bits of feces were my dog's outdoor signature.

I wished I could smell what he smelled to know his traveling direction, but we humans are centuries away from that ability. In what direction had he strained his head out of Anita's window? Raised his nose into the wind? The line of wind turbines ran south to north along the ridge. Pock had strained toward something at right angles to the project.

West. It might work. I pulled the compass from my pocket and saw its arrow leap toward north as I aimed west. As I walked, I ripped flagging tape off trees. I always eliminate every effort to survey wild places. Force of habit. It helped to think of flagging tape as an invasive species crowding out the rightful plants and animals that belonged.

Torn leaves and dirt cut by sharp hooves told me a deer had been too surprised to melt into the trees as Pock approached. He wasn't a deer chaser, so I continued west. Filtered sunlight caught spider webs he'd ripped apart on the run. I found a stream where he'd rolled in mud, leaving paw prints and mud-splattered ferns. He'd stopped to sample turkey scat, nosing aside dried older bits for something fresh.

All I had to do was find Pock before searching game wardens found either of us. I held my breath to listen. No fast-moving boots on dry crispy leaves. I had time.

Dizzy from panting and then holding my breath, I stopped by a bog ringed with wet plants and dropped to my knees. Leaning back on my heels, cool leaves pressed to my face, I heard a woodpecker dap-dapping insects out of a tree. A lone tree frog scratched out a gritty one-note song. Over my head chickadees hopped from limb to limb, twittering my presence to interested parties.

Someone else was interested.

Claws scratched bark in my direction, and inches from my face, a small brown face popped up over a log. The pine marten and I were eye to eye. Stuffed and displayed in a store window, it would have been the cute toy—rounded erect ears, shining eyes, a milky-yellow fur patch below its chin. Its coat rippled like melting chocolate. No wonder Russian women were desperate to drape marten on their bodies. It sniffed and showed me sharp weasel teeth, scolding me with barks that sounded like quick, wet kisses.

Up close with wildlife of all sizes and attitudes, I liked to create conversations that took me some place I needed to go. Sometimes the effort saved me from trouble. Sometimes it got me into trouble. I smiled at the marten. *Seen a black dog pass by here?*

It snarled back at me. *What's a dog?*

*Like a coyote but not as smart. He had something shiny flopping around his neck.*

*A trap? Was it a trap? Are you a killer?*

*Killer? No. He's . . . he's . . . family. I wouldn't hurt him.*

33

The pine marten cocked its head and rose on its hind legs, huffing at me. *You're all killers.* He wiggled into a hole in the log and slid out of sight.

As if to punctuate the flick of his disappearing tail, above me on the ridge chain saws buzzed into life. Tree trunks cracked as if split with lightning. Each crack was followed by a hoarse whoosh as hundreds of limbs slammed the ground.

The marten growled at me from an overhead branch. *Your kind is killing spruce and fir where I must hunt, hide, and live.*

*I'm not happy about that either.*

He turned away into thick balsam branches. *The animal you hunt follows a smell I teach my kits to fear. Not all children listen. Not all live.*

I pushed myself up and used the compass to find a west direction again, but it meant a steep uphill climb. I walked large circles looking to pick up Pock's trail. The effort seemed useless. The logging operation had probably spooked him. My dog hates explosive sounds. Thunder. Gunshots. Fireworks. They all send him howling under cars or tables.

When Pock's terrified howl cut through the chickadees and the chain saws, I aimed for it.

34

# FOUR

I counted five howls as I clawed my way through young trees crowding in on a patch of open woods. I didn't even think of working my way toward an easier route. I didn't want to lose the sound of Pock's distress. Then there was silence. Dead silence. Even the chainsaws had stopped.

I waited and imagined the worst. A life without Pock. Without his body, wet from the lake and soaking my feet at the foot of the bed. Without his insanely happy face—a face that said, *Get up. Get up. Let's get out-there. Don't care if there's a monsoon outside.* My dog pulled me out the door even if I was hiccupping tears.

I was two years into a life that Pock had helped make safe for me. Two years away from a husband who'd left me when my tan no longer camouflaged varicose veins. Two years away from a lobbying career that attracted more enemies than votes. I hibernated with the essentials: an ancient family camp no one seemed to want, a full woodshed, and a warm creature always happy to see me.

Listening hard, at first I didn't think I heard words, just a faint murmur that could have been disturbed bees. But it was noise and I moved up toward it. I didn't run. I placed each foot on moss or decayed wood, working my way around dry leaves and twigs. I didn't want to explode into something I didn't understand.

In a small clearing, a boy with a shotgun was standing over my dog. At the base of a huge beech tree, Pock lunged forward and then flipped back, landing on his side and struggling to stand before he lunged again. I heard the boy say, "Easy and quiet now," but Pock was strangely silent. Only the thump of his body hitting the end of each jump filled the clearing. He no longer wore a muzzle. Saliva foamed at his open mouth.

Suddenly the boy dropped to his knees, laying his gun on the ground. He crawled toward Pock until he was almost nose to nose with him. Trembling, Pock froze. "You look like you're used to being leashed, buddy," he said. "That's cool. You're cool. Don't push it. Lie down. Lie down. Makes this easier. I can get you out. I just need to check you out."

My dog cocked his head sideways to catch the boy's soft words. I slid down behind one of those huge boulders left in the middle of nowhere by glaciers. I have respect for guns and from where I crouched, the shotgun was within easy reach of the boy. Pock was no longer leaping manically, so I took deep breaths and leaned forward on the rock.

The boy must have been in his mid-teens, with military cropped hair that wasn't military because he'd dyed a patch over his right ear a bright green. He wore tall, dark-green boots, jeans patched on both knees with what looked like even older jean material, and a brown leather jacket that caught the sun in folds of buttery, soft, expensive leather. His glasses had sturdy black frames that were almost larger than his lean face. All of him was lean.

When he put a hand on my dog's head and slowly pushed him down to the ground, Pock whined, but he didn't pull away. When the boy's jacket fell open, I could clearly see the pistol in its holster.

"Hold it," I said. "Freeze."

The boy didn't flinch or look my way. "No, you hold it," he whispered. "Or the dog gets hurt."

Pock looked at me and then back at the boy. The tip of his tail wagged an inch or two, not enough to be friendly but enough to show he was hopeful.

"Now I am going to lean forward and do something quickly, so you'll have to trust me. Please don't talk." the boy said.

"What's your name?" I asked.

He froze. "You're talking. Really? My name?"

"I want to remember who you are." I said.

"Chandler. Chandler Perkins. And seriously. Do nothing. Stay cool so he won't feed off your freaking out."

"Can't promise that," I whispered.

"Well, don't move or twitch or lunge over here."

"OK," I said, but I didn't mean it.

"Your dog. What's his name?"

"Pock. Like rock," I said.

"Well, Pock's got his front legs caught in a trap. I can free him."

My heart jumped into my throat. Under my arms even more sweat soaked my shirt. "You know what you're doing?" I asked.

The boy actually smiled. "I should. I set it last night."

"Oh crap," was all I could say, but it came out more like a moan.

"Don't set him off getting all tense. He's going to be fine."

"I've got wire cutters in my pack," I said. "You need wire cutters?"

"I need you to sit by that rock," he said. "Really? Wire cutters? What'd you do? Break out of jail?"

Before I could answer, he lunged forward, pinned Pock sideways on the ground with both of his knees, and sang into Pock's ears. Pock was used to off-key singing.

"Pock, Pock. We got a lock I gotta knock 'fore you can walk. Let's knock the lock and walk, boy. Let's knock the lock and walk."

Pock seemed more interested in licking Chandler Perkins' face than fighting him. By the time I reached them, my dog was cradled in the boy's lap. I wanted to grab Pock and hug him, but bending over I saw the boy had pressed his hands on Pock's legs to stop any bleeding. There wasn't much blood, so I straightened up and stepped back.

"You crawl here, Ms. Wire Cutters?" the boy said. "There's moss 'an stuff in your hair."

He may have been smiling but his green eyes—almost the color of his hair patch—challenged me. His skin was toast brown. Either he lived outside all the time, or he wasn't from Maine. Most of us are whiter than white. He had a long straight nose that ran between high, regal cheek bones.

"You have a license to trap?" I asked, picking twigs from my hair.

The boy scowled. "You licensed to ask?"

My words choked on the obvious. "My d-dog could have died in your t-trap."

He lifted a tangled mass of cable and metal and shook it until it unkinked. "Not likely. It's the same snare biologists use to catch bears they study. They catch and release the same bears over and over."

"I don't know much about how trapping happens," I said, "but I know dogs aren't legal."

Chandler Perkins slid several fingers into a loop of cable and tried to tug it closed. "And your dog's gotta be special because this snare's designed to prevent this kind of thing. I can only trap bear this time of year." He held up silver cable. "This loop's got something on it that stops it from tightening down on small animals so they can get away. Pock must have pounded the trigger part with two legs. I think the snare thought he was large enough to be a bear."

I cherished Pock's vigor about exploring his world. Up until this moment, I'd only had to cope with porcupines and skunks. "What did you bait the trap with?"

"Bacon grease. Donuts."

"That explains a lot about today. Two of his favorites," I said. "Is it safe to walk around?"

"Yes, ma'am." The boy was busy, bent over and giving Pock a full body massage, which was usually my job. While Pock moaned happy moans, I tiptoed around the tree, inspecting the long end of the cable wrapped around the trunk. Beech nuts cracked under my feet, rolling open to pop out wrinkled brown nuts.

"Why use bait if you've got a tree dropping food bears like anyway?" I asked.

Chandler lifted Pock's head off his thigh and, limber in a way I'm not, easily stood from a dead sit on the ground. "Bears are way smart. I need something that overpowers my smell. I need a smell so strong a bear doesn't recognize danger. He'll only go for what he wants. The person who sets the trap always knows way more than what walks into it."

That certainly seemed to be true. I pointed to his gun. "Were you just going to stroll up and shoot a bear leashed to a tree?"

He hitched up his jeans and cinched his belt tighter into home-made, irregular holes. "Let's swap real names before we get into this," he said. "Most people call me Chan."

"Patton," I said, dropping my pack and rooting around for Anita's hat. I didn't notice the hat's PP&E logo—a white cloud puffing cartoon lips at turbine blades—but the boy did.

"You're Premier Power & Energy?" he asked. "Awesome.

Green power. Way to go."

"I'm not entirely sure about that," I said.

He rearranged the snare's cable around the lip of a can sticking out of the hole he'd already dug. Leaning over, but keeping one eye on Pock licking his legs, I saw how the trap worked. When a bear pawed its way down toward sweets in the can, it triggered a metal arm that sprang up to tighten the snare on its leg. A small, square piece of metal on the cable appeared to stop the snare's loop from closing on small paws and legs.

Chan leaned on a tree, watching me. "So what's your job with the wind people?"

I made a loop of Pock's leash and pulled him to my side after he stood and leaned toward Chan. "I'm not part of the wind people. I don't work for PP&E." I thought about the clipboard that Black Shoes had waved in my face. "I work for an organization it hires to study birds and bats on the wind power site. I'm on the team that picks up dead ones."

He made a sliding motion through the air with his free hand. "So you're smooth with some animals living and some dying." He bent to sprinkle leaves and twigs over the snare, now artfully arranged around the can so a hungry animal wouldn't see the metal loop.

"I don't think I'm *smooth* with tricking hungry animals into an easy kill," I said.

"You're an anti."

"Anti?"

"Anti-trapping. Probably a lot more anti stuff." He piled tree limbs and spruce boughs around the snare, narrowed them at the tree end, and opened them wide at my end. He stood with his hand on his hips and then waved them toward his creation. "It's like a funnel to push an animal toward the trap.

Helps them only look at what they think they want," he said. "It's called a cubby."

That sounded cute and cuddly when the entire process looked lethal. I shrugged. "Whatever," I said, and then I cringed. I'd always come down on Kate for tossing off that useless, snotty phrase. It was time to admit—at least to myself—that my entire trapping education had happened indoors in rooms where wildlife laws got hotly debated.

Trappers with long family histories in the woods showed up to lobby for what they loved. I liked their beards, clean flannel shirts, scuffed boots, and especially their genuine stories. If I hadn't been hired to help tighten up Maine's trapping laws, I would have invited the opposition to dinner. It was complicated, but I liked people who were close to the woods even more than many of the people who hired me to protect the woods.

I think the last public hearing on trapping regulations helped me resign, pack, and move to Antler Camp. First there was the woman from the U.S. Department of Agriculture. Who knew it had an Animal Services division? A government department that trapped, shot, or poisoned millions of animals, mostly predators. Coyotes, cougars, wolves, bears, foxes—all with our tax dollars. It seemed the main beneficiaries of this effort were ranchers out west, often grazing stock on public lands.

The woman sitting next to me, wife of a trapper who was fighting the new law I was trying to pass, whispered, "Good to know our tax dollars are hard at work, honey. I can't figure out if that fed woman is testifying for us or against us."

"You and me both," I said.

In my heels and tasteful navy-blue suit, I sat through too much YouTube footage of struggling animals—terrified, hurt, hungry, and thirsty—until someone showed up to end their lives. We heard graphic testimony about drowning beavers struggling to surface and breathe. We absorbed tearful tales about foxes and coyotes dragging leg-hold traps wired to logs so the bulky wood could eventually snag in brush.

The woman next to me kept shaking her head so hard my chair vibrated. "Too many squishy Disney movies as kids. That's what's the matter," she muttered. "I bet we love them animals more than those do-gooders do."

They showed footage about how to free dogs accidentally caught in traps, but as one limped away dragging his leg, I hid in the state house bathroom because it had chilly marble walls to lean on.

After watching Pock flip himself over backwards trying to escape a snare, I knew a dog fighting a trap was seared in my mind forever. I wondered if any of Chan's animals ended up on the dinner table. I came from a hunting family that was religious about making sure a hunted animal had a fair shot at escape before we ate it.

My father, brother, uncles, and male cousins didn't think fairness applied to giving a fair shot to females. We waited at home, sharpening butcher knives, and when the men returned, we wrapped up red-gray lumps that we dated and labeled. Venison roast. Venison burger. Venison steak. Occasionally we also got to write duck, rabbit, or squirrel on the butcher paper. I was welcome at gravel pit target practice, but unwelcome at Antler Camp in the fall.

Chan was still working on his cubby, mounding up brush to support the side walls Pock had smashed as he thrashed against the snare. I stood studying him while Pock whined on his leash. I wanted to ask about his impossibly expensive jacket, but he wasn't done asking questions.

"What are you up to anyway?" he said. "I never met a woman in the woods carrying wire cutters."

I looked down and tried to see myself as Chan saw me. I wore an old paint-stained shirt with sleeves cut off at the elbows and Baptist Thrift Store pants so soft and ancient they were like wearing air. My hiking boots look attacked by jellyfish because I'd patched worn spots with globs of Aquaseal.

My pony tail had no gray hairs because Cousin Liz treated me to appointments that returned my blond highlights. "You should not," she said, "resemble old moss on old trees." My face had forehead worry lines. My lips had enough wrinkles to give up on lipstick. I'd never liked lipstick anyway.

If I hid my arthritis-bent fingers, I could be anywhere from age fifty to sixty. I didn't think young people guessed our ages after forty. We were a foreign country.

"Let's just say my work and my life have been about trying to make sure the wild world has a chance." I looked at his brown skin, but thought it would be rude to ask about his origins. "I come from good Maine stock. There was wild meat on the table, but I wasn't raised to decoy animals and then kill them. Follow them, yes. Figure out their eating, hiding, and sleeping places, and often come home without seeing one—yes. But luring an animal to its death and not a quick one. No. Not me."

Chan walked to my pack and swung it into the air between us. He flicked at fish hooks and dry flies imbedded in the fabric. "I know that one. It's a Hornberg. Trout like it. And here's elk-hair caddis. Salmon are hot for that fly. You've got flies stuck all over this thing."

"My casts don't always land in the water," I said.

"Soooooo. You pick a fly that looks like food. You put the fly in the water and jerk it to look alive so a fish eats it. But you're not—," he smiled, "*luring* an animal to its death?"

Smart kid. I liked smart kids and I liked them even better if they outsmarted me.

"I release what I catch. Alive," I said. And while I didn't say it, I knew that freeing the fish— feeling it push off my fingers back into freedom—was the best part. That was another complicated thing.

"Is trapping your hobby or what?" I asked.

"S'not a hobby." He kicked a bit of dirt over the snare. "It pays some bills and stuff." He trailed off, and I stopped talking. The expensive jacket didn't fit with the boy's using animal skins for income. If trapping was a survival issue, I needed to watch my words.

Wildlife, how it got managed and how money got made off it, was the second hottest issue in Maine. Second only to anything to do with sex. Money from people pursuing any kind of wildlife recreation—trapping, fishing, hunting and even just watching animals—sent over a billion dollars to us each year. I was sure any benefits from sexual activity weren't as carefully tallied.

Chan wiped his hands down his jeans, rubbed his glasses on the hem of his faded T-shirt, and reached for his canvas pack. As a chorus of chainsaws rattled into life, he looked up at the ridge.

"You headed back that way to meet up with your people?" he asked.

"Not my people," I said.

"That's their flagging tape you got hanging out of your pocket. If you aren't with 'em, that's gotta be against some law."

I pulled out a crushed handful of pink flagging tape and shook it loose. Faded PP&E markings trotted up the center of the tape. "I'm on a mission to eradicate the world of invasive species," I said, sure he'd never understand what sounded like a good excuse.

"I'm not stupid," he said. "I'm just fifteen." He slipped his arms into his pack straps. "I get it. You think the tape doesn't belong. That's gotta be another anti thing."

"What I really am is stranded without a way home," I said, looking up to see tree shadows creep across the clearing. Leaves glowed in late afternoon light.

"Come on then. Patton. Right? We're going the slow way home until I get to Bertha. I got some places to check on."

"Bertha?"

"My ride. Parked downhill. First I got to snag the camera." He reached into a tree and extracted a tiny camera. "It's motion activated. Could you put it in my pack?"

He was tall and inches above me. I guessed six feet as I zipped his camera into an outside pocket. High on the ridge, cracking noises and dull thuds turned us both uphill.

"It's not a normal logging operation," I said. "The landowner here is going to cut every tree that makes any kind of money before he turns the land over to the power company that's going to build all over it. You must know this place like your backyard, so maybe that's not good news."

Chan stepped back to stare at me. "It *is* my backyard."

"It's going to get severely mowed," I said.

"Naw, I have a deal with them. I gave them a map where I trap and they said they'd work around."

"Did that mean they'd work around *in* it or that they'd avoid it?" I asked.

He snorted. "I know the crew boss. I'm covered."

# FIVE

My arms ached from the dive through the van window. My knees throbbed from the crazed scramble over uneven terrain, and my throat felt like sandpaper. Pock looked beaten up, too. He lay on my feet and licked his front paws where red welts cut through his chaffed fur.

"How long is this checking going to take?" I asked.

"We'll be out by dark," Chan said. "You handle that?"

"Sure," I said.

I unzipped my pack and waved a water bottle at Chan. "I've got an extra. You want some water?" I cupped my hand into a doggie water bowl and lowered it toward Pock's nose.

"Drink on the way," he said.

"You never had beaver fever?" I asked.

"You mean giardia? Sure. I lived in the outhouse for a week. Now I know where the good springs are."

A fifteen-year-old who knew his way around bacteria and water. Here was a kid—a person—who probably knew more than I did. Why hurry? Arriving anywhere meant Pock and I would find angry wardens, police, and crime-scene folks. With Chan, we might enjoy more hours of freedom before someone in uniform found us.

A chain saw growled up several octaves as it chewed through something tough. I nodded toward the top of the ridge. "Up there, they're removing big chunks of your backyard. How about a tour before it's gone?"

He shook his head. "You're making fun of me."

I unzipped a deep pocket in my pack where I kept emergency supplies. I felt through the toilet paper and dental

47

floss and pulled out a handful of chocolate bars. "Truce," I said.

The boy grabbed the candy and turned quickly away into the woods. Pock dragged me downhill after him, lured by the kid's stinky pack, but my leashed dog went one way around trees as I went the other. It was fifteen minutes before I caught up to Chan as he was turning over rotten logs.

"So what are you checking for?" I asked.

"Checking?"

"You said you had to check on things."

"Oh, yeah. Well, it's way too hot. I want to know if the salamanders are OK. I go around and see if everyone's where they're supposed to be and doing what they're supposed to be doing. If a place has the most important animals, the place checks out."

"Checks out?"

He lurched his head toward the ridge above us. "If there's goshawks and pine marten up in the big trees, you know that part of the woods is OK. You don't have to look for everyone if the mascot animals are OK. My mom's a bird nut. She knows all the names. I don't. If the pine martins and goshawks are there, her birds will be too."

Forty years ago, when almost no one knew what ecology was, I'd had a high school ecology class. Each morning Mr. Munn would huddle us up with pails and trowels and collecting tools. "Salute," he'd cry. We'd lift our copies of *A Sand County Almanac* into the air.

"And what does our forestry mentor Mr. Leopold say is the first rule of intelligent tinkering?" Mr. Munn asked.

Afraid of our indoor classmates' scorn, we whispered, "Save all the pieces."

"And what will we find here today? And louder please."

48

"All the pieces," we yelled. If we barked like marines and added "sir," he waved us into the woods.

From the bottom of dirt holes to the tops of trees in our study plot, we found all the pieces and all the animals that depended on them. I grew up thinking that "save all the pieces" was the best way to explain the wild world. No preaching. No shrill lectures. Just common sense.

Chan knew the pieces from putting his hands on them.

"And you trap—what?" I asked.

"Red squirrel and marten when they're up there, and they should be. It's fall. Squirrels are after the cones and marten hunt squirrel. I harvest the marten."

I didn't like the word *harvest* to describe hunting or culling or managing or whatever one does to kill the wild world. We didn't plant the animal crop in the first place, so we didn't get to mow it down like wheat. It's hunting. Or trapping. I liked a fair match-up.

I could see Chan's point of view. The person who sets the trap knows more than the creature that walks into it. But I grew up expecting to be outwitted by wildlife. My father always complimented deer for knowing more about moving around the woods than he did. He liked it that way, and I did too.

Chan seemed in no hurry to head down the mountain, so I let Pock off his leash. "You're scouting out where you'll set traps, right?"

He squatted over spruce cones mounded up into an untidy pile. "Trappers notice stuff. We watch a lot. There's a squirrel making a mound here, getting ready to make a pile he won't eat. He'll visit it all winter."

In a grassy area between fallen trees I saw what looked like a miniature graveyard. A rusted shovel missing half its handle leaned against a tree, and each small dirt-hill was marked with a popsicle stick.

"You might leash your dog," Chan said. "He'll be after my research."

Pock had already unearthed something gray that waved greasy-looking limbs as he joyously tossed it in the air.

"That's OK," said Chan. "No prob. I'll bury it again, but he might have some maggots or beetles on him. Better check."

Hoping nothing crawled up my hand, I pulled a twig from my hair and poked around on Pock. Black things fell off and scurried away. I pulled my jacket up over my nose. "What *was* that?"

"A hare I skinned out last March."

Different kinds of hairs on my neck lifted with fear. I wondered how deeply the mace was buried in my pack. This was not an average field trip. "This some kind of school project?"

Chan was bent over his shovel and digging a new hole for the hare. "Kind of. I'm home-schooled so I get to set up most of the learning I want to do. I'm making an inventory of what eats what underground—a buried food chain. And I think a skinned animal's gotta attract some cool insects. The sticks tell me the burial date and what I put there. Now I'm going to bury this." From his pack he pulled a zip lock bag. Bulging eyeballs pressed against the plastic.

I turned away and gulped great mouthfuls of air. Where did I need to go to avoid body parts? Grand Central Station? The Lincoln Memorial?

"I'm after the eyes. They're the first bug target." Chan said. He twisted the bag so it caught the sun and the eyes gleamed and danced happily in the bag.

I'm not a wimp. We ski patrollers deal with spurting blood

and bones that poke out through skin like mismatched chopsticks. Dizzy, I leaned against a tree and gulped long breaths.

"Hey. You OK?" Chan asked.

"Fresh air should cure it," I said. "I've had a bad day is all."

"Let's get you down closer to Bertha," Chan said. "Down low near water. Most everyone likes it down there."

Pock trotted by the boy's side, turning to see if I was visible. I caught up with them by a car-sized depression of black, rotten leaves. Chan was flipping them with the toe of his boot. "You know what this is. Right?"

"Vernal pool," I said, "but it's dried up now that everything's hatched out of it. As a kid I collected frog eggs in pools up behind my house." As the trail widened into an old overgrown road, we walked side by side.

I reached into my store of mind-blowing facts saved up to win people over. "Get this. Vernal pool creatures weigh more than moose."

"No way," Chan said.

"If we dumped all Maine's moose in one pile and all the creatures that hatch from vernal pools in other, they'd outweigh the moose. Probably in value, too. Frogs and salamanders and their kin are protein concentrators. No hooves or useless parts. Everything's digestible. Very yummy and efficient for creatures up and down the food chain."

"You're a biologist?" Chan sounded hopeful.

"No. Biologists like to do research away from the front lines where it can get tense. I used to get sent out to deal with people who sometimes weren't happy with salamander or frog conservation—groups not happy with wildlife conservation in general.'"

Chan stopped and turned. "What's the big deal?"

I kept walking. "Change is. It's tough to ask for change."

He fell into step with me again. "Like what?"

I couldn't remember the last time someone asked about what I really used to do for work. I knew I could get long and winded, so I stayed with the pools. "Like with vernal pools," I said. "We'd ask logging companies that were controlling road dust with chemicals to stop spreading them near pools. Just for a few weeks in the spring. Just till the adults could cross the roads, find the pools, and lay eggs. It's tough to find a mate and produce young if you've been poisoned. Some crews agreed to help out. Others ignored us."

The boy walked quietly for a few minutes. "I've got a lot to learn," he said.

"I think you're probably way ahead of most kids. You're out here every day burying stuff, digging it up, looking at it— way ahead of most kids."

We stopped at the lip of a waterfall that fell off bare ledges into a stream far below. In the distance, heat shimmered like a desert mirage. We could see a large marsh, its looping channels braiding their way into a stream that ran in and out of beaver ponds. A bald eagle lifted off of a dead tree near us and swooped low over the ponds. Warned by its shadow, ducks skittered into protected coves.

"That's Franklin," Chan said. "He used to have Eleanor, but she got electrocuted by a power line last spring."

"You name animals?"

"When I get to know them."

"What happens when you kill someone you know?" I asked.

Chan turned to face me, one hand clenched white on his shotgun.

"OK. OK. Down there around water is where most all the animals need to come and go from where they live, eat, hide, hunt. Me too, so I've met most of them." He smiled a soft smile that didn't make it to his eyes. "I've killed ducks, partridge, deer, bear, otter, mink, coyote, fox, beaver, muskrat, bobcat, raccoon, and squirrel. Add marten. And one fisher. And skunks under our house. If I won a permit in the moose lottery, I'd kill a moose, too." He tipped his chin into the air and looked down his long regal nose at me.

I watched a small log float over the edge of the falls where it popped up next to a grazing bull moose. Chan was already back in the trees, Pock on his heels.

"Wait," I said. "What was that all about?"

"To get it over with," he yelled over his shoulder, "so I don't have to wait around for a lecture I don't need."

# SIX

I usually trust my dog. There'd been one scary episode where he should have known someone offering him unlimited hot dogs was too good to be true, and we'd almost died in a cage full of wolves, but no one's perfect. He trotted behind Chan, ears up, tail wagging his whole body. It wasn't just the skunk aura floating after the boy. Pock had made up his mind to like Chan.

As we worked our way downhill, climbing over downed trees and skirting raspberry thickets, I could see Chan's generosity everywhere. Piles of cedar brush were mounded next to tall balsam firs, where sheltering deer could nibble cedar until the spring thaw eased their hunger.

In a marsh, old tree snags sticking out of a small pond supported square boxes with large round holes: wood duck nests built and nailed up by the boy. Wood ducks usually nest in trees, but these birds had luxury condos high above predators that would be hungry for spring eggs.

Chan sat on a log, pulled off his rubber boots, and waded toward a tiny island, bending to pick handfuls of grass as he sloshed ashore. Birds flapped around his head as he shook the stems and they rained down white kernels. He turned and pointed. "No dog," he said.

I pulled Pock into a sit. Two ducks swam so close that we could see each feather as if we had a magnifying glass. Pock shivered slightly but sat still. Long ago my dog had learned that his lips would never touch a fast duck. Their webbed feet treading water, the birds swayed back and forth, staring at us. The male wood duck looked like an extravagant art installation staged far from a museum.

He had bright red irises that matched the red of his bill. His wing feathers were iridescent blue slashes, and his vivid green head sported white racing stripes that folded into feathers pointed backwards like an aerodynamic bike helmet. Someone with minimalist tendencies had finished him off. His body was geometric blocks of brown shades, some with a copper sheen, other hues compressed between tiny white lines that looked like contour lines on a map. The basically brown female blended into her surroundings, but blue wing feathers marked her as a wood duck.

"Oh, Pock. Have you ever?" I asked. He was still trembling, oblivious to ducks as living, breathing art.

Scattering the birds and wading back to us, Chan grinned. "Wild rice. If I was hunting them, it might be illegal—feeding them during hunting season. 'Specially since I planted it. But I'm not hunting ducks, and I make sure no one else is either."

I wondered how he patrolled land that wasn't his. The maps Anita and I used were clear. Premier Power & Energy had leased land from the top of the ridge to the low valleys on each side of it. They'd hired the landowner, Great Nations Forests, to cut everything that grew on the eighty acres they'd use, and they were happy to let the company cut anywhere else it could find trees.

Somehow Chan seemed like this property's rightful owner for so many good reasons—some of which I didn't agree with—but his name wasn't on any deed. We crossed and recrossed a winding stream that reappeared from humps of moss whenever it wanted to run free. Ambushed by a memory that almost hurt, I sank to the ground and closed my eyes. Nothing smells as clean as moss washed by a stream—unless it's the stream as ice.

Long ago, sledding on kitchen trays, my brother Giffy and

56

I and the neighborhood kids had been a rag-tag luge team screaming around stream corners and rolling off into frozen moss when fallen trees blocked our route.

Chan walked back and stood over me. "What?" he asked.

"I had a place like this when I was a kid. We called it fairy land. Moss and stream water and in the winter—sliding on it. I didn't lose any teeth, but my brother did. We had to lie about what we were doing. We all protected fairy land."

"Still there?"

"No. Of course not. Eventually it got to be prime real estate."

"So?"

Ignoring his outstretched hand, I pushed myself off the ground. I also ignored grocery clerks' offers to carry my bags. "My dad sold it to a developer. We came home from school and it was gone. In one day. Maybe a century to grow the trees, and then even more years for the weather and tree-eating plants to create moss, and then I don't know how long for the stream to wear minerals off the rocks so that small chips looked like fairy dust. At least to us. Just a few hours and—gone." I slapped green bits off my jeans and looked at Chan. "Must sound pretty silly. Losing fairy land."

"No," he said, trotting downhill. "Nope."

By a massive beaver dam, Chan had chain-sawed a pile of birch for the beavers. Beavers don't usually need help from anyone, but drag marks under the water showed the residents were storing up the limbs they'd eat after ice closed the pond. "Wait, here," Chan said as he carefully shouldered his shotgun and navigated logs mudded into the top of the dam. Pock didn't even look back as he raced after him.

A mask and snorkel in a plastic bag lay by the edge of the dam. Why hadn't I thought of snorkeling with beavers, mink, muskrat, or trout at an age when I didn't mind bloodsuckers? I picked my way over the sticks on the top of the dam, snipping off late goldenrod sprouting along the top. I thought I'd plant my rear end where leaks trickled into the stream below, so I'd get nicely saturated and cooled off. I didn't see the deer carcass on the far side of the dam until a bald eagle landed on it. Each jab of his curved beak brought up something red and stringy. He may have been eating, but his intense yellow eyes tracked every move I made.

He wasn't bald. White feathers overlapped his head and cascaded around his shoulders in a fashionable shag haircut. His feet looked like bright yellow rain boots with knives at each toe. I had a flash of a James Bond movie where lethal objects snapped out of everyday items and killed people. A bit of white brow sagged over each eagle eye, gathering darkness into his stare.

I reached down to scratch my ankle. He swiveled his head almost one hundred and eighty degrees until his eyes locked onto mine—eyes so close across his narrow skull they didn't even look cross-eyed. He just looked like the most intelligent, pissed off being I've ever seen. The huge bird had eyes that didn't blink, not even when I sat on a log and hung my feet over the edge of the dam into the pond. Not even when I pulled off my shirt, dragged it in the water, and put it back on wet.

The eagle was offering a serious inquisition from a top predator to someone lower and more lackluster in the food chain. I felt like I was about to get arrested, so I thought about being polite. *That looks tasty. Bet that's something yummy the boy left you. Don't worry about me. I've got a granola bar.*

*No closer. I already spared you once when you arrived.*

*Got it. You on personal terms with the boy?*

*I watch him. He watches me. He leaves me meat when he*

*finds it on the road.*

*Roadkill? That sounds extra special.*

*Most humans would drive on by. You as well. This boy is not like other humans.*

The eagle and I watched a beaver rise from the pond and slap its tail on the water—a warning to his family about outsiders. I shifted on my log perch, wondering if these beavers were safe. I'd heard it took about eight minutes for a beaver to drown in a trap—maybe in front of its frantic mate.

I watched it carve a smooth water trail with a swinging tail until it dove back under the water. The eagle ripped off more red pieces, and I turned toward him. *Did you know beavers mate for life? Even I wasn't good at that.*

*Death will come when it will come.*

*Oh, great. An eagle spouting a line from Shakespeare. OK. OK. So far, my trapping experience has been seeing my dog bloodied in a snare and thinking about how that beaver might die. It's too much.*

*Too much what? Too much red tooth and claw?*

*Yes.*

The eagle ripped more flesh and gave it a slight toss so he could catch it in the air. *Tooth and claw everywhere. Your kind doesn't even eat what it kills.*

He buried his head in the carcass, and I turned my face into the sun, feeling the edge of cool as shadows grew longer over the pond. At the sound of a rough engine, the bird grabbed a stringy chunk and struggled to lift it and himself into the air. One wing cuffed the edge of my ponytail, so I bent double and grabbed my ankles. At lift off, wind from his wings rippled the water. His shadow was as wide as the pond.

Chan pulled up to the dam in a camouflage green and brown all-terrain vehicle outfitted with more lights than a mall parking lot. Pock hopped from an oversized apple crate lashed to its luggage rack and ran toward the abandoned carcass, but Chan kicked it over the edge of the dam where it vanished downstream.

"You met Franklin?" Chan asked.

"He's very impressive," I said.

"After Eleanor got electrocuted, I decided to help him out."

Chan clapped his hands for Pock to leap back into the crate. "Well, this is Bertha. Our ride." He straddled the ATV's seat and waved me up behind him. "Most eagles are impressive, but Franklin's got some parenting issues. Didn't step up after Eleanor died and left eggs in the nest."

The ATV's muffler stopped my questions. What kid knows an eagle well enough to weigh in on its domestic skills? With one hand behind me to feel Pock bumping in the crate and one hand around Chan's waist, I bounced up the rutted trails through an apple orchard so old its gnarled branches reminded me of bad arthritis. I could relate. My fingers were getting there.

I wasn't prepared for the house—the mansion. It was classic Maine. The new Maine, where a small coastal cape or lakeside cabin was razed and replaced by something the size of a bus terminal, often owned by folks who visit a few times a year.

My father's real estate office had been crammed with flyers of small, overpriced camps that almost screamed, "Tear me down and spend gobs of money." As a teenager I was tasked with sending these advertisements to people who probably would not love small, sagging refuges the way I loved Antler Camp.

Chan's home had pine logs stained a California redwood color, three stories of floor to ceiling windows that hurt my eyes with reflected sunset, wrap-around porches, sculpted stone chimneys, and covered walkways to a four-car garage. An entire south-facing roof had solar panels. Below it, wide lawns could have hosted a soccer tournament.

I smiled. Maine's weeds and wildflowers were moving fast, already choking out more expensive garden plants I didn't recognize. Lupine, tall and confident that it could win over any landscape, had grown its petals into large seed pods ready to burst open with millions of new Lupine recruits.

The house and grounds explained Chan's sumptuous leather jacket, but not his ratty clothes or his paying bills with animal skins. At least thirty bat boxes made of mismatched wood scraps interrupted the garage's tasteful façade. Thin slits in each box invited the bats to worm their way inside to a dark sleep.

"The bat boxes nailed to the garage are a nice touch, Chan." I said. "Are they your editorial comment on the palace?"

"My father tried to buy my mother with it," he said, waving a hand at the house and garage. "Didn't work. The bat boxes didn't either. Well, they did at first, but lately there's not many bats."

"It's called white-nose syndrome and—"

"I know. I know," he said, tossing a tarp over the ATV. "Fungus that kills bats. Last year someone showed up asking about caves and I showed him some. Then a whole van of scientists came with the Ken guy, put on booties, masks, and white suits, and took away all the dead ones. Said they'll be back next winter."

"Ken Douglas?" I said. "He's my old boss."

Chan dropped the tarp ropes he was tying and whirled around toward me. "You got to work with him?"

"Mostly grunt work. Last year I nailed up hunting regulations, wrapped animal evidence and froze it, and collected moose teeth in jars." I wiggled my toes and felt something squishier than socks. "This year I'm picking up dead bats and birds at wind power sites. I wouldn't get too excited about grunt science work."

"So," said Chan, walking out where he could see the entire driveway. "Don't you have someone who wants you back some time? Like soon? Like your boss?" We stood in the driveway, Pock sitting between us, and the boy shifting weight from foot to foot. I had a bad feeling he expected me to hoof it up the road away from his house.

"Can you give us a lift to Greenwood?" I asked. "I'll fill up your tank."

"I could," he said, "but I won't be legal on the way back. I only got a learner's permit."

Wondering about my boot, I limped to the nearest stone wall and sat on it, dropping my pack, untying my boots, and pulling at my wet socks. "I'm bushed, Chan, and I need to explore my socks." I held up one bare foot. It hosted several blood suckers. Like large worms avoiding daylight, their black bodies wigged frantically, but they weren't about to stop drinking me. My stomach turned over a few times. Pock came to sniff them and backed off, growling.

"Oh God! I hate blood suckers," I moaned. "Really bad childhood skinny-dipping experience."

Chan ducked under the ATV's tarp and came out with a first aid kit. "You want salt or heat?" he asked.

"What's faster?"

"Heat, but when I'm done I need you to go before they find you. The cops." He lit a match and bent toward my foot. "Hold still."

I looked away as I felt him trace the match slowly around the first blood sucker's mouth. "Was it the wire cutters that gave me away?" I asked.

When he laughed his voice cracked into deep chuckles that hinted at the man he'd soon become. "Sorry, but you were a total sweat-hog. I mean, who runs through woods when it's this hot?" He lit another match. "So I checked you out online when I came up here to fire up Bertha. State police. Game wardens. County sheriff. They all want you. But not me. I don't want you. I don't even want to know what you did if those people want you."

"What if I refuse to go?" I asked. "I mean, after I tell you I didn't do anything but find something in the road." He was closing up the first aid case. "And it was only one body part. Just one."

He used a burnt match to shove blood suckers off the stone wall, and then opened his hands and pushed his palms toward the driveway as if shooing away small rodents. "OK," he said. "Maybe we'll meet up sometime and you can explain stuff, but now's—"

He dropped the kit and was in the trees and out of sight before I heard gravel crunch around the front side of the house. I pushed myself off the stone wall and limped over the overgrown lawn to see who'd found me. A green truck filled the driveway and Pock bounced gleefully off of Moz, who fended him off with one hand while he held a phone to his ear with the other.

"I will collect her statement and use the fax in my truck," he said, reaching down to rub Pock's ears and then frown at his hand. "From the looks of Ms. Conover and her dog, useful evidence appears unlikely, but I will bring her clothes. Send the team home."

I patted my hair and found it bristled with sticks and leaves. I smoothed my shirt sleeves and pant legs and my hands came away muddy. Moz led me back to the wall and gently pushed me down on it. His body creaked with leather—wide heavy belt, gun holster, pouches for ammunition, GPS unit, citations book, and maybe even pouches that were just for intimidation. They didn't intimidate me. The fact that he was still not sweaty did.

When our respective children were small, I had listened for his leather noise as he collected his sleepy boys from our camp couch, chanting something low in a language I didn't know. After his wife had packed for Philadelphia and a life she called "civilized, paved, and varmint free," his boys had dragged their suitcases from her car and locked themselves to a swing set with their father's antique handcuffs. After that, Antler Camp became their second summer home.

I closed my eyes. I probably knew more about the sound of Moz than I knew about the man himself. I heard Pock sniff around his truck and re-pee each tire as a special welcome.

"That's not going to keep the dust down," Moz said, legs apart, arms crossed over his chest. Warden stance. Firm warden stance. "I see no blood on you or your dog. How did you find him?"

"He was howling in a bear trap. The boy who owned it released him and brought us here."

"Where is the boy?" Moz asked.

I looked back at the mansion. "No lights. Maybe he's in the garage." I hadn't made a conscious decision to help Chan, but there it was.

Moz sat with me and slowly scanned the swamp, ponds, and streams before lifting his stare to the ridge in a methodical sweep of the terrain, visualizing territory as if he crawled through it.

He took a deep breath and let it out with a low whistle.

"Young Mr. Chandler Perkins is watching us with a scope or binoculars. We will not find him," he said.

"How do you know that?"

"I taught the law to his trapper education class as he prepared for his licensing exam." The granite slant of his cheeks softened slightly. "Chandler does not visit woods. He is woods. Perhaps the only white boy I know who lives it as air he must breathe. He is aware of what he needs." Moz looked at me and paused. "Often, I think you are not."

After that, we were silent for minutes.

I slid sideways so I could face him—my two eyes on his two eyes. That was a scary thing to do. I could only compare the experience to chocolate sauce. When something is so compelling that one small bite of it has us plunging all five fingers into the pan, that's seduction at a cellular level. Seduction that wasn't about sex.

The wounded parts of me wanted to melt toward something in his eyes, but I didn't want him thinking I was wounded. And I didn't want him thinking he could diagnose me anytime he wanted to.

"It's no accident you're here," I said, grateful that Pock had jumped on the wall between us and put his head first in my lap and then in the warden's. "You helped me escape."

"I executed a remedy, not an escape. There was sickness on that road. Not what you saw, but what made it." He looked uphill. "Moving through the woods is a healing activity."

I thought Moz probably had lots of personal experience with that remedy. I had to admit it had worked. I felt strong again. Tired but strong.

Moz reached for my pack and unclipped a small orange disk about the size of a hockey puck. "I lost you for several hours, but as you stood above the pond, I retrieved your location."

I grabbed the device and turned it over and over in my hand, feeling the NWSS carved into its case. "You put that on my pack to track me?"

Moz retrieved it and closed a tiny rubber door on its side. "We should avoid the emergency button under this flap. The 911 people are not happy with you today."

Moz was his own security firm. Occasionally off-duty wardens worked security for various events, but Moz took no salary for his efforts. He activated North Woods Security Systems only when the world he cared about was at risk. Even trusted people he hired kept his side business secret. I'd never been hired, but I was trusted.

I knew I should thank Moz for the escape remedy. I'd avoided itchy police clothes and a badly lit interrogation room because he'd protected me at PP&E's parking lot. I just couldn't do it. "What gives you the right to engineer my escape and then track me like you hadn't made it happen?"

He pulled burrs from Pock's back and stacked them neatly on the wall while I inspected red circles left by the blood suckers and pulled on my boots. "Until very recently, my colleagues thought you and Pock might be connected to what we found," he said. "They wanted to quarantine him. They wanted to transport you to headquarters. I gave them time to reconsider, and I gave you time to find your dog. And yes, I tracked you."

I jumped off the wall. "Thaaaat's great," I said, boots squishing when I landed. "I could have avoided feeling criminal and paranoid for hours if I'd known you'd called off the search." I squeezed more water out of the socks I carried. "You're here to offer me a friendly ride to jail?"

He shook his head. "I will take you home if you give me a statement, your clothes, and agree to meet with investigators if they wish to question you."

Something had shifted. "Recently," I said. "You said 'until recently.' What's changed? Are Pock and I off the hook for something we didn't do anyway?"

Moz stood and stretched, shifting all his creaking gear so it rode low on his hips. "You may wait in the truck. I need to examine the house for—"

I put myself almost on top of his toes. My neck hurt looking up at him. "What's changed? I know you can't give me details, but maybe just a vague progress report."

He backed away and walked toward the house. "We found what appears to be the murder weapon at the site."

I trailed behind him. "Murder? It's murder if a blade falls off a tower and slices someone?"

He stopped on the top step, lifting one hand to rub late-day shadows growing on his cheeks. "A falling blade did not kill or dismember the victim. Ken Douglas convinced investigators that you could not operate construction equipment."

I thought that was a bit harsh. Ken had never asked me to learn big machines when I worked for him, and I'd only dented one trailer. Last winter at a ski area I drove snow cats up and down vertical slopes in genuine blizzards without wrecking anything. I closed my eyes and thought about PP&E's parking lot. Aside from Anita's and my cars, only a bulldozer was inside the gate.

"A bulldozer did the deed? A bulldozer?" I asked. I thought anyone could operate one of those. How much skill could it take? Climb into the cab. Turn a key. Fiddle with a stick control to move it forward. Fiddle with another stick to drop the blade on someone. Really? A bulldozer?

Moz was already through the unlocked front door. "That's it?" I called. "You're just going to drop that bomb and turn away? Don't you need a warrant to go in there?"

I knew better. Game wardens have the authority to check pockets, packs, cars, boats, homes, and any place someone might hide a violation. I'd seen Moz pull multiple trout out of ratty looking boxers worn by an equally ratty looking man—although I wish I hadn't.

He reappeared at the door. "Patton. I have already said more about this death than is wise. I would simply like you to know that you are not suspected of—"

I interrupted. "Murder? Someone got murdered right under Anita's and my noses? And I was a suspect?"

He placed one hand on my nearest shoulder. "I will need you to move on now," he said. "Much to do. Would you please step in and give me your opinion?"

Muttering, "Much to do. Right, much to do." I followed him inside.

Everything was Martha Stewart rich: stainless steel ranges, refrigerators, appliances, and stacked in corners, hi-tech phones, TV's, a sound system, and game consoles. Nothing hummed, beeped, or blinked because nothing was plugged in. Side hallways and the stairs to upper floors were blocked with large panels of rigid insulation.

The formal dining room was crowded with baskets of clothes next to four beds. Three beds were covered with stuffed animals, each pillow mounded with folded pajamas. The fourth bed's pillow was dented by a large, chipped cross.

I sifted through baskets. "No men. One woman and three girls, aged around four or five, seven or eight, and someone with a training bra."

Moz raised his eyebrows.

"The cups are just for practice so boys get to snap bra backs and girls get to squeal. It's a rite of passage that I hope has outlived its day."

Moz lifted each mattress and bent to look under each bed.

"Why are you searching the place?" I asked.

"I believe Chandler Perkins has been harboring eagles. Young eagles. Raising eaglets."

"Doesn't look like he's bunking in here. Don't you have something more pressing than eagle crime?"

Moz smoothed each bed and rearranged stuffed animals. "Your assessment?"

"OK. OK." I walked around the dining room that was now a dormitory. "They seem comfortable but are living low. Very low. Maybe off the grid and unplugged. They're heating just a few rooms and have closed off the rest of the house. It could be money stress, but they also might be hiding. Chan was antsy to get rid of me. Almost shoved me down the driveway."

A wood stove was plugged into the kitchen's fireplace chimney and four school desks, the old-fashioned one-piece kind, were arranged around it. Each desk had completed worksheets—assignments for children who might have ranged from first grade to high school. My fingers made dust trails down the middle of each seat. No one had used the desks for a long time.

I picked up a *Charlotte's Web* quiz and moved to a window for light. This was my all-time favorite book. A spider spins words in a web, hoping to amaze humans into saving her pig friend Wilbur from becoming bacon. The quiz used my favorite spider lines, the ones I scrawled on document margins while I waited my turn to testify about stressed populations of mayflies, salamanders, turtles, and butterflies. All creatures low on most legislators' evolutionary list.

Question two on the quiz asked the student to identify a quote. "If I can fool a bug, I can surely fool a man. People are not as smart as bugs."

I often thought Charlotte was right. Most people weren't as smart as bugs.

I blew on the paper. "There's dust on the seats, but not on the papers that have today's date. Looks like the boy's writing. He's kept all the papers and worksheets up to date." I didn't mention I knew his printing from popsicle sticks that marked carcasses.

Overjoyed barking took us both to the door. My dog had dragged skins across the driveway, nosed them eagerly into a pile, and was circling them, wagging furiously, preparing himself for a satisfying roll. I had seconds to save Chan's work.

# SEVEN

Moz and I followed Pock's drag marks, carrying the pelts downhill toward a dark grove of balsam fir. As I rubbed the skins against my cheek, I felt my resolve to avoid fur products grow weak. I'd never felt anything so soft.

"So. Chan lives in the property's original buildings," I said when we found the sagging camp, outhouse, and shed. Mounds and mounds of firewood were stacked neatly around a Ford truck that was colored light blue and rust. An antique gas-fired wood splitter covered with fresh wood chips and rust stood next to the outhouse. Of course. Woods shavings tossed down the toilet hole deodorized outhouse living.

The shed's open door explained Pock's theft of the boy's pelts. As we stepped inside, I reeled back against the outside wall before I swung back inside with a large gulp of air. Nothing smelled rotten, but it was like being inside an animal or an animal being inside me. The combination of fur, skin, and animal parts was like something I'd eaten without taking a bite.

Some furs were stretched on wire frames. The muskrats and raccoons looked like flat, oversized pancakes. Others hung by their noses. I thought the whole process must be slippery, because large buckets were under the table and the floor was deep in wood shavings. Knives and scraper tools were stacked next to short pieces of wood that looked like tiny ironing boards. I guessed the boards were for scraping pelts free of parts that could decay. Chan's rubber apron, streaked with stains, hung on the door.

We stacked the furs on a work table. Moz smoothed each

pelt as he checked for tags. I carried a pine marten pelt to the window where fading light caught the yellow patch on its neck. Was this quiet creature the marten child who didn't listen? The child of the angry parent I'd met in the woods?

I leaned my cheek into its fur. *I think I met one of your parents today. Very angry.* The marten was limp in my hand. Dead things don't often speak to me, so I returned the pelt to the table.

"All tagged and legal," Moz said, inviting me outside. "Perhaps a thousand dollars here. More if we add the firewood outside he's cut to sell."

Chan's small camp looked the way a bare-bones hunting camp should look. The round log walls had long ago been cemented together with mud. Here and there a darker smear showed recent repairs. When we stepped inside, it was so cool that bumps rose up my arms.

Through a hole in the floor, a ladder disappeared into sawdust sprinkled over ice. I was impressed. Chan's root cellar was his air conditioning. Dug deep in the dirt, it was well-insulated and filled with ice cut from the frozen pond. Barrels of apples and potatoes looked mold-free and edible. My stomach growled loudly in the quiet camp.

Faded green linoleum covered the floor until it reached the tiny woodstove and curled up against its edges. Chan seemed to be advertising his hermit status with just one of everything: one pot, one mug, one plate, one spoon and fork, and strangely, one plastic glass decorated with running wolves.

"You didn't tell him about the wolves, did you?" I asked, lifting up the glass. "No one else knows about that, right? Just you and me. Right?"

Moz nodded and moved quietly around camp, feeling his way through a sleeping bag and into the pockets of a fleece jacket so worn it looked like faded underwear. There was a toothbrush next to the sink and a full water bucket next to it. The only product on display was one bottle of Dr. Bronner's castile soap. Good for teeth, hair, face, body, counters, dishes, floor, and, as I happened to know, skunked dogs.

The laptop computer attached to a state-of-the-art laser printer didn't fit. Neither did the phone charger plugged into an extension cord that hung off the one chair. The Bible fit, but it looked oddly bulky so I opened it. Chan was doing what many boys his age do—hide behind something approved so he could read what he wanted to read. Only his Bible didn't host porn.

He'd pasted pages of nature guides and biology textbooks over the Bible's pages. Only a few lines of scripture remained carefully uncovered and underlined. *Ask the animals, and they will teach you, or the birds of the air, and they will tell you; or speak to the earth, and it will teach you, or let the fish of the sea inform you.*

Moz lifted the lid on a rusted box freezer and moved its contents around. Each wrapped fish had a date on it. I agreed. Always a good idea to eat the old trout first. Chan had marked venison, bear, and turkey with his hunting tag numbers and dates. Moz nodded his approval and kept digging. He was used to digging in freezers to find what was hidden. He pulled out a large plastic tub, lifted the lid, and slid the contents out on the floor. "This might reveal a problem," he said.

Foil-wrapped packages spilled around our feet. The dates ran from June into December, all printed in dainty script that was not Chan's. I bent to read the labels. Scout bake sale, marble cake. Library book sale, cookies. Homeschool Envirothon contest, shepherd's pie. There were four church supper packages. I felt drool gathering behind my lips when I saw the stroganoff. I wanted to open the track team banquet's fudge brownies on the spot.

"Given the amount of food his mother's put up to convince people she's here," I said, "we could eat well for a year." I was ready to assume Chan's mother was a truly gifted woman. "How's the freezer stay cold?" I asked.

Moz used his foot to nudge the stack of batteries next to the freezer. "I think our boy is using the solar powered roof and running power down here to charge batteries and operate the freezer and computer a few hours each day."

"He's not my boy," I said, lifting the tub back into the freezer. "Seems he's nobody's boy right now. Hiding out. What's with that? Chan as much as told me his father's gone, but where are the women? I mean where'd his mother go after she set up homework assignments for him and cooked months of food to fool outsiders?"

Moz frowned. "If she cannot be contacted, he may end up being housed by a state agency that cares for minors. We might wait here for a while."

He fluffed up the sleeping bag, lifted a pair of jeans onto a nail, and bent to collect tiny white-gray feathers off the floor and tuck them in his pockets. "He is alone here," he said, "but perhaps not this spring. The feathers are eaglet feathers. He must have operated some type of incubator to keep young birds warm."

Pock pawed the door until I let him in. Moz patted the cot. Pock jumped up, turned three times, and lay down. "He looks at home," he said.

"No way. I won't share Pock," I said.

Moz unsnapped his holster, removed his gun, and placed it on the counter by the sink. He pulled a large stump to the table, folded his hands on the table, and sat quietly interrogating me.

Because he was both a game warden and a Penobscot, his interrogations were inspired—like a yoga class where I was being guided to feel inside my body, moving from scalp to feet.

We were in a silent standoff, but the process had already reached my toes. I hung my pack on a moose antler nailed to the wall, pulled papers from Chan's printer, and sat in the only chair, my butt dropping low into the frayed cane seat.

Because I didn't want to look at Moz, I lifted the pages up to the remaining light. While Pock snored and Moz sat silent and watchful, I read Chan's book report. Kate had given me the same book for my birthday with a note thanking me for dragging her outside even when she didn't want to go.

*Last Child in the Woods* was a book about kids growing up without nature. The author called it "nature deficit disorder," but I just called it sad. Chan had a long list of good things nature did for young bodies and minds and a fine ending. "When the old folks die, we'll need an army of us to step up if we want trees, animals, air, water, and all the good stuff we take for granted."

I must have dozed off because I woke up to the sound of Moz lighting a kerosene lantern. Light flickered across his face, giving his sharp, high cheeks a warmth I'd never seen, but then I'd never shared a lantern with him.

I'd seen the canvas tent where he lived, pitched on a platform that angled out over a river. I'd spied into his barn where he turned wood into paddles, canoes, and animal masks so alive they looked ready to leap off the walls. I spent an entire afternoon researching Moz instead of looking for the "No Live Bait" signs Ken Douglas had sent me to retrieve. I even ended up rubbing sawdust on my face because it seemed more like perfume than perfume.

He was my ex-husband's friend, but always—somehow—

he was something like my silent partner. He used to ask for a second helping if Evan criticized my cooking. During Kate's nightmare phase, he'd seen the dark circles that smudged my eyes and swooped my daughter into his truck to play with his boys so I could nap. When I came to camp to live alone, Moz shoveled snow away from my mailbox and towed fallen trees from my driveway without my asking for help. Yet somehow, friendship wasn't sitting smoothly between us.

I pulled the stolen pair of wire cutters from my pack and tore a sheet of paper from the boy's notebook. Moz read over my shoulder as I scrawled.

*Hello Chan. Read your essay. It's first rate. I know someone who can help you publish it and get it out to kids 'cause they need it. P.S. You're busted. The warden and I know your mom's missing. Here are my wire cutters in case someone tries to arrest you and you need to get out the back window and find me. Patton. (And Pock too. He likes you.)*

"Those are not your wire cutters to give," Moz said, snapping his gun into his holster.

I had to agree with Anita. He didn't sound like anyone I knew in the warden service. His obviously wise grandmother, fed up with poorly funded reservation schools, had hired a British exchange student to tutor her grandson. That tutor must have been a very proper Brit. Even when delivered over the sound system of his truck, Moz's threats telling folks to give themselves up sounded like formal invitations to an exclusive event.

As we walked back toward the mansion, red lights that topped towers on the other side of the ridge winked on and off like warning beacons on airport runways. I'd never seen the wind project from Chan's side of the world. Windows in his massive, dark house reflected fiery streaks back out into the night. After settling us in his truck, Moz opened a small plastic bag and laid Chan's white feathers in it.

"May I keep one?" I asked.

"I am sorry, no. Even I cannot possess one eagle feather without an appropriate application to the government."

I had to lean across piles of communication gear to hear most of what he said as he started the truck. "We wait months or years to acquire ceremonial feathers, as if they were more precious than gold, but Premier Power & Energy has permission to kill eagles as if they are worthless. I do not know exactly how many deaths its license allows."

"I don't either," I said. I didn't want to add more gloom to the space we shared in his truck. Because I'd been fond of leaving fact sheets on legislators' desks, I already knew that the feds had a national total of allowable eagle carnage. All wind facilities combined could legally kill four thousand, two hundred American bald eagles, but who was really counting anyway?

I wondered if Moz knew that twenty-six more towers were planned for the ridge above us. He had to know, but he said nothing.

Moz parked his truck at the Road Kill Cantina and we waited out the engine's dying shudders. Given the day I'd had, eating from a carcass-themed menu might have been the last straw, but it was the only open place in town unless we wanted hot dogs from the gas station's steamer. Kate told me I must never be tempted. "A bacteria factory on steroids, Mummy," she said. "Not worth it for a night with the toilet."

A group of construction workers and loggers lounged outside the door flicking cigarette butts into the road. Each nudged the other as they saw the green truck and state logo. I thought I could tell the lawbreakers in the group. It was as if their shoulders got surly.

"I think my taking your statement might be easier if I buy you dinner," Moz said. He'd seen the men, but it was a game they played. He wasn't ignoring them, just taking inventory. Wardens are unfailingly nice at the start of any meeting. He moved his fingers over a small computer mounted below the instrument panel. "First I would like to research Chandler."

"What do you hope to find?" I asked.

"Often the Internet brings us helpful information."

Chan's personal YouTube channel, "Into Woods," flicked onto the screen. In two words Chan said what he liked and where he went. Clever. Moz scrolled down to the boy's spring videos. Chan was fishing, collecting fiddlehead ferns, picking up moose antlers dropped during the winter, and in one video, sleeping on fir boughs for long minutes of air time.

"No eaglets here," said Moz. He handed me one feather. "I will need that back."

I unwrapped a granola bar and reached behind me to find Pock's eager lips. "Are you going to arrest the boy?" I asked. "He could have found feathers anywhere."

"And spread them around his cabin? No. Chandler had young birds or one young bird, but I cannot prove it. Now I have time to guide him in a different direction." Moz pulled strands of hair behind his ears and settled his warden ball cap over them. "When I find him," he said.

I reached over and scrolled through the videos and stopped on one called, "Marten." We saw Chan's slow approach into a clearing. The camera picked up his hands reaching into a box-like trap hanging in a tree, and then it found the marten hanging upside down, metal jaws clamped around the middle of its stiff body.

"Turn it off," I said, jumping from the truck. "Had enough dead bodies today."

His hand on my elbow, Moz nodded his way through the men and offered up questions that didn't sound like the Moz I knew. "You boys have a good partridge season? And now you might be scoping out November deer territory?" He stopped near Ridge Dumais. "And Mr. Dumais. Our boys help you pull that new truck out of Shirley Bog? Well, we've all been stuck there I think."

As we went in the door, he dropped his voice warden low. "Be seeing you all later." It was the last line that clicked in the air and the men all knew what it meant.

I wasn't through the door before someone wearing too much purple threw her arms around me. Her head and pigtails only made it up to my armpits, so I was forced to smile over her head into a room of people who'd stopped eating to watch the show.

"You are not hurt? Why are you not hurt? All day I have to listen to customers' stories. You are with cut-up people. Your dog has finally done the bad thing. You ran away from badges people. You are hunted."

Francoise dragged me through her crowded restaurant to a back table piled with menus and newspapers. She liked to wear purple tights and clinging workout tops, claiming drunks could find "no grabbing places." With that much lycra fused onto her skin, she looked safe.

"Sit where I see you," she said. "I know you are with the big warden man, but so far, what good is he?"

Moz smiled and piled the table's contents off to one side. "Always a pleasure to see you too, Ms. Dodge."

We took side-by side seats under oversized hanging plants

that pretty much screened us from the room. Sweat shining on each forehead, the dinner crowd tried to pretend that the biggest news of the day, maybe the week, or even the month or year hadn't walked into the café. There was entirely too much swiveling of necks going on.

Hands on her hips, Francoise shook her pigtails. They were springing all over like indignant baby birds in a nest of black curls. "If you come back to town to live small life, Cassandra Patton, why are you big again?" she asked. "Now you are first page again. Most food is gone, but I will make you special."

"No need to name my meal after anything dead today," I said.

Francoise grabbed my cheeks and kissed each firmly. "Bien, mon amie. An omelette. For the man with long eyes, I make Flattened Before Grilled, Ham Hits Cheese."

She marched away to supervise butter-melting. Somehow, in a town that was the last stop before the woods met blacktop, she'd found a way to marry her native cuisine with tequila and a menu of dishes named after animals killed in the road.

Her Mexican nights had waiting lines out the door. I knew what Harvard economists might never understand. Francoise had a life-skills PhD—the kind where each day she learned something new so she would not fail.

I whispered to Moz. "What does she mean by your *long eyes?*"

Moz reached for a newspaper. "She believes wardens have eyes that see great distances."

"Because?"

"Because she never saw the spotting scope I used to see her netting fish in a closed stream."

"She never told me about that."

"It was a first offense. We think she did not understand that fish trapped in a pool are not the same as fish selected from a French grocer's tank. I arranged for her to cook a scholarship fund supper as community service."

He spread the day's paper on the table. In strong black letters the headline "Wind Farm Kills Unidentified Victim" was splashed across the top of the evening edition. Moz hummed a few descending notes of pleasure.

"They probably got it wrong," I said, rolling up my sleeves even further as onion-scented steam oozed from the kitchen.

"Misdirection is useful," Moz said. "We may have increased private time to reassemble the victim, reconstruct the death, and locate the responsible party. Or parties."

"You mean the murderer," I said.

Pulling a notebook from one side of his belt, he said, "I have already admitted too much to someone who is involved."

"I'm not involved."

He reached over and pressed his pen against my far cheek, turning my face toward his face. "I respect your desire to leave the world you knew before. I respect your choice to hibernate until you have decided that, for you, spring has arrived and you will reappear." He lowered the pen and lifted a stray hair strand from my forehead to the top of my head. "I respect you."

I opened his notebook and nudged it toward him. "You've got a job to do, and I'm being snotty and ungrateful. Dinner here instead of a sheriff's office vending machine is a very good thing."

In a rush, Francoise arrived with plates balanced up her arm, the dishwasher swooped in with coffee and mugs, and a large woman wearing overalls and suspenders pulled out two chairs across from us. She turned the chairs around and straddled them, pulling a mug close to her side of the table. She emptied the cream pitcher into it.

Francoise bristled and reached for the mug. "Private table," she said. "Pas pour vous."

The coffee tug-of-war spilled onto my omelet and floated several mushrooms to the surface. Moz leaned back, and under the table he braced both feet against the intruder's two chairs. His shove sent the chairs and the woman into a heap on the floor. Then he lifted my plate and handed it to Francoise. "If you don't mind," he said. "A fresh one."

On her way to the kitchen, Francoise hailed the rest of her dining room. "Closing," she called. "All to cash out. Vite, vite."

Moz calmly cut his grilled ham and cheese into four sections and chewed slowly on one. The woman on the floor sat up and glared at him. Huffing with effort, she righted one of the chairs and pulled herself up into it, never dropping the scowl she'd fixed on Moz. Apparently I didn't exist, so I lifted the other mug and sipped at it.

I guessed her age at forty-something. Like many women, she couldn't decide what kind of fashion statement she wanted to advertise, or maybe she wanted the world to know she was complicated. I'd already seen her steel-toed boots when she'd been upended on the floor.

Above them she wore rugged overalls that seemed impossible in a heat wave, except that underneath them was a filmy black camisole with slender straps. Severely cut straight hair pulled into mismatched barrettes couldn't hide recent salon expertise, and her short nails were sculpted into perfect curves. Calluses complicated the effect. Between her nails and the palms of her hands, each finger joint hosted raised, red lumps of skin that only hours with a hand tool could create. I voted for an axe or shovel.

The best part was her arms. From her biceps to her wrists, bright bluebonnet flowers were tattooed so thickly they rippled as if caught in a breeze. When she saw me staring, she said, "Cousins to your lupines. Texas cousins."

Moz cleared his throat so that we both had to look at him. "Cassandra Patton Conover, meet Lily Rose Baines Johnson."

# EIGHT

"I know who she is," snapped the woman, "but she's all alone now, right? All her green, save-the-forest groups are sucking deep what the wind industry gives them to smoke until they can't see the trees for that same god-damn smoke." She waved one flowered arm at me. "Sorry, honey. You're good. You got a lot of talented failures to your credit, and that makes sense since you don't have squat for money. That's something I can fix, ya know."

One hand, larger than Pock's two paws put together, lifted the newspaper and shook coffee drops off it. "That rag lies about everything. It says some monster workforce will get laid off if they shut that place down to find out why it blew up. The wind weasels don't deliver thousands of jobs. They move the same two hundred jobs around. Like those boys out front who work for Dent & Dent Construction. This fall they'll blow up Eagle Ridge and pave it, then get hired to rape some other virgin chunk of woods."

Moz pulled a card from his pocket, slid it across the table, and then lifted another section of sandwich. "Ms. Johnson. Ms. Conover and I would like to finish our meal, and then I have business with her. I already had business with you today when you handcuffed yourself to equipment that is part of our investigation." He lifted a set of cuffs off his belt and softly laid them on the table so they made no noise. "You may contact me at this number if you have information about today's event. If you do not vacate these premises immediately—without further comment—I will handcuff you to plumbing in the restroom and return for you tomorrow."

85

Lily Rose Baines Johnson ripped the card in two and mushed it into the coffee puddle. Then she stood, snapped her suspenders into place, and stepped into the middle of the restaurant. "You and I aren't done yet, honey," she yelled back at me. "You and me, we're gonna get this mess stopped."

Through the café's screen door, I saw Lily climb into a battered VW van—painted fender-to-fender with flowers—and drive away, luminous petals parting the darkness as she disappeared.

"What was that?" I asked around forkfuls of a new omelet that oozed spinach and bacon. I was a bit grateful for Lily Rose, as my first dinner had had no bacon.

"We believe she is somehow related to a former President of the United States. Lyndon Baines Johnson," Moz said.

"Get out."

"She has a distinctive pedigree, which was provided to me as I lay under the bulldozer unlocking her many layers of chains." He flipped his notebook open.

"I thought you were wrestling a man under there this morning. Lily Rose doesn't appear to be anything like lilies and roses," I said. "Except for her arms. What's she done?"

"The then-president's wife, Lady Bird Johnson—perhaps Lily Rose's great aunt or godmother, we are not sure—had most of Texas planted into wild flowers, and she also dedicated parks and wilderness areas throughout the country. Lily Rose used to be called Augusta Claudia, but apparently, she changed her name to honor Lady Bird's efforts.

"Both women have a history of actions in defense of the planet, but Lily Rose is often on the wrong side of the law." He lifted one page to the light. "She claims to be here to single-handedly stop wind power in Maine, where she says—and I will quote—'it's the worst pile of cow-and-horse-turd-stupid

I've seen except all the turd-stupid-regular stuff I'd expect from Texans.'"

I didn't think Maine's new wind-power law was my personal failure, even if Lily Rose thought so. Most of Maine's environmental groups—the ones that used to hire me to protect the woods—simply chose wind over woods.

In back room strategy sessions, I had laid out the silliness. How could they spend years fighting off condos and golf courses in wild, backcountry places and then support a law allowing three hundred miles of roads, towers, and transmission lines in territory they'd sweated to protect?

Moz wiped his mouth on a napkin and lifted his pen. "Are you ready to describe your day from arrival at the site until I found you at Chandler's home? Then I will take you home and wait while you change."

"You still want my clothes?"

Moz colored all the way from his green uniform collar to the edge of his blacker than black hair. I turned in my seat to watch heat work its way up his face. Here was a man who in the course of his work saw men and women in extreme circumstances that could often involve nudity, and he was coloring up over the mention of clothes.

Last year he'd undressed me to my underwear and crawled into scratchy warden blankets with me to warm me up, but I was too banged up to notice if his skin changed color. I remember his hands kneading my back and some chanting in my ear, though.

Francoise set a large take-out bag on the table and pulled a chair close to me. I hoped the grease stains on the bag meant chocolate croissants. She rested one hand on my thigh and listened as I talked and Moz took an occasional note.

"And you and your employer Anita Stockdale saw no other

people or vehicles at Eagle Ridge in the previous days?" he asked.

"Just the regular PP&E work crew coming and going. They never spoke to us and we didn't speak to them. We waved, but that was it. Oh, and we liked to eat lunch on the bulldozer. Cushy seat."

A hint of smile lifted his lips. "When you ate lunch on the bulldozer, did you see a key in the ignition?" he asked.

"We saw the key. To prove our theory that anyone could operate one, I took us for a spin to the outhouse and back. We figured that since we locked the gates at night, the crew felt good about leaving the key, so we left the key too. Of course, it would take nothing to hike around the fences and get in further up the ridge," I said. I hiked around the gate every night I camped nearby in the woods.

After a few more questions, Moz sighed and closed his notebook. "Is there any additional observation you wish to contribute?"

Francoise dropped the bag in my lap, blew me a kiss, and marched away to flip her "Open" sign to its "Not Open No Way" side.

I opened the bag to breathe chocolate air. My brain cells tingled. "You know," I said, "before I started picking up pieces of dead birds and bats, I don't think I would have had much to say."

"And now?" asked Moz.

"I think it's too much of a coincidence that a chopped-up person was keeping company with chopped-up wildlife." I stood and tugged one of Francoise's pigtails—a thank you she'd recognize. "And now I want to go home, forget about today, and when I wake up, eat this entire bag given to me by this wonderful woman."

———

It was dusk as late-season mosquitoes mobbed me and I handed Moz a garbage bag with my muddy pants, shirt, and underwear—but not my hiking boots. To make sure I could keep my only pair, I'd ducked into my bathroom and poured white vinegar over them and then flushed them around in the toilet for good measure. I was pretty sure I'd made them unattractive to the forensic team. "I only have two pairs of jeans," I said, gripping my bathrobe close. "When do I get that pair back?"

"You may have a larger problem," he said. I followed him into the gloom until I could see that someone had tied my rear bumper to the kayak rack on the top of my car. "It fell into the road as my men delivered your car." he said.

Pock circled the car, wetting each tire to renew his ownership. "Is it legal to drive it this way? Looks like the lights and body are fine," I said.

"No, but I think if you continue to carry it on your roof, officers of the law might believe you are on your way to a garage."

My throat simply closed up on the news, which I had no bank account to solve. Evan was still haggling over post-divorce finances, using his firm's stable of attorneys to craft new requests that I detail income from multiple sources of employment. I was hoping a judge somewhere would look at a calendar and realize that my seasonal jobs were simple, one-job-at-a-time affairs.

I turned and opened the screen door to my sleeping porch. Moz stood in the driveway until he heard my rocking chair squeak and my boots hit the wooden rail. Then he fired up his truck and disappeared up the steep hill that pretends to be my driveway. I hoped I was in time for the nighttime loon chorus. It was the best part of the day and free of charge.

I lived a life in which I prayed daily that nothing would break. Toaster, refrigerator, teeth, and Pock, of course. Then there was my Subaru. It cruised along offering up defects as proof of good stories: dents from a moose attack, scrape lines where I'd dropped through thin ice, a cracked windshield from an aggressive log truck. My car was a marvel of steady, uncomplaining utility, but there'd been something dishonest about the rust—something that rotted unseen from the inside out.

I didn't want to make too much of my car by comparing it to my marriage, but it had also rusted from the inside out when the outside seemed so serviceable. Until I was traded in for a newer model without dents and weathered body parts, I thought Evan and I were cruising along just fine.

From the screened sleeping porch, I heard Pock bite bits of water he thought were floating debris. The lake was his pool and playground, and he often had company. Wings tucked tight to their bodies, our resident loons torpedoed themselves back and forth under his belly, knowing he'd never catch them. From the far side of the cove, one bird raised a haunted cry.

Loons were supposed to be the soul of lakes, but there was edgy insanity in their laughter—high notes that sounded strangled as they dropped into silence. In coves all over the lake, other loons answered. Their cries echoed each other until the wild music was silenced by an unseen conductor who allowed one last lingering note. The loons defending their territories sang themselves into my blood like a transfusion. I stood and stretched, feeling suddenly stronger and more able to defend my own territory.

Sweat trickled down my back, collected in my elbow

crevices, and made the skin pocket behind my knees squeak. I couldn't remember a September that felt like summer. It even smelled like summer, when hot grass odors rise off the ground like steam you can't see. I shoved open the porch door so Pock could drip in a corner and pant.

Latching the porch door, I thought about how Antler Camp beat out Chan's closed-up mansion. I had three pine-paneled, smoke-stained rooms. One was a kitchen outfitted with tilted shelves trying to offload mismatched dishes, an ancient refrigerator that leaked water, and a single bed I'd squeezed behind the cook stove. Off the kitchen, a small bathroom had a shower stall for skinny people and a toilet that worked in warm weather. The outhouse worked all the time.

The second room surrounded a dining table and eight chairs I didn't use—chairs carved up by generations of restless Conover kids who knifed crude animals into the wooden arm rests until the wood looked like inspired cave paintings. A gigantic wood stove anchored the far end of the camp, surrounded by a couch whose sagging places fit my sagging places, two rocking chairs that broadcasted shrill squeaks, and shelves of children's books, mildewed *National Geographics*, and my library.

I had nature and tracking guides, everything Rachel Carson, dreary environmental tomes filled with dire warnings, and fiction that illuminated the wild world better than anything else on the shelf.

I had two copies of Edward Abbey's *The Monkey Wrench Gang*, a fictional hymn to lawbreaking on behalf of the natural world. The bug-smeared one had arrived from a steamy Brazilian port, sent by a Special Forces army vet who'd gone way beyond PTSD to involve me in what seemed to be a hopeless wildlife mission—until it wasn't.

I hadn't chained myself to anything, but I'd done some recent lawbreaking while helping wolves back into Maine. I was grateful the animals were so smart and skittish that few people saw them. I was even more grateful that someone else got blamed for their arrival, and extremely grateful that only Moz and I knew the real story.

So far, rogue squirrels hadn't attacked the unpacked boxes I'd stacked against the living room wall to keep out blizzard-driven snow. I thought they might be busy in the shed, chewing their way through old coolers I'd filled with reports about how much money the outdoors delivered. The squirrels helped me decide each *Bangor Weekly* column. Anything too chewed went into the wood box. Anything unchewed was elevated into reader-friendly language and sent to the paper.

Generations of Conovers' leavings were everywhere: yellowed recipes tacked to cupboards, rock collections on window sills, rusted scythes over the door, and fly rods and snowshoes hanging off moose antlers. My father's shotgun was propped by the bathroom window in case the squirrel population overwhelmed my bird feeders.

My father didn't care what I did with the camp because he wanted to subdivide the land and sell it. My mother wanted her daffodil bulbs divided in the fall and my marriage to reconstitute itself. I could do the daffodils. My brother Giffy wanted the tractor in the barn winterized, loose boards on the dock nailed down, and the tax assessor deceived by keeping the outside dumpy looking. Not a problem. Dumpy outside—inside it was the safest place on earth.

All I wanted to do was care for the camp and care for Pock, eat cereal over the sink, and make sure I had chocolate stashed where I'd forget about it and later be surprised. For two years I'd worked seasonal jobs as I found them and used the same mug over and over. I snowshoed and skied out the back door in winter, and in warm weather I biked dirt roads until I was hot enough to jump into the lake with my clothes on. Clothed immersion was more efficient than the town's laundromat.

Mostly I wanted to live moment-to-moment, wrapped in Antler Camp's past—just not *my* past.

I hadn't touched the fly rods for weeks, and fall was my favorite time to catch brook trout and then let them go. The heat had fish hunkering low in deep pools cooled by unseen springs. Probably the trout equivalent of panting. It wasn't fair to catch cold water fish in a heat wave. They would die from stress before I could wave them in the current and watch them revive.

My goal of reducing life to one simple place wasn't working. Machines that drowned bats in their own blood would have been enough to send me low, but there was the bloody shoulder, strangely more human than a whole person. And vomit. I hadn't thrown up since I was pregnant, and Kate was almost twenty.

My best friend Pock had been almost arrested, almost quarantined, and then definitely trapped. For the day's parting shot, an angry eco-crusader had leaned into my face and reminded me why I'd moved north, away from political theater.

And finally—Moz. Moz, who often failed to signal when he was a warden, when he was a Penobscot, and when he was maybe more than a friend. So much for a simpler life.

Keeping lights and lanterns off to keep the camp cool, I felt my way to the phone. The message machine was full because I preferred listening to old recordings. It was probably time to erase them, but if I kept it full, reporters couldn't leave me messages begging interviews.

My brother sang happy birthday accompanied by the Boy Scout soccer team he coached, all of them singing off-key to someone named Cassandra, although I'd abandoned my first name by fifth grade. My mother left a quote about walking through the valley of death, her voice gaily chirping grim Biblical proverbs.

My father hated leaving messages, so that explained some breathing and hang ups. After too many years helping out in his real estate office, I loved him and didn't like him at the same time. I think he knew that.

A deep voice washed down my shoulders, spiked through my chest, and settled hotly in my stomach. "I'm bringing Chinese and some British movies that you'll like, but I won't. That's OK. Love you!" Kate wanted her Dad's last recording wiped off the machine. I wanted reminders that a way of life could erase itself faster than a phone message.

I strapped a headlamp over my sweating forehead, its narrow beam lighting only a narrow path, and pulled *Charlotte's Web* from the shelf. Spider wisdom before sleep seemed like a good idea as the loon magic was wearing off. Lying naked on a porch cot, damp hair piled on my head, I opened to a random page. *OK, universe. Send a message.*

Charlotte the spider was talking to Wilbur the pig. "After all, what's a life, anyway? We're born, we live a little while, we die." I slammed the book shut. Perfect. Just perrr-fect. Maybe I'd been hasty—always one of my favorite faults.

I found a new page. "A spider's life can't help being something of a mess," said Charlotte, "with all this trapping and eating flies. By helping you, perhaps I was trying to lift up my life a trifle. Heaven knows anyone's life can stand a little of that."

There was the random message. I needed to get over myself,

out of myself, and help someone else, but maybe it was too late for the beetles committing suicide as they dive-bombed my screens. When they buzzed off in alarm and Pock rose into a lethal growl, I yanked a sheet up to my neck. Maybe I'd be helping the face that pushed up against my screen.

# NINE

"Front door. Go around!" I yelled, scrambling for clothes and dressing in the dark. After Pock had bounced off the door a few times, I opened it and let him bounce off Chandler Perkins. Lit by my headlamp beam, Chan dropped two duffels by my feet, pulled off his tall boots, and squatted to rub my dog's happy ears. The boy's face wasn't red and he wasn't mumbling, so I was pretty sure he hadn't seen all of me.

"Did you mean what you said? In that note? I could come find you?" he asked.

I didn't remember making an offer that included luggage. "Yes, I think I did, but you look very packed up," I said, lighting a kerosene lamp over the dining table.

"After you left with that game warden, I watched a woman with a clipboard also search my house. She left this." He pulled a card from the band inside his New England Patriots ball cap.

I turned it in my hand. "Child Protective Services. What's up?"

"You broke into my freezer. You know my Mom's gone." He shoved the bags further into the house and hopped up to sit on the end of the table. "Someone must have figured it out and called it in."

"So, where's your Mom?"

Chan looked away. "I can't say. It's not safe to say."

"You're not going to call this woman?" I asked.

"I checked it out online. Pretty sure they don't know what to do with kids like me. I'm fifteen. Under fourteen there's a law that puts me in a home. Sixteen and over, I can get emancipated by a judge. I think I'm in an age crack."

I liked the idea of age cracks. I thought I might be in one too. But mostly I was noticing that dark corners of my camp had been dumped on the floor. With the overhead lamp finally on, I could see books on high selves had been tossed to the floor, the doors to my mother's ancient sideboard were open, tablecloths kicked into piles, and the clean laundry I'd stashed in a basket under the dining table was spread all over.

I started folding clothes back into baskets, but they seemed creepy after being scattered on the floor by unseen hands. Instead I stuffed everything into a laundry bag. "You have any idea who reported your home life or lack of it?" I asked.

"Since my Mom left a few months ago, only you and the warden have come up the driveway. Last week a cutting crew walked down off the ridge to talk to me."

"About what?" I said.

"They wanted to know if I had permission to trap up there." Chan scowled. "I don't trespass. I got permission." He pulled a wrinkled letter from his pocket. "It's legal."

I glanced at the Great Nations Forest letterhead and thought about the shine on Black Shoes' loafers. "Maybe not any more, Chan. Great Nations leased that land to the wind power company. Today I got a lecture about how it can do pretty much anything it wants with it."

"They can kick me off?"

I nodded. "Sorry. I think that crew snooped around and turned you into Child Services to get you out of their hair."

"Nope," he said. "No way. I've been trapping the ridge since I was nine. People around here know it's home base for me. It's kind of where I really live. Who's gonna mess with that?"

For me, Fairy Land was a sad childhood memory. Chan would have to learn the hard way. I pointed to the porch.

"Why don't you take the top bunk near the lake? It gets a breeze. I've got sheets in the shed."

In the attached shed, I found paper littering the wood pile and dirt floor. Some file folders seemed to have earned special attention, tossed into overhead rafters where they stuck to swallow droppings. I sighed. My only steady source of income was my *Bangor Weekly* column, where I laid out facts about the jobs and money generated by outdoor recreation. I had accumulated decades of economic research, which now looked like nothing more than fire-starter material.

"You live like this? In this mess?" Chan asked.

I slumped down on the sill, buried my face in my arms, and wished I had enough moisture left for tears. Pock sniffed the open shed door, his neck hairs pointed up like small, stiff razors. Chan moved quietly around the shed, righting coolers and gathering papers into piles on my workbench. Climbing a step ladder, he reached for file folders and wiped off bird droppings.

"If someone's breakin' in here, you could use company," he said. "It's not so bad. The computer stuff has date stamps I can match up, and anyway, I think it's kind of clear what goes together. See? I got this file on hunters fixed already. Geez. It's millions. If you let me stay, I'll fix them all."

"Nothing will make it right," I moaned, as I opened an empty file that had had years of wind-power research in it. "Let's just dig out your sheets and pillows and get some sleep."

Before dawn the next morning, I was vaguely aware of Pock stealing off my porch cot and the squeak of the screen door before I put the pillow over my head and slept again. Later I ran a threadbare T-shirt under the faucet and put it on over running shorts that had long ago stopped running with me.

Ideal attire for heat without end.

I found my dishes washed, my books on shelves, the shed floor swept clean, and the workbench buried under neat piles of well-organized files. The wind file remained empty, its contents most likely stolen by whoever had searched the cabin. I couldn't imagine why anyone would want the stuff. For years I'd dumped anything remotely connected to the issue into one lumpy file. Chan was perched on the wood pile, his head bent over a mushroom identification book while my dog gazed at him with desperate adoration. Because they both had wet hair, I guessed they'd been in the lake.

"Gentlemen," I said. "Hungry?"

Chan followed me into the kitchen. I dropped bread in the toaster and kibble into Pock's bowl.

"There's bats in your freezer," he said.

"Yes, but we won't be eating them. Cheerios or Cheerios?" I asked, setting a box on the counter.

"And what was someone looking for—shredding your place like that?"

*Not money*, I thought, watching Chan empty one box and reach for another. I wondered if his mother would mind if her freezer food migrated over to my camp.

I picked up one Cheerio and sucked on it. "Well, the only stuff missing seems to be wind-power research from my last job—my last real job."

"Real job?"

"When I had a regular paycheck and health insurance," I said. I didn't think he could hear me over the crunch of toast and Cheerios.

My landline was ringing, and since the machine was full, I knew I had to answer it. I pointed to an industrial-sized jug of dish soap and my bathroom. "You need to shower up with that blue stuff, my boy. It cuts grease and stink. You're a bit skunky."

"You and my Mom," he said, thumping off through the kitchen. "Only happy if I lose skin."

On the phone Anita's voice was softer than usual. "Patton, you OK? I hate to bother you."

"I'm ready to come back to work," I said.

The connection sounded hollow. I tapped the phone. "Anita? Anita? Come on. All I did was find the human version of what we find out there every day."

Her voice hardened. "And then you ran from the law."

"And then I went after my dog and met up with the law later. By this time my clothes are in the state lab and all should be right with the forensic world."

I waited through seconds of silence, and then heard her sigh. "When Ken and I talked about your coming to work for me, he reassured me that hiring you wouldn't create problems. He said the reason he couldn't have you back again had nothing to do with anything you'd done or not done."

Ken didn't know about my wolf adventures, so he'd spoken the truth as far as he knew it. Unfortunately, wolves were such a hot issue that it was enough to have been found semi-conscious on a barn floor next to a cage that had clearly housed an entire pack of them.

She was silent for a while.

"He did say you were handy and efficient to have around, but here we are, possibly losing our contract to do this analysis for PP&E because . . . because . . ."

"Because my dog and I found a body part? We stumbled on it like we stumble on all the dead things we find up there."

"I know that," she said, "but my bosses at the New England Wildlife Consortium don't know that."

I slumped against the wall.

"You still there?" Anita asked. "How about you give it a rest for a week? Until things quiet down? We're not due for another site visit for five days. I think we're too far into the field work for anyone to want to change horses and riders at this point. And cheer up. At least today you'll get paid. Plus mileage."

"Today? Just today?"

"The Department of the Interior is about to grant endangered species status to at least one of the bats I stashed in your freezer. We'll be serious lawbreakers if we stockpile these animals. I won't ask you to sort out the northern long-eared bat from the others. They probably all look like beef jerky at this point. Just deliver them to Orono. The university's offered to hold specimens until legal matters get sorted out."

"Really?" I asked.

"Really. Just put them on ice in a cooler. You've got a shed full of coolers. Deliver them to the graduate assistant in the biology lab. Then we'll be legal."

"It can't wait?"

"Look. It's taken them years to realize that wind sites kill millions of bats. Add that to a bat-killing fungus no one knows how to get rid of, and they finally know which species are on the brink. When Interior is ready to act, you don't look a gift horse—a very slow gift horse—in the mouth."

"I was hoping to avoid people," I said.

"I thought you had a people career," she said.

"I quit that."

I heard keys tap as she typed. "You never told me why," she said. When people type through a private moment, they usually don't get much truth from me, but I was also trying to get my reasons for an early retirement into one easy phrase I could use over and over.

"Well. I was supposed to be a mouthpiece for the environmental cause, but I turned into a piece of mouth."

The typing stopped and I heard her breath closer to the phone. "Oh, that's really good, Patton. I like that. And I get it. It's just that my boss had no idea who you were before every paper's front page laid out your history. Having a high-visibility crusader work as an impartial researcher is a problem for the front office."

I slid down to the floor and drew my knees up until I could bend my head into them.

"You still there?" Anita asked. She waited.

"Listen, Patton, I can hear you breathing even though it sounds a bit like a wind tunnel. Now don't quote me on this, but when you used to predict something bad was going to happen, your track record was pretty good. I think you might have been right when you warned people that corporate wind was going to cozy up to corporate timber and kidnap Maine's forests."

She chuckled softly and started typing again. "I'm wondering if you have some kind of hidden agenda or something you regret that would cause you to work under the turbines when you fought them so hard."

I didn't think I could explain that I was simply tired. Fifty-seven and tired. Tired of fighting. Tired of trying to sound good and look good at the same time. Then there was the day about two years before my marriage collapsed that my fifteen-year-old daughter had casually said, "Dad thinks you let yourself go. He told me he isn't attracted to you anymore." Perfect. Always a relief to hear the news from a trusted source. Well, no. Hear the news from your daughter.

I was just so tired.

I could hear Anita close the lid on her laptop. "Maybe there's an easier way to handle the bats and avoid people who seem too interested in you right now. Isn't your daughter at UMaine working on a forestry degree? Maybe she'd meet you where there's no reporters and deliver the bats to the lab."

I raised my head. "That works. See you in a few days, Anita." I hung up before hearing her reply.

Chan reappeared to hang all the towels I owned on a clothesline outside the porch. Unless he was a pro scrubber, it was likely he'd transferred his skunky odor to all of them. Pock danced around his feet, tugging things off the line and rolling on them.

I wondered if Kate was still so buried in her lab that she hadn't seen the news reports. I should have been wondering about that a lot more.

After I explained the bat project, Chan easily identified each species, though they all simply looked brown to me. He stacked bags of them in separate coolers, emptied ice cube trays over them, and then heaved the coolers into the back of my car.

"Your rear fender's tied to the roof," he said. "We gonna leave it there?"

I realized that my dog and I had become a larger *we*. "For now," I said. "Where's Pock? He's usually leaning on the car so I won't leave him."

Chan sprinted toward the barn. "I'm on it," he called. Coffee and breakfast had defogged my brain enough to suspect something wrong in his eager offer, plus I hadn't seen his truck anywhere. Antler Camp isn't on the way to anyplace, so his hitchhiking there seemed unlikely. Something didn't smell right. I leaned around the corner of the shed and watched him chase my dog around the barn. They completed two circuits before I jumped in to grab Pock's collar and Chan's shirt collar.

I had to reach up for the boy's.

"Whoa, whoa," I said. "What's in the barn?"

"Nothing," said Chan.

"If I'm going to save you from a foster family that's already setting a place at the table for you, you must give me nothing but truth from now on. Right? Right?"

He leaned on the heavy sliding door and whispered, "No dog, please."

Inside the barn, the air was cool, damp, and heavy with hay dust that swam in the air between thick ropes of spider webs. In the center of the barn was a two-story, double-thick wire pen, a relic from the past—a last line of defense between door-ripping bears and plump livestock. Inside the pen, frantic brown wings leaped into wobbly take offs that ended as thuds on the dirt floor. When the eagle saw us, it emitted a screech that clawed up my spine in ways only a mother who's heard a terrified child will understand.

Chan cleared his throat "He . . . I think it's a he . . . he isn't hurt."

"You could have fooled me," I said, feeling my way onto a stack of dusty milk crates as Chan slipped into the pen. I pointed to the blue pickup truck pulled into the barn's shadows. It sagged under a load of firewood. "You're assuming a lot here, Chan. First you drive that truck here illegally. Then you come through my door with enough luggage to last until you're old enough to drink. Now the national symbol of the entire country is flapping around in my barn. You do know that having an eagle is far worse for us than a few frozen bats that have yet to be classified as criminal items, right? The game warden says we're not even allowed to own one feather of this bird."

I jammed my hand into the pocket of my shorts and found

the tiny white feather I'd transferred from my jeans before handing them over to Moz. It seemed that Chan and I were both criminals.

Picking up a pair of thick red gloves, Chan whistled softly and the eagle hopped to a low hay bale, hunching its shoulders and bobbing its head back and forth. "We didn't have anywhere to go," he said. "I think he wants to fly but just can't figure it out. I looked up the lunging behavior and it could be he's working on flight muscles. Getting ready."

"What are you feeding him?"

"Last night I gave him rabbit scraps from my freezer, and this morning mice I trapped in the barn." The pen floor was littered with mouse feet.

"Yummers," I said. "Maybe you need to dangle breakfast overhead so he has to fly up to eat. That might jumpstart the process."

"Please, please don't give me away. I think we're just days away from . . . from . . . "

"From escape?" I asked. "My warden friend found eagle feathers in your cabin, and he's very good at finding things. Have you raised—?"

"Teddy. He's named Teddy."

At the sound of its name, the eagle lurched toward Chan, almost knocking him over. Using both gloved hands, he quickly cradled the bird against his chest. They settled themselves on a hay bale. The boy smoothed the bird's feathers until the eagle relaxed, arching his head low and rubbing his neck against Chan's cheek. It was oddly intimate, something I expected from a dog or cat, or even a parakeet.

Only a few months old, the bird already filled Chan's lap. The talons draped over the side of the boy's thigh looked like weapons ready to pierce soft human skin. I tensed, ready to rush the cage, but Chan arched his neck into a comfortable curve, and his eagle burrowed into it and closed his eyes in what looked like ecstasy.

"You raised Teddy from an egg?" I asked.

"He's my best friend, Patton, but I know he's got to go. I'll do it. I'll do it. Just please don't turn us in."

The people I knew who understood both eagles and wildlife regulations had sworn serious oaths to uphold all of the laws Chan was breaking. Game warden Robert Atkins and wildlife biologist Ken Douglas would not be happy if I helped the boy and his best friend. But I also had an animal best friend — a friend I'd break the law for any day.

"We'll deal with this when we get back from the university," I said, waving an arm toward the barn door. Teddy spread all six feet of his two wings, exploding spider webs with the force of his aborted liftoff. Scrambling up on another hay bale, he fixed me with a stare that felt like a dare. *This boy's under my protection.*

*You're in a cage, Teddy. And I think you're just a kid yourself.*

*You don't know much about eagles, do you?*

*Not yet, but I'm worried I might.*

*We can dive a hundred miles an hour, soar to 10,000 feet, spot a rabbit two miles away, and knock a full-grown deer off a cliff.*

I sighed. *What do you want, Teddy?*

*I want to fly.*

Again, I pointed at the door, but Chan moved to the fence, singing softly to the young eagle that cocked its head and stretched bright yellow talons deep into the hay. Chan imitated the eagle's nervous bobbing, singing a soft tune. "Ted, Ted, just like I said, we'll get you fed. Then you'll soar, right out that door. So you can soar, right out that door." The last words sounded more like a sob to me, but I wasn't going to embarrass the boy by trying to comfort him.

Chan softly locked the pen and when he grabbed a small pack from his truck, a flood of beer cans spilled onto the dirt floor.

"You seem to be a fan of Bud Light," I said.

Chan didn't smile. "Men working the ridge are. I collect the empties and recycle them. Gas money."

Outside, I slid the locking bar across the door and leaned against it. Finding Moz before he came looking for me and found Teddy was more important than the bats thawing in my car. Antler Camp's thick barn door repelled bears, but no barrier could stop Moz if he heard an eagle behind it.

# TEN

Driving around with a rear fender tied to my roof was not a low-profile activity, and there were TV vans parked outside the Road Kill Cantina, so I took a sneaky escape on dirt roads.

I was tired of dead birds. I thought the eagle and Chan deserved a chance. Sure, cats and power lines and collisions with windows killed plenty of birds, but Maine's wild mountains were supposed to be a sanctuary, not an obstacle course where one wrong move meant death.

Chan still wore his knee-high green boots and patched jeans, but the leather coat was gone, replaced by a clean T-shirt decorated with an army of predators. Eagles, foxes, wolves, bears, weasels, and killer whales prowled around on his chest.

My phone rang with loon cries and Chan laughed. "Perfect," he said.

"Mum," said Kate, but she didn't sound like Kate, her voice clipped and cold. "Where are you?"

"Just outside of town but headed your way. Up to the university. Anita wants bats delivered to the biology lab and I was just going to see if you're free for—"

"Stop. Just stop right where you are and for once, do what I tell you." She sighed so loudly that I held the phone out in case her air blew out at my end.

"You know where I named Pock?" she asked. "That place. Meet me there."

"Why the secrecy? Is someone listening in?"

"Who knows," she said. Then she hung up.

Leaning out his window with my water bottle, Chan wet

down his bandana, wiped his face, and then tied the wet cloth around his head. "That your daughter? What's up?"

I tried to sound carefree when all of my mother-very-worried genes were charging around my body, ramping up my heart rate and soaking my arm pits. "Change of plans," I said. "And it's against the law to eat all the M&M's and leave me only stale peanuts."

Pock loved the Penobscot River. He was out the window and in the water before our wheels stopped rolling. Ripping off his T-shirt and losing his boots, Chan dove in after him. Any continuous set of Maine rapids that's tilted downhill is called a falls, and I'd parked at the bottom of Pockwockamus Falls where current swirled off rock ledges and reformed as mini-whirlpools. Massive boulders lined the shore. In the middle of the river, foaming current surged between more huge rocks.

Long ago I'd worked as a raft guide, and we'd named each boulder after an animal—maybe to soften its lurking danger. Stuck under a rock without air, there'd be no opportunity to appreciate geology. Drowning, no one would care that glaciers had once amputated car-sized boulders from Mt. Katahdin and abandoned them in the river as ice melted.

I stood on Crouching Rabbit Rock as Chan whooped and dove after Pock. They chased sticks tossed up by churning eddies. Animal gladness is a fine thing and in its purest form, pretty much lost to adults.

I watched Kate park her small red truck behind my car and lean against it, arms crossed, frown lines in place, so I knew I could relax. She was fine. I climbed off the rock and walked to lean against the truck beside her. Her sun-streaked brown hair was yanked into a tight bun and she wore black stretch pants that ended at her knees. Her sleeveless shirt showed off slices of pink sports bra and well-defined biceps. She was wearing her angry perfume—the one that smelled like burnt apple pie and attracted black flies. She was too busy gripping her arms to bother with the flies in her ears, so I waved them away.

"You remember the day we brought Pock here as a puppy and you wanted to give him the whole Pockwockamus name?" I asked. Silence. "I said we'd end up calling him Wockamutt or Pockywocky or worse." Not even a slight grin.

Kate lifted one hand to inspect a green-painted fingernail, recrossed her arms, and actually sneered. "I thought you swore you'd never again wear shorts once you got those big purple leg veins."

Ouch. A direct hit.

"Who's the kid?" she asked.

"Long story," I said. "Right now he's a house guest I can't get rid of. Pock's delighted, though."

She arched a made-up, darkened brow that telegraphed derision better than her entire body. I almost ducked. "Kate. What's going on? I'm here like you asked. Bats are melting in my coolers, and you're too angry to talk."

She closed her eyes and clenched her teeth until her jaw muscles rippled. "Do you really know anything about me? What matters to me?"

"Where is this coming from?" I asked. "This is me, your mother. Not your father who apparently divorced you along with me. I've been with you every step of the way. Two weeks ago I moved you into an off-campus apartment and then spent the day watching you dismember tree parts into petri dishes, scan them obsessively under a microscope, and scrawl calculations on whiteboards. The only words I recognized were tree and carbon."

She dropped her arms and picked a pressed black fly from

her lips. "OK, Mum." She stepped away from the truck and thrust her arms up in the universal *I give up* gesture. "Are you really going to skip over the fact that yesterday you were the most wanted person in Maine because you fell over a body part? Do you think I live under a rock? The entire University of Maine café stared at me this morning. And you didn't warn me?"

Well, yes. I did think college students lived under rocks. At least I thought Kate did. When she was working on a project, I couldn't get her to use any form of communication. When she was in high school, I used to slide flat wedges of cheese under her locked door. And yes, I should have called her.

"I can see you're not wearing handcuffs, so let's get to what matters," she said.

Eyeing us nervously, Chan tiptoed to my car, extracted my fly rod case, and dragged Pock back toward the river. I wished I had the rod in my hand, the river licking my legs, and the line singing by my ears, but instead there was family drama.

Kate stalked back and forth in front of me, index fingers punching the air, hair escaping her bun. "I thought you were going to quit that front-page stuff and lead—and these are *your* words—a small, quiet life. Good luck with that. Looks like I'm the one trying to lead that quiet life. Get a solid career that's science-based, not shrill and crazy. Have a life that's my version of planetary interaction.

"Now it's *all* about *you* all over again. When *you* are front-page news, reporters troll me endlessly, but it's only *you* who interests them. I'm working on my own story now, Mum. My own story."

By this time I'd slid down to lean on one of her tires. I slid a fingernail into the tread and found it too thin. I didn't know how we'd pay for new tires, but I did know that for the first

112

time in our lives, a mother-daughter chasm was cracking open, like an earthquake dividing us on opposite sides of a spreading ditch.

"I never knew you felt that way about my work," I said.

"You try growing up in the middle of some crisis that never ends. The phone rings at all hours, and there's never enough money in whatever dip-shit green group is paying you badly. They never have enough to hire genuine lawyers, so my mother goes off to do the work of ten better-paid people. Or she works in piles on the dining room table, on the couch, on the floor. Christ. On the toilet.

"Thank god I got earphones when I was ten. It follows you everywhere, even when you *try* to leave it. You took a job at a god-damned wind-power operation after you'd already lost that war. Right? You. Lost. The wind people got a law that lets them build stuff on any bump higher than an anthill. My god, it's like you're asking for trouble."

She slid down the truck near me, but not touching me. On the river, heat shimmered off rocks. Afternoon shadows made the boy and dog look like slow-motion silhouettes. Chan's right arm flew back and forth as he cast into pools below him. Pock's head followed the fly line in and out of the water.

"They're both hoping for a fish, but in this heat I doubt it," I said. "He doesn't know Pock will get to it before he does."

Kate snorted. "Hope he's good at taking hooks out of a hairy moving target."

And there it was—the quake cracks getting shoved back together—at least a little bit. She wiggled closer and squeezed my fingers.

I squeezed back, but sat up so quickly that gravel bit my thighs. "Kate, why can't I come to campus? Why are you worried about phone calls?"

She twisted a strand of hair around her fingers. She used to do that in her sleep when she was stressed, but back then I could rub her back and sing until her fingers relaxed.

"Someone broke into my apartment yesterday, and it's a wreck. There's nothing worth stealing. All my expensive stuff's at the lab. It's probably nothing, but I was getting hang-up calls. When I got home, my place was trashed. Thinking about it, someone had to be checking on me."

I heard sharp warning pings go off somewhere right behind my ears. I increased my grip on her hand. "What was the most wrecked part of your place?"

Kate waved her free hand. "Boxes I hadn't unpacked. Just old papers and books, but they were tossed all over. And my backpack. I think it had only tampons, energy bars, and project notes. And twenty dollars." She looked away, but I could see tears glittering in her eyes.

Before I could consider the wisdom of my confession, I said, "Our shed. Yesterday. It was also tossed. Files and papers all over."

Kate dropped my hand and pushed herself up on her knees facing me. "Was it locked?" she asked. "My apartment was locked."

"No, not locked."

She frowned and leaned toward me. "Well, even if you'd locked it, all someone had to do was lean against the rotting wall. Anything missing?"

"Yes, but it makes no sense. A file from my last job had some energy research. Mostly on wind. I'm not even sure what was in it, but only the empty folder is left. The papers are gone." I watched Chan bend low and slide a wiggling fish back into the river. "My house guest cleaned and sorted the rest of the mess this morning."

Kate looked away and then reached for my other hand and took a deep breath. "Last spring. I took a few papers from that file. I should have asked, but I didn't want to make a big deal out of my project unless I had something cool to show you."

"You took it? Months ago?"

She nodded. "Not the whole file. Only a few papers. It had plenty of your notes I couldn't read."

We sat in silence for minutes while the river roared, and Pock dropped log-sized sticks at Chan's feet.

"You should have asked. I'd give you anything," I said. "I'm only using what's in the shed to write columns for the paper. I don't get the secrecy."

Kate dropped my hands. "Don't you think it's more important that we both got robbed within days? That someone hunted for information they thought we had and probably about the same subject?"

I was thinking more about her adored backpack—how for years I'd washed out mashed fruit and melted make-up so she could keep it. Everything else from her childhood she'd outgrown. The pack was more like part of her body than an accessory. "I'm so sorry, Kate. Your pack."

"I know," she moaned, "but it's bigger than the pack. My advisor told me to transfer my notes to our shared site, but I guess I got behind on doing some of that, and I was just working and working on them until I was sure I had it right. I mean, if I was right, I knew he'd blow it up into some big thing. Then there'd be the inquisition of a peer review, not to mention all the college departments that get funding from industries who'd get royally upset, and—"

"Wait, wait, wait. Get what right? What would blow up? Who'd get upset and why?"

She held up her hands in a football time out gesture. "Don't interrupt until I get it all out. You promise?"

I nodded. Sometimes it's important for parents to only nod.

"I thought if I dug through your files, I'd find things to make you a scrapbook for Christmas. You know, keep the deal we made when Dad left. Give each other only home-made stuff."

"So who's going to be unhappy with what you've done?"

"I'm getting there. You had a weird phrase scrawled on the file—Trees Beat Turbines—so I looked through it. Turns out you were on to something you didn't know shit about."

I raised my hand to object, but she laughed and grabbed it. "Oh, come on! You know you're a math cretin. I do listen to *some* of your stories, Mum. I really do. Like the one where your math SAT score was probably lower than chimpanzees with pencils. And when I asked why you didn't go to law school to make better money, you said you were scared off by computation questions on the entrance exam."

Kate didn't know everything. I'd never shared my private oath to make sure she'd never end up crippled by number ignorance. When her math grades started to slip, I had a tutor sitting with her at our dining room table two times a week. Kate would have more choices than I'd had.

"You're a forestry major," I said, "but headed toward something so new I don't know what to call it. You need to explain the math thing."

Kate's face brightened. "There's tons of calculations in forestry. It's not just boys with axes anymore. Folks crunching numbers are all over the place analyzing the forest's outputs and versatility. My advisor's letting me audit his Climate and Carbon Dynamics graduate seminar even though I'm not far along in the program.

"Smarty-pants," I said.

"Yup. I am. Your idea about how Maine should appreciate

what it has—tons of trees rather than building big installations in remote locations? Well, it didn't look like you got beyond the public relations thing. It looked like you were working the spin part, but you never got to the math." She grinned a very wide grin that quickly disappeared. "I've got the math. The proof. And most of my notes were in that pack."

"How far did you get?" I asked.

"Well, my notes were kind of outlines of what's going to be a draft report. I created a few graphs and charts and things. It was early days."

"But," I interrupted, "you knew what you had might piss people off. It had to be something you thought was good. Who's going to get upset?"

She lifted two bright-blue damselflies off her knee and waved them into the air. "Too early to tell for sure, but I think corporations getting millions in government subsidies or tax breaks to build the facilities. And timber companies leasing their lands to energy developers—they get millions cutting and selling their trees and more millions for leasing the cleared space and they're also paid for each megawatt from each turbine, every year."

"And?" I asked. The pissed-off group had to be larger.

The damselflies were back, this time hooked up in mid-air to mate right in front of us. Kate ignored them. "And the math might disappoint some environmental groups who thought wind power was a climate change answer for us here. It's weird. I can run computer models based on real field research. I can show how growing trees and leaving them longer on the land before they're harvested pulls more carbon from the air than any other carbon reduction strategy we could go for."

She looked at me, eyebrows raised in surprise. "Weird they don't do their homework. The green groups. They claim that wind power closes down fossil fuel plants. No way. Those plants need to stay online to produce power when the turbines are down or when there's too little or too much wind. And every time they say wind will power so many homes, it's theoretical bullshit. Wind can't power a home twenty-four hours a day. Impossible. Would be like brown-outs in third-world places that only have one crummy power source that goes down all the time."

I was afraid that if I jumped up and hugged her, the moment where she'd gone far beyond anything I'd imagined would end badly.

She sighed a sad sigh. "Why isn't anyone talking about this? What does that mean? Either I'm totally wrong, or information's getting suppressed, or . . . or folks are so fixed on being right they only see one way forward. Can't see the forest through the turbines. Oh Gawd! I really do sound like you."

I started to get up, feeling that it would be easier to breathe, but Kate pulled me back down.

"And speaking of listening. I've got more to say, Mum, and I'm only going to do this confession thing one time, and I'm sorry I got so angry at you. Last year I was looking through the old Christmas cards, sorting like you asked, and I found one from your friend Shannon. Even though she's . . . dead." She dropped her eyes and voice.

"It had a weird painting of a crazed woman with super-intense eyes. Her mouth is wide open like she's screaming words. Not very festive, but she looked more alive than any Virgin Mary card I tossed out. Inside Shannon said, 'Sending you Cassandra's face. Know you will survive the Cassandra Curse even if she did not. I root for you. Every day.'"

I spread my legs straight out in the dirt so Kate could see I was a captive audience.

"Mum, I know you're named Cassandra, but we never really talked about why you only use your middle name. Why you want to be Patton. I never thought about it until I turned the card over and saw the story on the back."

"I know that story."

"I'll bet you do. Wish I'd known you were named after a woman famous for knowing stuff but who got ignored all the time."

"Not intentional. My mother wanted something feminine to counteract my father's determination to name me after a famous general named Patton. So, Cassandra Patton."

"Well. Anyway. I figured out the story fits you and hurts you at the same time. Who cares what's true and what's a myth? One god gave her the prophecy gift. Another god cursed her so no one would believe her." She reached for a stick and started to draw a large horse head in the dirt. When she was little, we spent hours drawing animals. Mine were stick figures that all looked alike. Kate fixed them with swipes of her crayons.

I drew a tail on the horse in the dirt. I could do tails. "Right. They didn't listen to her warning to leave the big wooden horse outside the city's walls. Not bring it in. The soldiers hiding inside jumped out and sacked the city, raping and slaughtering Troy's people. I don't think I'm in her league, Kate—am quite sure the gods haven't noticed me. At least not yet."

She chuckled. "True, but I agree with Shannon. You might try to avoid your first name, but the story fits you anyway." She nudged our dirt horse until its head tilted toward me. "Now this doesn't mean I'll listen more, but I'll try. I will."

Kate helped me up and we watched a family of merganser ducks negotiate the rapid on their way downriver. Brown babies, almost full grown, crowded their mother each time a wave washed them forward. Chan was laughing and whistling at Pock who was rolling on a gravel beach, all four dog legs pumping air.

"That would be dead fish he's found," I said.

Kate had a wind-chime laugh. "Yup. For sure."

Watching her face relax, I thought we pretty much agreed on most things. I slid an arm around her waist and tried to sniff her neck. "You're sniffing me again," she said.

"It's still the only way to find my baby in a herd."

Kate bent over, grabbed her loose hair, and with a move I envied, snapped it back into a well-behaved bun. "You know, I am proud of you, Mum. Just don't sniff me in public." She leaned into my car, lifted the cooler of bats, and walked toward her truck.

"Now I need to get back to campus. See if any of my work's on a school computer. I think I put a few graphs and visuals up on a site I shared with my advisor. I'll deliver the bats. You should hang out here for a while. Will do you good." She slapped gravel off her knees. "Are you OK? Should we do anything about the shed and my apartment? Tell anyone?" She winked and slid the cooler into the cab of her truck. "The game warden comes to mind."

Chan appeared, jumped in for the last cooler, and after stashing it in her truck, stuck out his hand. "Hi. Kate, right? You headed up to the biology lab at the university?"

"To drop the bats, yes."

"Got a class tonight?"

She nodded.

"Mind if I come along? I'd pretty much give anything to see the lab and go to a class."

Kate lifted her eyebrows at me again, but I gave her a

120

thumbs-up. "He's a good kid who's really been under a rock too many years, won't tell me what he's done with his mother and sisters, does chores willingly, and probably knows more about the outdoors than some professors. I don't think he has a toothbrush though."

Chan leaned into my car and pulled out his backpack. "I'm set. Your rod's on the rock. I had a few hits on a caddis fly. This time of year, even hot fish go for that."

Pock jumped into Kate's truck, but she dragged him out, emptied a can of baby wipes on the front seat, and pointed at Chan. "Chores start now and that includes fish slime on your hands."

I jogged after her as she drove away and called, "Wait! Your draft report. Did it have a name?"

Kate put the truck in neutral, took a long drink from a water bottle, and screwed up her face. "OK. I know it's safe to tell you since it's too long to fit on a bumper sticker." She skipped her voice up to a high-pitched, pontificating tone. "Enhancing Maine's Forests for Carbon Sequestration to Obviate the Need for Industrial Fragmentation and Devaluation of High Value Silvicultural and Recreational Lands."

"Oh, that's a crowd pleaser," I said.

As she blew me a kiss and drove away, she yelled, "It's easy. Trees beat turbines."

Without looking up from one of Kate's textbooks, Chan yelled, "My freezer has frozen raw food if you can't score mice. Shred it up though."

Right. Teddy. He liked his food shredded.

# ELEVEN

Kate was right. The river would do me good. I didn't want to think about how a piece of shoulder had probably changed my life. I didn't want to think about the thief who'd searched our homes. I lifted my phone looking for a signal, and sent Kate a message to change her locks and press Chan into guard duty.

Whenever life stacked up against me, I went to the Penobscot River to feel clean and whole—it was better than having someone dress me in a white robe, dunk me in water, and pray over my head. No one was around, so I left my fly rod by the edge of the pool and stripped down to a black sports bra that covered way more than just my chest, tied my short's drawstrings, and kicked off my rubber sandals.

An endless supply of sticks teased Pock further out into the foam—foam that looked somehow whiter and higher than before. I thought about moving my car to higher ground, but this wasn't like Utah where flash floods from bad weather routinely trap people in tiny canyons. On the Penobscot, upstream dams were automated for predictable flows that moved water downriver from lake to lake. I snapped the band off my pony tail and dove toward Pock.

Luscious cold bubbles crawled up my arms and legs as the current shoved me around the pool, massaging my skin into goose bumps. Goose bumps! I hadn't felt cold for weeks. When the drawstring floated free and my shorts slipped to my ankles, I realized that whole parts of my body were missing a free wet massage. I tossed my shorts and bra up on shore and floated in the current until Pock's bark made it through the water in my ears.

Somehow he'd crawled onto Leaping Lion Rock in the middle of the river and was tugging at driftwood snagged low on one ledge. I didn't even try to yell over the churning rapids. I knew he'd be there till after dark pulling on what he couldn't have. Leaping Lion was a house-sized boulder that divided the flow and sheltered a patch of calm water behind it, so all I had to do was swim through the calm water and try to coax Pock off.

When I climbed up to fetch him, I left skin from my toes, knees, elbows, and tender parts on the rock's sandpaper face. I didn't look back at my car, because I couldn't bear to see if anyone was parked next to it enjoying the show. If I had, I might have seen the river lick my tires in a warning.

I did hear the roar. There's nothing like the sound of water shearing off rock fragments and shoving them downriver. A flood is so much more than water. It's everything the water destroys and bulldozes in a cruel torrent of trees, rocks, sand, and any building in its way.

Thankful that this rock had once been useful to men who managed log drives, I knew it had an iron ring bolted deep into its granite core. "Don't look," I yelled at Pock, dragging him up the rock. "Don't look at the bad thing. Just don't look!" I couldn't resist a peek.

Instantly I wished I'd never seen that perfect wave in *The Perfect Storm*. The wave swallowing the top of the rapids seem to hang in the air, heavy with pulsing weight. Then without breaking, it rolled downriver toward us like a giant white fist. I dropped to the rock and wrapped one hand around the iron ring and another around Pock's collar, twisting it tight so it wouldn't slip off.

I took a deep breath and curved my back into what was

coming. The river lashed us with biting spray and tugged viciously at Pock. I tugged back. On its final lick, it tossed uprooted trees in the air to our left and right. Gone in seconds, the wave disappeared downstream.

I stumbled upright, hands locked into bent claws from the death grip I'd had on the ring. I raised them both in the air while Pock leaped a happy dance on my toes. "That's it?" I yelled. "That's all you got? One wave?"

I didn't remember I was naked until I saw Moz on shore next to where my car had been. With two hands he held out a blanket as if all I had to do was walk into his arms. When of course getting off the rock, swimming up to him, and getting out of the water naked would be more complicated.

First, I had to deal with everyone who'd been stranded with us. Pock had a large black water snake cornered in a crevice, hissing its displeasure. Three beavers groomed themselves on the only ledges that allowed me to get off the rock. The mother duck, guarding what was left of her family, quacked at my ankles. *Just get the hell off and we critters will sort it out.*

*You ever seen one wave like that before?*

*No. It's got to be a human thing. Bad things usually are.*

*How many of your kids are missing?*

*All the ones who couldn't keep up with me.*

I grabbed a stick and nudged beavers off the ledges, whistled for Pock who was trying to dodge the angry duck, and climbed down into the pool behind the rock. I'd avoided looking at Moz, but Pock saw him and hit the pool with a hard smack, his tail wagging like a propeller.

By the time I reached shore, I found the gray blanket thoughtfully draped over a rock and I wrapped its scratchy folds under my arms like a beach towel. Revving his green warden truck to gain traction in fresh mud, Moz pulled my car from the ditch where the river had parked it. I looked around for Pock. I needed to get my hands on him and feel him all over—make sure he was OK, but he was perched in the seat beside Moz, head out the window like the perennial kid he was. I knew my dog loved me, but he also loved anyone who owned a truck.

Carrying a handful of Band-Aids and the small pack that always lived in my car, Moz joined me on Crouching Rabbit Rock. I couldn't meet his direct gaze even though I knew he was signaling something like, *everyone has these bad days. Think nothing of it. I didn't really see anything.*

I imagined that wardens monitoring radios would be howling with laughter if Moz were the tale-telling kind, but he was my friend. He handed me my pack. "I assume you have a change of clothes in here, and I believe your car may be driven. It seems to have slipped sideways into the ditch when the road became mud."

He turned toward the river, pulled a knife from a sleek leather case at his belt, and whittled the log Pock had dropped at his feet, while I slipped into threadbare sweatpants and a T-shirt I'd promised Kate I'd never wear.

Moccasins on his feet and legs hanging over the rock, Moz sat facing Mt. Katahdin's jagged ridgeline. He flicked his knife toward the mountain's deep ravines—dark gashes in the day's late light. "My Penobscot family would say the god Pamola flew down to take his revenge on you. Have you angered him?" he asked.

I expected this chit-chat before the serious talk—a tactic Moz had used on me and hundreds of others whose hands shook after a near miss. I'd worked on the river for years and knew its rapids were not necessarily forgiving. We'd been lucky. I folded the gray blanket and sank onto it, sliding my hands under me so my butt could enforce discipline on my shaking fingers.

I could do chatter, but I was better at leaping in. "No. Don't think I've upset any mountain gods lately, but I'm on someone's shit list. My camp was broken into sometime in the past few days. And yesterday, someone raided Kate's apartment. From the look of things, someone was interested mostly in our paperwork."

We watched Pock dismantle a woodpile that the river had twisted into an angular sculpture. Moz wiped his knife and laid it on shavings that minutes before had been a solid log. He pulled a small notebook from his breast pocket and held a pen over it.

I pasted three bandages over a knee missing skin. "There's nothing more I can tell you. Kate and I don't have a clue about it." I tapped his notebook. "Now you need to tell me why my paperwork problem is officially interesting."

Against his green collar, blood flowed north into his face. "I have advance knowledge of what other investigators may discover later." He sighed and lowered his pen. "Anything unusual in your life may be relevant."

"First things first," I said. "Except for the fact I was without clothes, I am very, very grateful you showed up. So, let's clear that part up." I lifted a few shavings and blew them toward the river, waiting for them to be swept away. "How did you come to be here? No accident, right?"

More blood rushed to his face.

I nudged him. "I was the one mid-river, standing naked on a rock while coping with a dog, a snake, beavers, and ducks, so why are you the embarrassed one here?"

Moz put his notebook on the rock and reached down for the top log in Pock's pile, digging his knife blade into it.

"No sir," I said, reaching for his arm. "It seems to be a day for spilling stuff, so spill it."

Moz continued to whittle. "You should know that many people know what I am about to tell you, and that I was not the one responsible."

Dread started to work its way from my toes up toward my stomach. "OK. Now I really want to know."

"A patrolling warden spotted fishing activity at the falls. He set up a spotting scope upriver where he could observe the activity. He observed a boy with a dog, fishing. After the boy left, an older woman carried the rod to the river, but she did not fish."

"Older? Older woman? No. Don't tell me the rest. I know. He watched me float naked around the pool—the spotting scope good enough to see my every mole and certainly identify me. Then he went on the radio so everyone could hear and it probably went something like this, 'Tell Warden Atkins there's a naked woman he knows in distress at Pockwockamus Falls.' He might have even used my name."

Moz nodded.

"Your peers and underlings don't get to prank you often, right? Even though they try all the time? So. After the radio message, you drove to the falls. What did you see?"

He rested his knife on his thigh and squinted up river where the last sunlight lit up spray on wet rocks. "From the access road I heard a noise that sounded like spring."

"Spring?" I asked.

He swallowed several times and cleared his throat. "Spring, when a melting river held by ice breaks free and carries everything before it. I heard rocks grinding against each other and saw the wave approach as you climbed a boulder in the river. I saw you stand. I saw you grab Pock and sit. I saw you

128

disappear under the wave." He pulled his black ball cap so low I could see individual green stitches in the tree embroidered on it. "Had you not worked this river and known its seasons and moods and remembered the ring, I believe you both would be dead."

Pock jumped up to rest his wet head on Moz's lap. My dog knew when someone needed attention. He'd moved faster to comfort the man than I had.

The knife was loose in Moz's hands. Slowly I reached for it and wiped it clean on my shirt. Then I turned it and offered it back to him, handle first—but not before I'd squeezed his fingers so hard both our hands turned white together.

I wanted to tell him about the duck who'd blamed the wave on humans, but that seemed like a private conversation. "Moz," I asked, "who now owns the upstream dam? It got sold last year, right?"

"Premier Power & Energy. I have already called in requesting information. I want to know if today's flows were managed by computer at the generating station or at the dam." He paused and lowered his voice. "A river, by itself, does not make a single rogue wave."

"Well, that's a duh. Is anyone hurt or missing?"

"When the warning siren sounded upriver, boaters and fishermen had time to move to higher ground. Down here, you would not hear it, and floating on your back, it is likely your ears were submerged."

Yes, on my back, floating naked around the pool, I'd been on display like a cake slice on a rotating dessert carousel.

We sat for long minutes. Maybe Moz was thinking about the river and the rogue wave, but I'd moved on. "Before I sidetracked you, you said you had advance knowledge others might not have. Yet. Since everyone seems to know what I look like naked, what's the advance knowledge that only you have?"

He leaned forward to reach into a side pocket and pulled out a small plastic bag filled with what looked to be black underwear. "I found this in the victim's sweatshirt pocket. I believe this item belongs to you." It was Warden Atkins who raised the bag up level with my eyes.

"Those aren't mine," I said.

He squeezed the bag so that white SA initials pressed against the plastic. "When I helped you move your friend's belongings to your camp after she died, you said you would be proud to wear Shannon Angles' clothes."

This was another strange moment when perhaps Moz wasn't just my friend. "There's no way to make this look less creepy, right?" I asked.

His voice was low. Even lower than his serious warden voice. Low like sadness. "Did you know the victim? Yesterday, the fact that you found part of a body at PP&E's site was everywhere on the news. Today, your location on the river was public information. Today you may have drowned from a wave we cannot explain."

I knew Moz was trying to connect some dots and warn me, but my fingers strayed to the bag of underwear in his hand. It was probably too late to hope that the item was not a used pair. "First off," I said, "I never gave anyone my underwear. I'm sticking with *creepy* on that," I said. Shannon would have said sleazy, icky, and pervy, but then if she were alive, I wouldn't be coping with her undies in plastic.

Moz lowered the bag. "If you had a relationship with this person, it will be discovered."

"I haven't! I haven't! I haven't even contemplated a relationship with anyone but my dog!" I said. That was a bit of a lie. I was starting to look at some men and wonder if anyone would want to undress a fifty-something woman once they uncovered the varicose veins along the way.

We sat in silence on the rock—except for the river. It always murmured.

The events of the past two days were sliding downhill into a messy pileup at my feet. "There's more you should know about the papers taken from my shed and Kate's apartment."

He looked at his notebook, but didn't pick it up.

"Kate had taken some papers from a file I had on wind energy, back when I was working on that new law. The one that makes permitting the sites easier. She used my notes to make a case for something that might get very touchy. She's not even sure she can replicate what's been stolen until she checks the computer in her advisor's office to see if some of her information is stored there. She says she's not ready to go public with it yet."

"I am not the public."

"Alright. Alright. She's put together solid data that might give the lie to wind power's claims to be a magic save-the-planet solution. At least here in Maine." I pulled the blanket from under my butt and wrapped it around my shoulders. It didn't seem to matter that we were in a September heat wave. My teeth chattered.

Pock nudged my hands until they lifted, and I rubbed his head. I bent into his ears to whisper that he was my best friend, and we must avoid more life-threatening adventures. My fingers pressed in on the hard lump in his left ear. "There's only so many times I can quietly rescue you, boy," I said, "before we get discovered."

Moz lifted the blanket so it covered my neck. "Have you testified to or published information that might bring a thing like this wave upon you? Can you think of any work or activity that might make someone angry or desperate enough that they would steal from you or . . . or . . . "

"Try to drown me?" I asked. "Of course, I've pissed off people. Mostly scummy folks hiding under rocks who needed daylight on what they were doing. But I always use information that's already public. Sometimes it's buried and I give it new life, but I use what anyone can find. And my newspaper column talks about how Maine's outdoors brings in money and jobs. Maybe it's been gathering dust on a researcher's shelf or buried in tiny footnotes, but it's all out there. Readers like it a lot. They keep sending receipts to the paper's editor with notes about what they've spent."

Moz pulled his legs to the edge of the rock and rose smoothly over them. He reached down one hand to pull me to my feet as he slipped his notebook into a chest pocket. He slipped off his moccasins and lifted each of my legs into them. I felt like a kid wearing her dad's slippers. "Until you find shoes," he said.

We navigated around smaller rocks to get to his truck. I watched him pull on dry socks and lace his feet into black warden boots before I handed him his blanket and moccasins and slid behind the wheel of my car. It sounded fine, even for a Subaru with too many hard miles and a rusted fender on the roof. Moz waved Pock into my back seat, pushed him down onto a worn sleeping bag, brushed wet hair away from my left ear, and handed me the underwear.

I squashed the baggie into my car garbage bag and slid chocolate wrappers over it. I should have thanked him, driven away, and said nothing. But I didn't.

"You don't need this? It's not evidence of some kind? You put me through that for what?"

132

"Please know that I will not ask you about this again." He stepped back. "There are times we must prove we are alive. Intimacy with another is strong proof."

"Oh, so now you're not going to believe me, and you're going to infuse a baggie of underwear with a message about spiritual growth? No thank you. I told you. I don't know how my underwear migrated to this person."

He straightened and his black brows knit together into one long dark warning cloud that spilled anger into his even blacker eyes. His stride ate ground as he stalked to his truck, but he didn't peel out. Very slowly and very deliberately, he inched past me without turning in my direction.

I was hoping for some splattered mud. While I hadn't planned the anger sparking between us, maybe he'd be angry enough to avoid Antler Camp—avoid me and Chan and Teddy the eagle.

Slumped and miserable, I sat in my car until it was almost dark. I tried to think my way out of recent events, but they seemed carelessly splattered over all my plans to simply breathe, drink tea, listen to loons, and find chocolate where I didn't expect it. One thing seemed clear. Moz thought the severed shoulder belonged to a man. If so, this was a man I'd have to deal with, even if he was in pieces.

# TWELVE

Confused by my headlights and the summer-like heat, late-season bugs committed suicide on my windshield as I drove past the road that led to Antler Camp. The prospect of trapping mice and dangling them within reach of Teddy's talons seemed like the perfectly horrible end to a perfectly horrible day. If I picked up some skinned rabbit for the eagle and also raided Chan's freezer for the shepherd's pie, maybe feeding us both could be easy. I could also help the frozen brownies find their way to Antler Camp. Brownies for dinner was fine with me.

The air blowing in my car window felt like a hair dryer set on stun. Every few feet, lightning silhouetted animals in various states of disarray. An owl dipped low over the road, pursued by a mob of small birds. From the safety of a ditch, a fox glared just long enough for me to see a mouse squirming in its jaws.

I swerved to miss a road-killed porcupine, unsure if quills could flatten a tire. A dark streak bled from it across the road; someone had been hungry enough to flip the animal over and pull a meal from its soft belly. Probably a fisher cat. Porcupine meals don't scare them. Just before Chan's driveway, three deer exploded from dense cover, twisted away from my car in an airborne ballet and raced ahead of me, their flicking tails bleached whiter by lightning.

Whipping into the Perkins' driveway, I almost collided with a mound of debris that hadn't been there two days ago. In my high beams, rain pelted the pile where chains glinted like silver snakes trying to escape into the mound's dark center. I backed the car up a few feet, eased my way out the door, and, fitting my headlamp's elastic band around my head, slanted the beam into the pile.

It seemed that every one of Chan's traps had been dragged off the mountain and tossed in his yard. His white name tags winked at me from the tangle. He'd been careful to comply with the law, even if someone else had ignored it. It was a crime to touch someone else's traps, let alone remove them.

The voice came out of the dark, accompanied by heavy boots crunching gravel. "You're going to tell me I done wrong, ain't ya? Of course you are. That's what you do. That's what you all do."

Leaving the lights on and Pock trembling in the car, I stepped further into the road. The rest of what Ridge Dumais had to say was swallowed in thunder so loud that the windows in the empty house rattled. The rain stopped feeling like sweet relief. It pelted me as if it had a grudge.

"Hello, Ridge." I waved my hand over the mound of traps and then lit him up with my headlamp. He was shirtless and walking toward me, rain streaming down his chest. "The boy has permission. He was legal," I said.

When Ridge jammed his red ball cap low over his eyes, his arms came alive with muscles that rose and twisted like rope. He must have been in his fifties, and except for a fleshy beer cushion pushed up by his belt, he was the hardest man I'd ever seen. Decades of wielding chain saws and repairing whatever broke had sculpted him more than any gym's heaviest weights.

He spit tobacco chew near me, and the glistening mound was lit up by more lightning. Although Ridge was the crew boss for Great Nations Forests' cutting operations and probably had more important things to attend to, he seemed to like my boots as a target. He'd hit them dead on before.

"I know he's a real good kid and all, but my crew's behind

on our cutting schedule over here, so—" He nudged a few traps with the steel toe of his boot. "He can relocate his trapping operation."

Distracted by Ridge and the storm, I hadn't noticed busy headlights above the pond. Now I couldn't miss the growling skidders as they ramped up engines and forced massive tires over logs and rocks, towing trees toward the nearest road. Lit by spasms of lightning, the gleaming arms of other large-toothed machines grabbed clusters of standing trees and sliced them from their trunks. I didn't need to see the forest gone when I could hear it going. I threw my hands up in the air.

Ridge put one hand in front of my face and waved it up and down as if to snap me out of what he knew was coming. "Well, Missy. Save it. Just save it. Don't work yourself up into a rant that goes nowhere but the dirt here. You don't work for anyone who gives a god-damn what goes on here.

"I got history. My granddad lost his job because you greens closed the Belfast chicken-packing plants. My dad got laid off the Millinocket mill after you all stopped the dam they needed for power." He laughed a hoarse smoker's laugh and marched toward his black ATV. "Now, it looks like the green people you used to hang with actually like what I'm doing. Soooo maybe I got this job for a while. Makes my day to see an enviro lose out. Makes my day," he called.

Gunning the ATV's throttle, Ridge circled me slowly. I was used to people blaming job losses on me. That was easier than wrestling with the far-away forces that exported jobs to places where labor was cheap and environmental laws non-existent.

The scene in Chan's driveway was new though. I'd never been blamed for generations of hard loss. I'd never been herded by an ATV lit by lightning either.

"You're running machines straight up and down the

mountain, Ridge," I yelled. "You know that dirt's gonna move!"

The ATV's headlights turned and lit me like I was on stage—a very wet stage. Hair soaked loose from my ponytail felt like wet spaghetti down my neck. I tried rubbing my face with my shirt, but it just delivered more water.

Even above the storm, we heard the new noise and snapped our heads toward the ridge. I thought quickly about Moz. Earlier that day, what he heard must have sounded the same way—water that doesn't sound like water—more like a train that's left the tracks but is still going, grinding up rocks and cracking limbs and shoving everything before it.

"I got to go get those boys off the hill," Ridge yelled. Wheeling tightly on two wheels and sliding sideways in the driveway, he disappeared into the rain. Darkness dropped on me more heavily than water. I ran to my car, pushed Pock out of the driver's seat, and drove up Chan's elevated lawn, strangely mounded up higher than the rest of the property. I snapped a leash on my dog and dragged him up three flights of deck stairs to the top of the mansion, where flashing red lights from the wind turbines competed with lightning.

I didn't know what I expected to witness, but I hoped that deep in his trembling soul Pock trusted me to do the right thing. Most of the time that worked out, so we hunkered down under the overhanging roof and waited. Pock hated explosive noises, so I sat with him, hugged him, and together we waited out the storm.


Before we left the safety of Chan's upper deck, I watched for lingering lightning and squinted toward Chan's small shed and cabin. I hoped his pile of firewood had deflected the debris and water, but I knew I couldn't wade through the mudslide that had broken the beaver dam and flooded everything below the pond. There would be no trip to his freezer. No frozen rabbit. No shepherd's pie. No brownies.

As thunder faded, out on the lawn I heard fish flipping in the mud, hoping one last twist would land them back in the pond. There were some squeals that could have been otters or mink. The appeals ended on high notes, like someone hoping for replies in the dark. I heard only one loud tail slap on wet mud. Maybe that was the remaining beaver headed out to create another pond.

I knew that buried under the mud was an entire suffocated ecosystem of rich life, most of which wouldn't be mourned by anyone—unless, like Chan, they'd dived into the pond to watch insect larvae evolve into winged beings or see jellied egg masses explode into thousands of wiggling frogs and salamanders.

Pock and I climbed off the deck and left before the mud went completely silent.


Back in Antler Camp's barn at midnight it was clear that Teddy liked red meat. Pock, leashed to Chan's truck, was drooling and jealous. I was jealous, too. On the way home I'd spent a week's food budget on steak. I ended up chasing soggy Cheerios around my bowl while Pock ignored his kibble, and Teddy ripped through the steak. I thought that as long as we kept our distance outside the pen, our presence might comfort the young eagle. Maybe sitting in the barn with still-living creatures was what *I* wanted—animal comfort after the storm's violence.

Teddy was a noisy eater. Inside the wire pen, he gargled strange clucking noises as he weaved back and forth over the meat, not wanting to take his eyes off us—greedy for the next bite, but struggling with the large pieces.

I started to get to my feet, thinking I might help him out by cutting his meal into smaller bites, but he half-flew, half-scuttled to the far side of the pen, ducking his head up and down angrily. I slumped onto a tractor tire. *Maybe I should have cut it up more for you.*

He slashed his beak through the chunk he carried. *I can figure this out. I got it. Where is the boy who is always with me?*

*He'll be back. Eat up.*

*What is the animal with you?*

*He's a friend.*

Teddy cocked his head. *Friend?*

*He's someone who's always with me, like Chan is with you.*

*You don't smell as good as he does. Neither does your friend.*

*Well, it's been a long day.*

I must have fallen asleep slumped against the side of the tractor, because Pock was up and wagging at the door before I heard the sound of Kate's truck backing up to the barn. Teddy was perched so nervously on a hay bale that his talons vibrated. I heard the hose being dragged away from the barn and water sluiced over something.

"Mum? Mum? We are soooooooo here," she called.

Yes, they were, and I was caught red-handed in the barn with an illegal eagle and a dog that probably shouldn't have been used to soothe him. I pulled Pock behind the pen and asked him to lie down. "Down," I said, "and later, you can lick all the dirty bowls in the sink." Issuing rigid dog orders never worked, but promising him good stuff often did.

"What's up?" I said, sliding the barn door closed behind me, instantly awake to the color changes on Kate's truck. While I could see streaks of its original red on the hood, the rest of it was caked with brown mud. There were even ripple marks where some of the goo had dried in the wind.

The eye-roll she gave me enlisted her entire head, including the muddy arms she thrust toward Chan. She ran for the lake, flinging off her sandals and stripping down to her sports bra and underwear. I could never do that: keep clothing on in all the right spots until the moment of the dive, but Kate could. Chan was bent over the rickety fish-cleaning table that leaned against the barn, whipping the hose back and forth over a huge pile of fish.

"Are you going to clean them all?" I asked.

He looked up, tears running down his face.

"I'll get the knives," I said.


We silently worked our assembly line until almost noon. Chan sliced off heads and gutted the brook trout. I slipped their small bodies into baggies. A few still had the lovely but dimming red spots I loved. I always released fish. When brookies with attitude flicked their escaping tails at me, watching their iridescent spots blend into gravel camouflage was the best part of the whole transaction.

I was painfully aware that all was quiet in the barn while we worked hard to take care of Chan. We could never eat all that fish, but the boy's jaw was so set and his tears so endless that we bagged the fish just to let him know how sorry we were.

Kate defrosted my freezer, filling garbage bags with lumps

of food that probably predated carbon dating. She layered the trout between trays of ice cubes. "Good thing the frozen bats have migrated to the biology lab. Nothing in here was edible anyway. Cheer up, you've been eating cereal and toast since Dad left. Now there's trout." She laughed and handed me a cold glass. "And your iced tea will taste suspicious."

Lifting her own tea, Kate pointed at the porch and said, "Let's rock. The boy's busy." Bent over, Chan was balanced on the truck cab's sideboard using my hose. Mud coated my driveway. I didn't see footprints heading to the barn and wondered what might happen when he finally checked on Teddy and found Pock.

On the porch we eased into rockers, careful lest their sagging frames disintegrate. Rubbing the arms of a chair where I'd nursed her nineteen years ago, Kate said, "When this one goes, don't throw it out. I'll come get it and fix it."

She rocked back and forth a few times and then stopped, sipped some tea, and leaned toward me. "So? You gonna tell me stuff?" she asked, looking around to see if Chan was out of sight. She slipped off her T-shirt and wiggled into one of her father's old shirts. "You should change your stinky fish stuff, too, Mum. Bears from far away will come here."

"I hate clothes," I said.

"No, you don't." She tossed me an old Evan shirt that still had beetle parts on it from cleaning screens. "You just hate shopping. I don't blame you. And what have they done to jeans, making them so low that women's middles are squeezed up like ripe fruit?"

I smiled. "Some of us have ripe fruit layers we don't want to advertise." I sucked in a breath and experimented with something that sounded breezy. "I don't know much, Kate. The wardens and cops knew from the get-go it wasn't an accident though."

"You only saw one part of someone? I mean, was it a full-on chainsaw massacre scene or something more manageable? Like roadkill?"

My hands trembled on the buttons of my shirt and there was nausea that fish guts couldn't explain. "The blood I saw was brown, dry, and cracked. Like the mud on your truck. And stringy parts dangled."

When she saw me struggling with the shirt, she leaned forward and reached for buttons I couldn't see through my tears. "I'm sure there's not much else to say about it," she said gently. "And it's got to be obvious you had nothing to do with it."

I wasn't sure about the obvious part. "How did Chan do up at the U?" I asked.

"Well, first I left him in the biology lab where they were dissecting a moose calf—part of a project to understand why ticks are killing so many. Friends said he smiled the whole time. Later, he sat in on a panel discussion for my Bioethics class. We discussed civil disobedience, and there was lots of chat about whether one person could make a difference.

"He filled a notebook and was literally on the edge of his seat the whole time. I mean the outer two inches of it. Something strange though. The instructor asked him to introduce himself, but he just shook his head. He smiled. Just didn't speak."

"There's a lot we don't know about him," I said.

"Well, he's good at sleep and eats. He slept on my couch and he ate enough toast to pave the road from there to here. He wanted to swing by his home, but when we arrived we ran into a wall of mud."

Kate frowned and sipped her tea slowly. "He didn't ask me

to help, but there was so much misery I wanted to keep busy. We tossed a pile of his traps into the truck. We tossed dead fish in on top of them. He went down to take pictures where the mud was mounded up over something that looked like it used to be a stream. He sat in the middle of it, sweeping his phone up and down, then he disappeared and came back with a bag of filthy books. He didn't speak the whole time."

I decided not to tell her about how Pock and I had heard the entire hillside avalanche down on Chan's world. I thought she'd had enough drama for one day.

Kate stood, opened the porch door, and squinted at the lake. "Mum, where's Pock? How could he miss a fish-gutting party?"

# THIRTEEN

Before I could answer her, something with no muffler roared up the hill away from camp. When we heard Pock's howls, we raced for the barn. Teddy and Chan were gone. Pock jumped frantically up and down inside the pen, howling as if he'd been speared with porcupine quills. As I unlatched the pen door, he pushed past me and raced after the truck.

"What's going on?" yelled Kate as she took off after Pock. "What the hell is going on?"

Nothing good I thought, nudging a pile of name tags and a few remaining traps littering the driveway. I picked up the wire cutters he'd used to cut off his tags and make his traps anonymous.

I recognized a few cable traps, the kind Chan used for bears. The kind that had caught Pock. There was at least one large conibear trap—something lethal with heavy jaws. I shoved it out on the driveway to make sure it wasn't set and then picked it up.

Chickadees in the trees were nearly apoplectic, the tops of their black heads bobbing over their white cheeks. They looked like clustered fans wearing identical baseball caps, peeved about an umpire's call. They added lots of extra dee-dee-dee's to their calls to signal bird anxiety. *Big scary bird. Big scary bird.*

*One at a time, please.*

One bird teetered far out on a limb. *We watch. We watch. We know these birds. They take loon babies from the water. We watch and hide.*

*The bird here couldn't fly.*

*The green-hair one raised his hand. Something big and red on the hand. The big bird flew. Flew to the hand. Big thick hand. Big scary bird.*

I watched the chickadees scatter toward trees that offered more protection. Sometimes truth arrives in strange ways before I actually get to witness it. Real or not, my bird conversation simply told me what I'd already guessed. If Chan could call Teddy to his side, he already had a different relationship than rehabilitation and release. He'd soon be training his eagle to hunt.

A small blue car slowly inched down the hill. Kate talked to the driver as she tugged Pock on a piece of flagging tape my neighbor had used to mark driveway ditches. They were followed by a van painted with scenes of dark-green trees huddled around blue puddles. I guessed the puddles might be lakes. Large black letters snaked along the top of the van's trees asking us to "Join Up with Conservation Maine to Keep Maine . . . Maine."

Kate reached me first, leaned in low, and whispered. "Millie and who's ever with her aren't supposed to know about Chan, right? And whatever was going on in the barn, right? So, when do I get to know?"

"Later. I promise. You might want to escape. Millie's car looks filled with campaign signs and she's brought reinforcements."

"The mountain bike's out back?"

"Yes, and Motor Mark mowed the path so it's scalped. You're good to go."

Kate ducked into the camp, Pock on her heels. Millie opened her door, turned, and rummaged in her back seat, dragging out lawn signs and stashing a staple gun in her apron pocket. I really did love Millie. She was married to Ken

Douglas, and while I didn't work for him anymore, both of them had become deep friends in different ways.

Millie was my unofficial kitchen boss, pushing my hands into her bread dough until I felt every cell in my body hunger for something warm and delicious. Squat, with frizzy hair that hung around her head like a gray cloud, she wore glasses trimmed with green glitter and, always, an apron. "It's the only bit of lady clothing with deep pockets," she said.

She wore a clean apron to her monthly Greenwood selectman meetings. Her insistence on being called Select-A-Woman instead of the traditional selectman title so unnerved her male peers that they'd renamed themselves the Select Board.

Tugging large posters onto my lawn, Millie was clearly seeking reelection. Each sign yelled "Select a Woman: Vote Millie!" in huge letters. The small print at the bottom read, "Paid for by my husband Ken and donors who know I listen a hell of a lot better than the rest of 'em put together."

The door of the van opened and Dan Figarello unfolded himself from the front seat, whipping out a smile that radiated confidence even though a narrow tooth-straightening band crawled across his teeth. He was so lean he'd used his belt to gather up extra pants' material around his waist and so tall I had to force my head back as far as it would go to work on eye contact.

Still in his twenties, he was young enough to remind parents of their earnest sons and daughters, fresh-faced and full of optimism. "Hello Patton," he said, staring at Antler Camp's rough log walls. "I've always wanted to see where you lived. Am thinking now you might make sense." Dan was the head of Conservation Maine's communications team, but he reliably lacked tact when he was simply chatting. He was, however, supremely gifted at devising strategies that delivered new members who'd never considered themselves environ-mentalists. They thought they were signing up to love Maine more than they already did.

I didn't realize I was holding a conibear trap in my hand until Dan pointed and said, "Seems like the last time we met, we'd hired you to lobby against these up at the legislature." He pointed at the trap. "What gives?"

"Hello to you too, Dan," I said, watching Millie disappear toward the outhouse. "Well, it almost worked. Now traps this big are mostly illegal—except for beaver and those have to be set underwater."

Dan smiled down at me. "Right. You did some good work on that. Thank you." He swiped one hand over his blond hair, which was carefully cut to look only slightly shaggy, and asked, "How'd you like to endorse Millie's campaign?"

"I'm assuming that would be free work," I said. "I don't think Millie needs any help from me. Folks love her."

Dan wandered over to moose antlers hanging over the front door—ones I couldn't reach. He ran his fingers over the bleached bone tips. "Didn't expect to see animal parts on your door. Kind of beat up though."

"We didn't find them until other animals had chewed out the good stuff. This camp belongs to my whole family. Some hunt. Some don't. I used to until my father had me field-dress a deer I'd shot. Turns out I like both venison and deer, but apparently want to keep them separate—venison on my plate, deer in the woods. Go figure. I can't."

I looked at Dan's dusty van. It didn't make sense for him to come this far north to work a local election when barely a thousand residents called Greenwood home. Walking to the swing, I nudged some apples so shriveled by unexpected heat, they'd split apart like crushed crackers. "What's up? Something's up." I swung back and forth and waited.

Dan looked toward the outhouse as Millie let the door bang shut and trotted up to us. "You have the nicest one in town," she said. "TP in a coffee can so it smells good and mice can't nibble it. Wood shavings to toss down the hole when all is done and hand sanitizer sitting on one of those shelf fungus things that stick out of trees."

She swooped over, grabbed the swing's ropes, and bent to plant a kiss on my cheek and whisper in my ear. "I'm still invited to next year's no-balls canoe trip again, right? Just us ladies? I'll bring dumplings we can cook on top of hot soup."

I realized I was the object of a campaign to make me feel good about the two people staring at me. "What's up, Millie? And, please, I'm not about to discuss anything that happened to me yesterday. I'm trying to move on."

She gave me a thumbs-up and sank onto the grass near my feet, giving a small squeak as she sat on the staple gun in her pocket. "You always deserve it straight, just like you try to give it to the rest of us, so here it is. The first Select Board item we'll vote on after the town election next month is a statement of support for Premier Power & Energy's wind-power expansion into more of Eagle Ridge."

I backed up the swing so my feet were straight against the ground and I had some distance from them. "Not just *more* of Eagle Ridge. You mean take the whole thing, don't you? All of it that overlooks the lake and town?" Dropping my feet, I whooshed past Millie and slid off the swing to stand facing Dan's chest.

I thumped it a bit with my most crooked, witch-ugly finger. Dan grimaced and backed away. I'd never thought of weaponizing arthritis, but there was always a first time and I had very ugly fingers. "You both know the town's written statement of support won't be enough, even if Millie votes for it. PP&E needs useful bodies at the microphones. Someone else local will have to show up at the permitting hearing to testify." I poked Dan again. "Dan or someone from Conservation Maine will step up to say that wind in the woods is wonderful, and I guess you might hope a local with green credentials could back him up. Right?"

Dan raised his eyebrows at Millie in a look that said, *here she goes. Thanks for setting her off.*

I stomped around the apple tree, muttering. "Lotta good it's done ditching the briefcase to carry around bats. If a dirt road in the middle of nowhere can't quarantine me from the goddamned war . . . ."

Missing my mood entirely, Dan shrugged. "Well, anyway, yes. We thought you'd be a good person to show up and speak. You'd be a volunteer untainted by those of us who are . . . who are legal parties supporting the application."

I bent my head sideways, trying to look like I was giving serious thought to his proposal. For me, the wind issue was all about money—except I wouldn't be getting any. The energy companies got subsidized by millions of federal dollars in tax credits. Great Nations Forests LLC was getting millions for leasing its land to PP&E. The state power company building the transmission lines would get millions of dollars from raising our rates to pay for new poles and lines. Dan got a paycheck.

And then there was Conservation Maine. I didn't think he knew about his organization's quiet deal with PP&E—but I did. I did because I'd often lurked in the legislative dining room, choosing a booth behind people huddled over something. If my nose was pressed into a romance novel that had a cover with a woman whose shirt was strategically ripped, no one ever took me seriously.

PP&E planned to offer Dan's team six-hundred thousand dollars for something it called mitigation. In return, Conservation Maine would not oppose the project. It could boast that it was buying up and protecting lands and waters elsewhere in Maine to mitigate the project's downsides even as it supported alternative energy. A win-win. Of course, those protected lands and waters would be far from Greenwood. Far from what got destroyed.

"There'll be good things for you up here," Dan started to say, "Money for the town, jobs."

"Spare me," I snapped. "I've memorized the last six project applications and final permits. Nothing new in this one, including your arrangement with the developer. After Conservation Maine gets its six-hundred thousand dollars in the deal it brokered with PP&E—"

I paused for effect. Dan frowned and shoved driveway pebbles in small piles. Millie smiled at me. I had no idea why, but she smiled.

I started pacing, kicking apples so they flew apart around us. "So. After Dan's group gets its money from its PP&E deal, Greenwood will get some money each year for about fifteen years. Spread around, it lowers our property taxes by about twenty-seven dollars a year. The power all goes out of state. No town's been able to negotiate cheap electricity as a license condition.

"And jobs? Maybe a few doing some trucking for the Dent & Dent construction crew, and yes, motels and restaurants will have a good bump for about a year during construction, then PP&E will hire one or two people to deal with the site. They're usually not local. And the future? No town or county's been able to strike a deal that gets close to the full cost of the decommissioning to take the stuff down and return the roads to forest. Turbines only have a life of fifteen to twenty years, so that's kinda important if we want to invite the tourists back.

"Oh gaw-awd!" I yelled, thinking the Maine way of saying god in two syllables was way better than a short, unemotional *god*. "My brain's already fogging over from having to think about this shit all over again."

I dropped down next to Millie and felt apples collapse under my butt.

Kate and Pock careened down the hill into the yard. Pock's tongue was out so far I thought he might step on it. Kate's face was red enough to glow in the dark. She dropped her bike and sprinted toward the dock. "Any takers?" she called. Pock was by her side when they both hit the water, scattering a family of ducks and sending our loon family into deep dives.

"She's looking marvelous, Patton," said Millie. "Not the red part, just that she's looking more and more like a young woman and less like a girl. It suits her. I always thought she was about twenty-eight even when she was ten."

During my rant, Dan had pulled a stump from the woodpile into the driveway to use as a stool. He looked at us and tapped his head.

"I'm not nuts. Just done," I said. "Without going into details, let's just say I think wind turbines on our mountains are not good for anyone in Maine who isn't making money off the deal."

I rolled up on my knees to face Millie, grateful for the sweet smell of apples firmly pressed into me. "Millie, of course you'll be welcome on the no-balls trip." I looked at Dan who'd screwed up his face. "That's a canoe trip we do without men we might know—without men we might even love," I added, turning back to her.

"I can't endorse you this time. Not if you're going to vote for a factory to replace the woods and views the town needs. You know we get millions from tourism. When they put this law together, they drew a big circle around the north woods and essentially said 'build wind power here. We'll make it easy.'

"And you know what, Millie? There wasn't one tourism person at the table. Plenty of energy experts salivating after government subsidies. Plenty of environmental folks chanting green mantras, but no one from the business end of the woods. No one to speak up for the Rangeley Lakes folks, or the Moosehead Lake folks, or even the Grand Lake Stream folks. No one to speak up for business people who need wild landscapes to get people into their cars driving north."

She started to speak, but I reached into her apron pocket for the staple gun, put it in her hands, and shook my head. "I will help you put up your signs, so you can leave that." Clutching a low limb, I stood. "Whatever happens, you'll be in my canoe next summer."

I walked toward the dock, thinking I'd jump in fully clothed except for my flip flops. Kicking them off, I stopped, faced Dan and Millie, and pointed at the Conservation Maine van. "I know folks like you are inspired by well-intentioned activism, but lots of times, it looks like green wallpaper to me—just a thin veneer that covers up your not knowing what really matters up here.

"If you're going to 'Keep Maine, Maine,' you may need to find it first. Sleep on some pine needles so your clothes don't smell like lattes. Jump into a stream that's so clear you can see mica grains in small pebbles. Listen to coyotes howl so close, hairs on your neck pop up. Stay too long high on a mountain, and find your way down by starlight. Can't do that in Portland. Lights. And if you get your way, we won't be able to do that here, either. Lots of lights on those turbines."

Dan was vigorously rolling up his shirt sleeves even further than they were already rolled up. I knew I was making him angrier, but I couldn't stop. "I might believe that slogan on your van if I knew you'd dived deeply into what's worth conserving." I turned away. "I hope you'll forgive me for some of this."

"Too bad, Dan. We tried," Millie called as she stacked posters on my lawn. "She can turn a room silent and light the fire under folks at the same time when she's good. And I mean just like that. I thank the lord she's a friend."

After that, Moosehead Lake closed over my head. Bubbles escaping my mouth, I swore to never, ever, give another useless lecture. I aimed for Kate and Pock and hoped they'd wait for me.

# FOURTEEN

After they'd gone, we climbed out of the lake. Kate changed into dry clothes and hugged Pock as he stood on his hind legs, a paw on each of her shoulders. Then she hugged me and climbed into her clean truck. The outline of my wet body on her dry shirt made me feel better about losing her to school.

"So, Chan's gone somewhere with an illegal eagle he's raised from an egg," she said, lifting a new finger each time she added something to her list. "He thinks the bird's his best friend. The game warden—your game warden—knows the boy's an eagle criminal. The boy's driving a truck full of traps he's made anonymous by cutting off his tags. Who knows where his mother has gone. His entire mountain and shack of a home are under mud, and the boy certainly knows who caused it. You were there with Pock in the thick of it despite your stated desire to not be in the thick of it. And at this point, I think *thick* means your clothes are in the state crime lab."

I nodded.

"Oh, and someone cares enough about our personal papers to execute home invasions."

I laughed despite the dire list. Evan and I had never discouraged our daughter's tart takes on reality. She'd been right-on since age four, but we'd kept our faces expressionless. She was too young to know how often she was right.

"I think that's it, unless you want to add that I've probably lost my job," I said.

"Of course. So added." She reached over to lift a dripping lump from the passenger seat. "And then there's this. The boy slogged through the mud to retrieve it."

155

I pulled up a handful of dry grass and swiped it over Chan's Bible.

"He kept looking at the folded-over page on our way here," Kate said, leaning out the window to squeeze a stream of water from her hair. "I'll make you a deal. You stay off the front page. I'll try and dig up the graphs and charts I stashed in computer files somewhere. See if I can reconstruct my original data on trees and turbines."

She tapped her car keys on my chest before she started the truck. "And *you* have to file a flight plan with me if you go somewhere. That's our deal. You could do way better on that, Mum. Anywhere at all. Let me know where you've gone, or you haven't seen me really pissed-off."

I agreed to the flight plan, leaned in and kissed her, and held Pock's collar while she drove away. Then I opened the Bible and with my finger, cleared off the folded-over page.

Just one sentence was visible between pasted-in paragraphs on moose mortality and tick infestations. I felt my heart dive toward my toes and more sweat—if that was possible—trickle down my back. Chan had underlined only one sentence from the book of Hosea. "For they have sown the wind, and they shall reap the whirlwind . . ." He'd underlined it so many times, small rips like tiny wounds cut each word.

He was clearly in a vengeful Old Testament mood, where men advocated an eye for an eye as a good solution. I wondered what kind of whirlwind the boy planned.

It was late afternoon by the time I'd hidden my car behind a pile of granite slabs that construction crews had piled up on either end of the Eagle Ridge Project's security fence. I had only a weak signal, but I texted Kate a short message. *Off to check*

*out my tent at wind power site. Probably stay the night.*
Checking for road dust that might announce traffic, Pock and
I walked around the fence and into woods no one had cut yet.

I'd camped in a small clearing next to a stream that bubbled
up from underground springs. Cool and shaded by alders and
birches, its waters never failed to soothe me, whether I had my
feet in them or was drifting off to sleep.

My tent was collapsed in a large puddle. Old Christmas
cookie tins littered the ground. Clearly, animals had wrestled
with our food stash. The clearing was a track soup of coyotes
who'd walked everywhere, deer who'd come and gone from
the same matted-down game trail, and numerous small prints
that signaled a pine marten or weasel convention.

I didn't mind. In a way, it was like coming home to find lots
of family who felt so comfortable in your space that they'd left
litter and mess, sure you'd forgive them. I did. Pock sent the
remaining squirrels scrabbling up trees. A squadron of Canada
jays swarmed onto low branches, but they seemed unnaturally
edgy, jumping to high limbs whenever I moved an arm. Pock
licked his bowl clean of kibble I salvaged off the ground, while
I chewed on crackers so stale they stuck together. The jays
shifted hopefully overhead.

*Sorry, no crumbs here fellas.*

*He already fed us.*

I looked around at the gathering darkness and saw an
opened sardine tin perched on top of a stump. *He?*

*He with green on his head.*

*Green? Like what?*

*What wood ducks wear, silly.*

*After he fed you, did you see which way he went?*

There was general cackling agreement and even some
whistling as they puffed up their gray feathers to almost twice

157

their size. *Not going to help you. No help without food.*

Canada jays had to be the toughest birds in the forest. Who else would lay eggs and hatch them when it was full-on winter and way below zero? I'd seen them eat ticks off of moose and snatch a baby bat from its mother. I tossed crackers wildly around the clearing. *Move fast before the dog gets it.*

The jays ate all the crackers, even diving at Pock as he raced toward the farthest bits. As fast as they'd flown in, the jays flew out, not keeping their side of the bargain. It didn't really matter since the empty sardine can had confirmed Chan's arrival. And I already knew that the wind project was the best place for him to exact eye-for-an-eye revenge.

I shook water off the tent and righted the collapsed poles. My sleeping bag wasn't soggy, but it was a damp, cool mat to lie on. I pulled Pock into a loose spooning position so his back was cradled in my arms and his breathing almost matched mine. I heard more animals visit and that made sense. I'd left a few stale tins open, except one with Pock's reclaimed kibble and one filled with chocolate. We'd need breakfast.

As I fell asleep, I had a hazy recollection of Evan, not when we'd been married, but after he'd left. At that time, I often fell asleep imagining him spooning with his new young wife. Thinking of them curled up together was unexpected comfort that I could never admit to anyone because it was so weird. At last, I thought, at last he'd be happy. I wouldn't be happy—but he would. Pock yipped softly a few times in his sleep and I tightened my grip. Hugging my dog was way better anyway.

I woke alone in the tent, groggy and wondering if Pock had learned to unzip it. Then I remembered I'd let him out at dawn when he whined. He wouldn't go far. He'd be busy wetting foliage to let everyone know he was home. I lifted bits of sleeping bag to my nose, thinking I must have spilled coffee on it, it smelled so good. Without my contact lenses, I could only see something white waving in front of the tent screen. I crawled over to squint at a hand waving a paper plate over a tin mug.

"Francoise has also sent croissants," said Moz, fanning more coffee in my direction. "It is time to follow the boy's trail." Hauling on the previous day's sweaty shirt and shorts, and licking my contact lenses so they'd stick back in my eyes, I realized I was not at my best. I also owed Moz an apology for how I'd snapped about underwear—evidence he'd hidden from his search team. Evidence that linked me to whoever had owned a sweatshirt and probably more body parts scattered in the woods.

"I'm sorry," I called, licking more fingers to even out my eyebrows.

"Is that sentiment for recent events or for what we may do today?" he asked. I could hear the smile in his voice. "Meet me down the trail, please."

By the time I'd gulped coffee, laced up my hiking books, and hoisted my pack to my shoulders, Moz and Pock had disappeared. With a mouth full of chocolate croissant, I headed down the game trail, marveling at how economical deer must be to re-use a narrow path that often disappeared. Only pine needles, rearranged into patterns more intricate than Persian rugs, gave them away.

I almost bumped into the rear tires of Moz's ATV. "The game trail ends in a road?" I asked. We stood on an unused logging road where raspberry bushes competed with dead brush, herbicided so future crews wouldn't have to deal with a regrowing forest. I wasn't tempted to eat the last berries.

Dressed in old jeans that sported a neat crease, a warden softball-team shirt, and worn hiking boots, Moz sat waiting for me. Two helmets dangled from his hands. "Deer conserve energy whenever they can. They use paths they make and paths others make, and so do the coyotes who stalk them. Pock will ride with me where he will not be tempted by either species." The front paws of my dog were draped over the machine's handlebars, and the rest of him was shoved into Moz's lap.

He slipped a bright orange vest over his shirt and laid one behind him on the seat. "Moose-hunting season," he said. I pushed the mug into my pack, wiggled into the vest and helmet, and swung one foot over the seat behind him. "There's so much I want to ask," I said, pulling the pack into my lap and finding his tracking device still clipped to it. That answered one question.

Moz nodded at dents in the grass in front of his tires. "Chan rode this way last night, perhaps thinking dew would hide his tracks. The heavy load he carries will make it easy to follow him." He sat quietly rubbing Pock's ears and didn't ask me about Chan's heavy load. I figured he already knew about the traps.

"We going?" I asked.

Moz lifted his arms. "You must reach around my waist."

At least he couldn't see the blush as I leaned forward, crushing everything in my pack except the wire cutters Chan and I seemed to be sharing. They squeezed my chest but didn't hurt as much as the burn that started in my throat and spread to my hands as Moz locked them tightly around the middle of him. His muscles moved smoothly under my hands. I was grateful that engine noise stopped conversation.

We made a wide arc around the wind project, thumping up over haul roads and smaller trails used to extract trees from the

160

side of the ridge they'd just cut. I had a clear view of sun reflecting off the solar panels that covered Chan's empty mansion. We stopped in a small clearing surrounded by piles of logs. Moz turned off the engine and tilted his head toward a cooler breeze blowing at us from Canada.

I tried a whisper. "If there's a hearing coming up on the project expansion, and some state agency still has to decide the outcome, how could Great Nations' crews cut the proposed site ahead of time?"

Moz watched a red-tailed hawk circle overhead, its calls a falling crescendo of ragged sound cut off in mid-screech. The bird had the classic raptor cry—so piercing and threatening that movie sound crews dubbed it in to replace eagles' voices. Our national bird has a limp and wobbly cry, like someone whining over something unimportant.

Moz didn't whisper, but his voice was quiet and low. It was his most serious voice, the one that made lawbreakers drop illegal ducks, or fish, or anything they had in their hands after hearing only a few words. "Those who once stood up to protect the forest no longer stand for the forest if wind power is located in it. The timber landowners are confident there will be no opposition and all permits will be granted. They have given themselves permission to cut the project corridor and anything nearby that will justify the expense of moving machines and crews to this location."

In front of us the hawk dove into the grass and rose with a thrashing rabbit. The bird dipped so low, I could see the wailing rabbit's jaws open wide and its ears blow back with the force of the bird's take-off. I buried my head in Moz's back. A rabbit's scream sounds exactly like a human baby.

We rode further uphill, and I kept my head down on the man's back for what seemed like miles until the ride suddenly smoothed out. We'd joined a project road almost as wide as three lanes of the Maine Turnpike. I eased my grip on Moz and found my chest covered with tiny wood chips sweated off the back of his shirt. My arms smelled like I'd hugged someone more tree than man.

# FIFTEEN

Moz slowed to let Pock jump from the ATV as he parked by a trail littered with Bud Light cans and cigarette butts. Scrubby and stunted from high-elevation winters determined to kill them, the trees by the trail had locked their limbs together like people in a protest march who refused to be separated by threats and force.

"You think Chan's in here?" I asked, crawling off the ATV into a stretch I hoped would restore my spine.

"Pock does," Moz said. He whistled him back up the trail and reached for the cargo bag lashed on the back of the ATV. "Do you have a leash? I believe we must arrive together." He unbuckled his helmet and stripped off his orange vest. "We can hike without these. It is too hot for moose to be anywhere but bogs or deep forest, and most who hunt them prefer roads close to their vehicles. Seven hundred pounds of meat is hard to carry over rough terrain."

Down the middle of the trail, we followed a deep groove where something heavy enough to displace small rocks had been dragged downhill. What we found looked like a set from a Disney fantasy film. Pock stooped to drink from a pool surrounded by sheer rock walls, a small beaver dam, and a beach studded with white pebbles. Thick clumps of mountain ash rustled with birds feasting on berries, and birch trees dropped leaves that floated into bright yellow piles on beaver-chewed logs. Under the tiny waterfall that dropped into the pool, energetic damsel flies darted up and down, blue wings opening and closing like bursts of bright confetti. "This must be some kind of oasis," I said.

Moz knelt by the water, fingers exploring deep grooves that disappeared into the pool. A beaver slapped his tail, warning his family that more interlopers had arrived. As I looked around, I saw that previous guests had not been kind to the beavers' home.

A few birches had been chain-sawed and made into a rough table, their naked stumps stripped of bark and blasted by shotgun pellets. In the shade, toilet paper warned me where not to walk. A full six-pack of beer cooled in shallow water. Most impressive was a can sculpture arranged like a naked woman, pop tops flipped up for nipples and a clump of moss positioned between her Bud Light legs.

"Oh, come on!" I yelled to no one in particular. Moz had slipped into the pool for a closer look at whatever had disappeared into it, and Pock, tied to a tree, was panting in the shade. Obviously, the pool was a backwoods break room, where anyone who worked the roads and woods had arranged toilet, target range, and bar amenities. I tied Pock to the table and started dismantling Bud Woman.

First, I heard Chan's scream. "Traps. There's traps. Help him. Help him!"

Then Moz exploded from the pool, gasping for air before he went down again. High above the pond, Chan's terrified voice bounced off the rocks.

"Go down. Pull the chain. Get the chain. You have to—"

I didn't hear the rest of what he had to say. I was already underwater, headed down as Moz struggled past me toward the surface. Disturbed mud churned all around me and Moz slammed me sideways as he bent back down toward the bottom. I grabbed his hair as he went past and tugged him toward the surface. Spitting water into my face, he coughed and struggled.

"Can you stand?" I yelled. "Can you keep your head above water?"

In answer, he gasped in another breath like he was ready to dive, but I lifted my hand and cuffed him across his nose. "Damn it. Just stop! Can you keep your head above water? Even if you just tilt your head." I tried to cuff him again, but he ducked, spreading out his arms to tread water. "Well, can you?"

"Caught. I'm caught."

"I know that. Let's first see if you can breathe." I started to back up, but Moz shook his head. "Don't put feet down. Not safe."

I figured if he could tell me what to do, he could breathe. "Ok. Got that. I'll have to dive down and pull out the chain that anchors the trap. I need you to be still and kind of float. I need to see what's going on."

"Get the mask," he said. "On shore. Mask on table."

"Only if you promise not to dive again," I said.

Panting short breaths and grunting in pain, he rolled his eyes at me.

I took that as a yes, paddled to shore, crawled out on the beach, and grabbed one of two masks on top of his gear. On my first dive, helped by the mask over my eyes and the settling mud, I found the trap's chain anchored into two thick sticks crossed over each other in the mud. I surfaced for more air and dove again, this time prepared to kick the sticks sideways. Legs are always more powerful than arms.

Each time I surfaced and gulped air, Moz's face looked grayer and grayer and his eyes stayed closed. It took me four dives before I kicked the chain free, watched it dangle below the trap on his leg, and surfaced next to him.

"Can you make it?' I asked, but he was already stroking

165

toward shore, dragging one leg. On the beach we threw ourselves onto our backs, coughing and spitting out muddy water.

Moz lifted one arm and pulled off my mask. "Are you alright?" he asked.

"Oh, sure," I said. "Nothing to it. You?"

His chuckle ended in a soft moan. "The boy around to help remove this?"

I looked up. "No."

Moz turned his head so I couldn't see his face.

"I don't think you have to hide how grim all this could be," I said, sitting up. "You're in luck. Just catch your breath."

I got up, twisted water and sand out of my hair, and rummaged through Moz's pack. "Got rope?" I asked.

He shook his head.

"Well, Pock has." I attached one end of the pack to the table and the other end to Pock's collar and unclipped his leash. "Don't pull too hard on this," I said, rubbing his ears. "Don't want to worry about you right now."

On my knees, I inspected the trap and the leg it held. "Good news. No blood. And it's on your thigh which is nice and fleshy and somehow you also got some stick in there so it's acting like a buffer between nasty teeth and more of your leg. I think the wood took the full force of it." It wasn't a good sign that Moz didn't seem curious about my assessment.

"Hard to get these off," he said, eyes closed again.

"Agreed. But lucky for you the only video I watched from beginning to end when I had to sit through hearings revising our trapping laws was the one showing us how to get a dog out of a trap like this. I paid very close attention."

Up on his elbows and paying close attention, Moz didn't look gray anymore.

I wove the leash through the side springs on one side of the trap and stood, both ends of the leash wrapped around my fists. "I think I can get this side open enough for you to roll your leg out sideways. You ready? When I pull up and relax the springs, you move."

Groaning loudly, I pulled. As Moz rolled away, I dropped my fists and released the leash. We didn't discuss my rescue. The trap's snapping jaws echoing off the rocks around us was enough conversation.

On his feet and limping to grab logs from the dam and stack them on the beach, Moz looked too angry for questions about the long red scar that started on his chest and disappeared into plaid boxers. He'd stripped to go in, but I was still wearing all my clothes. It seemed like a good idea to keep them on but lose my hiking boots. They overflowed with runoff from my body.

Waving me away and sliding carefully into the pond, a second mask on his face, he grabbed a log, disappeared, and reappeared without it. While he repeated the disappearing log maneuver at least five times, I looked around for Chan but found only a beaver already repairing his dam.

*The young one is gone. But not before he left killing things in our home.*

*I don't think he was after you. He was after the men who came here.*

*When we swam in our pool, they threw rocks at us so we hid in our home.*

*Well, that's over now.*

He turned and slapped his tail. *You will be here tomorrow to stop them when they return?*

Becoming the pond's guardian was a very seductive idea, but Moz swam to the beach, offered me a mask, and slipped his own mask over eyes so dark I could see nothing I recognized

167

in them. "Keep your feet up," he said.

I swam next to him, looking down except when I needed to snatch air. When I saw the trap holding a dead beaver and touched Moz's shoulder, he didn't respond. All around the limp carcass, tiny fish poked at tiny wounds, and bits of soil hung in a brown haze where the animal had clawed into mud.

Near the far shore we floated above a pile of rotten leaves and bark slouched against a few unopened beer cans. Bud Light bait. Moz tapped one can with the last sapling he carried and metal teeth rose from the leaves and snatched the wood away from his hand.

On shore lying in the sun, hot pebbles on my back and Pock leashed to my foot, I asked, "If an entire crew cut Chan's side of the mountain, what did he hope to achieve by setting traps? As soon as one man was hurt or even drowned, the others would know the danger."

"He is not practiced at hate," said Moz. "I believe he tried to locate his bait near the edge of the pond where someone with a hand in a trap might be able to stand and breathe or jump to the surface and breathe. I am not sure that plan would have worked well if a short man reached for the beer."

"Or someone somehow stuck a leg into it," I said.

"That," said Moz.

I rolled over to let the sun cook other parts of me and watched Moz dress and repack his gear. "Are masks standard warden gear?" I asked.

"My sons, when they visit, like to watch fish pursue their lives." He heaved the pack over his shoulders and shrugged it into place. "A mask helps me find evidence people may throw into the water as they see an approaching warden."

I tied on my soggy boots and started pulling Pock up the trail.

Walking behind me and shoving litter out of the bushes with a long stick, Moz asked, "If you think the boy's revenge was ineffective, what would yours look like?"

I felt out of practice, but thinking the answer out loud helped me ignore dust as we climbed. "First, I'd do some deep breathing and make sure I wasn't delivering revenge, just exposure. I'd make the target's behaviors and choices visible so whatever came down on them wouldn't be watered down by publicity focused on me.

"If this goes public, it will be all about Chan and what he's done here, rather than the harvesting and mudslide. I'm pretty sure that the harvesting operation resulted in an illegal discharge downhill to state waters. I'd have photographed the dead animals and maybe fish flipping their last flips—and used it as anonymously as I could."

As we trudged uphill, Pock snuffled through trailside bushes hoping a partridge might fly up into his face. "I'm sure setting traps here had to be some kind of crime," I called back.

"Yes. Let's talk about breaking the law," came a much-too-happy voice from the PP&E truck parked in the shade at the top of the trail. Pock dropped into a crouch and inched forward until his leash had no slack, and I had to lean back against his weight. I pushed him down into a stiff-legged sit while he growled something low—a well-behaved warning, but still a warning.

Smoking, Ridge Dumais and Matt Pruitt leaned against the truck. I looked back for Moz and found him gone. I guessed I'd have to call the black shoes man by his real name as it was clear we were going to have an ongoing relationship. He'd changed into spiffy brown hiking boots, but he still looked quite corporate, even without his clipboard. "Mr. Pruitt," I said. "What are you doing out of the office?"

He waved his cigarette at me. "We're checking for unauthorized ATVs now that we've increased security. Our roads seem to be popular with folks who are not on our payroll. Your mortality inspections are not scheduled today, so you might be trespassing." With an annoying sucking sound, he inhaled stray smoke. "And we've still got questions about yesterday's events. Law enforcement done with you yet?"

I raised my middle finger.

Ridge reached into the truck and pulled out several trail cameras. "We got motion-activated cameras that saw two machines come up here." He dropped his cigarette and ground it out under his boots. "What would you know about that?"

Behind them, Moz slid out of the woods. When his shadow crossed over theirs, they jumped.

"Jesus, Atkins," cried Ridge. "Don't do that."

Moz lifted his pack onto the back of his ATV, sliding it over the top of Chan's traps to cover them. He held up a clear bag of empty worm containers. Stuffed inside some of them were bits of brown-stained toilet paper and a few beer cans.

"Your crews appear to be in violation of fishing regulations. This is a fly-fishing-only pond and stream. No live bait permitted." He turned the bag so they could see all of its contents. "They are also in violation of littering laws and they have harvested trees in violation of Maine's Remote Ponds Protection Act."

Ridge sighed and leaned against the truck. "See any of our boys down there?" He waved a hand at the trail behind us. "Might be that woman who likes chains. You never know. Her and her Texas pals might be plain ignorant of Maine law."

Moz strapped his bag on the luggage rack, motioned me up

behind him, and lifted Pock to his lap. Pock half turned and licked his seatmate's face, but it didn't change how rigid and angry Moz's back felt against my front.

"You're not dressed warden-like," Ridge said.

With his hands on the ignition, Moz paused and snapped on his helmet. "I was hoping for a picnic."

"As if shit," said Ridge. "You don't look authorized."

"Hey," I said. "You can . . ."

Moz leaned back so far I was laid almost flat on the luggage rack, but I got the hint. "It is a sad fact that our recreation days are often interrupted with opportunities to enforce the law," he said, starting the engine. "Now instead of taking this woman to dinner, I will be driving to our evidence lab and asking for DNA analysis on the bag's contents."

Matt stepped in front of the tires and held up a hand, his cigarette strangely pressed between thumb and forefinger like someone who'd spent more time with marijuana than tobacco. I hadn't seen anyone do that in decades. "We'll see this area is cleaned up and posted off limits," he said, "but keep that woman and her eco-Nazi friends off our site, or we'll have to do it."

Moz drove us back a few feet and then turned his wheels. "Posting it would be wise, Mr. Pruitt. You must agree we would not want people eating fish that must live below what you spray to kill plants up here."

As we rolled away, I leaned forward. "Can you really talk that way as a Maine game warden? Even out of uniform? I mean, the snark? That was fabulous."

He didn't answer.

"And what are we going to do about Chan and what he did at the pond? Ridge said they'd seen two ATV's on a trail cam. One had to be Chan, right?"

Moz just shook his head. I didn't realize he wore a gun under his T-shirt until my arm bounced low into it. It hadn't been there on the uphill ride. I shifted my arms higher around his torso.

Outside the front gate, Lily Rose Baines Johnson's van was parked at an imposing angle. Moz slowed us to a crawl. She still wore her steel-toe work boots, but she'd changed into a sleeveless shirt and what looked like a very old pair of Millinocket high school basketball shorts. Maybe, like me, she shopped at thrift stores. "I won't bite," she called.

"That's not what concerns me," Moz said quietly. Pock leaped off the seat and ran to the gate wagging his whole body. "May we trust his judgment?" he asked.

"Not really," I said, standing to stretch. "He seems drawn to troubled souls."

Moz turned and stared at me, black eyes bright with his own private joke.

"What?" I asked. "What? And is the dinner thing you said up there a real offer? I think I earned it today."

"We should see what animates Ms. Johnson," he said, striding the last few yards to the gate, but stopping well out of reach of her arms that stretched though parts of it. One hand waved a piece of paper and the other reached low massaging Pock's ear. Next to riding in big trucks in the front seat, Pock loved ear rubs the best. I could hear his groans.

"Message for you, Patton," she called. "From your boss. Found it on the gate here."

Moz reached for it and then handed it to me. "What else is your business here, Lily?" he asked.

"We're on a first name basis now, Warden? You do know that a gate wouldn't stop me if I wanted in there, don't you?"

"I do," said Moz.

"I was hoping for some help," she said. "But not from anyone who works here, so this side of the gate seemed safer." She waved an arm at her truck.

"Your tires are flat," Moz said.

"Just two now. I carry two spares and I've already changed those tires. Two more slashed ones to go. They got all four while I was out for a walk." She grinned. "Always good to know when one is appreciated for what one does."

"It is," said Moz. "And what are you doing here?"

I was so busy reading Anita's message and absorbing its surprising requests that I wasn't really listening until Lily said, "I need to talk to Cassandra. Or Patton. Or whatever her name is."

I lifted Anita's note and smelled gear oil on the picked tape hanging off its edge. "You read this, didn't you? It was sealed up and you read it. Anita would never leave something like this hanging out in PP&E territory. My mailbox. You've been to my mailbox. My mailbox in town."

Lily shrugged. "I need to talk to you before that hearing on Monday."

"How come everyone seems to know where I am?" I asked. Moz turned away and adjusted his shirt lower over his hips.

Lily snorted. "Where else are you going to go if you're not at home or that weird cafe? You have easy-to-follow ruts."

Moz walked toward the porta-potties, his fingers traveling over his cell phone. "What are we going to talk about?" I asked. The day was slipping away and although we'd heard Chan yell and found his traps and essentially saved his butt, we didn't have hands on him. Or Teddy. The breakfast croissants had long ago disappeared into my pond swim and hike, so I unwrapped a granola bar and dropped Anita's note into the pack.

"Wanna share?" Lily asked.

I handed another bar through the gate's mesh barrier. "These always taste like sawdust," she said.

"You're welcome. That's the idea. If I carried around something worth eating, it wouldn't remain emergency food when I need it."

Lily looked up, chewing. "You're good. Strategic. Your mind covers lots of territory at once. Back-up plans, alternatives. But I already knew that. Not only are you easy to track, you're all over the Internet, too. No wonder the PP&E folks don't like you."

"It's a little early in our knowing or not knowing each other to know that, isn't it?"

She stuffed the empty wrapper in her pocket. "I don't think so."

I grabbed Pock's collar and pulled him away from the fence, even though he was straining for the crumbs Lily tossed at him. I was pretty sure there was nothing Lily Rose Baines Johnson was going to ask me or tell me that I wanted to hear, so I was pleased to hear Moz walk toward us. Lily popped the rest of the granola bar into her mouth and stepped away from the gate.

"The tow truck will be here in an hour," he said. "It will tow you to Medway where there is a garage that sells tires."

"I found another body part," she said, hitching up her shorts to perch on the hood of her van.

# SIXTEEN

In less than half an hour, wailing sirens signaled a law-enforcement invasion. Before it could trap us and make me hear more about body parts, I leashed Pock and slipped away into the woods. There was no way I could rescue my car if roads leading away from the gate swarmed with official people.

At my campsite I tied Pock where he could have his feet in the stream if he needed a drink. I stretched out on the moss I'd been eyeing as a possible mattress if and when my tent grew mold in the heat. Moss can be so deeply green that it casts a green shadow on bare skin. I raised my arms to admire the effect while springy parts of it massaged my back.


Hunger pangs woke me. I was desperately hungry. I found a chewed but intact can of Spam up the trail where coyotes, pine martens, or something toothy had given up on it. I scraped off droppings deliberately left in animal frustration and rinsed the can. I knew Kate would never approve, but I crawled around on my knees collecting raisins from the shredded gorp bag. Apparently, my guests liked M&M's and peanuts, but raisins were off the menu. I found lemonade drink mix in my pack. It's always useful for drinking stinky water, but this time I planned to upgrade canned Spam to edible Spam.

I righted my small stove, placed my small fry pan on it, and tossed in some slabs of what is really just pork shoulder and ham with a bit of potato crystals. While the Spam sizzled in its own fat, I swatted bugs and thought about how my life was going. Sometimes in the Maine woods everyone decides to compete for blood at the same time. Black flies, mosquitoes, deer flies, and one species so huge Kate and I called them moose flies. After an energetic bout of arm waving, I found myself miraculously free of the entire hoard.

A smile worked its way over my lips. I hadn't even used that much energy to get free of my entire previous life. When my husband divorced me, I divorced my lobbying career. Like my husband, most legislators were done giving me quality time anyway. Nothing seemed to fit. I wanted it all gone. Within minutes of becoming single again, I chucked my tasteful heels into a dumpster outside the courthouse and went to a Goodwill store for used overalls and flannel shirts.

With her home broken, Kate used her high school Advanced Placement credits to move out and jump-start college. My mother moved into Sea View, a Boothbay Harbor nursing home with no ocean views. My father set up a small apartment at his real estate office and continued selling high-end coastal homes to folks who could afford taxes the locals could not.

I appeared to be quite free, so I packed everything that would fit in my Subaru and moved north. I assumed Antler Camp would offer me a safe, simple life. I might have been wrong about that.

I picked a dead moose fly from the browning meat, and just for a moment was tempted to eat it because it looked like a crispy appetizer. I tossed it to Pock who caught it with a happy crunch. Lining up the next ingredients in a neat row of raisins, lemonade, and one lone nut, I wondered if I could line up the week's events in the same orderly way. I imagined calendar entries with cryptic notes.

Monday, someone had chopped up a body before I reported to work. Thanks to everyone's expectations or suspicions, I felt responsible for that shoulder and whatever else came with it.

That day was a busy day, as Pock and I had escaped the scene only to meet up with a bear trap and its owner—who seemed to also be hiding out. I had a close encounter with an eagle's raw power, and then a close encounter with a game warden who was going to complicate my life.

I'd conducted surveillance at an empty mansion where I had no right to be, followed by dinner where it seemed that everyone for miles around had an unhealthy interest in my life, especially someone named Lily Rose Baines Johnson. The day's icing on the cake was a motherless teenager showing up as my new roommate.

Tuesday was even better, beginning with the news that my boss Anita was getting pressure to fire me. My barn was commandeered to hide an illegal eagle. At the Penobscot River, I transferred bats and my houseguest to Kate, but not before she fingered me for what sounded like a chaotic childhood where she'd had way too much of me. Someone engineered a wave that turned my skinny dip into a survival moment, and Moz saw me naked.

I added raisins, lemonade mix, and a bit of water to the almost-done Spam. With luck, the sugar and raisins would congeal into a fruit sauce. I could make Spam taste amazing.

Tuesday finished up with a catastrophic mud slide shared with Ridge Dumais, who seemed to work for Great Nations Forests and Premier Power and Energy at the same time. He was, however, a good reminder that I'd abandoned the war for the forest—a struggle that could quickly turn nasty. Why people who worked for corporations that owned over nine million Maine acres should get bothered by a woman living on a tight food budget was always a mystery to me.

Tuesday night, Teddy and Pock and I had dinner together in the barn.

On this day—which was only Wednesday—my goal to have Antler Camp as a sanctuary was tested by Chan, Kate, and dead trout. Then Millie and Dan filled up my afternoon with a volunteering offer I could easily refuse. Thinking that some secret parts of Eagle Ridge might offer more privacy, I'd returned to my tent site only to find it invaded by animals who smelled opportunity.

I eased the fry pan onto a rock so I could stir the final touches into the hot Spam. Cataloguing the rest of the day's events was easy. I was grateful that I'd avoided Chan's traps, no one from PP&E had arrested me, and Moz was coping with Lily.

Pock whined, his cocked head asking if we'd share dinner. I dropped onto the ground beside him, snapped off the leash, and rolled him over for a tummy rub. "It's got to cool, boy; then we'll split it. I know you adore Spam." Pock was a Labrador Retriever. He loved every food, everything about food, and even the word *food*.

I could answer Pock's dinner question, but I had no answers for all the others I thought up while picking twigs from his fur. Where was Chan? Where was his family? Where was Teddy? If Kate hadn't stolen my entire file on wind stuff, who had it? The same person who had Kate's pack? Did someone want to bury what we had on paper, or use it? And the rogue wave? Not an accident. Maybe some kind of message, but not an accident.

The really big question was simple. What would happen if I did know the person who'd left his shoulder in the road?

I reached for the pan and spooned more sauce over the meat. "And what was that huge scar across Moz's chest?" I asked out loud.

"Impalement," said Moz, stepping past my tent. Pock

leaped up, knocking the frying pan into stream gravel. There was a small sizzle as fat found cool water.

I leaned over, grabbed the pan, and poured out greasy water. "That was dinner," I said. "Unless you're serious about taking me out somewhere."

Moz walked to the stream and scooped up the Spam. "I think your friend needs this more than we do." He dropped all but one slice back into the pan. Pock licked it up while I stared at Moz.

"Impalement?" I asked. "OK. I need to know about that. Then . . . maybe dinner?"

"You are not interested in Ms. Johnson's find?"

"Not if I have to hear more about Lily."

When Moz laughed, the tight skin around his high cheekbones relaxed. Not something I'd often seen. He pulled a stump upright and took out his knife to shred the remaining Spam. "In my life, the scar came early. Each year four Wabanaki tribes' people travel from Indian Island Reservation in the Penobscot River to the base of Mt. Katahdin. I was too sure of myself, too certain I could pole a canoe upriver through rapids others avoided. The pole jammed between rocks and splintered, traveling up under my skin. It stopped before reaching my heart. I was lucky."

I jumped up. "Lucky? Lucky? How many important organs were rearranged or punctured?"

"I was a long time healing after the helicopter ride to Portland and then on to Boston. The doctors told me I was healing but losing weight. At night they whispered over my bed. One day after the snows melted, my nokemes came and sent them away. She made me drink her tea. I awoke to the sound of birds and her chants outside a teepee on lands where there are no roads. I do not remember the journey. Only the birds and the sun and her songs."

The Canada jays must have liked his bird story. They chattered in trees above us. Pock patrolled below, vacuuming up crumbs they'd missed during the first visit, occasionally putting his front paws up on a tree trunk to send them scattering. Most dogs ignored small birds, but Pock was keen on everything that moved.

"OK. What's with body parts and Ms. Johnson?" I asked.

"I can only report that on an errand into the woods to relieve herself, she found more of what we need to find. It was, however, not enough to reveal the victim's identity."

"No hands? No face?" I asked.

He shook his head.

"So, no fingerprints and nothing people could recognize?" I thought about the next question, which I didn't dare to ask. *So, nothing that gets me off the hook?*

Moz bent into his pack to pull out the two masks we'd used earlier in the day. He dropped the Spam pieces he'd saved into a small baggie he pulled from his pocket.

"And Chan? Any news of Chan?" I asked.

"He and his bird were here."

Teddy was busted. Moz knew about the eagle. Pulling another baggie from his pack, he emptied out small rolls that looked like shaggy bark. "Please lie down, Pock," he said. Even prone on the ground, my dog could stretch himself into a longer dog. His nose was inches from the bag's contents.

I didn't tell Moz that I'd already figured out Chan's visit to my tent. Only Shannon knew about my animal conversations and Shannon was gone. "I don't have to figure out if you're sane or insane," she'd said, waving a canoe paddle in the air. "Look at people visiting zoos. They talk to animals and think they know what the animal says back if it roars, does a head fake, or twitches its tail. You're just better at sorting out what the actual conversational exchange might be and getting benefits from the process. There's other ways you might be slightly insane, though."

Thinking about her closed my throat. I dropped to my knees and stared at the gray bits on the ground.

"You have never seen these before?" he asked.

"They look like tree bark."

"They are castings." I reached for one and Moz grabbed my hand. "They are not sanitary—perhaps a danger of salmonella with items that are not fully digested." He reached behind him for a handful of stream water, sprinkled it over one piece, and then pried it apart with a twig.

"Not digested?" I asked

He sank down next to me, comfortably cross-legged while my knees were already screaming. "Many birds regurgitate items they cannot digest. What do you recognize?" he asked.

Moz had a habit of leaving animal puzzles in my Antler Camp mailbox, and while I appreciated bits and pieces of animals' leavings and chewed-on things, it seemed a strange way to communicate. On the other hand, it worked for us. Somehow the wildlife world was a bridge we could cross toward each other.

"Hair. Feathers. What's this?" I shoved the twig against something tiny and white. "It's a skull. A regurgitated bird skull."

"Yes. The skull has no teeth. In these casts, the eagle left proof it was not dining on a mammal. It dined on something that could fly. Something it might catch in the air."

Of course Chan's bird could fly when it wanted to take down dinners that weren't served up as mice platters. I looked sideways at Moz. His black brows were drawn so tightly together they almost met in the middle of his forehead. "Young Chandler Perkins is in deep water. Now the bird is hunting, or the boy is deliberately training him to hunt."

"Teddy," I said. When Moz didn't reply, I said, "Teddy is the eagle's name."

He sighed. "I found these casts under a tree." He rose and pointed to a white pine whose upper branches were coated with white smears of bird waste. "The eagle was perched—hunting."

Pock rolled in spilled grease while my stomach growled. "You don't happen to have any food on you, do you?" I asked. "I think the Spam was all I had left."

Moz stripped off his shirt. A river of scar tissue poured from his chest to his waist, but he made no move to hide it from me. He kicked off his moccasins and pulled the belt from his jeans.

I stared, guessing that few people had seen his torn-up chest or heard its history. Here he was, comfortable with my seeing proof of how he might be flawed—even beyond his skin. I wore old, pre-varicose-veins shorts and hadn't thought about my legs all day. What a relief. I pushed off a rock and got to my feet. "Changing for dinner, are we?"

Whistling to Pock, he rubbed dog ears and reattached the leash to both dog and tree, then picked up a mask and handed one to me. "Yes. I believe we are. However, it may be very private. If we ate a meal together two times in one week, game warden and police gossip would not help either of us right now."

"Speak for yourself. I think my job's already disappeared." I raised the mask. "What's next?"

"Trout," he answered, quietly wading the stream, a small net tucked under one arm.

182

# SEVENTEEN

I considered my clothes. Swimming apparel choices appeared limited. A black sports bra gripped me firmly from collar bone to navel. "That's not a bra," Kate snorted when she'd seen it. "That's a straitjacket."

*Exactly*, I'd thought.

I pulled off my hiking boots and T-shirt, tightened my pony tail, hitched up my shorts, and waded after Moz. No ripples parted the water as he waded, not even when he lowered his mask and slid down to float on the surface. I slid my feet over pebbles and around larger rocks, imitating his stealth moves. An unseen current tugged my legs, but I lowered my mask, sank to a floating position, and anchored my hands in gravel.

We were floating on the thin film that divides the fish world from the human world. I could feel hot air on my rear end, but every other part of me was cool. Hair on my arms drifted up and down like water plants seeking microscopic food. Rotating my head only slightly, I could breathe and then return to the wet, green world.

The water was so clear I could see every grain of sand and each cloud shape that, far above us, shadowed rocks and drifted on. I thought about the mask I'd seen next to Chan's pond. His magical green world was buried under mud. I was lucky to have one before me.

In slow motion, Moz turned over rocks, lifting tiny things into the current. Soon they were bumping off my mask and I could recognize them. When I smiled, escaping air bubbles bounced the stonefly larvae toward shore. Their shelled segments arched in the effort to find new rock homes for their outstretched waving legs. Until now I'd known them only as empty shells left on rocks near shore after mature flies had hatched and flown away.

Something glittered and I held out a finger to snag it. Not much bigger than an inch, a future caddis fly had woven a hard pupa case around his larval self. This one must have been an artist. It had chosen tiny pebbles flecked with bright mica flakes and glued them together to make its cave. The creature inside waited to emerge as a winged insect that would feed fish—if it lived long enough. Caddis have short lives. The stream's current rotated the pupa case into my hand. Inside it, tiny wings vibrated. *Is it time?*

I turned the pupa toward the end that looked like it could open. *Time for what?*

*Time to become what I am supposed to be.*

*A different kind of bug?*

*My wings are folded and pushing against the wall. I ache.*

*Someday you'll fly. I imagine it will feel great. Pick a windy day though. Fish have a hard time feeding when the water ripples.*

*Maybe your hard shell will fall off one day. You know. The secret one?*

I tucked the pupa next to a protective rock, thinking it sounded like the therapist I'd seen since my divorce. I knew about secrets.

My husband Evan had saved up his huge secret. "I'm done. I've waited for ten years until Kate was old enough to start applying to college. I want to take this thing apart," he'd said.

I sat sewing a ripped Antler Camp pillow. "What thing?" I asked.

He circled his arm out to me and back again.

"Our marriage is a thing?" I asked.

He smiled, almost bouncing on the couch with anticipation. "I don't want to live in some loveless marriage like my parents."

It took only an hour for him to pack the spare clothes he kept at camp, unscrew a trophy brook trout mounted on the wall, and slide it all into his monstrous SUV.

"Where are my fishing flies?" he'd yelled.

I was on the coach, clutching the pillow. "Don't know," I yelled back, but I did. Evan hated the outhouse, so that's where his box of fake bugs waited out the awful day my life changed. When he drove away with our best canoe, I stood in the driveway with his flies and watched his car's dust.

I'd been looking forward to Kate's college years, too. I wanted a return to the couple companionship we'd put off for years: canoe the Allagash, ski in Canada, play scrabble with headlamps, and squish mosquitoes on the tent wall. I'd taped a list of my plans on the refrigerator, adding clippings about western trout rivers. Evan had stashed his plans deep inside.

The unstained wall behind his absent mounted fish grew dark during two winters of persistent woodstove smoke while I researched insects and scrawled tiny tags to identify all their life stages. I'd cast the flies into ponds, and streams, and rivers, tricking fish toward my hook, but I'd never actually seen how real creatures lure real trout. Apparently, my head needed to be underwater.

Two brook trout, eager for the floating larvae, glided from rocks near shore and rolled over on their white bellies to signal hunger and the chase. Slowly Moz reached for his net and squeezed Spam scraps into the current. I didn't actually see how he caught both trout in one swipe, but as we stood, they thrashed in his net.

I sputtered water. "Is that legal? The net trick?"

Moz lifted the brookies so the late-day sun caught red spots pulsing along their flanks. "I am fishing with flies and avoiding live bait. We are legal."

Watching the net dance with fish, Pock was wild at the end of his leash. I pulled on my T-shirt and tugged at my soaking shorts. They were glued to my thighs like plastic wrap. "What were the Spam scraps for?" I asked, unclipping the leash. "You already lured them with familiar bugs."

Moz turned away. I heard two wet slaps as the brook trout ended their lives on the nearest rock. His knife flashed, scraping off scales and opening the fish so cleanly, they already looked like dinner. "Like all animals, trout are curious. I also was curious. Would they investigate new odors?" He tipped the blade of his knife next to one fish eye and poked at a small opening. "They smell through holes here," he said. "Nares."

"Nares? Not called noses?"

He grinned. "Nary an underwater smell escapes them."

I groaned.

Bending over the stream, he rinsed the fish and tossed their heads and parts into the current. Fish guts left in the woods invited unwelcome guests.

I was always surprised when a different Moz came out to play and tell a joke. Even though I was a very white person, I could feel the Penobscot side of him, schooled to keep his inner life secret from my kind.

I thought I might understand his caution—his hard-learned silence. Sometimes I thought there was a whole tribe of men who'd forced women onto smaller, meaner plots of ground where we were also supposed to be content and silent. I knew the scale of intimidation was different, even if the pain was real. My relatives had never been hunted down and slaughtered, so I never shared this thought with Moz—or

186

anyone else. I didn't want to sound like a whiner.

As Pock swam circles hunting fish parts that were already feeding downstream creatures, we concocted dinner. Coated with Spam grease, my frying pan sizzled with trout. Moz produced a crushed baguette dusted with leftover croissant flakes. He must have used the Road Kill Cantina's back door to beg Francoise for pre-dawn breads. I poured more lemonade mix into my water bottle, and we sat side-by-side in the shade eating trout sandwiches and watching Pock search the river.

"He does not know how to quit," said Moz.

"No. I'll have to call him in soon," I said, wiping my hands on viburnum leaves and handing him a sturdy one. "Napkin?"

"Perhaps wait until his ears drop low in the water."

I tilted my head toward Moz. He was not a cruel man.

"When he is tired, he may leave us to ourselves," he said.

That was a conversation stopper. And there was so much to discuss. Chan. His eagle. Lily Rose Baines Johnson and her crusade. The thefts of Kate's and my papers. The mystery body appearing a piece at a time.

Moz reached behind me, put his arm around my waist, and pulled me closer. It didn't look like there was going to be much discussion. I thought about all the lady-like things I could do with a blow dryer, eyebrow pencil, and other strategies to offset dark eye circles and hair that had to be mad at me for its permanent pony tail. I'd covered the camp's mirrors when I'd moved in full time. Personal grooming was limited to soap in the shower.

"I know no easy way to say this," Moz said, pulling me closer, "but I believe you sit on something an animal left behind, and it is now melting under you."

I tried jerking my arms away. "You mean I smell like some kind of scat?"

Moz tightened his grip, turned, and leaned down to my neck. I think I went limp, the way birds do when you've got a good grip on their body and wings at the same time.

He laughed low into my neck. I think more of my small skin hairs floated free. "Yes and no. The part of you at my nose smells like pine and trout and clean water."

I was a great believer in sniffing one's way toward shared intimacy even if my daughter rebelled against the practice. It never crossed my mind I'd be on the sniffed end of such a moment. I stayed limp but whispered, "Not having a problem with the part that's furthest from your nose?"

His chuckle pressed teeth against my neck, but I felt their pressure all the way to my toes. "No," he said. "What animals leave behind does not bother me."

I closed my eyes, inhaled deeply, and found a not unpleasant horse-barn odor. I could feel a Moz smile spread wide on my skin. It seemed like we were suspended, breathing each other. He also smelled like pine, trout, and clean water.

Even Pock smelled that way when he landed on us, fish head in his mouth and stream pouring off his body. Moz rolled away and leaped to his feet. Pock dropped the fish head in my lap.

"Oh, many thanks, Pock." I picked dog hair out of my eyes. Drenched, we all stared at each other. My dog wagged his tail and laid a protective paw on the fish. "I think this is some kind of test," I said.

"Have I passed?" asked Moz. He bent, picked up the fish head, and winding it up like a frisbee, hurled it back into the stream. Pock dove after it.

"Depends," I said, reaching up to grab the hand he offered me.

Pulling my hand into both of his, he said, "Many tests here today."

I didn't have time to explain that he'd passed them all because Lily's boots snapped a few tent pegs when she charged us.

"No shit! No shit! And you flunked all them tests because I could use some help here. That's you the game warden isn't it? You're the help?" She jammed her hands on her hips and scowled. "Well, aren't you the law out here?"

There wasn't much to suggest Moz was the law. His shirt was off, and while I was getting used to the scar that bisected his chest, the wound should have been a conversation stopper for anyone else. Without a belt, his damp jeans had slipped a bit below his waist, and he was barefoot.

As he turned to face her, his entire body seemed to take in one long breath. Whatever he'd been seconds before simply expanded. It didn't matter that he was without uniform, gun, and leather implements. His black eyes glittered a warning.

Pock placed the retrieved fish head on top of Lily's boots. She ignored it and the storm on Moz's darkening face. "I need to talk to Alexandra or Patton or whatever she calls herself. And I can't do it with the wind-weasel men harassing me. Call them off."

I didn't see anyone, but Moz grabbed his shirt and turned to face the spot where Lily had appeared. Branches she'd wacked aside were still twitching.

"The cooked fish smell," Lily said. "Followed it."

Matt Pruitt and Ridge Dumais wacked the same bushes as they charged the clearing. "Arrest her," Matt panted.

"No. Arrest those dweebs," Lily said. "I got a right to be here."

Ridge advanced on her and snarled, "Like hell you do. You're trespassing."

Lily reached for the net hanging next to her head on a tree.

"I have a right to walk to any stream, any time I want. 'Specially if I'm fishing."

Both men looked at Moz, who'd put on his moccasins and shouldered his pack. "The charge would not hold up in court as she has claimed her right to access this stream," he said.

"You mean anyone can just walk in here anytime they want?" Matt asked.

Moz stepped slowly toward the woods on the other side of the clearing. "If the stream has—even one time—supported navigation by any craft—and this one has—anyone may walk to it as long as he or she does not travel near established development. Maine navigable waters are public property. Many legal challenges have failed to change this law, and I believe judges and juries also find fishing access sacred."

Pock, eager for more play, dropped the fish head near Ridge, who raised his boot. Before the kick landed, I picked up the fish and tossed it back toward the stream. Pock landed with his paws spread wide. The splash drenched Lily's back, but she didn't flinch.

"What the hell's a gate for then?" asked Matt.

Moz slowly wound his belt through its loops. Somehow it worked. His getting dressed without embarrassment meant he had the outdoor stage all to himself. "Access to navigable streams is only guaranteed to foot traffic. You do have the right to post your actual facilities against trespassers. That would be your roads and what you build."

Matt shouldered Ridge aside and stood, arms out, in front of Moz. "Where are *you* going?"

Moz looked at me. "When Ms. Johnson is done fishing would you please retrieve the net? You may give it to me Monday before the public hearing. Many of us will be detailed into the region that day. When all eyes are on a large event that gathers people into parking lots, poachers feel there are no eyes in the forest." He raised both eyebrows until they almost met in his forehead, signaling bad personal weather on its way. Without looking around the clearing he asked, "Has this man moved away from my path?"

Feeling sad for so many reasons, I shook my head.

"Do it, Matt," said Ridge. "Game wardens got more power than God." Matt backed away and Moz disappeared. Whatever force had held us in place, listening and behaving, it evaporated when the warden stepped away into the woods.

Lily tossed me the net and retraced her steps out of the clearing. "Yup. Monday. That probably makes all of us. See you there, Cassandra or Patton or whatever. Make time for me. We've got plans to finalize."

"What are you cooking up with her?" asked Matt. "This is the second time I'll have to warn you if—"

"That's it!" I yelled. "I am so done with whatever it is you boys think you have on me, or can do to me, or just even threaten me about. I am so DONE!" I picked up the fish head Pock had dropped on my toes and shook it at them. Bits of pink flesh spurted in their direction. "Get out! Just get OUT!"

At the screech in my voice, Pock started a slow crawl, growling low in his throat.

"Ditto on my dog's message," I said. "So do it now."

On those words, Matt's head snapped up and he almost smiled. "Right. Do it now, she says." He lit a cigarette, tossing the match toward my tent. The cigarette between his thumb and forefinger, along with his soft "do it now" reply, tugged at my memory. Somehow, I knew this man.

"Do I know you from a previous life?" I asked.

"Not sure I had one," he answered, sucking smoke deeply into his open mouth. He was about to say more, but Ridge shoved him away toward the sound of Lily's disappearing boots until we were alone. He pointed one crippled finger at me.

Pock rose from a crawl to a crouch, and Ridge backed away.

"Quietly, Ridge. Go quietly," I said, reaching for the masks Moz had left behind and stashing them in my pack. "I will too."

It was time to abandon my camp site. My dog knew how to pull tent stakes out of the ground. He dropped each one at my feet. After I packed the tent, I checked the mound of dirt where I'd buried finds from our night-time forest walks, piling more brush on top of it. I pulled Anita's note from my pocket and groaned.

*Patton. You and dog ok? Premier Power & Energy expects all subcontractors to be at the hearing on its Eagle Ridge Expansion Project application. We're needed in case someone brings up dead wildlife. Can you dress appropriately? Bring earphones and share my phone. I've got the Eagles, the Byrds, and Cornell's bird call library. This is not optional.* She'd scrawled a few bat wings in the margin instead of her name.

As I heaved my overloaded pack onto my back, pans and camp stove clanked together in ways I knew I'd regret. I might have missed the eagle if I hadn't tossed the fish head to the far side of the pool when Pock was busy.

Chan's bird circled once, short, sharp cries announcing his find. He stretched his talons to snatch the carcass, lifted off the water, and banked away toward an upstream tree. Of course it was Teddy. Chan was perched half way up the tree, arm and red glove extended in the air. I knew they'd be gone by the time I got there.

I started up the path toward my car.

Chan was reckless to hunt the eagle on a wind-power site.

Maybe he thought wide roads made it easy for Teddy to spot and hunt food. I sighed, realizing the boy and his eagle were strangely welcome in my home.

I also knew I wasn't done with Eagle Ridge—even if Anita fired me. Kate's carbon explorations would link her directly to Eagle Ridge and the coming controversy to build more towers on it. Our stolen paperwork was somehow aimed at its future. She didn't know that, but I did. Parents never stop thinking about lurking danger. At some point, we can no longer send children to their rooms or take away the car keys, but that doesn't mean we aren't hyper-vigilant.

Unlike stumbling on buried treasure that gave the finder great press, I was publicly tied to the discovery of a violated body. It was a strange and intimate relationship, and another way Eagle Ridge was testing my goal to lead a simple life. I wasn't done with the person who'd shared a shoulder with me.

It seemed every event of the past week kept pointing back at me and the ridge like a stubborn compass bearing. Lots of people ignore compass bearings despite the needle's determination to point north. We can miss the whole point of a compass. It's an unfailing corrective to human willfulness.

If everything kept bouncing back toward Eagle Ridge and the wind-power facility on it, it would do me no good to deviate from the route being laid out for me. I needed to find out who'd been murdered on the job site where I worked— maybe murdered in the woods where I camped. Definitely taken apart with a machine I'd driven. The compass needle pointed at me, but if I didn't know who belonged to the shoulder, what could I do?

Stopping by my car, I looked uphill at the towers and roads. If I narrowed my eyes to tiny slits, they looked all squished together and tilted down toward me. Nothing actually loomed over me, but my chest suddenly felt squeezed for air. I dropped my pack and bent toward my knees, forcing air down toward the ache—down toward the weight of it all.

I straightened up and scattered biscuit crumbs onto Pock's car blanket. "You want a vote about what we should do?" He wagged his tail and dropped onto his blanket.

"Right. Tackle one thing at a time. First, sleep." I leaned in to rub his ears and whisper as if the deserted road wasn't deserted. "I don't think wind power is inherently an evil force sent to test our moral relationship to the natural world. But right here, right now, really bad forces are at work and bad things attack our mountains and woods. I can't be the only one who sees the danger, right? I can't really be alone on this, right?"

Pock licked my face so hard that it felt like the one facial I'd never had. Over and over, his rough tongue lapped my forehead, cheeks, and nose. I leaned in to let him. "OK. I'm not alone on this. Thanks."

# EIGHTEEN

I spent the weekend in and out of the lake, hoping evaporation would cool me as I wrote overdue posts for my Bangor Weekly column. Before he'd disappeared, Chan had reorganized my research into perfect files, so catching up on my "Valuing Nature" articles looked easy.

I decided to start off with bats. I couldn't find a local money figure for them, but nationally they were worth twenty-two billion dollars—what it would cost farmers to replace these flying, insect-eating machines with pesticides.

Hit hard by disease, Maine's bat populations had already declined by ninety-seven percent. I didn't try to calculate the pesticide-replacement math for my state. It was enough to know that without nature's help, we'd put more poisons on the land.

I desperately wanted to share good news, so I whipped off an upbeat piece on how wildlife pursuits like hunting, birding, fishing and my favorite, moose-watching, gave us thousands of jobs and over a billion dollars a year. I wasn't used to celebrating good news, so I had to use two fingers to firmly push down my computer's "send" key.

On Monday I walked around Antler Camp touching special places. I sat at the long pine table and ran my fingers over its stains and gouges. I could have sanded them away long ago, but each came with a memory. I could see where Kate and her friends had danced divots into the surface, using it as a concert stage. A corner of the table where my mother had tie-dyed us ugly T-shirts would be forever purple.

I didn't want to leave the camp's quiet, safe space. I didn't want to attend another hearing about the future of Maine's woods and wildlife. It wasn't that I didn't care. I simply knew another regulatory brawl would activate the pain.

I rubbed my fingers on the table until they warmed and the morning's stiff joints relaxed. I thought about the decades of hearings I'd sat through—how they hadn't really slowed down forces determined to wear away an intact, healthy outdoors. The whole thing seemed a lot like arthritis. After decades of doing the same old thing, our bodies invited the disease to eat away the cartilage that protected our bones. Only the grinding pain of hard things rubbing up against other hard things remained.

It was a very hard thing to sit through a hearing that gave developers permission to wear away what I cared about. It was an even harder thing for wildlife to rub up against what people endlessly bulldozed, blew up, or built.

I left Chan a loaf of banana bread and a note saying he could still find me if he needed to. I didn't open his duffle, but found myself hoping he'd return for clean clothes. I didn't worry about him living off the land and feeding himself and Teddy. Whether he grilled fish or roasted squirrel, he was probably cooking more than I was.

Anita's request to dress appropriately proved impossible. In return for receiving all my tasteful pantsuits, the Baptist Thrift Store had dressed me in overalls already bent at the knees, soft flannel shirts, and a down vest with only one piece of duct tape on it.

Kate was not impressed. "Mum, you should save one outfit so if you get hired back some time you can show up at the legislature."

I'd wrapped a scarf around my waist to compensate for the

stretched front of my pants. "Burning bridges," I said.

I did have two of Evan's discarded white shirts and a pair of black jeans, so I swept my hair into a barrette and stuffed it under a PP&E ball cap. I tucked a starched Evan shirt into the jeans and added a swipe of mascara to compensate for the lack of formal wear.

After driving up the west side of Moosehead Lake, I left Moz's fishing net and masks visible on my car seat and hiked a dirt road past cars that also couldn't fit into the parking lot. I'd started the day with an early swim, thinking dripping wet hair would solve half the day's heat challenge, but after a quarter of a mile, sweat stains and lake water looked no different on my shirt. I was soaked. Pock was soaked too. He'd visited every roadside bog and puddle.

The Birches Hotel and Conference Center parking lot was jammed with over a hundred vehicles of all sizes, makes, and budgets. Gun racks decorated the rear windows of most trucks. Their owners didn't want to be far from what gave them pleasure or protection—or both.

I leashed Pock and thought I felt the same way about my dog. I never wanted to be far from him and some days I couldn't really believe he was all mine. Evan's new wife was probably not allergic to dog hair, just to anything from his previous life. The best part of the divorce settlement was not having to share my best friend.

There was a neon sign over the Birches' giant metal shed door that flashed, "Meeting in Progress. No Weapons or Chew Allowed." I smiled. Having a regulatory hearing in the hinterlands was much more fun than a stuffy location in the state capitol. I detoured to the waterfront and tied Pock under birch trees that shaded the lake. He flopped in wet sand, wagging his tail to let me know how happy he was to miss the meeting.

The Birches wasn't really a conference center, and its ancient log cabins weren't a hotel either. It was a sporting camp with entrepreneurial zeal. The dock and floats were crowded with aluminum fishing boats, large flat party boats for wedding events, jet skis, canoes and kayaks, and a canvas-covered excursion craft advertising moose-watching tours.

A floatplane taxied up to the dock, its wake rocking boats so they appeared to be nodding a greeting to the people the pilot helped out of the plane. One of his guests wobbled past me wearing three-inch heels. "Where's the bar?" she panted, not waiting for an answer.

I looked at my feet. Anita's request for appropriate dress was vague and that was good. Aside from hiking boots and frayed running shoes, I only had my walk-in-the-water sandals. The neoprene straps were still a lovely shade of blue that I hoped would make up for their sturdy defects.

I turned toward the shed. It was really three or four steel Quonset Huts welded together to form one large space under arches that easily shed snow. I'd already signed up for the Birches fall tipping crew. They paid only minimum wage, but I'd be in the woods all day snipping the ends off balsam firs to supply their wreath-making operation. I'd smell good, and the free lunch would last me overnight. Pock could roll in discarded branches that smelled better than his usual outdoor choices, and as a bonus, he could chase snowshoe hares.

Balsam fir always made us feel better.

The resort's winter snowmobile operation had been moved outside. Trail-grooming machines, work benches, and tools were parked next to the shed. As the wreath business faded into real winter, the Birches crew was paid to groom hundreds of miles of snowmobile trails. Inside, warmed by multiple woodstoves, mechanics repaired machines that weekenders broke with careless abandon.

I loved the Birches. It testified to rural Maine truths—truths I'd tried to explain to legislative committees that were too eager to give corporations tax breaks to locate in parts of Maine that didn't need help. "Every bite I put in my mouth from childhood on came from Maine's outdoors—from its resources directly or its natural appeal. Me and thousands of other Mainers," I'd said. "Let's figure out the rural formula and support financial aid for that formula."

Many legislators had trouble understanding and funding the tourism economy. If they couldn't walk a factory floor and count the widgets or garments or cans of chowder, they didn't want to bet money on it—even when tourist businesses had no higher failure rate than widget factories.

In business for generations, the Birches family followed smart, unwritten rules. Figure out all the activities tourists will buy and offer them. Hire family whenever you can. Hire people with season-to-season skills so they'll always be fixing and painting and repairing. Don't fire a great employee because he or she is working several other jobs to make ends meet. That's just what people have to do when they sacrifice to live where they want to live.

Many Mainers made that sacrifice. I had tried hard to explain it, leaning into a microphone to explain why land conservation was good for the average worker. "It's the second paycheck," I said.

My favorite old guy leaned down to his mic. "Did you make that up, little lady?"

I handed the clerk a slick report. "No. The Montana economist who wrote this report did."

"And exactly what is meant by a second paycheck?"

"It means access to the outdoors has real financial meaning to folks. It has real value in their lives. Especially if the first pay check is small."

The chairman tilted his white head.

"Duck hunting before breakfast," I said. "Fishing during lunch break. Hopping on the snowmobile at night. Ten to fifteen hiking trails near home. Ponds with picnic tables and family campsites. That kind of thing. Most of it cheap or free."

He held up his copy of the report. "But that's Montana. Got a Maine report? We'll need a Maine report."

Often Maine's liquid border functioned more like a thick prison wall than a river we could easily cross to get west of New Hampshire and learn more.

Their satellite dishes rotating on roofs, two media vans parked at the front door. Reporters I'd worked with for years jumped out. I lowered the visor on my ball cap, but the public-radio reporter snatched it off. "Nice shoes, Patton." He laughed. "And about yesterday. I could use something on the body scavenger hunt you started."

"Musgrave. I have complete amnesia about yesterday."

I liked Brett Musgrave. He was my age and hadn't lost any of his zeal. His gray eyes were almost as eager as the drooping handlebar mustache that blew in and out as he spoke. Even though he outweighed most people by at least a hundred pounds, he always leaned back a bit so his heft didn't put people off.

"So, give us a comment about this show here," he said. "I already got someone on tape who says a wind tower can't crumble like that without someone's cutting corners in how it got put up. Says there's got to be structural flaws if there's no hurricane. But he was really dry and boring. We could use something from you."

I patted him on the way by. "I'm still scared of your facial hair, Brett. I don't know if you have an upper lip."

I ducked in the open door to find a wall-leaning spot near the action. Double-bay doors wide enough to winch float planes in for winter storage were open. Across the lake, Mt. Kineo looked down into lake water that perfectly mirrored its severe gray cliffs. No breeze.

Off to my right, on a raised platform of pallets, Department of Environmental Protection hearing officers were testing microphones. Two women were setting up stenotype machines and tape recorders. Off to the side of the makeshift stage, tall easels held displays. Some posters were technical renderings of the proposed towers and turbines. Other posters were artist renderings of the site during and after construction.

Posters are my favorite developer exhibits. Always creative. While I didn't have proof, it looked as if PP&E had hired Walt Disney to draw dense forests and cavorting wildlife at the base of each tower. I was tempted to dash up and draw in Snow White, but when I stepped up and peered closely at the drawings, the real art was clear. By drawing tall trees at the base of each tower, the company was avoiding an accurate representation of each installation's height. The towers looked like part of the forest rather than a replacement for it.

There was no poster showing what the site currently looked like. Nothing to show that Great Nations Forests LLC was already prepping the site for wind power—already leveling ninety acres for roads, concrete pads, transmission facilities, and construction staging areas.

I'd witnessed an entire mountainside slide into Chan's pond, so I knew the timber company was cutting more than the project's footprint. Having men and machines geared up to harvest wood, it made no sense to shift them elsewhere when Great Nations owned the land, the trees, and the income they'd deliver.

Squealing microphones sent people into rows of metal folding chairs. The overflow crowd shuffled onto the oil-stained floor to stand behind the seated crowd. Sweat glistened on every face. Most folks had folded PP&E's colorful brochures into paper fans, and the shed's vigorous fanning activity looked like a mass butterfly migration.

In front of the stage, two long catering tables were covered with piles of paper, computers, and water bottles. The table hosting opposition to the expansion was staffed with three people. Two men wore creased khaki pants, neat pinstripe shirts, but no ties. Brown hair cascading down her back, the one woman wore black pants like my pants, but she'd added a small string of pearls and a thin green shirt that softly defined her erect shoulders. Her glasses caught the light as she glanced up and nodded in my direction. I nodded back. I had often been one of the few people at an opposition table. She'd taken the time to send me recognition and a kind message.

PP&E's table was surrounded by a huddle of men and women in dark suits, their heads bent toward Matt Pruitt. Behind this table at least four rows were filled with their consultants, researchers, and expert witnesses. Even more seats had full water bottles on them, saved for more witnesses.

Anita looked in my direction, grinned, and shook her head slightly to warn me away from her seat in the PP&E section. I sagged with relief. She knew I was seeking out an invisible space. Her suit coat had field hockey and basketball patches sewn on the pockets. She must have had it for decades. She'd draped her long blond hair over her shoulders to hide earphones. One knee jiggled to rhythms that weren't Cornell's bird-call library.

I stood on tiptoe to see into the middle of PP&E's witness team. Conservation Maine and at least four other environmental groups wore dark and ominous suits. Millie wore a sweater jacket she'd obviously knit herself, decorating it with buttons that looked like small apple pies. She didn't belong in any neat category and I loved her for it.

Ridge Dumais and some of his crew filed in to lean against the far wall. No one made any effort to hide the four Great Nations Forests' vans parked outside. The men looked happy. They were earning a day's wage to lean back on their heels and fill their cheeks with chew.

Ridge raised his ball cap at me. I nodded back. It was always adversarial between us, but I appreciated him for being honest about who he was. I didn't have to like him to appreciate him. He was often the scrappy public face of Great Nations, and I'd been the scrappy face in his face. I knew he appreciated my scrappy self even as I knew he was GNF's man every day of the year.

Premier Power & Energy had asked the woods crew to be visible during the day and then testify at the evening's public comment session. Their job was to undermine any tourism argument directed against the expansion. Gruff and real at the microphones, they'd say that logging jobs were more important than a few tourist bucks.

Just because I'd heard the message hundreds of times didn't make it true. Maine's forests delivered more non-forestry jobs than actual woods jobs. The old days of cutting, delimbing, and loading trees by hand were gone. Modern harvesting machines had chopped thousands of jobs out of the woods, but on the other hand, fewer loggers died, and more fingers and arms got to live unsevered lives.

While the timber companies no longer delivered lots of jobs, they did deliver for their stockholders. Each year forest landowners made millions off partnerships with energy companies.

The leasing contracts were supposed to be secret, but a few years ago I'd found Pock sitting on one in my car's backseat. I wasn't surprised. My Subaru was an undercover mail box. People left me information they hoped would see daylight while they remained in the shadows.

I'd read the contract under my car's dim interior lights, and then turned on my phone's calculator. It seemed the energy developer would pay the forest landowner an upfront fee to lease terrain it needed for roads, towers, and all kinds of hardware, but that was just the start. More millions would get forked over as the landowner got paid for each megawatt generated on each turbine for each year of operations. Millions and millions and millions of dollars.

I'd mailed the contract to Brett Musgrave, but guessed his network couldn't find sources to verify what I'd sent. Financial partnerships between the energy companies and the timber companies remained secret. I couldn't figure out why no one seemed curious about the arrangement.

No vans of well-paid workers would arrive to speak up for tourism, even though I was always hopeful. Those business owners were busy repairing roads, training staff, making beds, raising sled dogs, selling hiking boots, taking out garbage, or arranging reservations.

I definitely had no optimism about the Office of Tourism. No official would arrive to remind the room that it represented Maine's largest employer. No one would bring nifty posters to illustrate how natural landscapes were a priceless business asset.

The tourism office just sold Maine. No one thought to give it the job of taking care of what attracted visitors in the first place. I wondered if the marketing staff even knew much about inland Maine. When lobster and lighthouse ads tipped me over the edge, I glued pictures of moose and rivers over the lobsters and mailed the revised ads back to Augusta.

People were still filing into the saved seats. Nudging my shoulder, Ken Douglas joined me at my wall. "I collected the warden's net from your car. I might see him before you do. He says you can keep the masks for a while but says you should stay away from big-water rivers,"

I smiled but didn't reply.

"OK," he said. "Must be a private joke."

"It certainly is. Anything else?"

"He told me not to tell you they found more of the mystery body, but I figure you're somehow invested and deserve to know. They found the arms with hands attached. Very, very black hands it turns out. White arms with black hands. More mystery. The forensic people seem to know the victim's a man. They've sent the latest find to a federal lab that identifies fingerprints from decomposed evidence."

I winced and felt more sweat make its way south of my bra. I hoped they found the rest of the body in one place so people would not share more updates with me.

Ken pointed into the crowd. "Who's that kid coming to sit with Kate behind the opposition table?" he asked.

# NINETEEN

I almost didn't recognize my daughter. Her brown hair was gathered into gold clips that held soft curls near her face. On her feet, delicate sandals sported red straps and heels. Gathered into folds around her lap, Kate's blue dress could only make her blue eyes more blue. I didn't know she owned a dress or could turn straight hair curly.

While most PP&E women were clones of their male seatmates, Kate was dressed to turn heads. I'd used this strategy to unnerve men predisposed to reject whatever I hoped to share. Maybe skirts melted ear wax. I didn't think Kate had noticed the few times I'd done myself up and gone off to work, but perhaps she had. I wasn't proud of the strategy, but it made me less threatening, and it was—occasionally—a useful weapon.

Sitting next to her but slumped over a large mud-stained backpack, Chan was shaded under a baseball cap. Despite the heat, over his rumpled jeans he wore his tall green rubber boots. The T-shirt looked clean. It usually hung large on Kate when she wore it to bed, but it fit Chan. When he sat up and turned to look toward the front door, the shirt's slogan spread out across his chest, "May the Forest Be With You."

"Oh crap," I said and started to push myself off the wall.

"No," said Ken. "Whatever's going on, if you walk across this room to talk to them as famous as you already are on top of this week's news, what the kids want to say will get swallowed up in what you are."

I thought back to the river and Kate's anger and knew, if anything, I should disappear. I started for the door.

"Not so fast," said Ken, reaching for my arm. "I checked the witness list. She's registered under her Dad's last name, Kate Crawford. No one will know who she is if you don't show it."

"What comes after her name for credentials?" I asked.

Ken looked at writing he'd scrawled on a PP&E brochure. "University of Maine Carbon Sequestration Project."

"And Chan? What's his witness credentials?"

"Ms. Crawford's assistant working on something called . . . ." He looked at his notes. "Something called Project Night Skies."

"Oh crap," I said again.

Huddled over a large notebook in Kate's lap and deep in quiet conversation, they ignored me. The public radio reporter did not. Brett Musgrave slid next to me and lifted his slim tape recorder. I collected it, turned it off, and returned it. Ken chuckled.

"Why are *you* here, Ken?" I asked.

He tugged at his loosely-tied tie. "Eagles might come up and I am the department's go-to person on that."

Brett whipped out his notebook and scanned a page of scrawl. "Eagles. How's that an issue? Isn't the developer allowed to kill some? Maybe not on purpose, but in building and operating?" He flipped more pages. "I mean the feds hope to cap eagle mortality around four thousand. Birds. I mean eagles. Per year. Except goldens. No one's allowed to kill golden eagles. Declining populations."

We stared, but Brett was back in his notes and talking fast, his mustache twitching. "Most of these energy companies don't apply for these incidental take permit things in the first place, so who knows about the real dead eagle count." He looked at Ken. "I know you're the wildlife biologist around here. Explain this. The companies that follow the law and get an incidental take permit have to report mortality numbers every five years. Don't you people write up yearly reports on wildlife? Numbers? Trends? How are you gonna find any eagle problems if a company sits on its data for five years? Or doesn't report it at all?"

Ken sighed. "You know? Public radio is the only thing I contribute to. Homework. Good homework's done there."

I lifted my hands to quietly clap. Many times I'd been on the receiving end of Brett's deep dives into wildlife controversies. I counted on him to drive at us like a bird of prey who'd scouted out something vulnerable.

"Well," said Brett, "I thank you for that compliment. Soooo. If someone asks how you're going to keep current with eagle mortality rates on wind sites, what do you say?"

"Good question, but don't think it will be the hot issue this time," said Ken. "At least not eagles all by themselves. Maine Fish and Game's on the record expressing concern for this entire PP&E expansion. That's what will come up." Brett was scribbling madly, but Ken handed him his card. It looked like tiny gnats had died on it. "I'll send our official statement to you."

"What's the meat of it?" asked Brett. "You folks haven't pushed back against a project before."

Ken stepped away from the wall. "Well, we've demanded some operating changes to shut down turbines when the wind's just right for bats to migrate, but that's pretty much it. When Maine created fast-track permitting and speeded up the wind process, we didn't have any hard bird and bat data to take to regulators. Now we have a bit more. It looks like if we put too many of these things in the same location—the same flyway— bird and bat mortality might get ramped up."

209

"Soooooooo." Brett liked to hang on the *so* word. "The law making it easier to build wind towers happened before the science did."

Ken winked at me and turned to go. "Don't ya just love public radio?"

I planned to follow, but Brett tapped my shoulder and whispered, "Your way. Nothing from Cassandra Patton Conover on the record. Just give me your inside take on some of the players. You worked this scene for years."

"No recordings. No quotes. No notes," I said.

Brett flipped to a clean page. "Only what I need to look up later."

I grabbed his elbow, walked him over to the PP&E side of the room, and ducked behind a few easels that didn't hide his bulk. "Look deep into the middle of the corporate scrum there. What do you need?"

"I already know that woman handing out T-shirts," he said.

Lily Rose Baines Johnson, steel toe boots banging on metal chairs, was tossing T-shirts down the aisles. "Share them out. There's tons," she yelled above the din.

"I don't think she knows she's in the PP&E camp," I said.

Brett chuckled. "She's in both camps. In Maine she's chained to bull dozers and raising a fuss. In Texas she owns a ranch where her cattle graze under hundreds of wind turbines."

I gulped and took another careful look at Lily throwing shirts to the crowd. It's one of my private rules to never underestimate how women can dress for completely different lives and then live them successfully—often at the same time. I wondered what she wore for cowboy boots in Texas.

Most of the PP&E side of the room acted like the shirts were contagious, stuffing them under chairs or tossing them back into the aisle. On the side of room opposing the project, men and women scrambled into shirts and helped Lily hand them out.

"Now we'll know who's in what camp," I said. "She's a surprising woman. Ya just never know, do you?"

Brett pointed at Dan Figarello. "Yup. That's why I could use some decent background."

"Dan Figarello's from Conservation Maine," I said. "They fought hard against a huge development project in the backcountry a few years ago. You'll find reports, ads, and interviews where they say the biggest threat to Maine's forest is large-scale development that splits it up into small, separate chunks. Chunks of trees here and there don't function like a real forest. God knows how he can sit with developers who'll chew up more woods than fifty Walmarts and their endless parking lots."

"Oh please," Brett whined. "That's a good sound bite."

I pulled my hat lower.

"OK. OK," he said. "Maybe what we've got here is green energy in one corner and green tree people in the other."

"No. There's hypocrisy and then there's huge hypocrisy." I pointed out Anita. "Off the record, the woman with the long blond hair who's wearing ear phones will give you the real zone of death around the turbines. She's got company maps of the small areas she's allowed to survey for bird and bat mortality, and she's made her own map of where carcasses actually land. You can ask her what days and seasons she's allowed to work, and then you can imagine how carnivores are partying when she's not there."

Brett scribbled frantically. "You work with her, right?"

"Not sure anymore. Last week I got very public." I nodded at the back wall. "The boys in hard hats are Dent & Dent construction. They move the same hundred or so jobs from site

211

to site. That thousands of wind-power jobs thing? Bogus."

Brett smiled over his notepad, eagerly chewing on facial hair between his lips.

I groaned. "The man in the plaid vest under an awful green coat is the Pennsylvania tourism consultant PP&E likes to import. He spends more time in their offices than in the field surveying tourists and tourist businesses. Try to get his itemized billing records as evidence; they should reveal where he's parked himself. And he's never done a displacement analysis like any genuine expert would offer up."

Brett lifted his pen and tilted his head. "Displacement?"

"It's possible to assess how destroying or altering tourism landscapes sends people elsewhere to spend money."

I pointed at two women sitting with Dan Figarello in the last row of PP&E witnesses. They'd been part of a fly-fishing class I'd taught last year. Each morning at five they waited outside my door, laughing at my attempt to sneak to pools before the class stampeded fish. We'd become friends.

My chest started to ache. "The women talking to the red-haired man are also with Conservation Maine. In return for dropping its opposition to this project, the fund is getting six hundred thousand dollars from PP&E to protect territory somewhere else. Some bogs and uncut lands they've wanted for years—far from Moosehead Lake."

"What? What?" whispered Brett. "That makes no sense if it doesn't help the locals."

"It's still called mitigation when a developer can hand over money to the state or a willing organization so a different place gets protected—supposed to make up for what gets destroyed. I don't think they'll testify. PP&E wants them to sit here as proof the company cares about nature."

"I love this shit," said Brett.

"I don't," I said.

Millie Douglas turned to look at me as I pointed out her multi-colored coat. She wiggled a few fingers at me and I wiggled some back. The ache in my chest moved up to my throat. "Someone from the Greenwood Select Board may testify that it supports the expansion of twenty-six more turbines on Eagle Ridge. You'll find PP&E money or a promise to buy or build the town something it desperately needs. I expect the deal's already been cut."

Brett drew big dollar signs on his pad. "That's not public info," he said.

"Go to the next Select Board meeting, stand up, and rustle some papers like you have evidence. They'll confess." I wasn't going to mention possible campaign contributions given on the sly. Millie and I had too much history, and I needed to breathe.

"Wait, wait," said Brett walking me to the door as voices started to boom from microphones. "You're leaving?"

"No one's paying *me* to be here, Brett."

He pointed at the table with only three people. "Don't think folks fighting this are getting paid," he said, "or paid much."

I turned away. "I know."

Down by the dock, Pock had excavated a hole in the sand so deep that seeping lake water made him a wading pool. His tail slapped water when I dropped down beside him and shoved my feet into his pool. Minnows swam up to investigate my toes.

Lake water smells better than bottles of expensive water. I wasn't tempted to drink it, but it was lake-clean. It smelled like lily pads and marinating tree bark. Millions of creatures flavored it with scales and cast-off skeletons, but it was so clear my feet looked magnified. How a lake can be clean and full of life at the same time was a better mystery than anything going on in the building I'd just left.

At least that's what I thought, until bagpipe music drifted toward us and set off loons in the cove. Rising so high their white bellies rose out of the water, they beat spray into the air with frantic wings and screamed warning cries to loons further up the lake. Long after our pair dove and disappeared, frightened bird echoes bounced off Kineo's cliffs in a duet with the wailing pipes.

# TWENTY

I untied Pock and turned toward the parking lot, thinking I could duck behind the protesters, the line of police, and whoever was playing bagpipes. A large hand squeezed my shoulder so hard I was lifted off the ground.

"Sit," Lily whispered to Pock, but he was already on his butt. I almost sat, too. "Let's just see what's going on here," she said.

"And then what?" I asked, peeling each of her fingers off my shirt.

"We might have a moment."

"Oh good. Can't wait. Maybe we'll talk about your Texas ranch and how cow poop seems to be growing tall metal things out of the ground there."

Lily's laugh was musical. Like Kate's, it ran up a few notes and ended with an enticing chuckle. "Sure thing, honey."

A state trooper shoved two men from the hearing into the no-man's land between protesters and the woods crew lounging on dusty trucks. Matt Pruitt waved a booklet in the air as he tried to shift himself back into the suit coat a trooper had manhandled off his back.

A second man wearing bagpipes landed on his feet, clutching his swaying instrument and smoothing his kilt. His braided beard reached almost to his belt. He looked old and ageless at the same time, wind-burned, wrinkled skin making his face resemble a desert landscape cut by ancient ravines.

"My camps sit across the lake from this abomination you're going to build," he yelled. "It's like you've parked them things in my bank account and they're going to suck it dry. People who've been to me for years say they won't spend money to

215

look at metal shit they already got outside their city windows. You can't do this to me."

Lily sucked in her breath and gripped my arm so tightly her fingers stopped circulation. I made a fist and squeezed it to send blood where it needed to go.

"The enviros are all on board, old man," Matt yelled back. "It's just you and a few crazy troublemakers out here."

Spit glistened in the man's beard. "Them enviros walked right into your trap, didn't they? You dangled some fancy language about climate catastrophe and doing the right thing and getting rid of coal and oil and gawd knows what else, and it all looked bright and shiny so they got blinded and didn't see . . . didn't see—"

"Didn't see what?" Matt asked. "What?"

The bagpiper looked around at the TV cameras. Slowly he turned a complete circle until he came face-to-face with Matt again. "Didn't see woods death, that's what. The greenies can't see what's dying for the bait you set out to tempt them away from what they used to help take care of. Well, I can smell what you set out and it stinks. People come up here for real woods. How it looks. How it sounds. Smells. Feels. It's not woods when you're done carving it up. You even got death rays."

Matt circled a finger by one ear as a comment on the man's mental health.

The bagpiper swatted Matt's hand away. "I'm not nuts! Them blades are god-damn deadly, whipping around shooting shadows that'll flicker all over my docks and porches all day. Can make folks sick to be on the receiving end of 'em."

By this time, the old man had everyone's attention. No one shuffled feet or coughed or made faces at neighbors.

"At night, we don't get peace neither. Not with lights blinking at us like we was criminals surrounded by cop cars.

216

It's all stink. You're stink." Leaning over his instrument, he spit near Matt's shoes. I could feel a smile crack dust on my face.

Matt leaned so close to the bagpipe; it sighed a small, exhausted squeak. Then he shoved the crumpled booklet he carried into a plaid sash spread across the other man's chest. "You can't become a witness by marching in and creating a god-damned show. You're not signed up. You're not approved to leave evidence. Come back tonight when they'll let any wingnut talk." He turned away. "Thank God, you'll only get three minutes like the other nuts."

When the bagpiper swayed, Ridge Dumais shoved himself off a truck and trotted to the man's side. "Come on, Ross. Let's get you home," he said.

"Not yet. I'm waiting."

"For what?"

"My own people."

Ridge tipped his red hat back and patted the man's shoulder a few times. "They're long dead, Ross. Your Clunie folks are buried up near my Dumais folks. Now come on."

The tramp of marching feet announced Clunie's people. Eight kilted men and women marched into the circle of onlookers and with smart salutes to Ross and more bagpipes blaring, they marched in the shed's door.

Tears gleamed in Ross Clunie's eyes. "Thought they wouldn't show up. Would have to do it all my myself," he said. "They come a long way from Clunie to get here. Signed up official and then come over the seas. They swore they'd make it and god-damn, they did."

Brett Musgrave appeared out of nowhere, juggling a notepad and his phone. "Do what by yourself?"

"Give evidence," Ross said, raising the booklet. I don't

remember moving my feet, but somehow Lily had shoved me into the group's inner circle, snatched what the man held, and then tossed it at me.

I knew it well. "Wind Farms and Mountaineering in Scotland" was strong evidence that wind turbines sent tourists elsewhere. I guessed the troop of marching men and women who had thighs like Greek temple columns had to be Scottish mountain guides or part of the group that created the report's survey.

I'd put that same document on each legislator's desk. But again, that was Scotland and this was Maine, so few of them read it. What could we possibly have in common? Tourists? Mountains? Lakes, or was it lochs?

Ross Clunie wrapped Lily in a bear hug that rocked them back and forth in the dust. His bagpipe bounced off their swaying bodies. "You're all grown up! You're all grown up," he sputtered.

Muffled by his beard, Lily sniffled and coughed. "And you're the same. You're the same."

When she dropped to her knees and her coughs stretched into labored wheezes, the crowd fell silent. Ross bent and handed her something she pressed to her face, then he held her as police moved the crowd and Brett Musgrave away.

Ridge stepped up beside me. "You partnering up with that woman to cause trouble?"

"Not really," I said, walking around Lily and Ross. "What's going on?"

Ridge shook his head. "Some kind of reunion I'd guess. Clunie's hosted zillions of people at his camps and probably hired just as many local folks over the years, so who knows?"

I could hear Lily panting into Ross's ear. "How could you know I'd be here? I'd need this?"

Ross stroked her hair. "I always have an inhaler in my pocket. Ready to go. 'Case you came home."

It took a while for the police to escort Lily and Ross into the shade and sort out a scene I could make no sense of anyway, but Pock was easy to find. In a break with tradition, he was still sitting where Lily had told him to sit, ears pressed flat to his head to signal his displeasure about being left out. His tongue drooped so low his toes were wet with saliva.

It is possible to be so drenched with sweat that clothes become like plastic wrap tucked tight around the body. When that happens, I have to look down to make sure I was covered up because nothing hung loose to remind me I might be dressed. I was there.

"Let's head back to the lake, boy," I said. Pock collapsed into the pool he'd already made. I draped his leash over a tree limb and was almost up to my waist in water when Millie found me.

"Come quick, Patton. Oh, come quick! It's Kate and that boy, and all hell's gonna break lose."

I heard the hearing officer's gavel pound wood and his shouts for "Order! Order!" before I spotted them. Kate was standing at the witness microphone in the middle of the aisle. Half the audience was on its feet, yelling and pointing at Chan, who darted in and out of the field of easels, swinging something over each PP&E poster. Chased by a stenographer who kept tripping over upended displays, he was running toward the hearing officer when a state trooper tackled him.

The sound system squealed as someone bellowed into a microphone. "Order! Order! God-damn it! Give us order!"

The trooper stood up, holding Chan by the collar. The room sat down and resumed frantic fanning with any paper they had, and the hearing officer adjusted his tie. In that silence, Kate cleared her throat into the witness mic and asked, "May I continue, Mr. Zaitlin?"

The hearing officer rearranged an overturned card so his name again faced the crowd. "Do you need this young man or should we arrest him?" he asked her.

"If you will hear me out and then permit security to assess and plug in the cord he has, we would like to turn out the room's lighting for a brief moment," she said.

"Young lady, you are asking a great deal."

"If you please, I am here as this boy's voice as he is unable to speak in public. He's a registered witness for Project Night Skies. Before you, you have a map of the United States I will refer to. Have each of you a copy?"

All four members of the Department of Environmental Protection's hearing team put hands over their microphones and leaned together to confer. Leaning back, they looked at the one woman on the platform. She glanced at a form in her hand. "Kate. Is that your name, Kate Crawford?" she asked.

Kate nodded.

"Let the record show the witness has nodded," she said. "Kate, you should have requested, in advance, a special accommodation for a disabled witness."

"He looks alright to me, but it's clear he ain't local," yelled a voice from the wall leaners at the back of the room. "Awful tan for these parts, but fast as hell in them boots."

Zaitlin's gavel thwacked his table.

"I am sorry," said Kate. "This is my first time before the department. In the future I will use that advice should I need it."

The woman nodded to Kate and then to Zaitlin. "Well," he said, "I'm trying to imagine what you might get up to when you return later all well-prepared." He looked at the trooper who was almost dangling Chan in the air. "The boy needs his glasses, officer."

"Christmas lights," the trooper said, bending to retrieve Chan's glasses. "No phone. No detonator. Nothing but this string of lights."

"Now I've seen everything," Zaitlin said. "Or I'm about to. Proceed Ms. Crawford—but carefully."

Before Kate could draw a breath, he leaned back into his mic and addressed the PP&E table. "Evan Crawford. You are Premier Power & Energy's lead attorney today. You related to this lady?"

My ex-husband stood and said, "My daughter, sir."

"You put her up to this?"

Evan signed so loudly we could all hear him. "No, but I have some ideas." He turned to look at me, but Millie was quick, opening her coat wide and stepping in front of me. Except for the puddle of lake water on the floor, I was invisible.

"You have objections?" asked Zaitlin.

"No. I'm as curious as everyone in here," said Evan.

The hearing officer leaned back in his seat and said, "Well, let's hope your daughter makes you proud. Proceed, Ms. Crawford."

Chan bobbed thank-you nods at Zaitlin and plugged one end of the cord into a power strip on the stenographer's table. Kate looked at me and pointed to the shed's doors before she cleared her throat and smoothed her dress. "I am reading the testimony of Mr. Chandler Perkins into the record. He asks that you enter the map before you into evidence. It is a NASA satellite map of the United States taken from space at night. On it you will note that except for the Great Lakes, the only remaining region that retains any dark mass in the entire eastern United States, is Maine's north woods.

"Mr. Perkins wants you to know, and I quote, 'The white areas on most of the map are lights you can see from space. The lights signal people, development, highways, and built-up places that aren't natural. Please note that the bottom half of Maine is all white and lit up along with about half the rest of the country. Maine's inland wooded area is dark, so the map is telling us Maine has the last real forest east of the Mississippi River. Not bits of trees here and there between roads and houses. Maine has the last real forest."

Zaitlin leaned into his mic. "I don't see how putting a few tall towers in between trees changes that, young man."

I let out the breath I didn't realize I held. How could this possibly end well? I pulled my ball cap so low I could barely see my feet and aimed for the door.

"Wait," hissed Millie. "They're up to something. Let's do the doors."

# TWENTY-ONE

Millie moved to close the front door. I slid around the outside of the room, hoping someone would help me with the tall bay doors that faced the lake. Brett and Ken appeared and together we slid all four panels into place.

Boots clomping on the concrete floor, Chan walked to a bank of switches and waited for the trooper to join him. The trooper nodded and the boy turned out the lights. In the dark shed, red lights blinked and glared like airport runway beacons. I heard people suck in astonished air. Somehow Chan had managed to tag every turbine on each poster with a red, blinking light. The crowd muttered and moved restlessly.

"Silence," barked Zaitlin.

Kate's voice was older than I'd ever heard it. In the dark, she didn't sound like my daughter anymore. She belonged to the room, and Chan, and the moment, and the person she was becoming.

"I am reading Mr. Perkins' words again," she said, moving her cell phone's small beam over the paper she held. "He wants to say the following: 'These lights imitate the security lights on top of each turbine. Each tower has a red flashing light. All lined up, they look like an airport—a huge airport in the middle of the Maine woods. Please don't be fooled by calling these places wind farms. They are not farms. No one's raising chickens on top of our mountains. They are industrial installations that destroy night. They are heavy industry that does not belong in our deep woods.

"'As you look at these lights, please know that under each one is a tower taller than any building we have in the state, a tower set into a huge concrete pad and all of it surrounded by leveled, blasted, and bulldozed acres and acres of land. Please look at these lights and know that our forest is cut and will be cut to build hundreds of miles of roads wider than most highways, roads where herbicides are used to kill plants trying to regrow. Roads that are plowed and salted so trucks and cranes can get to each tower every day to make repairs and in the winter, remove ice that stops blades.

"'Please look at these lights and know that toxins from this development and its roads leak into our streams and lakes. Know these industrial installations destroy high-up places that aren't common in Maine—places special birds and animals need to live and eat and hide.

"'Please see these red lights as a warning to stop. Just stop. Please stop while part of Maine has woods and night that's vast and awesome. While we have something that's going to be rare not just here, but all over the world.

"'The Maine woods is my future. It's my generation's future. Don't make us blame you for destroying our future.'"

Half the room stood and cheered. Lit by flashing lights, the other half of the room looked frozen in place. Zaitlin's gavel banged and banged. After the state trooper slapped on the shed's lights and pulled the plug on Chan's exhibit, people resumed their seats and dropped into whispers shared with their neighbors.

"Holy shit," whispered Brett, pocketing his phone. "I got it all recorded for tonight's taping. He'll be headlining the news. You know this kid?"

"Actually, he's my house guest," I said.

"More holy shit. What can you tell me?"

"Nothing. You'll have to ask the boy," I said as the lights came back on. "But take him somewhere one-on-one away from the crowds."

Evan was on his feet, shifting his weight from one foot to the other, a habit I knew came from deep rage that didn't look like rage to most people. I saw Kate square her shoulders. She was ready for it.

Ken leaned toward my ear and whispered, "There might be some genetics at play here. I wouldn't miss this for the world."

"Mr. Zaitlin," Evan said, "I ask that the previous testimony be stricken from the record. Subjective testimony belongs in the public comment period you hold later tonight, not here with expert witnesses and proper documentation."

Kate had been joined at her aisle microphone by Chan. She grabbed for his hand, and held onto the mic with her other hand.

"May I speak to Mr. Crawford's objection?" she asked.

There was a grin on Zaitlin's face. "Please," he said.

"If you and your colleagues will turn the map over, you will find Mr. Perkins' statement fully footnoted with relevant reports and research—including notice of illegal toxic discharges to state waters at Premier Power & Energy's current project site. We expect more charges will be coming relevant to the project you consider here today because a significant erosion event into state waters occurred last week after site harvesting at the proposed expansion site."

Kate turned toward her father with a smile and then back to Zaitlin. "You will find that Chandler Perkins often references PP&E's most recent studies and application materials in these footnotes."

Zaitlin and his people studied their maps and bent again to talk quietly. I couldn't see Evan, but he was very quiet.

The woman who'd given her advice on how to sign up an unlikely witness said, "We agree that Mr. Perkins' final comments did arrive in the form of a plea, but we will accept those comments as a summary of his position based on the tenor of the research and reports he's cited here and his familiarity with facts included in PP&E's application. We feel the night sky map is especially helpful."

Zaitlin pulled his microphone close to his chest and smiled. "Well, Mr. Crawford, what do we think of your daughter now? Looks like no one put her up to it but herself. Herself and the smart youngster in boots there. Let's all take a fifteen-minute break while he removes the lights from our exhibits and someone throws open the god-damn doors."

Zaitlin waved his team toward the Birches kitchen porch and giant metal tubs full of ice and bottled water. Rivers of condensation dripped off the tubs and glistened in the noonday sun.

Millie came to pat my arm. "I'll snag some water for us and then maybe we can talk."

"Everyone wants to talk about things I don't want to talk about," I said, looking around for Lily. She was not the type to quit in the middle of a battle she wanted to fight. How could Lily miss the best part of the day?

At least that's what I thought until Chan lifted his backpack and emptied its contents on PP&E's table. Someone screamed. Chairs crashed into heaps as lawyers and witnesses lurched away. I saw Kate kick off her heels and climb up on the nearest table, her head swiveling left and right looking for Chan.

I clawed my way forward and reached up for her. "Get down. Get down, Kate. What in hell?"

She jumped into my arms. "The eagle was not part of the deal. The eagle wasn't in the plan. Good Christ, once a dumb kid, always a dumb kid."

Ken was trying hard to clear a space around the PP&E table,

and then Moz was there, raising his arms straight into the air. If people couldn't see the gun on his hip, they could see his green uniform. "Exit the building," he said. "Exit the building."

The law enforcement team, rivers of sweat staining their uniforms after hours in the parking lot, quickly formed a line that passed people from officer to officer until the room cleared. The trooper who'd grabbed Chan pointed at us, but Moz shook his head and said, "They are with me."

Kate and I stepped up to stand next to Ken as he smoothed eight feet of twisted feathers down the table. Despite one splintered bone, the underside of one wing was like a sand panting of rich brown hues that rose and fell into more shades of white. In a soft, husky voice, Ken said, "She only had a few days of freedom. Only a few days."

Spread across several laptops, Ken's golden eagle stared up at us with vacant eyes. The smell of a wild animal not long dead has no taint of decay. Ken's eagle smelled musty and wild. Even in an airless room, I thought she smelled like wind.

"I don't mean to sound harsh, Ken," I said, pulling a garbage bag from the can under the table, "but if you and Moz remove her before Zaitlin and his crew return, the last image they'll have of Chan is what he said, not what he's done here."

Kate gave me a hard stare. I knew what it said. *Of course my mother is thinking politics at a time like this. She's doing strategy stuff when Ken's heart is broken.*

Ken looked up with wet eyes. "She's right, Kate. You and the boy did more for wild ones today than my department has done regulating turbines in the last fifteen years. Let's not waste it. We can cut your mother some slack." He unclipped the eagle's radio collar and wiped it on his shirt. "I'm gonna know exactly when she died and where she died," he said.

227

"She's mangled like someone snapped her neck and dragged her down a road. Who does that?" Kate asked.

Moz pulled evidence gloves from his pocket and said, "Eagles hunt with their heads down, Kate. She never saw the blades coming at her. Perhaps her last thought was for a rabbit dinner far below."

"I don't need to ascribe human feelings to her," Kate snapped.

Moz eased the eagle into the garbage bag. "Then I will," he said, lifting the bag.

Kate grabbed Ken's elbow. "Walking out with you, Ken," she whispered.

I collected her red shoes and left them on top of the opposition table where she could find them, and then I went back to the lake and waded into water up to my neck. Anything was better than facing Brett and his notepad, or a riled-up crowd, or car seats so hot I could cook on them. My shirt and pants floated away from my body as water traveled up to my armpits.

When I turned around Moz was sitting with Pock. Two water bottles and his bare feet were planted in wet sand.

"Again. Meeting by water as we often do," I said, opening a bottle and drinking almost all of it. "Thanks."

"I am not sure sharing water locations means that a genuine meeting between us has yet occurred," he said.

I sat heavily in the sand, nudging Moz and chuckling. "Speaking of meeting-up stuff, did you know the woman you unchained from PP&E's bulldozer owns a Texas ranch with wind power turbines all over it?"

Moz leveled his black, bottomless eyes at me. I could see nothing in them, no recognition, no spark of fun to share about Lily's secret life. The look was stony and hard.

"What?" I asked. "What did I do? What did I say?"

He twisted the cap off his water bottle and held it without drinking or speaking.

I'd often seen his face harden into lines that looked like rocks laid down under great pressure, but I'd never been on the receiving end of Moz as a hard man. I thought he saved those flat black eyes for lowlifes who abused animals. With two fingers he collapsed the bottle cap until it was flat in his hand.

"What?" I asked again.

Why he worked in white law enforcement given our crimes against his nation and so many other nations wasn't a question I dared ask. I only knew that when he wore black boots, he belonged to Maine's Warden Service. When he wore moccasins, he belonged to the Penobscot Nation. No one could wear boots and moccasins at the same time.

I looked at his bare feet. There were no footwear clues about how to handle the situation. "OK. OK. Looks like you don't think it's funny that Lily's here fighting the towers when she's making money off them back home, but I do."

Moz reached down, cupped water into his hands, and rubbed his face. Then he slid back up the bank and reached for his boots. "I am thinking someday I may have to tie you down in order to have conversations you now avoid."

I tried to get the last words in, but they bounced off his retreating back. "This is because in the middle of a nuts day, I couldn't shift gears and do some genuine meeting up? And your solution is to tie me down? Who says that to a woman these days?"

I sent more messages that he couldn't hear. *How could you end up sounding like other men who don't know what to do with me? And since when was I such a problem?*

Well, I knew the answer to that one. From birth apparently.

Pock whined and tugged at his leash. He wanted to follow Moz. I wanted nothing more than to sink into the lake by the Birches and get magically spit out miles south onto Antler Camp's docks.

As I walked away from the lake, Ridge waved me into the parking lot, but I pointed at outhouses located at the end of a long line of rental cottages. He watched until I tied Pock to a tree and disappeared. Through the classic half-moon window carved on the door, I watched until he disappeared, but I didn't like the way he stared at my small sanctuary as he backed away.

I cut through the woods behind the parking lot, talking to Pock who was too busy chasing squirrels to really listen. "Oh sure, Mr. Game Warden. Pick a really good time to talk about our relationship. Been pretty busy, ya know. Shoulder in the road? Bear trap thing? Home break-ins? Homeless teen and illegal eagle? And the wave? I could have met up with that and had a pretty intimate conversation for sure."

I couldn't say out loud the worst thing in a list of bad things—Moz turning hard eyes on me.

Parked in deep shade that obscured an abandoned camp's driveway, Chan's truck attracted Pock before I realized we'd found Teddy. My dog lay wagging in front of a portable dog crate I'd last seen stored in my barn. In its dark interior, one huge, yellow eagle eye found me. *Where's my boy?*

I knelt before the cage. *Causing trouble, but maybe not as much as you'll cause.*

Teddy swiveled his head from side to side, catching filtered light from overhead leaves. I was inches from him. *Holy cow. Your eye's almost the largest part of your head.*

He blinked. *We have eyes and brains almost the same size. You should be so lucky.*

*Well, we're going to need all the brain power we can find to figure out your future. You can't stay with the boy.*

*I'm hungry. The boy lets me catch food.*

*I saw that. Nicely done.*

Teddy thumped his wings against the cage's sides and beat his beak on the front bars. *Let me out.*

I pulled Pock away from the cage. *Sorry. Can't do that, but I'll see if I can find your boy.*

*He's your boy too.*

I nodded. Chan had to be someone's boy. Right now, he was my boy.

# TWENTY-TWO

Leaving the trees, I found I'd correctly estimated the half-mile distance to my car almost to its front tires. A shirtless Chan rubbed my rear bumper. I stood in the road and watched him fold and refold Kate's T-shirt as he leaned all his weight into the car.

"What gives?" I asked.

Without stopping, Chan started on my back window. "The guys from Dent & Dent are working their way up here, spraying something black on cars that have bumper stickers they don't like. I'm taking yours off." He looked up, wiping his face with one free sleeve. "Not easy though."

"I bought the car used. The 'Care for the Planet' stickers came with it." I grinned. "But thanks."

"Didn't know this would be so mean," he said.

"When you dumped a dead eagle on PP&E's computers you didn't think it would piss their lawyers off? And if we are going to talk about mean, we'll have to discuss the traps you left in the pond. We're going to need a long talk."

Chan stepped into the road and dropped his arms. I walked up to him and handed him a wet bandanna from my wet pocket. "Last time I went head to head with the Forces of Darkness, someone slashed my tires, ripped my kayak off the car roof and ran over it squashing it flat, and I had to have the cops tap my phone to see if they could trace threats. There's millions of dollars and hundreds of paychecks involved here, Chan. And reputations that lead to even more millions and even bigger paychecks."

"We're just bugs."

"Bugs perhaps, but don't count out bugs. Remember that

locusts pretty much brought an Egyptian king to his knees so he had to free people he'd enslaved."

Chan kicked up dust with his green boots. "That's just a bullshit Bible story. "

"OK. Remind me to lend you *Charlotte's Web* when you get back to camp. She was a bug in a story too, but I think the book changed my life. It might help. I think it's all about how one person—sometimes—can make a real difference. One person or one bug."

Chan turned away. "I lied to you."

"Yes, you did. I know Teddy can fly and you've been hunting with him. Moz the game warden knows too, but he likes you. I think the safest place you can be now is Antler Camp. Take Teddy and go there."

Chan handed me Kate's shirt. "Kate's so great. She helped me get the words I wanted down, and then she spoke them for me. I ruined it with the eagle, didn't I? I probably screwed things up with Kate, too."

"You've got time to get better." I leaned close. "Time to get better at unleashing *the whirlwind* on folks without getting flattened yourself." Chan winced. He had to know I'd seen his favorite Bible page. "I think you were both brilliant. Powerful and truthful." I handed him back the shirt. "We removed the eagle before news people or regulators got to see it, and I think Kate will understand. She's had to put up with my trying to get people's attention for maybe too much of her life. She won't want this shirt back though."

"I owe you some more truth. My Mom's over in Saudi Arabia trying to get my sisters back." He pulled the shirt over his head. "My Dad came and stole them, and she's gone to get them back."

I let out a small groan. "She have any help?"

"We worked out a plan, but I can't talk about it."

He grabbed my hand and pushed a paper into it. I squeezed his hand back.

"The woman with the T-shirts told me to give this to you," he said. "You're gonna do something, aren't you? You're not going to let them blow up the rest of the mountain. The T-shirt lady said you're famous for fighting stuff."

"But not winning much."

"I'll help you. I want to help."

"I think you've done enough today." I wanted to hug him, but I wasn't his mother, and I could hear the Dent & Dent crew moving up the road, laughing and hooting. I wrapped him in a sweaty hug anyway and whispered, "You need to go before these gentlemen get any closer."

As he trotted into the trees I called, "And don't let the eagle hunt at my camp. The loons and everyone there are friends. Use the fish in the freezer."

I tightened the ropes holding my bumper to the roof and then lifted up the car's rear door and invited Pock to join me. We sat on the edge of his blanket, sharing the last crackers I had in my day pack. I rooted around inside it checking for tracking devices. If I found one, I wasn't sure if I wanted to clip it to my waist so Moz could find me again, or toss it into the back of a passing truck.

I conducted a quick pack inventory. I found the wire cutters, flares, map and compass I'd removed from the crime scene van, a squashed roll of toilet paper, broken dog biscuits, and two chocolate bars melted in their wrappers. I usually try to limit pack contents to emergency items. The first aid kit, water bottle, headlamp, and batteries made sense. So did the chocolate. I made a mental note to remove the cracked windshield scraper. I added Moz's diving masks. Maybe I was just hopeful.

The Dent & Dent posse was two cars away, howling at a bumper I'd appreciated earlier on my walk toward the hearing. The car's owner had obviously stolen a "Pass at Your Own Risk" sign and blacked out the first letter. I was sure the men wouldn't spray paint over the "Ass at Your Own Risk" message.

Suddenly they grew very quiet, listening to a man who'd stalked up and waved them back toward the Birches. Evan Crawford stood alone in the road. He'd rolled up his shirt sleeves to show biceps that hadn't aged, and he'd unbuttoned his shirt to show chest hair that had. It matched his close-cropped gray hair and a beard that was just a faint shadow on his cheeks. Walking toward us, he pointed at my car's roof. "Love what you've done to enhance your vehicle's appeal, and that's my shirt you're wearing."

I tucked the shirt more firmly into my jeans.

Evan crossed his arms and leaned toward me. "You used Kate," he said. "You set her up to do *your* work."

I slid from the back of the car and faced him. "Last I checked I was collecting dead things up gravel roads and Kate, aided by high-tech computing gear, was working on a carbon project at the university."

He sneered. "Well, she's carbon famous now."

"She's our daughter, Evan. Not your enemy. I didn't put her up to anything. The last thing I heard from her, I was a math cretin, and I'd wrecked her life."

He turned and paced the road, still near me, but at least he was moving. "Well, she might have wrecked mine."

"Oh please, spare me. You'll get paid thousands for billable hours no matter how this turns out."

"So where were you when *our* daughter put up her slideshow testimony?"

My stomach twisted with disappointment. Escaping, I'd missed Kate's big moment. Neither of the children had shared their agenda with me, so I was technically off the hook for leaving. No. I wasn't off the hook. Ken had been clear that Kate was a scheduled witness.

I studied Evan while he studied me right back. I wouldn't get good information by being snarky. I thought I could be on my best behavior for a good cause even if I didn't want to tap dance around his ego. "Are you able to summarize it, counselor?" I asked. "Without bias?"

Evan frowned. "No."

I pushed Pock down on his blanket and walked toward Evan, pointing the dog brush at him. "Try, or I'm flinging dog hair at you."

"Empty threat. Nicky's the allergic one, not me."

"I'm sure she expects you home sometime. By then you might be toxic." It felt strange to send him home to someone else, but there it was. This roadside chat was more conversation than we'd had since our court date.

After twenty-two years of marriage, he'd said only six words as I sat collapsed on a courthouse bench. Six words. "Leave me a few house plants?"

When I could stand, I planned plant vengeance—easy because Evan had returned to work. At my former address I cleared the last bits of me from his life, loading up photo albums he'd tossed in the leaky shed loft. I looked through Nicky's clothes to see her jeans size. I pocketed all their expensive energy bars. Finally, I took an eye dropper and added bleach to the plants I'd never liked, hoping their mysterious death would be annoying. The good plants went to Antler Camp with me and twenty-two years of photos.

I went to sit with Pock on the edge of the car, ready to be well-behaved after my dog hair threat. "Whatever Kate did, it must have been good to get you so upset. Come on. Sum up her testimony in one sentence. Less painful that way."

Evan pulled dark glasses from his shirt pocket, shoved them over his eyes, and directed his comments toward the road, not me. "Her research showed that if we increased our forests' carbon storage by only one percent (you'd have to include dead wood and increased soil productivity—whatever that means) and allow trees to grow longer before they're harvested— that bit of extra carbon would do it."

"Do what?"

He looked up at the trees around us, tall and uncut by generations of Birches owners who wanted guests to feel a real forest during their stay. "Just a one percent increase in our forests storing carbon would equal three times what Maine emits in fossil fuels. A year."

I jumped up. "That's three sentences, but I'll take them." I grabbed Evan's shirt sleeves, but only for a moment because he pulled them away. "Can't you see what she's done? Her forestry department works to figure out growth rates for trees—mostly to help owners plan cuts and heap up profits.

"She was working on trees as a solution, not a profit center. Every researcher she needed was in walking distance from her lab. All she had to do was collect their data, apply what she was learning about carbon storage, and prove trees are an alternative to wind. She did something huge I don't think anyone else has done—bring trees and carbon to the debate over wind power." I danced a bit in the road. "Oh, way to go, Kate."

Evan wasn't pacing. That was a good sign.

"Did she have some charts and stuff?" I asked.

My ex-husband finally looked at me, but I was reflected in his sunglasses and couldn't get a clear read on his attitude.

"Come on. I'll bet it was good. What happened?" I asked.

When Evan pulled his glasses down and his laser-like green eyes found me, I thought he was headed toward sarcasm, but when he spoke, it was the man from our early days—days when we'd hang on every Kate word, even toddler gibberish. His voice was gentle. "There was an actual groan from execs sitting behind me when they saw how she'd graphed the build-out of wind power compared to what trees sucking carbon could do."

"Details?" I asked. "Oh please."

He cleared his throat and then laughed. Pock jumped from the car to join us, his tail thumping on Evan's legs. "Making your day, am I? OK." He raised his right arm. "The line depicting carbon removal using trees went up and up. The line showing wind power's actual record of carbon removal based on fossil fuel displacement–you know—power plants cutting back or shutting down—flatlined near the bottom of the graph." He dropped his arm. "Flatlined. Yes. She's good."

I skipped a bit in the road. "How good?" I asked. "I hate to sound desperate, but I'd really like to know."

"I think she knew as a very young witness she'd be suspect. She knew not to make it about herself or talk much. She used evidence from trusted sources we couldn't undermine."

I tugged my drying shirt away from a stomach that still had C-section sag—something my husband had never missed when I undressed. "I can't imagine anyone you could not undermine," I said.

He nodded. "Well, me too. But she had a Department of Energy map showing only one reliable wind site inside the state."

"Mt. Katahdin," I said.

"Yup. Tiny, red dot of decent wind on top of our most exposed and protected mountain. Only hot spot in the state. You could have heard a pin drop when she put that slide up on the big screen."

Evan went silent. I could feel his attorney brain formulating a final closing statement. "She's so good, you need to hear this. Two things I know from working with these people for years. One. Trees must always deliver a profit. If you follow Kate's scheme forward, someone has to come up with millions of dollars to encourage land owners to delay harvesting. Wall Street drives its corporate decisions toward quarterly profits, not long-term strategies like waiting for things to grow."

He buttoned the top button on his shirt. "Two. And this is more practical and personal, but it's still about money. Because there's millions on the line here and the stakes are enormous, it's possible someone will come after you thinking you created her testimony. Or come after Kate—even if they just try to smear her."

"Oh, come on. This isn't some kind of spy story gone wrong," I said. "She just took available data from a public institution and recombined it toward a new thesis."

Evan picked dog hair off his sleeve. "Cassandra Patton, I try not to listen to grumbling that borders on criminal matters I'm bound to report. I am hearing borderline grumbling because my clients are not used to being thwarted. I'll warn them to behave. I'll warn Kate to look over her shoulder." He bent down to rub Pock's ears. "All three of you should now consider yourselves warned."

I thought maybe the river's big wave fell into the warning category, and certainly the thefts from our homes. I also wondered about the truck aimed our way, a dust cloud exploding behind it. We jumped to the side of the road as Matt Pruitt gunned his PP&E truck past us.

I blinked dust from my contacts. "Somehow I feel I should already know who he really is," I said, "beyond the parking lot where I met him and his too-clean black shoes and his officious clipboard. Where's he going?"

"He's off to set up a field trip at Lily Bay State Park overlooking the project site," said Evan. "I have to tag along." He sniffed and returned his sunglasses to his face. "Waste of time even though Zaitlin and his staff asked for it. New law. Maine's regulators no longer have to give as much weight to scenic impacts when they rule on wind permit applications."

"Isn't that some kind of oxymoron thing? An environmental protection agency protecting development instead of woods?"

I knew I'd ruined the moment when Evan slapped his hands over his ears. "Christ! You do know you can't fix the universe, don't you? Years and years of listening to you until, until—" He stopped.

I thought I could finish his sentence—*until I left you.*

That put Evan in the Kate camp of having had too much of me. I could forgive Kate. A child wants good reasons to flee home, and at some point, I think all parents are just too much.

I'd had as much legal Evan as he'd had of political me, so I shrugged. "Well, I think you'll enjoy the Scots, Evan. They're here to talk about business and since the wind law was written by business folks who didn't expect other business folks to turn up with business problems, it might be good theater."

I pulled my wet hair back into a pony tail. "So. Moving on. Should I know Matt from a previous life?"

He slapped road grime from his dark suit pants. "Of course you know him. He's Soap from your river days. He pretends he has no history as the grungiest raft guide that ever lived. I remember you used to hug your gear bag in your lap so it wouldn't touch anything of his."

"Holy shit," I said. "Soap? I haven't heard that name in decades. No wonder I didn't recognize him—except for the way he held his cigarette. Like a joint. I sort of knew he had a deep relationship with weed, but we thought more about his aversion to shaving, shampoo, and hygiene products. Holy shit. Soap."

"Holy shit's a good place for you to start and stay with," said Evan. Walking away, he pointed at the car up ahead. "And that 'Ass at Your Own Risk' message? I'd pay close attention to that. That and the ongoing investigation into your relationship with a dead piece of someone." He tossed a wave into the air without turning around.

I stuck out my tongue at his back, but only felt sad. I didn't miss him anymore, but I missed having a family. Kate's high school graduation had been a sea of hugging, whooping parents. I felt beached waiting for Kate to take photos with Evan and his young fiancé and then find me in the parking lot. She understood. All she said was, "I don't want to talk. Maybe not talk about it ever again."

I opened the note Chan had left in my hand. Lily had drawn me a map, but I didn't need directions to the state park. I gave Pock a hug and closed him in the back of the car after I retrieved his electric collar. Lily Bay State Park was a long piece of waterfront property with dozens of wooded campsites on Moosehead Lake and acres and acres of woods trails. It also hosted the most concentrated population of deer anywhere near Greenwood.

Deer were not stupid. They chose forests where old, tall trees offered shelter from winter snows and wind. Great

Nations Forest and other logging companies didn't need big trees to make it through the winter. They had bars with big-screen TVs and snowmobile suits that weathered blizzards. Without those luxuries, deer concentrated themselves into the nearest uncut patch of forest they could find.

Pock loved the park too, but mostly I thought he was grateful that deer had come together to give him the gift of a good chase. I checked the battery and tested the collar against my wrist. It buzzed and vibrated. If I needed to send him a quick reminder, the pressure on his neck would say, *ignore anything remotely connected to deer—scent, trails, scat, and tails flipped up in the air over fleeing butts.*

As I slowed to leave the Birches driveway, Francoise pulled her purple van to a stop so it faced me. She jumped out and trotted over to us, pigtails bobbing around her head. Pock lunged forward into my lap to greet her.

"Donut for doggie," she said handing one through the window and dropping a bag of croissants in my lap. "Are made yesterday, but heat with butter. Beaucoup butter."

I assumed Francoise worked at speaking a language that was not English and not French because she was the smartest business woman I'd ever met, and she knew it worked for her.

"You made my day," I said. "There's no way I'd invite you to eat what I cook."

She smiled. "You make mean banana bread."

"OK. Next loaf is yours. I'm collecting dead bananas in my freezer. I just hope they don't taste like trout. You catering for the official state folks?" I asked.

She nodded. "Maine is cheap. Très mauvais. Only money enough for crumbs on pans." She stepped back, but didn't leave.

"There's more?" I asked.

243

"Your name is much at coffee counter early."

I lifted a croissant and thought my car was probably as hot as an oven, so it would taste just fine. "Look Francoise," I said, my mouth full of pastry, "you don't have to tell me everything you hear. Especially from people wearing uniforms."

She shifted her feet back and forth. That set off her pig tails again. "The uniform people say they know home of cut-up person."

I lowered the croissant and slipped the rest of it to Pock, who was already drooling. Francoise continued her nervous shuffle. "A tent far in woods."

I knew I had to be in there somewhere, so I waited for more.

"You know this place? You go there?" she asked.

"No. No. I don't know anything about the cut-up person. Why? What's going on?"

"They say tent walls full of words. Your words on paper over walls."

I dropped my head down on the steering wheel, but way down in my soggy sandals I could feel something start to fire up. Even my toes felt hotter than usual.

Francoise stood on tiptoe and reached for my shoulder. "The long-eyes warden told the other badge men he would find you."

Well Moz had found me and said nothing about my words wallpapering a dead person's tent. I pounded the steering wheel. "That's it! That's it!" I yelled.

Francoise jumped back, crossing herself and whispering, "Mon Dieu! Mon Dieu!"

"I'm not mad at you, Francoise. Not mad at you. I just want some peace. Eat cereal over the sink. Sleep with my dog. Listen to the lake thaw and then listen to it freeze again. I've got to figure out how this person in pieces knows me—figure it out before the law does."

"I can't leave unless you are alright, Patton," she said, dropping into perfect English. "Promise me that you'll find the game warden and let him help you."

"Just so you know," I said, "I won't tell anyone you can talk like the rest of us."

She clapped her hands and backed toward her van. "Now I know you fine."

"Would you find Kate and tell her I've gone out to Lily Bay, and if she's part of the field trip I'll see her out there?" I called.

She gave me a thumbs-up as she pulled out a small stool, climbed into the cab of her van, and pulled the stool in after herself.

I figured it was about time to give Lily the private audience she wanted. I aimed for the park and just inside it, a narrow, rutted road that led to a wooded spit of land and a forgotten campsite. When the lake was high, the site was an island. When the lake was low, anyone could walk over exposed rocks and find a small clearing between ancient trees, a splintered picnic table, and a caved-in outhouse.

I knew the campsite was far away from toilets, parking lots, and information kiosks where Matt Pruitt would set up his official field trip. He had to know who I was and who I'd been decades ago when we'd guided rafts down the Penobscot River.

At least I was recognizable. I still had a pony tail, drove a Subaru, and owned a Labrador. Friends told me I'd hardly changed at all, but of course they hadn't seen me naked. I knew that sometime I wanted to catch up to the Soap side of Matt Pruitt. We had history.

First, I had to find Lily Rose Baines Johnson, and then find the mystery cut-up man. Both were making my life miserable.

# TWENTY-THREE

When I turned onto the dirt road to the forgotten campsite, I stuck the phone in my shirt pocket so I could listen to messages. My father left an actual message, his voice strong and sure. Even though he was close to eighty, he still made his YMCA aerobics classes march up and down the gym until sweat glistened on the floor. All six feet five inches of him were working well in ways I envied.

I could hear his fax clicking away and someone typing furiously to the rise and fall of muted voices. His office was always busy with people working on dreams of owning Maine real estate. I wasn't surprised that he planned to send an appraiser to assess Antler Camp's worth. I wasn't worried. He couldn't sell Antler Camp without my mother's consent, and she was firm. Her camp was priceless.

She'd left a long message, singing a hymn in a cracking voice. I sang along and felt better. Hymns were fine. Preaching I avoided. My mother was in a Boothbay Harbor nursing home that had no ocean views, but there were days when dense fog rolled up over the lawns, bringing such a strong tang she said she didn't need to salt her food.

The last time I'd gone to visit, I brought her chocolate she wasn't supposed to have and Pock whom she and everyone loved. The residents called out to him using the names of their long-dead dogs. After he licked crumbs off the dining room floor—layers of them—he eased up on my mother's bed until she could reach his head and stroke it.

"I'll never sell it," she'd said. "In my will I've left my share to you. Now your father doesn't know that yet, and he doesn't need to. I adore the man, but he's on his own planet. Sometimes he looks up to see who's orbiting around him and tries to exert a gravitational pull if he thinks we've floated too far away from appreciating him.

"I have loved seeing how you fought that. Now that I'm headed out, you should know that I always rooted for you to have your own solar system." I'd poured lotion into my hands and massaged her face until she fell asleep, thanking her quietly for rooting for me even if it was new and surprising information. If I'd known as a child that speaking up was a good thing and I was a good person for doing it, maybe I wouldn't have caught the girl-be-silent disease.

It was often a secret disease—not visible as it worked its way through our deepest selves. After enough messages telling us we weren't acceptable, we took over the infection process. We helped the disease metastasize to our brains so no one had to remind us that our words and voices needed careful pruning to get and hold jobs—get and hold most men we met. We carried scalpels inside to accomplish our own voice reduction surgery.

Hiding at Antler Camp was, after all, a familiar silent-girl strategy. Taking myself out of the effort to be heard took me to familiar childhood haunts where I could lie in grass near grazing deer or sit on the dock wrapped in leaf noise as a storm riled the lake around my toes.

As a child every day after school I ran to the woods to be alone, but I was never lonely. Every plant and animal in it seemed happy to have me just the way I was. Antler Camp offered me the same genial and tolerant company right outside my door.

Kate left the last phone message. "Good news. Dad told his team to ignore the eagle incident and they all snapped to attention. I looked for you after my testimony, but Francoise said you'd gone to the park. I'll see you there, but maybe you should pretend you don't know me. I think that's working well for me. I think you can sit back on this one."

She signed off with a laugh and a phrase I hadn't heard her use in years. "Love you more than all the chocolate chip cookies in the world, Mum."

At the end of the road as I parked next to Lily's van, I thought about a similar message I always mentally sent toward Kate before I slipped into sleep. *I love you more than ALL the cookies in ALL the world.*

I slipped Pock's electronic collar over his head and activated the hand-held device that sent a buzzing reminder about tantalizing wildlife. I tied his leash around my waist and slipped a backpack strap over one shoulder. I found Matt Pruitt's truck parked on a dry, wide pebble beach. Ground water slowly seeped into deep ruts under his tires. He was recently arrived. I wasn't sure why I clipped Pock into his leash and slipped into the woods instead of following the path to the campsite. Maybe it was the drag marks in the dirt path.

I did know why I didn't rush in to rescue Matt when I saw him tied to an upended picnic table. I needed to assess the entire scene. I circled behind the decaying outhouse, crouched behind one of its collapsed walls, and pushed Pock to the ground. Seeing humans to greet, he started to wag his tail. He stopped when Matt wailed.

"Oh, for shit's sake, woman, what do you want?"

Lily was busy looping blue ropes over a tree branch above him. "You're on camera," she said. "You might want to keep it clean."

It wasn't an empty threat. Set up across the clearing on a small tripod, a video camera's lights winked at them. Lily had pushed the picnic table vertical up against the same tree where she was busy coiling and uncoiling ropes. Matt's hands were tied to the ragged table slats over his head. His feet were anchored to table edges resting on the ground. It was the essential crucifixion position.

I was just about to leap forward when Lily dropped her arms, and I saw the taser dangling from her belt. I respected tasers. While I didn't have a serious heart condition, occasionally it surprised me and my cardiologist with a siege of irregular rhythms. I guessed that electrical current applied to any part of me wasn't going to make my doctor or my heart happy.

I assumed that Lily and I were both on the same side—the side of the wild world. I knew I could break the law to protect that world. I'd already done that in ways that I didn't want public. On the other hand, tasering and kidnapping someone was unlikely to remain a private operation.

We first-aiders know that when someone is crying for help, the airway and most of the rest of the person is essentially alright unless there's blood on the ground. There was no blood on the ground. I thought I had some time to wait it out.

Matt continued to swear and yell at Lily until she reached for a long pole leaning against the tree holding up his picnic table. Standing on the tips of her steel toe boots, she lifted the pole and whacked a gigantic hornet's nest high above them. On the third thwack, insects poured from the nest and circled it to determine damage. Yanking on the longest rope, Lily gathered the entire hornet's nest into a fine mesh net she'd hung between low branches. Hundreds of angry insects found they had nowhere to go. Their angry buzz filled the clearing.

Matt stopped struggling, frozen against the boards behind him. "You have no idea what you're playing with here, lady," he whispered. "I could die."

"Well, I think that applies to most of us," Lily said. She pulled on a rope and the net full of hornets rose into the air. "If you answer only a yes or a no to anything I ask, the hornets stay up in the tree. If you chatter on, I'm dropping them down on your face."

Matt screamed. "You're crazy!"

Lily started to lower the net.

"OK. OK! Your way. Your sick game. Just get to it."

Lily lowered the nest so close to Matt's hair, I thought he could feel the wind from frantic wings. "See those camps across the cove?" she asked.

He nodded vigorously, but that only made the hornets buzz louder.

"That's not a yes. That's not a no," she said.

"Yes," he whispered.

"I grew up there, and I worked there for fifteen years. You know how many local people work at Ross Camps each year, pretty much all year?"

"No."

"Of course not. Must be the hard hat and a fat salary obscures your vision. Cooks? Guides? Mechanics? Housekeeping and grounds?"

Matt stared.

"Of course not. Why would you know anything about other people's jobs? The little people's jobs." Skipping the rope a bit, she bounced the hornet nest once on Matt's head.

He groaned, "Please, lady. Please."

Pock whined in my ear. I agreed. It was time to save Matt, but just then Lily raised the net and nest high into the tree. She sat on a stump, the rope wrapped around her hand, the taser hanging from her belt.

I wasn't proud of myself for sinking into a more comfortable position with an even better grip on Pock's leash, but I wanted to see how Lily's drama played out. I wasn't sure I could forgive Matt for waving a clipboard at me like he hadn't known me from a previous life.

"Time's a wasting," she said. "So only a yes or a no. This is not a public relations assignment. I will not allow corporate spin. Nod if you understand."

Matt nodded so hard his head bounced off the boards behind him.

Looking at crumpled paper she pulled from her pocket, Lily said, "I will try and ask these questions fairly." She glared at Matt. "Not that fairness is part of your company's DNA."

Matt licked his lips and gulped large mouthfuls of air.

"You're an engineer who specializes in industrial wind power. Right?"

He nodded.

"Yes or no out loud from now on, Matt. And you've worked in installations in Texas and several other states?"

He hesitated.

"These are the simple questions, Pruitt. I own over two hundred turbines in Texas with thousands of blades turning smoothly in what seems to be a steady breeze, so I've already checked out your employment record."

"Yes," he said. His eyes grew wide at the thought of Lily owning turbines.

I considered the ant hill I'd disturbed and shoved a board on top of it. *I'm with you, Matt,* I thought. *Doesn't make much sense.*

Lily crossed her legs and leaned back, glancing up at the humming, thrashing ball of hornets. "So. We've established your expertise even though you're probably only forty something." She consulted her notes. "First real question, Matt. In this part of the country, since wind power has been added to our energy mix, have any plants using fossil fuels to create electricity closed down or essentially changed their operations? And don't include coal in your assessment. That's on its way out all by itself."

I couldn't tell whether being tied up or not being able to explain his side of it was more torture. Matt swiveled his head back and forth, muttering whole sentences.

Lily twitched the rope and the net dropped a few inches.

"No!' yelled Matt.

Lily looked around. I slumped lower behind the wall even though I could smell marinating waste in the outhouse. "Good. We're clear. Wind power has not affected our use of fossil fuels. Now we'll move on to prove why that is."

She lifted her notes and frowned. "Is it true that while wind power installations theoretically have about ninety percent operating availability, they actually only generate power about twenty to forty percent of the time?"

Matt looked puzzled. "Repeat?" he asked, looking up to see if the net would drop.

"Asking to repeat is good. That's allowed." Lily repeated her question and then added, "Obviously I'm getting at how little time the turbines are actually working, allowing for too little wind, too much wind, ice freeze ups, explosions when the machinery's on fire, and general maintenance."

Matt twisted in his ropes, desperate to dispute her. So far, Lily had used information I'd already found on websites that had no rabid agendas. I picked some exploring ants off my arms and Pock's back. At least they weren't red ones.

Lily sighed. "Compared to the theoretical opportunity to run most of the time, do most facilities actually operate only twenty to forty percent of the time?"

"Yes," muttered Matt. He twisted his legs in the dirt, testing the ropes. I heard boards crack.

"And in fact, your current project on Eagle Ridge has an average yearly history of generating electricity thirty two percent of the time. Correct?" Lily asked.

Matt glared at her.

She waved her paper. "I'm quoting PP&E's corporate reports. Well?"

"Yes," he said.

"That's better. We're getting there." Lily stood and walked to check her video camera. I grabbed Pock to push him closer to the ground. He was so close to the anthill, his eyes crossed trying to follow escaping insects.

Matt hung his head. When he raised it, his eyes had deep shadows and his cheeks were white and blotched with red patches. I pulled myself up on my knees, ready to end it.

Lily resumed her seat on the stump and nodded at him. "I'll speed it up. Even when electricity generated from wind installations is getting to customers through a well organized, central system, are any fossil fuel plants shut down?"

Matt almost whispered, "No."

Lily's voice grew louder as she paced back and forth in front of the table, flipping the rope end to punctuate her words. "In fact, all the plants burning fossil fuels are always needed for back-up because wind is not fully reliable. Oh yes, you need it as a question. Are these fossil fuel plants always running, even in stand-by mode because it costs too much to shut them down? Are these plants always running and using fossil fuels?"

Matt straightened up. "Yes! Yes!" he yelled.

Lily lowered her voice, but leaned close to his face so both of them could face the camera. "Do the green groups, the environmentalists who support Maine's wind power—do they know these fossil fuel facts?"

He turned his head sideways and spit at her.

Lily didn't flinch. I was on my feet, trying to untangle Pock's leash from my legs.

"Last question, Mr. Pruitt, and it's personal so buck up. What's the best part of having a job with this company?"

Matt looked at the camera. "Not having to work with assholes like you," he hissed.

I was halfway across the clearing as Lily, inches from Matt's face, yelled, "You killed someone to keep your job didn't you? Chopped him up? Silenced him? What did he know? What did he know?"

Matt arched his back against the table. "No," he panted. "Yes! Wait! No. And yes! Are you happy now?"

When Lily leaned on the table it collapsed, dumping both of them on the ground into a heap of boards. I chased the loose rope writhing over the dirt as the net, unattended, swung toward the ground. Pock, chasing me, was under the net when it fell on his back and hornets exploded all around him. There was a lot of screaming, mostly me, yelling, "In the lake. Everyone in the lake! Lose the Taser!"

Lily, Matt, and I made it into the lake, ducking under water as long as we could before we surfaced for quick breaths. Pock did not.

After long minutes when we could no longer see hornets in the air over the clearing, Lily and I had to drag Matt out of the lake, a few boards still tied to his limp wrists. We laid him in the grass, but I only had eyes for Pock. I circled the clearing looking for him, kicking bushes to see if he'd been taken down with hornet injuries. A massive attack by stinging insects is not a slight medical emergency. Matt however, was having a major medical emergency.

"His face is turning blue! He's got red spots everywhere," cried Lily. "Didn't we all get air? Unbutton his shirt or something!"

Leaning over him, I could almost see his neck and lips swell as he wheezed and started to thrash. I leaned low. "Matt," I said, "I can fix this fast. Try to purse your lips almost closed and take short sips of air. I'll be right back. Do. Not. Panic."

Lily was throwing her arms all over, winding up her own panic. "And you," I called as I raced back to the outhouse for my pack, "Freeze! Do nothing. Say nothing."

By the time I returned to Matt his eyes were bulging with the effort to breathe, but they begged me with a prayer I couldn't miss. "I got this, Matt. You know I do," I said. Ripping through bags in my pack, I pulled out an epi pen, dropped to the ground, and pulled one of his thighs across mine.

In seconds, I had the cap off the pen and the device pressed hard against his thigh. "Just seconds, Matt. Seconds." With my free hand I rooted around in the ripped package for another device in case one dose of epinephrine wasn't up to the most intense allergy attack I'd ever seen.

Slowly his breathing eased and a weak smile lit up his face. "So," he croaked, "those things still good after twenty-five years? You were always the go-to person for bandages and shit like that."

I brushed wet hair away from his forehead and untied the last knots on his wrists. "You're lucky the ski patrol resupplies me. These things cost a fortune. And I'm guessing, Soap, that your old first aid kit was full of rolling papers and condoms."

Matt reached up and grabbed my hand. "Pretty much," he said. "Thanks, Ms. P." Decades ago when he'd been Soap, I'd been Ms. P, said with a buzzing emphasis on the Ms. part of my name—male guides adjusting to a brave new world and having fun at the same time.

We looked at Lily who'd retired to the last remaining picnic table where she sat rubbing raised stings on her bare arms. "You got some of that for me?" she asked.

I pointed to a patch of leaves with thick stems and spiky middles. "Pick a whole bunch of those plantain leaves, chew them up so they're gooey, and slap them on your bites. And I still want you to do nothing and say nothing."

I turned to Matt. "Why didn't you tell her you were deathly allergic to stings like that?"

He tried to sit up, but I laid him back down and propped his feet up on rocks to jump-start circulation. "Lie down until you get some color in your face or you'll just end up falling flat on it." I said. "Why didn't you tell her?"

Matt nodded at Lily who'd stuffed her mouth with leaves and was chewing them so hard green saliva dripped down her chin. "Look at her," he said. "You actually think discussing my medical needs would have stopped that? Does that green stuff work?"

"It can, but you're better off with an epi pen." I started to cram spilled first aid kit contents back into my pack, but I'd already moved on from the current emergency to the next one. Where was Pock? I fingered the control device in my pocket, unsure if I wanted to call him in or go find him.

Matt raised himself on his elbows. "As if I knew I'd be tasered and dragged out here and tied up. I've got epi pens in the truck."

"How did she get you down the dirt road?"

"I don't know. I've never been to the park, so I followed signs to the beach picnic area and the road ended here. When I got out of the truck, she was waiting for me."

I'd been to the park so many times, I didn't need to look at signs Lily must have switched to lure Matt to the island campsite. Out by the main park road, I heard air brakes echoing up the cove toward us before starting up again in the direction of the public beach. The field trip bus driver knew his way around the park even if the signs were wrong. I could hear traffic following the bus, all except for one engine slowly heading toward us.

# TWENTY-FOUR

"Quickly now," I said, thinking Moz would be preferable to PP&E's security team. "We're going to have company and it might be the law. I need to know the truth."

Matt sat up. On our knees facing each other, we ignored Lily, who was slapping wet green leaves on her arms.

"Shoot," he said. "Just don't limit me to one-word answers."

"You had to recognize me in the parking lot after I'd found the body part. Right?"

He nodded.

"Why did you pretend we didn't have history?"

"I don't know. Honestly. Maybe there's a gut instinct to wall off parts of one's life from earlier parts that don't fit." He rubbed his throat, which now looked normal-sized but had to be sore.

"I think I'm in the middle of trying to do something like that," I said, "so I'll take that reason. For now. But you were still a giant snot at the gate and an even bigger snot when you and Ridge Dumais barged into my campsite to threaten me."

"Yeah, I was a snot, but I thought I'd get away with it. Didn't look like you recognized me."

"I didn't. Haircut, clean face, clean clothes, shiny black shoes. Officious voice." I reached down to squeeze water from my shirt. Having the lake drip slowly into my underwear was unnerving. "I do, however, owe you my life, so I can let some of that snot go," I said.

"We might be even now," he whispered.

When he looked directly at me and bent his brows in

concern, I saw the eyes of the young man who'd crawled over an entire boulder field in the middle of a river to keep me from drowning—or worse. Trapped in my kayak and stuffed sideways into a crevice where current poured through a small slit and pinned me to rocks, I'd seen Soap appear above me, dangling a rope that looked like the best gift I'd ever had.

"Trouble?" he'd asked in guide-speak, which was always understated. "Have trouble making that safe move to the right side of the channel?" We didn't discuss the fate headed my way, because my kayak was already changing shape. Long before my boat would crack open, the force of the escaping current pressing it into rocks would bend the hull enough to break my legs in multiple and agonizing ways. When the kayak finally snapped open, I'd be stuffed into the crevice to drown.

"Look at my eyes, not the boat and not the river," Soap had said. "Always my eyes and do it now. Do it now." I had no idea how he wound the rope under my armpits and angled me perfectly so my escaping body slid out of the boat seconds before it filled with water and snapped in two. I just remembered his eyes.

I waved away a few mosquitoes and lifted my eyes to his. I sighed. Why was nothing ever simple?

"I never paddled that rapid again," I said.

Matt slid his hand across the grass to cover mine. "Most likely a sign of mental health."

I squeezed his hand back. Lily was running around the clearing gathering up ropes, folding up the tripod, and eliminating any evidence of her interrogation. She'd also heard the approaching vehicle.

I pulled my hand away. "Soap. Or Matt. Or whoever. I've

260

got to get out of here and find my dog, but I have to know this one thing because I'm involved even if I don't want to be."

Matt sat back on his heels. "I didn't kill that man."

"You knew he was a man."

"Yes."

"So, the yes and no you yelled means you didn't kill him but you . . ." I waited. "Look, Lily's video footage is going to have people asking about this very thing—your weird reply to her question about killing someone. She's going to use it somehow. If I can help, I will."

Matt's voice seemed to come from very far away, almost like a bit of wind that blows itself out before it reaches anyone. "No, I didn't kill him, but yes, I used the bulldozer to cut him up."

Air whooshed out of my lungs as I tried to imagine anyone raising and lowering the blade over and over to sever someone. What kind of person would do that? Certainly not the Soap I knew. Not the nineteen-year-old boy with the kind eyes. Maybe his early life on the wrong side of the law had started something else. Weed had been more dangerous back then— federal prosecutors were eager to hand out hard time, and ruthless cartel middlemen salivated over college kids' ignorance. I'd lost at least one college classmate to that hard scene. Maybe Matt's soul hadn't escaped intact.

"Why, Matt? What possible reason could you have for doing that?"

He stammered, "My job. My job—"

"Job?" I asked. "Your *job*?"

He looked past me toward the edge of the clearing and whispered, "He was dead, dead when I found him. I . . . I just wanted to create a bad scene at the site—a really, really bad scene."

"You wanted to create a mess? Aren't you the site manager? What's going on that you thought it was a smart move to dismember someone? Matt? Matt?" I reached over and shook both his shoulders. "Did you know him? Recognize him? I really need to know this. Matt? Matt!"

His head snapped away toward the path, and I felt him trembling. Even though it was early afternoon, headlights from an approaching vehicle lit up tree bark where we'd parked. I dropped my arms, and Matt turned his head to stare at me. I heard his silent challenge as someone turned off a motor and slammed a vehicle door. Was the kayak rescue enough for me to rescue him from the awful thing he'd done? I scrambled to my feet, but he stayed on the ground, his head bent.

When Moz walked up the path and stood, legs apart, arms crossed, taking in the entire scene, I leaned down and said, "I don't think I can cover for you with this man." Matt moaned and hung his head even lower. "Here's what I can do," I whispered. "I'll tell Lily that if she releases the footage she's shot, she's also going to jail. Even if she edits herself out, it's clear you're still tied up and struggling."

"Much appreciated," Matt whispered.


After walking around the clearing, Moz sat on my side of the table facing Matt and Lily. No one had much to say. Matt explained that he'd followed the wrong road. Lily said she'd invited me out to have a private chat. I nodded agreement.

"You look ill," Moz said to Matt.

"I'm much better, thanks. Got stung, but the women were on it." Matt's hair dripped from his forehead down to his cheeks. "Seems they think lake water is the way to go."

Lily took the cue and handed Matt some of her wet leaves.

He slapped them on his neck. "And the women seem to like weird herbs. I need to get to the beach, meet people, and get back to work," he said.

Moz listened but had a hard stare fixed on Lily. "Turn right after you leave this road," he said as Matt pushed himself up and staggered a few steps.

"I'm fine. I'm fine," he called. "Got some medicine in the truck."

We watched him leave and waited. Lily picked at her arms. I wanted to leap off my seat and head after Pock, but thought our common code of silence had to play out.

"And Pock?" asked Moz.

That question felt like permission to leave.

"Must be exploring," I said. "I'll go get him."

Moz finally turned to look at me. "Where the lake is low near where your car is parked—Pock is rolling in mud."

I stood and looked at Lily. She'd been trying to get me alone for days. I had so much to ask her. I was sure Moz could feel the heavy air between us, but Lily figured out a smart exit.

When Lily lifted herself off the picnic table bench, green plant bits rained off her arms. "So, it's a date. Right, Patton? Tomorrow for breakfast? Your place?"

I was so eager to have her gone I would have agreed to anything. "Done," I said, reaching for my pack. "Hope you like Cheerios."

She laughed without mirth, gathered up a large duffel that clanked as she lifted one strap to her shoulder, and trotted off down the path.

Moz pointed at the seat I'd just left. I sat on the other side of the table, pulling Pock's collar control unit out of my pants and wiping water off it. We shared the same table, but sat in different worlds.

He opened his chest pocket, lifted out its contents, and spread them on the table. The empty epinephrine pen, a mound of dead hornets, net fragments, and Lily's crumpled cheat sheet of questions pretty much summed up the afternoon.

"Good work," I said, "but before we get further down this road, Matt Pruitt has something to tell you. Or at least he does if he takes my advice. It's about the mystery body, and I only learned a little of what he knows before you showed up."

"Do any of this afternoon's other activities get us closer to what happened to the dead man at the Eagle Ridge Wind Power Project?" he asked.

"You mean the man who has my work taped to his tent wall?"

Moz poked at a few hornets. Their wings and black bodies disintegrated into yellow and black fragments.

I slid down the bench seat until I was across from him. "You could have mentioned the tent discovery. I had to wait for the Francoise grapevine to find out that a dead man who's now in pieces was wallpapering his home with items stolen from my home. Oh, goody. Now I'm really connected to someone I don't think I know—or want to know."

Moz reached for the control unit and examined it. "Does Pock feel pain if you use this device?"

I leaned away from the table. "I get that you can't tell me much. I keep showing up in the middle of your investigation, but maybe you could simply say that instead of finding something else wrong with me?"

He closed both hands over the control unit, fingers exploring all of its buttons.

"OK. The collar," I said. "You ever had the barber get too close to your neck with electric clippers? Makes you sit up straight and maybe turn around to see if he's focused on something outside the window? I've pressed Pock's collar to my neck and tried it. It took a lot more current to make my neck hair stand on end than what his collar is now dialed into."

I leaned forward. "If you're implying that I'm cruel to my dog, I've made the choice to protect him from people who shoot dogs that run deer. You wardens know this better than most folks. A shot dog gets maimed or dies a slow death after crawling off. In a way, the collar is my gift to Pock."

Moz put his elbows on the table and leaned in, waiting for me. A good sign, so I kept talking.

"When I first got him, it was clear he'd never been free. He was a brown blur halfway up a mountain rockslide before I got him back. Now he gets to run most all the time, and when we're in deer or moose country, he wears the collar." I looked at the path and tilted my head to listen for dog noise. "If you think Pock's busy and happy in the mud, you can tell me more about the mystery man. Right?"

Moz looked down at his hands. "He reused your papers to write a story."

"Story?"

"It appears to be the story of his life, written on the reverse side of what I know to be your research."

I was slightly disappointed that I'd only been a recycling opportunity. "And what can't you tell me? I already know about the black hands headed toward a lab."

"Ken?" he asked.

I smiled.

"We are piecing together events and are close to his identity. Until that time, those of us investigating may not comment."

I picked up a bit of hornet and flicked it into the grass. "Am I on the list?"

"The lab is done with your clothes, but I am not sure

investigators are done with you. Your papers in the dead man's tent connect you to him. His camp was illegally located on PP&E's lease, and your tent was also located on leased company land. It is likely that on many nights you and the unknown man may have been unauthorized guests in shared woods."

I knew what I'd ask next, but Moz was busy stuffing bits of net and Lily's crushed list into a plastic bag.

"I never met anyone else while I was camped there," I said.

He raised the bag to consider its contents and returned it to his pocket. "There is also your Premier Power & Energy history."

Testifying before numerous legislative committees, I'd been very public about PP&E's environmental record—or lack of it. I'd given slide shows of bulldozed streams, destroyed deer yards, and miles of forest cut to bare ground. "There's no way I can duck that, and I'm proud of it," I said.

Moz lifted a few rotten fragments from the picnic table and started to shred them into a neat pile of flakes. "There's more?" I asked.

He gathered the wood bits into his hands and lifted them into the breeze off the lake. "While I understand the pleasure of driving the bulldozer to the toilets, your fingerprints, among others, are on the machine's controls," he said.

"Thaaaat's great," I said. "Seriously, what could possibly be interesting about a woman and a dog who have nothing to gain by chopping up a trespasser?"

The edge of a smile lifted his lips. "To me, you and Pock are always interesting."

I could see Moz wanted to move away from anything official. I could do that. "But today I might be both interesting and disappointing. I think you're not pleased with me. Right?"

For an answer he lifted Pock's collar control unit and tapped the red recall button. Unless mud had coated the sensors pressed into his neck, Pock would find us in minutes.

"I believe I am angry over what I cannot change, and I am sorry for how that feeling comes at you. I have no claim over you to ask that you behave differently—to ask that you retreat from this developing situation." He looked at me with softer eyes, but I think I'd already started to snort a reply.

I slapped the table with both hands. "You mean you want me to be less than I am. To take whatever is Cassandra Patton Conover and divide her by some acceptable quotient. I can do that kind of math. People have been asking me to do that my whole life. Just be less. After all, it's simple subtraction." I dropped my voice to a whisper when I really wanted to shout. "Do you have any idea how you just pulled out a knife and stabbed me? Of course, you'd have to find a place I haven't been stabbed already."

He winced and a dark red flush lifted from his throat to his cheeks. I'd stabbed him right back.

We were so still that wildlife invaded the campsite. Chickadees flitted into balsam branches above us. Two squirrels investigated the ground where I'd ripped open my pack. They balanced on hind legs and chewed granola bar crumbs. So brown and shiny he looked fresh-waxed, a mink slid from the water with a meal in its jaws. Seeing us, he froze, but the crayfish waved its lobster-like claws and flipped its tail against the mink's clenched teeth.

Both of us smiled when the mink disappeared into tall grass—smiled at the mink and then at each other.

I almost slapped my head when I got it. Moz wasn't part of the world that wounded me. We'd known each other through marriages, children, and too many blizzards, and shared

267

sandwiches stuffed with more black flies than peanut butter. All of it—all of the background or soundtrack or whatever it was that we'd shared when he was supposed to be Evan's friend, but was really my friend, was about a shared hurt and a shared faith.

What else could bring two people together who were so very different? An ache in the back of my throat answered before the words lined up in a clear sentence.

We both believed the wild world would heal us if we needed healing.


Even when I was married, Moz had offered me doses of what I needed. One day in late winter after a brutal, name-calling legislative session and months of Kate's pre-teen sniping, Moz invited me on what he called "a bit of personal business." He blindfolded me and drove us to a remote mountain where moose had waited out the worst of winter, shedding their antlers in great brown heaps of curved bone.

Moz removed the bandanna from my eyes. "We do not want people to know how moose may yard up together. Maintaining the fiction that they are usually solitary and hard to locate in winter may save them from becoming easy targets. Remote locations often seduce lawful people into criminal behavior."

I'd folded the bandana, strapped on my snowshoes, and followed him up through the melting March snow. "I'm guessing female moose were here too, but they're obviously tidier than their men," I said.

Around us and as far as we could see, hundreds of small trees were rubbed bare where moose had satisfied the itch of drying antlers against rough bark and then stripped the loose pieces and eaten them. The forest looked raw and naked. I knew that when blood stopped flowing into the weight of what male moose carried around, their antlers toppled off, but I'd never stood in a field of antlers.

Some were snagged in low, leafless branches. It looked like sculptors had entwined angular bones and twisted tree limbs as a wilderness commentary on arthritis. A few yards away from a snagged antler, I held up my hands, closed one eye, and saw how my gnarled fingers neatly fit into this artistic vision.

Other antlers were almost buried in late winter snow. In the sun, their tips glittered in melting hoarfrost that I knew would recrystallize at night.

We helped each other strap antlers onto the packs we wore and then hiked down to stack the sheds in his truck. I retied my blindfold. "I'm alright with not knowing how we got here," I said. "It should probably be something I get to do once in life anyway. Something magical should stay that way."

That night, while Evan and Kate slept, I nailed my antlers to the outside wall and painted a large Antler Camp sign for the door. I sat in the driveway and pressed my hands over my nose. My fingers smelled like wood, dried moose blood, and the leather conditioner Moz used on his pack. I was good to go again.

I rapped the picnic table with my fist. "Moz, wait a minute." He wasn't trying to stand, but I felt him leaving before he actually left. "Let me think about what's going on here. Wait. Please. I need to think."

He folded his hands on the table. Maybe his head moved. I wasn't sure.

This man moved between two separate worlds, the white

world and the Penobscot Nation—worlds that were often at war with each other. Both were hard on him for not choosing one and letting the other one go. It was the dance between his black boots and his moccasins. I knew he moved carefully in and out of those worlds, aware he didn't fit comfortably into either one—aware that each wouldn't accept him for the man he was. It made sense he was a hard man, but he'd never been hard with me.

If I trusted him, then I had to ask what he knew about me that I didn't know. I looked at his face across the table. Not one part of it moved. It looked chiseled out of ancient rock.

"What don't I know? What should I know?" I asked.

"After you left your old life behind . . . "

"Or it left me."

He shrugged. "You now speak and act as the crusader you once were, even as you live a new life. I am not sure you are whole yet."

"Whole?"

"I am not sure your spirit has made peace with the location of your body."

"Well, that was predictably inscrutable."

"No."

"No, what?"

"I was clear. If you are no longer a lobbyist or a wife or the mother of a young child, with the ways you spoke and acted before—what will you be?"

"How does my spirit catching up to me have anything to do with what you said about having no claim over me? What you said about having no right to ask that I pull back from what you called a developing situation. I'm lost here, Moz."

"Yes, lost."

"No, I'm not lost-lost. I just don't understand you."

He put one hand to his forehead, pushing so hard against it that skin around his hand turned white. "You are freer than you have been in a long time. Free to be lost, to not know your new life well. Caught up in what is new, you may be less vigilant."

"OK. I think I understand that." I thought he was trying to say I didn't fit anywhere yet, and maybe he was the right person to know about that. "So, what did you mean about having no claim on me?" I asked.

"I have no right to ask that you avoid danger. I have no hold on you to try and make that happen, but it is a wish I have."

I did another mental head slap. I'd missed something unexpected. He wanted to have a claim on me, but not like property he owned. He respected my right to act in ways I chose to act, but he was afraid I'd be hurt. Or worse.

I reached over the table and took his hands, but they didn't respond to my grip. I ran my fingers over his calluses and up and down the ridge lines of his fingertips. "I am sorry," I said. "I am so sorry. I will be careful, I promise."

His eyes remained stony and endlessly black. Then we had company.

Mud flying off every part of his body and yipping for joy at seeing two of his favorite people, Pock charged up the trail. I grabbed the collar control and pressed the red button, yelling, "Sit. Sit where you are." I tapped the button again. Confused, Pock shook his head, but he sat, mud sliding off his body into a pile by his tail.

"What do you want me to do? I'll do it," I said.

Moz pulled his hands away but reached over the table and slowly ran one finger down the side of my face, touching the line of my bones down into the curve of my cheek. He looked at me the way people in airports stand and stare at someone they may never see again—wordless and sad, absorbing every line and curve.

"What? What is it?" I asked.

"The last time I warned you about people with power who would not give it up, I believe you almost died."

Only Moz and I knew about Pock's and my night penned with captured wolves. Only Moz knew the woman who'd hoped desperate wild animals would kill me. We'd agreed that my relationship with Maine wolves should always remain secret. "I don't understand. Why is this the same?"

"Threats are gathering around you. The river and the wave. The theft of your work. The break-in at Kate's apartment." He looked away toward the lake. "Your private clothing appearing far from your home. Premier Power & Energy's anger aimed toward you. Lily Rose Baines Johnson's unexplained interest. They may be separate events, but I feel them circling you."

Mentally, I added Evan's warning about his upset corporate clients to the list. "What do they feel like? The circling things."

"Money. Money without limit and perhaps only you and Kate stand in the way of people who want it."

I tried a smile on him. "And Lily. Don't forget Lily."

He frowned. "And Lily."

Again, I said, "What do you want me to do? I'll do it."

"Do I have a choice of where to locate you?"

I wanted to say don't push it, but instead I said, "Yes. You call it."

"Kate is safe at school," he said. "I have arranged private security that neither she nor her peers will recognize."

"You'd use your private company?" The people Moz hired were always good news: ex-wardens, guides with decades of stealth experience, and people from the Penobscot Nation so loyal they often refused paychecks. "Thank you," I said and meant it. Half of my body relaxed and half waited for my fate.

"Your camp, however, is not safe," he said.

That was true for many reasons. Antler Camp was down a remote dirt road. The shed door and all the other doors were just a kick away from collapsing. While I had a shotgun for squirrels who ganged up on my bird feeders, I was better at aiming it in the air to scare them. And most of all, everyone knew where the camp was.

Moz slid off the picnic table's bench seat and readjusted all the implements he wore around his waist. "Do they let family members sleep in with relatives who are in hospice care?" he asked. "Share their rooms for a visit?"

I sighed and slumped. "Good one, Moz. Who would look for me where most of the residents can't remember my name?" Nursing homes were mentally porous locations. No one would remember if I'd come and gone, stayed three years or only three hours. I liked the setup. Moz would arrange to have someone check up on me, but I knew all the exits. The doors Pock favored were close to dense landscaping, so we'd use one of those. I had work to do.

I shook out my wrinkled sleeves. Evan's shirt was probably used to a laundry service, not a dip in a lake. "Yes, Pock and I can sleep at Sea View. There's no ocean view, but there's unlimited chocolate pudding, and everyone adores my dog. I'm not sure if my mother is still technically in hospice care. Cousin Liz brings her double cheeseburgers, so she's gained enough weight to slip back into a future."

Finally, there was a smile. I was sad to bring up anything that would fade it.

# TWENTY-FIVE

I moved my hand low, telling Pock to stay in his pool of mud. More than anything I wanted to go rub every inch of him and feel that he was alright. He lifted each paw to rub the side of his head until he'd added even more mud to his face. I sent him some thoughts. *Hang on. Whatever needs fixing or cleaning or removing, I'll be right with you. Hang on.*

"I have a problem," I said.

Moz raised his eyebrows as he if couldn't believe I had only one.

"Chan is staying at my camp. At least his luggage is there, and I think he expects to find food there as well. My freezer, the lake, and my barn are all useful to feed his bird. What should we do about eagle boy? If I'm at Sea View I don't think he should stay at camp all by himself with only Teddy for company."

His official voice returned. "Today, all wardens received video of Chandler's dead golden eagle dropped on a table at the public hearing. We are instructed to find him."

I watched Pock rub his face. "Actually, I think the eagle at the hearing was Ken's bird."

"It is the federal government's golden eagle," said Moz. "Every feather and every bone of it. Alive or dead, he should not be in possession of any eagle."

I felt for the eagle feather in my pocket. It was still there. "He's got a cell phone. Can't you trace that?"

"I followed his signal to the park, but it often disappears."

"What's to be done with him? I mean if we find him first?" I asked.

Moz reached for his phone, studied its display, and returned it to his belt. "I have a plan that may work if my supervisors will forgive his inexperience and ignorance."

"Does he get to keep Teddy?

"No. Not until he and the eagle are trained by a master falconer, the boy becomes a licensed apprentice, and a parent appears to supervise him."

I reached for my pack and slid off my seat. "Oh, right. I'm sure that's all close to happening."

"On the Indian Island reservation near Bangor my cousin is a master, licensed to teach Penobscot youth falconry skills. He would accept Chan and perhaps retrain the eagle, although I believe hunting with a bald eagle will involve special permission from my department."

"Really? The bird looks very eager."

"Yes, to grab others' food or feed on available carcasses. I believe bald eagles are more often scavengers than predators. They are rarely approved for the sport of falconry."

"Bald eagles are lazy? Maybe they're just smarter than other raptors."

Moz stepped into the middle of the clearing. "I am more concerned that Chandler's eagle is imprinted on the boy who has raised and fed him." He walked a circle around the picnic table, raising his voice. I thought the blueberry bushes enclosing the clearing were too low to hide anyone, but then again Chan was very good.

"His eagle may not fear humans and may even become aggressive. It is illegal for apprentices to obtain a wild bird taken from a nest, and they are not allowed to raise a raptor that has formed an attachment to a human being." Moz stopped and lowered his voice. "Only experienced falconers may manage the training of an imprinted bird, so it may one day be freed."

"These birds don't live forever with their trainers? Their owners?" I asked.

"The sport has an ethic of returning birds to the wild after several hunting seasons. Teddy should have that opportunity."

Chan wasn't going to be good with turning his best friend over to anyone else, but I thought he'd appreciate Teddy's chance to live free and wild. I could see the boy releasing the eagle *if* both of them didn't end up in detention facilities.

I looked at my best friend, who was lying in a pool of mud trying to rub his eyes with his paws. I knelt next to him, but he ducked his head as I reached fingers toward his face. Gray layers of dried goop covered most of his body. I peeled a few hard pieces off his back.

"I'll have to get Pock cleaned up so I can hug him and Sea View folks can spoil him." I lifted my pack to one shoulder. "When I know you've got some kind of good plan for Chandler Perkins, I'll go home to pack.

Moz waited for me to start down the path. "I have already shared my interest in the boy. Should he be found, he will be turned over to me. Ken Douglas will meet you at your camp to make sure you are not alone with unwelcome company."

I stopped and whistled for Pock to join us, but he was busy working on his face. I walked back to leash him and gently guided him toward the path. "You're not overreacting?" I asked.

"I am if there is no threat." Moz faced me and tilted his head, waiting. "I have never inspected a crime scene that contained this kind of evidence. I also have no doubt Mr. Pruitt suffered abuse as he was the only one who had difficulty walking."

I shrugged. "You'll have to speak to Matt. I told him I trusted you. I urged him to tell you what he knows before it comes out anyway."

"I respect that you may have reached an understanding with these people, but you may not see what I see. Whatever happened here escalates the coming fight between Premier Power & Energy and the forces determined to stop the company's expansion at this site."

"What if what happened here was just Matt and just Lily?"

Moz slowly shook his head. "Matt and Lily are larger than their names. Every person has a larger shadow—something you know and use well."

I almost dropped the leash. I thought no one knew my secret—the one where I tried to imagine shadows and agendas floating in the air around someone. When I was working, I saw more than a cartoon thought bubble hanging over someone's head. I imagined a hidden self I could either expose, manipulate, or accommodate.

"I think I left my X-ray vision in Augusta—right by the State House vending machine. It has Kit Kat bars I like. I don't try to see past people's clothing much anymore."

Moz grinned at me. An actual grin with teeth showing and eyes lit with a few sparks shining out of their back depths—eyes that wanted to share the joke.

"What?" I asked. "Oh, I get it. You've been doing some X-ray vision on my shadow self. I should have figured that out by now."

The sun was sinking. Its low rays bounced off the lake, slanting heat sideways at us. If anything, the day was hotter in late afternoon, but I could still feel more heat crawl up my neck to my face.

"What about my shadow?" I asked.

In the middle of the trail to the mainland, we simply stared at each other. Pock leaned on my legs, rubbing his face on my pants, but the rest of the world around us was suddenly still. No birds. No lake sounds. No creak from the leather at the game warden's waist.

His answer surprised me. I'd hoped for something striding along, hair flowing out behind—the shape of a woman on a mission. "It is not upright," Moz said. "The head and shoulders are bent low and forward to protect the heart. It moves with great care. There may be wounds."

I had to admire his X-ray vision, but I didn't feel generous. "Great. Crippled," I snapped.

"Not crippled. Wounded."

I was tired, and I suspected that women didn't make good decisions when we were exhausted from unrelenting resistance. The resistance didn't even have to be big—just endless. It could be anything from arguing with a mechanic when we actually knew the car's transmission was about to go, or asking "what did you say?" when someone called us "little lady" after a brilliant professional moment, or even being right about eyelids.

When I'd told Evan that I could see filtered daylight with my eyes closed, he told me I was ridiculous, and I didn't know what I was talking about. "My eyes, my eyelids," I'd shouted. "They're *my* eyes. I should god-damn know."

I was tired. "Yes, Moz. Wounded sounds about right. Are you offering up—"

I couldn't get out a snarky line about first aid because his arms were around me, my head was buried in his neck, and I felt his lips in my hair. I knew there were warden belt implements making indentations on my skin, but I didn't care.

"I am perhaps offering up me," he said.

I sagged even further into him and felt tears start down my cheeks. No sobs, just tears he couldn't see. Somehow, we'd synchronized our breathing. I couldn't tell where my chest ended and his began. Despite the crisp uniform, he smelled like living plants and good weather.

I thought we both could hear approaching traffic, but neither of us moved. "Is there another way off this island?" I asked against his chest.

Moz leaned back, but he also tightened his arms. "I believe we would be gone now if we had an escape route."

I reached up inside of his arms to wipe my cheeks. "Whoever it is, I don't want them to think you made me cry. Bad press for the warden service."

He leaned down to one of my ears. "You may joke about the tears. I know humor is your way to create distance. It will not work with me."

I wasn't completely comfortable with having someone deliver such a sure diagnosis of strategies I might and might not use. "Moz, the things I appreciate about you are also the things that scare me."

"I know."

"Really? You simply don't know everything."

He dropped his arms and moved his hands to hold my face. "Then I have much to learn."

I reached up to squeeze his hands as they left my face. "Yes, you do."

# TWENTY-SIX

We could hear Chan's yells before he and Lily burst into the clearing. "Teddy's gone! Teddy's gone! He's gone!"

Despite the confusion of Chan retelling his story, Moz repeating questions as he tried to calm the boy, and Lily offering help to search for the eagle, I was most aware of Pock. Instead of running toward Chan, he shadowed every move I made, his nose next to my ankles. I needed to get the dried mud off his face, but when I tried to peel away bits around his cheeks, I heard his faint, low growl. It was gentle, but it was a warning. *Please don't touch me.* I gripped the leash to help him walk beside me.

By the time we'd reached the mainland, we knew what Chan knew. After he'd left me on the road to the Birches and returned to his truck, he'd found an empty crate, the door open and bent. He searched the roads, borrowed a canoe to paddle the shoreline in case his eagle hunted over the lake, and called and called. On his way to find me at the park, he met Lily replacing the signs she'd switched earlier in the day and drafted her to help him. Chan wanted all of us to help him search for Teddy.

Lily bent to lace her boots even tighter. "Chan thinks the bird might return to Eagle Ridge, the last place he hunted with him. He's terrified about his eagle getting chopped up in the turbines."

"I can give you three or four hours of search time," Moz said to Chan, as he lifted a travel crate from his truck and checked it for porcupine quills and anything else his last passengers had left behind. "That is the daylight we have left.

If we find him, he will go in this crate to the nearest licensed wildlife rehabilitator who will help decide his future."

Chan hopped from one booted foot to another, his new, carbon-themed shirt already stained with sweat and road grime. "I don't care. I don't care. Just find him."

Using a stick, I lifted a wet undershirt that Matt must have abandoned in the road. I tossed it onto the floor of my car. Pock needed help finding the door, but his nose guided him onto his blanket. Chan's arm, waved urgently out his truck window, only made me sad.

When we parked the two trucks, Lily's van, and my Subaru outside the Eagle Ridge project gate, I saw no security. Maybe with the project shut down, protesters dispersed, and towers locked up, no one worried about intrusion. Despite the company's jobs claims, after Dent & Dent built a site and moved on, only two or three PP&E workers rotated between different sites. The promise of plentiful local jobs was an empty promise.

The bulldozer was the only vehicle inside the gate, but someone had moved it to the edge of the lot, far away from uphill roads. Trampled protest posters were stacked outside the gate, and stained coffee cups left by last week's crowds littered roadside ditches. All manner of wildlife had enjoyed a fast food buffet. Like bits of snow, chewed burger wrappers blew up and down the road.

Chan had to know our search would fail. I couldn't see how an eagle or any free bird would want to return to captivity. The dead squirrels explained his hopeful attitude. Pulling a pile of thick red gloves and a large handful of limp squirrels from the back of his truck, Chan gave us each a glove and a squirrel.

"Lift the glove high in the air while you hold the squirrel between your thumb and the rest of your hand. Teddy knows the raised glove is his signal to return, and when he sees food, he'll land. Leave your arm out, and lean your head away. His wings have gotta be six feet wide. Plant your legs extra good on the ground. He can hit you like you're being checked by the biggest guy on a hockey team."

Lily and I looked at each other and shook our heads. Moz frowned. "You and Lily do not need to participate. What Chan suggests is dangerous for novices."

"And you're not a novice?" I asked.

"No," Moz said. "I am not."

I thought we could safely volunteer. The odds of us snagging Teddy were less than slim. We watched Moz and Chan roll an ATV off the back of the warden truck. Moz left to drive uphill to the pond where we'd cleared Chan's traps. Chan left to hike to my old campsite and the stream where Teddy ate our discarded fish. Lily and I were to walk up the project's widest roads. Raptors like to hunt roads where small creatures take big risks darting from one side to the other.

I leaned into my car to find Matt's filthy wet shirt, still snagged on the stick I'd used to handle it back at the park. I hung it on the gate where I thought he might find it.

"You can hunt squirrels anytime?" Lily asked. Clearly, she didn't want to talk about the hornet episode, and I felt the same way.

"Hunt them anytime, most anywhere," I said, slipping into on my pack and leashing Pock, who showed no enthusiasm for the squirrels we carried. That was a first. He loved squirrels no matter what they looked or smelled like. His coat was gray with mud, and he held his head at an angle, listening for the smallest sound—the way he located rodents under snow. Like a coyote or fox, he'd lean his head one way and then the other until he was sure someone tunneled beneath him. Rising on his hind legs, he'd drive his front paws deep into the snow, exploding hidden tunnels and stunning mice.

The message was clear. Pock could use his ears, but not his eyes. "Lily, I need to get my dog to a vet. He hasn't been right since the hornets. He won't let me touch his face. There's a twenty-four-hour clinic in Bangor that knows us as frequent guests. We can do this quickly. We only have to travel up one road to get a few good views."

"Maybe talk while we walk," she said, bending down to pick more plantain leaves and stuff them in her pocket. "My arms still hurt. Not as bad, but they hurt."

I led her up a side road toward tower number five as she wheezed and coughed, but she waved me on whenever I stopped to wait for her. "I'm OK. I'm OK. It sounds worse than it is," she panted.

Together we stopped and stared at a missing chunk of mountain. Acres of missing mountain. Everything that was supposed to grow there was gone, replaced by gravel bulldozed into a flat plateau. Boulders blasted from the ridge's granite spine had been tossed into heaps. Glinting in relentless sun, mica and other minerals shone from rock piles, but that was nothing compared to the glare coming from a tower looming forty stories above us.

I was used to the sight. Lily was not. "Holy shit," she said, shielding her eyes. "Back home they roll into my cow pasture, toy with the dirt a bit to get it ready, add the concrete and rebar, pop in a tower, and then hoist up the blades. Most cows don't stop chewing."

"You mean you haven't walked up here?" I asked. "Most of it isn't fenced. I thought you'd seen all this."

284

"I had some operatives sneak in for measurements and pictures, thinking I'd save myself for the protesting part. Now I know you have to stand in the middle of it and get righteously angry. Genuinely, royally, furiously, call-up-the-rage, hot and angry. This is nuts. This is totally insane."

We walked to the base of the tower, and I climbed up a short ladder to the concrete terrace that surrounded it. "We should be looking up," I said, reaching down an arm to boost her up. I had to climb back down to lift Pock, who kept trying to tug me back downhill. As I put him down, I felt all around his middle and ran my hands down his legs. No growl. Only his head was off limits.

"For Chan's sake, we should be looking up. While we do that you should tell me how you can own wind in Texas and then be here to fight it."

Lily leaned back against the tower's base, her face tilted into the last of the day's sun. "Jesus, it's almost as hot as Texas out here. What gives?" She unbuttoned her shirt to her waist and then bent over coughing. "We can start out on Texas, but I've more important things you need to know." She wrestled an inhaler out of her pocket and jammed it into her mouth.

"Texas," I said. "Then Ross Clunie and his camps."

"What's up with your dog?" she asked.

Pock was leaning off the edge of the platform, his nose lifted and busy.

"Texas," I said, moving to stand over my dog. "And then we'll go. I'll head to the vet. I don't care where you go."

"Alright. Alright. Ross Clunie saved me when I was fifteen and that's all you need to know on that—for now. Let's do Texas. Maybe then you'll be ready to hear what I need to tell you. I think you might be mad about Texas. I inherited the ranch. I make millions off leasing land to energy companies who let me graze cattle under their windmills.

"Towers and turbines don't ruin the basic Texas terrain or hurt my ranch operation. There are plenty of good places where wind power and all its paraphernalia won't destroy the terrain and the lives of people around 'em. Plenty of places where it's a good thing. It's early days, so I think we're still making mistakes. Maybe someday wildlife and tourism research will catch up to the permitting process so we don't screw up. We're not there yet, so I intend to use the millions I make in Texas to stop Maine wind, because here it destroys what's left of the woods, and it ruins people's businesses."

She cleared her throat. I recognized a speech headed my way. I'd given years of them.

"First you need to know how cows and wind power are a lot alike. I don't particularly like either of them, but I've made my peace with their existence."

Anticipating something unusual, I tied Evan's white shirt into a knot above my belly button so air could reach more of me. I used my ankles to rub Pock's sides so he'd know I was thinking of him.

"Cows and wind power are both vulnerable to weather. A freak winter storm with a hard freeze kills beef almost as they stand, and here it freezes and kills the turbines that get clotted with ice. At least until crews get to them—and there's more winter here than on my ranch. And then both cattle and wind power are products that get sent to far-away markets so they can earn top dollar. My beef goes to Japan where they'll pay anything for it. The power here gets sent to Massachusetts where it's got a guaranteed contract with a good, high price locked in."

I wondered if Lily could be bottled and poured into the water pitchers placed on legislative desks, and I wondered where Moz was. Although we were on a side road, we'd be able to hear his ATV.

Lily rasped words as she struggled for breath. "Both cows and wind are subsidized by government. My best grazing is on public land the government owns, and I'm damn lucky it has great water and abuts my ranch. Wind-power developers get millions of dollars of federal tax subsidies, and state and local governments throw more money at the process. Tons of people like steak and burger, so I think federal lands allowing grazing is a good investment. Not sure about wind."

I closed my eyes against the last of the sun. Teddy's wing span was so wide, I thought I'd recognize his shadow behind my lids. "Aren't cows a big part of greenhouse gasses?" I asked. "You know, cow gas ramping up climate change? And doesn't wind power have just the opposite reputation?"

"Well, aren't you a good little girl scout." She coughed and laughed at the same time. "The reputation word is the right word. The energy lobby launders what it wants to say through friendly think tanks and congressmen. These sources turn that propaganda into reports and sound bites that read like facts. The greenies then pass them along as green-verified facts. Yes, cows are a problem, but wind power won't solve it."

Against my better judgment, I was starting to like Lily, but then I remembered Matt and the hornets. "Speaking of facts, Lily, I think your video can't get any play. When you tortured Matt, you became the center of attention. Anything you wanted to expose couldn't compete with a man writhing around on ropes. What were you thinking?"

She sighed. "I'm not good at publicity stuff. I know I blew it. I think I'll give the show to you."

"I don't want it," I said.

Trees back down the road were developing long shadows,

my stomach complained about missing lunch, and Pock, his paws draped over the edge of the platform, leaned heavily on his leash. I put the red gloves in my pack and laid the squirrels where I thought someone hungry might find them.

As I helped Lily down the ladder she said, "To be fair—and here's something else cows and wind share—they oversell their shit. The fat lobby, that's dairy and meat people, they oversell the health values of beef. The energy lobby oversells wind's ability to get us off fossil fuels. What else is new?"

"I think Pock's onto something," I said, pulling hard against a fresh lunge that tightened his leash.

Lily wheezed and started walking, one arm through mine and one holding her inhaler. "At least it's downhill," she said. "And the dead rodent things are uphill."

Pock still wore his electronic collar. Letting him off his leash so a burst of current could remind him I mattered didn't seem like a good idea when I was also in charge of Lily. Whatever she still had to tell me, I wasn't sure she'd have the breath to do it. All I wanted to do was hoist her into her van at the front gate, where I hoped she had more inhalers, and then drag Pock to my car and head toward the vet. He had other ideas.

"What's he want down that road?" Lily asked. "Doesn't look used much."

"I think it's an old dump site," I said, checking my phone. I wanted to call and give the vet clinic a heads-up on our arrival, but there was no signal. I texted Moz a message that I was heading to Bangor and the vet. At some point our phones would find a signal and snag the messages out of thin air.

Lily wobbled toward the first ruts of the overgrown road. "Maybe it's the eagle."

Pock, his nose glued to the ground, leaned after her. "OK. OK. Just a quick look and a pee and we're out of here," I said.

Pock sniffed his way forward and then dragged me down the road with an urgency I'd never seen, his nose bouncing off rocks he couldn't see. Behind me Lily's breathing was loud and hoarse. Ahead of me, his collar digging into his neck, Pock panted loudly too. Just before the road ended, I managed to wrap the leash around a birch sapling before Pock could drag me down into an immense gravel pit.

Almost the size of a football stadium, the pit was a moonscape of steep dirt sides filled with metal and debris. Old rusted beams, shipping containers, upended trailers, and even twisted railroad trestles looked like they'd been emptied out of a child's toybox to lie neglected and jumbled on the pit's floor. Old refrigerators, freezers, air conditioners, and stoves had been added to the industrial mix. And culverts—acres of culverts tossed together as though a tornado had twisted its way through a city's water system, spitting out every round thing that drained water.

The bottom of the pit was a stagnant pool stained with rust and god knows what other poisons. It fed a red-colored stream that gurgled through piles of tires and disappeared into raspberry bushes trying to reclaim the site. Raspberries could grow anywhere.

Sometimes, bushwhacking around the woods, I came across old family dumps with beat-up wood stoves, hand-crank washers, and glass bottles empty of the cures they'd promised. It used to be standard procedure to pile rejected stuff out behind the house where anyone could find the right nut or screw to repair possessions.

This pit was different. It had a malevolence about it, as if the effort to recycle or store material in a safe location was some evil idea—as if the Maine woods was the perfect place for an industrial graveyard, and every stream and pond within miles didn't matter.

Lily caught up with me, wheezing so hard that her breath whistled out between clenched teeth. "Well, ain't this lovely. Looks like a giant middle finger pointed up at the folks who like to regulate everything." She put a hand on my arm. "It's taken me . . . long time . . . get you alone."

"I can't image what you want. I'm quite sure you don't really know me," I said.

When she inhaled a deep breath that struggled into her chest, Lily could spit out whole sentences. "Yes, I do. I'm you, but with money. I want what you want. You want what I want. I could try this by myself, but you'll do it much better."

"Assuming we both agree on what *this* or *it* might be, I'm getting tired of people appearing out of nowhere who've signed me up to do battle without my consent. It's getting weird."

Lily put her shaking hand on my arm and shuddered in another breath. "In South America on a beef-selling trip I met a crazy-looking man who wasn't really crazy. He told me he'd tricked you into helping him get wolves back into Maine a while back. He gave you a great recommendation."

"Oh, my God! Is there some misfit, underground grapevine sharing my name around for projects no one else will touch?"

She smiled. "Kind of."

I scowled at her. Pock cocked his head one way and then the other, listening. Then he leaped up, drove his paws down on the ground, and snapped his leash. He was in the bottom of the pit before I had time to reach into my pocket and push the recall button. I had visions of him getting ripped open by every jagged piece of debris he couldn't see. Running with his nose close to the ground, he followed a straight, open trail to the largest culvert. As he disappeared, I saw his white flashing light blink into culvert darkness. I'd activated his blinking light instead of his return-to-me button.

"Stay here," I told Lily as I slid down loose sand toward the culverts, my feet riding waves of collapsing gravel pit wall.

"God-damn," I heard her yell. "Just like skiing. I can do this!"

We slid to a stop near a culvert surrounded with scrubby trees and junk piled around it. Pock's faint light winked deep inside.

"It's big enough," coughed Lily. "Got four feet of crawl space."

"Hang on. Hang on." I turned around. "It's been cleared so it's easy to get into it." Railroad ties lined a clear path that narrowed near the culvert. More heavy ties were tossed haphazardly on top and heaped up against the sides. In the heat, the smell of creosote off the treated wood burned my nose as if I'd shoved too much Vicks VapoRub up it.

Inside, something banged against the side of the culvert. Lily tried to talk, but I raised my hand. "I know. I know. Either my dog's in trouble or he's met up with something in there."

I bent, reached inside the lip of the culvert, and picked up three white feathers. Reaching into my pocket I pulled out my own eagle feather. "Teddy," I said. "Teddy's in there."

"No shit," Lily wheezed.

"Nothing's right about this." I pulled out Pock's collar control and pressed the recall button. I heard his toenails scratch on the culvert, but as soon as he saw me, he turned and ran back inside. His blinking light retreated until it was a faint blip. Three times I recalled him, and three times he trotted to the entrance and then retreated. Each time he disappeared, the banging started up again.

Lily had stopped using sentences. "Looks OK. What. Going. On?"

"He wants me to come in with him. He's asking for help." I tucked in my shirt and rolled its sleeves down to button the cuffs. "Now you really must stay, Lily. None of this feels right. Stay and keep watch. Use more of that inhaler."

Bent double with coughing, she nodded and wheezed, "No one. Around."

I gave her my phone. "Get out to a signal and use the phone if you hear anyone coming, or if I somehow get trapped. You know how to use one, right?" I asked.

She frowned. "Antique," she said. "Will buy you. New. Later."

"Focus," I said bending over to step inside. Small shafts of light filtered through rusted slits above me, and beetles skittered away as I lumbered forward, grateful I'd added squats to my stretch-on-the-dock routine. Tiny things skittered over my bare toes. The slower ones got crunched under my shoes. "Right. Sandals are perfect for this," I whispered.

It was like walking on M&M's, except there was no redeeming release of chocolate odor. The culvert's air reminded me of my parents' cellar, where cans of paint, insecticides, weed killer, and other tainted products slowly corroded into the concrete floor until the air was so vile, we held our breath the entire time we sat on the basement toilet.

I could feel the chemical sting at the back of my nose. Swallowing only delivered the burn to my throat. Not trusting the gloom ahead, I slipped off my pack, took out my headlamp, and shifted the pack to one shoulder.

However hot it was outside, the culvert's heat was like a sauna on steroids. Forget the fires of hell, I thought, bending lower when my head scraped the ceiling and rust rained down on my neck and fell inside my shirt. Hell is an abandoned culvert in a heat wave. I slammed my hand against my chest to kill whatever was crawling toward my bra.

"Pock?" I called. Ahead of me his named echoed back, each version growing fainter. "Po-ck. Po-ck. Po-ck."

Behind me a loud crash set off another echo that seemed to race past me into the tunnel ahead. Pock came out of the dark and bounced off me, crashing us both to the floor. "It's me!" I yelled. "It's me." Whimpering, he crawled into my arms and would have crawled into my clothes if they weren't already glued to my body with sweat and fear.

"It's me. It's me. Shhhhhhh." My dog hates loud noises and I agreed. Hearing a loud noise from the culvert entrance was the worst noise I could think of. "Let's just breathe," I said, stroking him. "In. Out. That's good."

"Shine light," Lily called. "Can't see." The battery on Pock's collar gave a ping and died. I had the only light, and I aimed my head in her direction so she could find us. As she crawled slowly toward us, her tortured breath bounced off the culvert walls. It sounded like the metal itself was hyperventilating. *More hell*, I thought.

"You. Won't. Believe," she said dropping down beside us and taking her time to cough out each word.

"Try me."

"Logs, alive. Rolling. At me." She took a deep shuddering breath and blew it out as a sentence. "Only way out was in."

I thought she'd perfectly summed our predicament. The only way out was in.

"Let's go," I said. "Stay low. Try to crouch and not crawl. There's rust and creepy crawlies overhead and below."

"You don't want. Know more?"

"Did you have anything to do with the guy in the tent? The one that got cut up?"

"No."

293

"Do you have my phone?"

"No. Dropped."

"Was there any daylight left behind you when you called out to me?"

"No."

"I don't need to know more. Let's go find Teddy."

# TWENTY-SEVEN

As we moved, Lily crawling while I crouched and staggered, my light played off rivets that connected two different culverts into one long tunnel. The rivets were shiny and new. The culverts were not. We found Teddy at the end of the third culvert. He was in a large cage that once must have hosted a gigantic parrot. The cage had rounded ornate sides welded into a floor filled with bright green feathers. Each time Teddy flew himself against its bars, some of his feathers drifted down to the green floor.

Coming out of the dark with bent shapes and a shaft of light that bounced ahead of us, we must have seemed like a nightmare. Quickly I pulled off my headlamp and held it over our heads. "Just us, Teddy. Your friend, Pock. Chan's friend, Patton. And your new friend Lily Rose Baines Johnson."

He squawked and pressed himself against the back of the cage. *Keep back.*

*OK. We can do that.*

*Where's my boy?*

*He's looking for you.*

*I want my boy.*

*Well, we all do, I think. If he's on the outside, that's where we all want to be.*

"What. Doing?" rasped Lilly.

"Shhhhh. The bird and I are thinking," I said.

Teddy cocked his head. *She's very loud.*

*She is, but I think she's in trouble, too.*

*Can you get me out?*

*You'd just fly into another wall. Let me work on it.*

"Pock," I said, "you seem to get along with Teddy. Lie

295

down over here." He bumped into culvert walls until he found my hand and dropped down in front of the cage. I found his head and rubbed it enough to know his eyes were watering. Dog tears had made tiny rivers, washing away some of the mud under his eyes. "Good boy," I whispered. "Soon, it's the vet. Remember, he's open all night. We'll get there."

I swept my light around to see where we'd landed. Dozens and dozens of barrels and cans were stacked near the end of the culvert where a dirt wall loomed brown and solid in my headlamp's beam.

Lily had crawled to lean on a large white can marked with an outdated skull and cross bones logo, but there were newer containers with luminescent yellow squares and biohazard symbols. I didn't bother to read the fine print still visible on some of them. We'd been stashed out of the way with other problematic items.

Lily wasn't coughing. She was chewing. "Here," she whispered. "Take. For Dog." She transferred a fistful of green, slimy plantain from her hand into mine. I squeezed saliva out of the wet leaves, mashed them into a thick paste, and smeared the mess over Pock's eyes. "Thanks, Lily," I said.

"We trapped?" she asked.

"For now," I said.

I really did think we'd escape until I heard the growl of a very large engine outside the culvert walls. The sound of something large stopping, backing up, and then advancing was repeated over and over again. What sounded like heavy rain was not rain. Through a thousand rusted slits, dirt and gravel bits rained down on us. I grabbed the bird cage and dragged it back into the second culvert, almost tripping over Pock who seemed glued to my legs.

"Lily" I yelled. "Follow my light back out here."

She didn't move. Hands over my head to ward off falling dirt and keep my headlamp useful, I scrambled back, bent over, and grabbed her hands. They were strangely chilly. "Move now, Lily. Someone's trying to bury us. We have to move."

She moaned and raised her arms. I slipped my hands into her armpits and dragged her backwards into the first culvert where Pock trembled by Teddy's cage. I looked at my team. Not much to work with. I thought at some point I could rely on Pock, but not until the racket overhead stopped. Each time something hard banged against the far culvert's walls, he flinched but stayed by Teddy's cage rubbing his eyes on its bars.

I slipped off my pack and dug around until I found the two diving masks Moz had left in my care. I put one around Lily's head so her eyes were protected and forced one up over Pock's jaw until I could position the mask over his eyes. "Stay," I said, pressing his paws to the culvert floor. "I mean your paws. Have them stay down."

Teddy fluttered to the edge of his cage and stuck his beak through the bars. In my headlight beam, it was even yellower than the barrels' hazard labels. *Let me out.*

*Nowhere to go, Teddy.*

*There's air. I can feel moving air.*

*I can feel it too, but I think there's a plan to bury this culvert when someone's done with the one we just crawled out of.*

*Who do they want to kill?*

*Good question. You're too young to have enemies, and everyone loves Pock. Lily rubs people the wrong way and she's got money that could scare people who recognize her agenda. I've upset lots of folks who want to mow down the natural world, but recently I thought I'd lowered my profile. Maybe not.*

297

*The boy brings me treats. You have any?*

I reached in my pack and my hand brushed across items I recognized. I still had the wire cutters, flares, compass, duct tape, and map I'd taken from the crime scene van. I felt the jagged edge of the old window scraper. I pulled out the first aid kit and tucked it into my waist band, and then moved on to the dog biscuits and chocolate. I broke one biscuit in two and gave half to each animal.

Pock, panting heavily, inhaled his and the tip of his tail wagged. I felt a tiny jolt of happiness. Teddy spit out his biscuit. *Not meat.*

*Don't tell the dog that.*

I crawled toward Lily, holding up one hand that was dark with melted chocolate. I slid to the floor until I could look directly into her face. I slipped off her mask. "You think you could suck a bit of chocolate? Might revive you. I've got water, too."

She moaned but opened her eyes. A headlamp makes ghosts of each person it illuminates. Lily was whiter than a ghost.

"Can't. Revive," she said.

Rolling on my back I rifled through my first aid kit but could find nothing to counteract an asthma attack unless her throat closed up and she passed out. On ski patrol I'd always prayed successfully for the ambulance to arrive before I had to insert an artificial airway, but I knew how to do it.

"What do you mean can't revive?" I asked.

"Not. Asthma."

The air was so thick with dust blowing in from the far culvert that I could barely see Teddy and Pock a few feet away. Teddy had his head tucked under his wings and Pock, the dive mask enlarging his eyes, simply stared off into the darkest part of our tunnel. When I blew my nose onto my sleeve, black, grainy goop trickled out.

Lily waved one hand into the swirling dust. It parted like thick cocoa. "This will do it," she whispered.

"Do what?"

"End it."

There it was. What Lily had to tell me. Not all she wanted to tell me, but it was the heart of it. It took her almost half a minute to explain. "End. Stage. Pulmonary. Fib—fib—"

I reached for her hand, held it up against my chest, and knew she'd been sentenced to death. "OK. I know. I understand. Fibrosis. Pulmonary fibrosis."

Lily pulled me close to her lips. "Was hoping. For quick end. This. Good."

"Not sure of that, Lily," I said.

"You. Will. Get. Out. Know you." Coughing shook her whole body.

"Will gum help?" I asked. I didn't wait but pulled out a pack, wiped her lips with a chocolate stained finger and placed a piece inside her cheek. With a small smile, she chewed and her coughing eased. "I always use gum for dust," I said. "Essential for roads up here."

She smiled again and whispered, "Pocket."

I didn't want to let go of her hand, but she pushed it against my chest. I reached down to her pants and fumbled around until I pulled out a lumpy envelope.

"Spoon," Lily whispered. "Read later. Spoon me now."

I crawled over to Pock and Teddy and pulled the cage with one hand and Pock's collar with the other until we were all together. I'd been so busy listening to Lily that I hadn't paid much attention to the far culvert, but the silence was loud. Unbearably loud. The air was still filled with boiling dirt, but the machine noise was gone. All I could hear was Teddy clicking his beak against the cage, Pock licking his paws, and Lily's shallow, irregular breathing.

"Spoon," she said.

I crawled around behind her and wrapped my arms around her body. I'd spooned with a few men, most often waiting until they fell asleep so I could slip away and claim my share of the bed. I liked a lot of space. This was the first time I'd ever wanted to press my body deeply into the shape of someone else's body—the first time curving myself to fit someone else seemed utterly essential. I turned off my headlamp and fit myself into the sideways curve of her, pressing one arm up over her shoulder.

"Thank you," she whispered.

I tried to synchronize our breathing, but she started to rasp short breaths followed by longer and longer pauses. I tucked my chin into her back and breathed through the fabric of her damp shirt. It seemed like hours we lay together. Even in the oven-like heat of the culvert, her cooling body cooled mine. I knew what was coming, but when she raised herself on one elbow, I was surprised to feel her back muscles tighten and hear her voice.

"Shut it down. Shut it god-damn down."

She collapsed back into my arms. The pauses between short breaths grew longer and longer. I felt Pock lift his head onto my leg. It was just what I needed to remind me that the rest of us were living because Lily was dead in my arms. I waited minutes after her last breath while her body relaxed in a way that no sleeper's body ever relaxes. Her neck muscles sagged too low. Her shoulders slowly shrank beneath my touch. Somehow, she got heavier and lighter at the same time. I finally understood the simple phrase people used to describe death. She's gone.

Slowly I removed my arms, rolled over on my back, and lifted Pock's head to my stomach where I could remove his mask and rub his ears. I didn't feel like crying. I felt hollow. I'd never been this hot, this dirty, and despite my best friend Pock and the eagle, I felt terribly alone. Maybe having someone die in one's arms did that to people.

Teddy squawked and flew up to his perch as the largest spider I've ever seen dropped down to swing on one slender thread right before my eyes. Her deep brown body glistened with clear drops of water. I wondered if she was surprised to see us. I could have used a surprise visit, but if Moz found my message, he'd think I'd gone to Bangor.

The spider lowered herself until she was level with my nose and crossed and re-crossed her legs energetically.

I blew out a small breath and the thin rope swayed. *You have some spider wisdom? I could use some help here.*

*I came from the outside.*

*It's raining?*

She rubbed her legs even harder. *Big rain. Gone now.*

I tilted my head toward the culvert's cracked ceiling. *I think it's early, but it's getting light.*

She pulled herself up a few inches. *Better get a move on.*

*Oh, right.*

*I spin webs over all the holes. There are many, many holes in the rust. Better get a move on.*

Pock's patience with watching the spider ended, and he gathered himself for a leap. My dog loved everything that moved, especially bugs. I held his collar. "We need to thank this creature, and after all, she's not a bug. Spiders aren't bugs. See? Two body parts. Eight legs."

When I looked up the spider was scuttling away into the first culvert. I crouched upright, replaced the batteries in my headlamp, and swept its beam over the ground around us looking for more signs of tiny life.

Pock and I jumped when Teddy screamed, but I was the only one slammed back down by the culvert's ceiling. I didn't know eagles could scream, but pressed against the far edge of his cage, Teddy screamed. He fluttered against the bars, eyes narrow slices of rage.

"Alright Teddy, I'm coming." I bent even lower, lighting up a trail of dead birds and bird parts. A dead sharp-shinned hawk. A dead red-tailed hawk. More dead birds had to be in the jumble of wings and bones cooked dry by the culvert's heat. Teddy's cage must have rested on them, and when I'd dragged the cage, I'd also dragged the birds' remains. Apparently, the culvert dump was used for dumping all kinds of problems someone wanted to hide.

I was just as angry as Teddy, but all I could do was yell, "Oh, stupid people, come on!" It echoed back as "on, on, on, on."

"Right," I said, "I'm on it." I moved Lily away from the bird parts and used a foil emergency blanket from my first aid kit to cover her body. I shoved her envelope deep into my deepest pocket along with a few feathers I scooped up from the floor. *Got it, Lily. We'll be back for you, but right now I'm on it.*

"Pock," I said, "now we really have to get out. There's a lot to do." I considered my pack's contents. I had wire cutters, three flares, a compass, a map, a windshield scraper, the two dive masks, duct tape, and a first aid kit. I drank half my water bottle and poured the rest into my hands for Pock. Slipping one dive mask over his eyes and the other over my eyes. I dragged Teddy's huge cage over to Lily and covered him with a corner of the foil blanket.

It took hours to find the most rusted side of the culvert and scrape it thin. Using the wire cutters, I cut a hole I hoped was big enough for escape. I looked at my team. The cage was too big for the hole, and Pock, with all four legs dangling, was also too big for the hole. I thought I could squeeze out, but my hips might lose skin. I could have made a bigger hole, but the bulldozer's silence was also a threat. How much time did we have before its driver returned?

I wasn't going to leave Pock, so after I padded the jagged edges of the hole with duct tape, I lifted one flare out through the opening. If I ignited it, either help would come or the bulldozer operator would be scared off. Pock whined and bumped up against me. *Slow down,* I thought. *Slow down.* I pulled the flare back inside the culvert and read the directions. Even one flare was suicide. A stray spark falling near the stored cans would bring every hazmat team and fire department from multiple counties, but we'd be ash.

Pock needed a vet. I wanted to hear Kate relive her hearing testimony. Chan probably needed adult supervision. Teddy needed a future. I had overdue library books. I tried to swallow, but my throat felt thick. I was pretty sure Moz wanted to see where our unfinished hug would go. I wanted that, too, so I swallowed anyway and thought about other options.

I leaned out of the hole and aimed the metal back of the compass so it reflected the rising sun. I'd never sent an SOS message, but it seemed logical that alternating three short and three long exposures would work if anyone looked down into the gravel pit. I added lots of yelling to my compass work until the sun disappeared behind clouds stacking themselves on top of each other. The breeze from a new direction turned leaves below me onto their backsides. My top half felt cool while my bottom half still fried in the culvert. The heat was gone.

Bouncing up and down through the air like they were riding little roller coasters, chickadees swarmed into the poplars trying to grow up around the culvert. *What's up? What's up?*

*Where'd you come from?*

*All over. Flashing and noise. Noise and flashing we cannot resist. What's up?*

*Seen any people?*

They bounced from limb to limb, trying to outdo each other with shrill chick-a-dee-dee calls. *What is people?*

*Two legged ones that look like me.*

*You're it. None near. Going back to trees now.*

Like a school of frightened fish, they lifted into the air and peeled away toward the tops of distant pines. I pulled my head back inside the culvert.

"There's no good way to do this," I said, dragging the cage to the hole. "The eagle's going out free, and you, Pock, are not." Lifting the cage to the hole I slowly started to open the door. "Teddy, I have no idea what life will hand you next, but stay away from the tall things on the hill. They aren't trees, and Chan loves you. Remember that."

The eagle was busy forcing his beak between the opening door and the cage bars. He fell into the trees before hopping to the ground and preening a few feathers into place. Running and flapping, he took off before he could hit anything, losing and regaining elevation a few times before he disappeared.

I looked at Pock. "Sometimes I guess there's nothing left to say. Now it's your turn. Down, boy. Down." I was hoping for centuries of innate dog trust as I folded his legs close to his body and wrapped the leash around his body until he looked bound and mummified. "Ass end first," I said.

It wasn't pretty but wrapped into a more cylindrical

package, Pock went out the hole. His muzzle was the last canine item to exit, and I kissed it as I lowered him to the ground. I tossed my pack and headlamp out after him and greased my mid-section with peanut butter from a snack tube stashed deep in my pack. It was like hot, liquid oil. I squeezed out of the hole sure I'd either burnt off skin or permanently dented my thighs.

As I landed, I felt the envelope in my pocket bend into an unnatural shape. I rolled over and up onto my knees and found I was staring at black boots.

"I would be happy to untie Pock if you like," said Moz. "Unless you also need help getting up."

# TWENTY-EIGHT

Untied, Pock hobbled around stiffly, wetting the culvert in what looked like dog revenge. He wasn't bumping into as many obstacles, but his head was cocked at an unnatural angle.

Moz squatted before me and looked around. "Lily?" he asked.

"She died." I pointed. "In there. With me. I mean I held her until she went." My voice started to break. "I can explain most everything, except who put us in there, but not now. I need to get out of here."

Drawn together with worry, his eyebrows threatened anger. "Are you able to stand?"

I nodded but didn't move. PP&E's bulldozer, its shovel filled with dirt, was parked up against the far culvert. Long cables snaked from it down the length of the connected pipes to the blocked entrance. There, every cable was wrapped around a railroad tie. Just a twitch of the dozer's controls had reorganized them to seal us in and prevent escape.

The eagle's scent might have lured my dog to the dump, but the trap that caught us was set with my best friend. I'd seen wood suspiciously stacked around the culvert's entrance, but the bait inside—Pock—was too urgent to ignore.

I took a ragged breath, inhaling the past week's lessons. Bait always appeared as something strongly desired. Traps set so we ignored danger—even when we should know better. Pock lunged into Chan's bear trap without taking time to notice and react to an unfamiliar human scent. Bait probably seduced one of the angry pine marten's youngsters into ignoring the box contraption that didn't belong in a familiar tree.

Bait could be anything. Even pollution-free electricity was so tempting, people who should have seen the forest didn't see it at all. Perhaps all they saw were humming power lines snaking toward fuse boxes far away. I kicked at a few cables.

Moz studied the silent machine. "Someone did not complete the intended work."

Severe understatement was probably a useful law enforcement tool. Victims of something traumatic could be put at ease, and whatever needed investigating wouldn't be tainted with guesswork, but I wasn't the law.

"Intended work?" I sputtered. "Intended work? Someone tried to kill us! I mean Lily turned out to be a very sick woman, but the dirt and dust that got inside finished her off."

Moz lifted me so swiftly off the ground that my feet hung in the air before he set me down. His arms lingered until I sneezed out more of the culvert's grime. Reaching into his uniform pocket, he pulled out a clean handkerchief. I rubbed it over every surface I could reach, including Pock's face and eyes. I tried to return it, but he waved away what had become a black cloth stained with leaf bits.

My words gushed out. "It was hotter than hell. There were bugs. It was loud. The engine noise got louder. More dirt got dumped on us. Had to inhale dirt with air. And then—and then—it got quiet. Someone wanted us dead, but then it was so quiet."

Moz called Pock and leashed him to the nearest bush. Walking slowly to the bulldozer, his back stiff with what looked like barely restrained rage, he nudged pebbles with his boots and stooped to pick up items he added to plastic bags pulled from his pockets. I started toward him, but he raised both hands to stop me.

"How'd you find us?" I called.

He called out but didn't turn from the bulldozer. "Your chickadees. They sounded like a large posse of birds who had located something exciting. Their noise directed me to the pit after I found the road."

"Really? Birds? That just makes my day." I vowed to make sure my feeders never went empty again. "But what took you so long?"

His pockets bulging with bags, he came to stand by me, shouldering my pack and untying Pock. "Yesterday, near dark, I was at the top of the ridge when my phone found a signal and texts from you and Chan. Chan said he would continue searching. He has night eyes, so I was not concerned. Your message said you would take Pock to Bangor. I traveled down the backside of the ridge to Ross Clunie's camps as someone may have seen the eagle. Fish remains left on shore may have lured him. Ross fed me dinner—"

I started walking quickly toward the edge of the pit. "You were eating while we were getting buried?"

Moz easily caught up with me. "That timing sounds accurate."

"I don't want to bring up your extensive search and rescue expertise, but what happened to it?"

He reached for my elbow and guided me away from small streams running red with rust. "Rain happened. It cleared the parking lot of tracks. Your parked vehicles warned me that I must search. On the old road I found deeper marks where someone had staggered more than walked."

"That had to be Lily," I said.

"I did arrive in time to see the eagle fly from the culvert and the backside of Pock being shoved out after the bird."

"I don't think I shoved," I said.

"You did, and it was a fine strategy. Even if I had not

309

tracked you to the dump, you would have survived. I am sorry about Lily Johnson. I liked her spirit—not in ways I may officially admit, but in ways that appreciate resistance against what should be resisted." He bent toward me and inhaled. "Was the peanut butter for the birds or was it your only available food?"

Holding my hand, he helped me up the pit's slippery sides and held it all the way back to his truck. My freshly washed clothes sat on the passenger seat. "The crime lab does laundry?" I asked.

"If we request it."

We stood in the project parking lot staring at each other.

"Require assistance?" Moz asked.

"With what?" I asked. "Clearing my name from the cut-up man's fate when his tent was covered with my words? Making sure the corporate forces of darkness don't derail Kate's career because she made a good case against them? Getting Pock to the vet after Lily weaponized hornets to pursue her attack on PP&E? Finding my house guest and his eagle before one of them encounters a spinning blade? Not getting fired for finding someone lying cut up in the road?"

I started pacing. "Maybe—just maybe—you could help figure out who wanted Lily or me dead at the dump site. Good Christ! Maybe it was both of us."

He smiled, but it was only a slight twitch upward of his lips. "I was going to ask about helping you change. There is blood on your pants. I thought perhaps you might be in shock. From your extensive list I see that you are yourself again." He reached into his truck and handed me my clean clothes. "I believe there's a washing station in the porta potty. I will feed Pock, assuming your car continues to have emergency supplies."

I tossed him my keys and he walked away toward my best friend who was already exploring the tires of Lily's van, Chan's truck, and my car—none of which had moved since we'd all gone off to search for the eagle. Pulling plastic bags from his pockets, the game warden lifted his phone to his ear.

*Right, feed the dog. My ass. He's calling the entire uniformed posse. You there, Lily? Out there somewhere? I can shut this all down faster than he can. Hear that, Lily?* I turned toward the porta potty.

I didn't make it in the toilet door because Chan sprinted into the parking lot aiming himself at us. "I need help. I mean Teddy needs help. Quick! Quick!" He turned and ran in the direction of the stream where I'd pitched my tent. Dropping my clean clothes, I was only a few steps behind Moz, but Pock raced past all of us.

By the stream Chan stood with his arms out so we wouldn't stumble on Teddy and Ridge Dumais. Half of the struggling man was under an overturned ATV. The rest of him was under the eagle. Teddy sat on the back of Ridge's head, wings fluttering madly and a red ball cap in his beak. His talons were so deep in the man's neck, I could only see the tops of yellow eagle feet dance on skin when he repositioned his claws for deeper penetration.

"Control Pock," Moz whispered, but it was too late. On his belly, Pock crawled forward to lie under Teddy's bobbing head. He whined softly. Clutching the hat, the eagle squawked back. The conversation veered back and forth between the two animals while Ridge used his arms to flail at Teddy's wings.

"Don't fight it, Ridge," I called. "Try and breathe as slowly as you can. Relax every part of your body. Play dead."

Ridge paused, his arms in the air.

"This is Patton out here, Ridge. You can believe me on this

one. Best to believe me."

He lowered his arms and slowly went limp.

Chan seemed frozen until Moz reached out an arm to pull him back. "We need to calm this scene," he said, keeping one hand on the boy.

Chan started to object. "Chan," I said, my voice very low. "Right now, Ridge looks like he's moving all the body parts we can see. If even one of the eagle's talons finds the man's spinal cord, that's game over for both of them. You have a red glove?"

He nodded.

"Good. Walk slowly to the far end of the clearing where Teddy can see you, put it on, and raise your arm just like you told us to do."

Moz released Chan's arm. "If you have another dead squirrel, now would be a good time to advertise it."

The drama ended quickly. Chan raised the glove and sang something that snapped the eagle's fierce eyes toward the boy. Then Teddy dropped the hat into Pock's open mouth and the eagle struggled to extract his talons. Ridge did such a good job of playing dead that his head flopped loosely on the grass. After the bird landed on the boy's red glove and picked at the squirrel, Chan slipped a hood over the eagle's eyes and all was quiet. Too quiet. Ridge was unconscious.

We rolled the machine off him, and Moz knelt at his side, fingers on the pulse at his neck. Chan, Teddy, and Pock were quarantined on a large rock by the stream. Planning my next moves, I walked back and forth between the two groups, grateful everyone was breathing normally, but hopeful they would all simply disappear.

The ATV trail Ridge had mashed down to motor to the stream proved useful. An ambulance crew easily trotted in and then carefully walked out, flanked by two game wardens who arrived to huddle with Moz and then help with the stretcher.

We stood and watched the men disappear. "What did you and the boys discuss while the paramedics were packaging Ridge?" I asked. "And what did you pull out of the ATV to give them?"

"Our friendship does not mean that I can share an investigation," Moz said.

I'd expected that answer and shoved my elbow into his side. "But if it's a very good friendship—a very, very good one— you'd want to ease my mind."

He scowled. "You are *very* good."

"I am that," I said.

He pulled a plastic bag from his pocket. "I found these on the floor mats of the bulldozer."

It looked like Matt Pruitt's white undershirt had been shredded into tiny flakes. "It was Matt? That's bits of his shirt. It was Matt?"

I turned away so I could think without Moz's eyes on me. Apparently, the old days of Soap the river guide were long gone. As off-duty guides we often flirted with the lawless side of acceptable behavior. We paddled flooded rivers local sheriffs had closed. Lying on soft sand, we slept soundly under No Trespassing signs. Sometimes bandages got removed from first aid kits so cocaine, magic mushrooms, or hash could bed down with the tweezers. We lived within a risk-taking, permissive culture, that at the same time, did not forgive reckless, selfish behavior with paying guests.

Our work had practical and ethical boundaries. A happy guest who tipped us well was a guest who'd been surrounded with the best safety practices and stories we could offer. We picked up river litter, buried toilet sites left by ignorant campers, and cheerfully rescued hundreds of people who should have paddled a lake before trying swift current. When a river was at risk, we car pooled to hearings and wrote letters and convinced attorneys on our trips to roll up their sleeves and get involved.

The guide community was the most ethical group of people I'd ever met, but I had to face facts. If Matt could cut up someone with a bulldozer in one location, he could certainly use that machine to bury us at another location. His mutterings about wanting to create a mess at the site and save his job made no sense, but then burying us to stop opposition to the project wasn't smart either. Other warriors determined to save the woods would step up—or at least I hoped they would.

I turned. "You should know something about Matt. He—"

Moz held up his hands and the baggie of shirt bits to stop me. "We found what looks to be the rest of this shirt in Ridge's ATV. I should have said whoever used the bulldozer at the dump site was careful to leave incriminating material where it would be found. If the shirt is Matt Pruitt's, I believe Ridge Dumais intended to implicate him."

Ridge. Ridge Dumais. I put both hands over my face and felt my mouth open wide under them. Ridge and I had a history of sparring with each other, but I never considered us enemies. Mostly it felt like we yelled at each other from opposite sides of a forest. He'd essentially yell, "We can cut any god-damn way we want. It's not your land. Not your trees. Nothing growing here belongs to you."

I'd essentially yell back, "We own what's tangled up with your dirt and trees. We own the wildlife, rivers, most streams, lots of lakes. If you lay waste to the forest, you mangle or destroy what we own."

There were plenty of times we could grin at each other—

kind of shake our heads and accept our respective scrappy selves anyway.

"Was he after Lily or after me?" I asked, dropping my arms. My legs felt shaky, but I thought if I sat down, I wouldn't get up for days. Maybe weeks.

Moz lifted his hands and spread them wide.

"OK. So no clue on that, but why did he stop burying us? I mean I'm grateful, but why would he stop when he had us trapped?"

Out in the pool a fish jumped. I watched ripples spread out until they disappeared. Under the surface in that cool, green world, fish were hunting. Crayfish and amphibians and other bugs were also hunting and killing. Even water spiders jumping in spasms across the surface were hunting. Maybe every smooth veneer hid mayhem.

"I think what Wardens Adams and Kane have carried away contains answers to your questions, Patton. We need to wait for what they may discover," Moz said.

"But why would Ridge try and frame Matt?" I asked.

He bent his lips to my ear and left them there longer than he needed to speak low to me. "Again, what Adams and Kane are taking away should explain Ridge's choices and actions."

I leaned into him. "And the dead man with my underwear and papers?"

"That as well."

"And the giant wave?"

He leaned away and frowned. "The company operating the dam has not been cooperative. Because no one was hurt, no property damaged, and an upstream siren warning was used, we may never know about the wave."

I reached up and lifted his hair away from his forehead, smoothing out deep lines between his eyebrows. "I'm OK. It might take a bit of time, but I'm OK. Or I'll be OK. I'm not sure about the boy and his eagle."

Teddy, hood over his eyes and dried blood dark on his talons, was perched on Chan's knee. Under one of the boy's shaking hands, the bird rocked back and forth, dipping his beak low to ruffle hair behind Pock's ears. Whatever had happened in the barn when they'd been shut in together, the eagle and dog had an impressive interspecies relationship. The eagle groomed my dog. My dog bent his head to enjoy it.

I wondered if a relationship with Moz would also be a kind of interspecies experiment. We were so very different. I watched him bag Ridge's hat and hoped no one blamed the eagle for assuming any red thing meant food. Chan walked slowly to the center of the clearing, his arm supporting the eagle, his fingers tight around rawhide thongs attached to Teddy's feet.

"Can you talk?" asked Moz.

With red-rimmed eyes the boy looked at me and shook his head.

"Maybe you can explain what's next, Warden Atkins," I said.

Moz crossed his arms, but his voice was soft. Maybe it was a voice he'd used with his own boys when they'd crossed some line. It was a good mixture of the law and someone who understood genuine pain. "You and I will put the eagle in my carrying crate and take him to Avian Haven. People there are expert at raptor rehabilitation and they are very fond of eagles. There, you will need to say good-bye to him. Your hatching him from an egg and raising him is an unusual circumstance. Avian Haven's staff will be excited and want to know how you accomplished such a feat. I will not hurry you once we are there."

He reached down to smooth one of the bird's wings. "My department may want to charge you for violating wildlife regulations, but I believe, Chandler, that if you enter training to become a falconer apprentice that you will be forgiven. I have an uncle who is willing to help you."

Chan looked up and raised his arm. Teddy fluttered and settled back on the glove.

Moz bent until his eyes were level with Chan's. "You now know that an eagle is a powerful bird and even a danger to people if it has been raised from birth by someone—if it is deeply imprinted on a human. I will not protect you from what you should know. I believe the best outcome for you and for the eagle is that Avian Haven equips him for a life in the wild."

Tears dripped down Chan's cheeks. "They'll teach him to be scared of people?"

I reached up to put a hand on his shoulder. I was still shorter than he was. "When rehabilitators believe an animal can safely be returned to the wild, they teach that animal to avoid people. It's not brutal. They help animals without breaking their spirit," I said. "Perhaps later on the warden will return you to Antler Camp until we sort out your family situation. I'd like that. Pock would like that. Would you like that?"

Chan nodded, and with my dog trotting by his side, he led the way out of the clearing. I didn't move. "I need some time alone, Moz," I called. "I need to sit by the stream and breathe. When Pock realizes I'm not with you, he'll come back. Catch up with you later?"

Together, the warden half of Moz and his other Penobscot half looked slowly around the clearing inspecting every tree and blade of grass. Neither one of them trusted me, but they left together without speaking.

It was a shame to waste such a perfect day on revenge. No vicious heat. No brutal humidity. Blue skies so sharp they made the green woods around me look washed out and slightly artificial.

By the time Pock trotted back to me, I'd put on medical gloves from my first aid kit and almost uncovered our hidden stash. He helped me drag away tree limbs and brush I'd used for concealment. He sat, head cocked, as I pulled plastic baggies of limp bats, rare warblers, silent thrushes, and dozens of their migrating cousins out of a large, plastic tub.

Pock had seen them all before. On our nightly walks outside PP&E's official search perimeter, I'd removed his muzzle. He'd carried their bodies gently in his slightly open mouth. I had no real plans about what to do with my collection. It seemed important to remember their small lives, how hunting bats sliced through night air—how migrating birds answered messages humming in their blood.

Watching from the edge of the woods, my hand tight on Pock's leash, I waited until every official vehicle had left the Eagle Ridge Project parking lot. The last was a crime scene van driven slowly up the road from the dump site. Lily had to be inside it. Outside the fence, the driver left a new padlock on the gate and stepped over to peer inside Lily's van and my car before he drove away.

We took twelve trips from the stream to the dump. I rigged my pack to hang off Pock's back, and I used garbage bags I found in the porta potties. By the time dusk shadowed the road and slowed our marches to careful steps, Pock and I had transported three hundred and thirty-five birds, ninety-two bats, and I'd found my phone where Lily had dropped it.

As I slid small bodies out of plastic bags and gently pushed them into dark culverts, I smoothed wings and tucked legs neatly under each creature. I didn't know all their names, but I looked into each animal's sightless eyes, gone black without light and wind. I touched hundreds of faded colors that spoke to me of gender or camouflage or maybe just the pride of plumage, but in death, all their eyes were black.

Resting, Pock and I sat at the top of the pit and watched night fall on it. Red lights from some of the highest wind towers strobed across the dump's debris like garish neon signs. I drank the last of my water and shared granola bars with Pock. Chocolate chips didn't seem to bother his canine system at all.

I smiled thinking about the reasons Moz kept the winter moose yard a secret. Remote locations certainly did seduce people into criminal behavior. "Guess what?" I asked Pock. "I might have broken more wildlife laws today than Chan has. Maybe having good intentions will mean something if we get caught." He licked feathers off my hands and wagged.

Then I talked to someone I hoped could hear. "I think you'll agree, Lily. Premier Power & Electric's secret and flagrant violation of the terms of its permit—hundreds of toxic cans of waste and hundreds of dead birds hidden in culverts—is just shocking. Shocking."

I lifted the envelope out of my pocket and found a copy of her will. "Clever woman, you are, but I've got a better use for this envelope. I hope you've carried it around a long time and your prints and stuff are all over it. Let's send it to Ken Douglas with a short message, a map to the culverts, and a few migrating warbler feathers, shall we? He's the right person to uncover this shocking story. He'll be good and angry about the birds. There'll be great press and you'll get the credit."

I raised my empty water bottle in a toast to her and patted the will in my pocket. *Bet you've hatched some surprises for me. Right, Lily? Well, good for you.*

I put both arms around Pock, squeezed him, and then wiped more mud from his muzzle. He squinted up at me from half-swollen eyes. "The vet clinic has beef flavor biscuits," I said. "After that we'll go see what young Chandler is up to at camp. If we're lucky, Kate will be there." I didn't mention Moz, but mentally I added him to my hopeful list.

I adjusted my headlamp and followed his waving tail into the trees.

# TWENTY-NINE

We didn't make it to the vet. After a few miles, I turned around and drove home to Antler Camp. I only trusted my regular vet. With his eyes half-shut but also half-open, Pock looked like he'd make it through another night without medical assistance. I planned on lying on the porch with him as I lifted wet towels to his face. In the morning I could be first in line when my dog's doctor opened her doors.

As I stood in the driveway listening to Kate's and Chan's laughter, camp light falling on Pock's panting body, I felt guilty and beyond exhausted at the same time. I had no energy for taking care of anyone else. I had just enough strength to lie down. "Maybe we'll sleep in the barn," I said. "After a swim. Just us. You good with that?" I asked.

"We're good with the swim," said Kate running to me and swinging me off the ground into a powerful hug. "But not the sleeping in the barn part. You don't have to speak or do anything. Go out on the dock, strip, and dive in. I'll leave you something to wear. Is that blood on your pants? That looks like dried blood."

I must have sagged in place, because she grabbed Pock's collar. "OK. We got Pock. We got it all. You go."

Chan stood outside our circle of light, not speaking but nodding his head helpfully.

There's nothing like diving off a dock into water that's blacker than night. There's no way to figure out where air ends and water starts until the lake rises up like a surprise slap in the face. Splashing water across the cove meant someone didn't want to share the lake. Hooves clattered on rocks and vegetation squeaked around the body of a departing moose. Deer were too dainty for careless noise.

When I hauled myself out on the dock, my filthy clothes had disappeared, but the scraped sides of my hips began a slow burn. I found a neat pile of clean underwear, sweatpants and a pajama top Kate had borrowed from her father years ago. A tall mug of ice cubes, lemon slices, and cold water sat next to a plate of banana bread. The bread tasted like trout, so I knew Kate had used the over-ripe fruit I'd stashed in the freezer.

She'd also left me a note, my headlamp, and a small booklet. I lay back in the pool of water that dripped off me and read her note. *Thrilled you and doggie are safe, safe, safe. Take all the time you need. No chat needed. Chan told me most everything.*

*Guess what we found in the shed? Poems your counselors wrote about you for summer camp events. They explained a lot about who you are—who you've always been. As far as I can tell, starting at age ten you got mostly crap for who you are. I don't want to be part of that pile-on. Even though you're my mother, I will work on appreciating who you are and how good you are at what you do. You do that for me, so I'll try harder.*

*And who was the counselor who wrote this so I can find her in some old folk's home and beat her up?*

I lifted the yellowed booklet to my light. Even before I read the first words, I was back in the decorated dining hall. Its walls were covered with balsam, green leaves, and tinsel. Candles softened the room into something magical. I remembered the dread I felt as I stood to read my special end-of-session poem—written especially for me to read about myself.

*I did well in tennis. Reached almost the top.*
*The same in jacks and ping pong.*
*But the place in which I really succeed,*
*Is talking all summer long.*

I switched off my headlamp, surprised the sound of the dining hall's laughter was as vivid as my memories of balsam and candle wax. What had I done when everyone laughed and clapped? I'd forced a smile and waved. Maybe that was my first be-silent-girl lesson.

Two loons swam near the dock, white checkerboard patterns on their feathers flickering in bits of light. Maybe they hoped Pock would come out so they could swim under his belly. I rolled over on my stomach. That was giving too much human stuff to the loons. Maybe I'd have to stop doing that and end my animal conversations as well.

All I could think about were hundreds of silent birds lying in a poisoned dump, rust drifting down on them, spiders and beetles tunneling through their beaten bodies. They should have been resting on Maine's islands before the next day's flight or safely south, fluffing up feathers before sleeping in thick jungle.

I was so tired I didn't think I could dress myself. I would have walked into camp and climbed into bed naked if I only had to face Kate. She'd make a grossed-out face, but she had to love me as I was. Right?

Staying in shadow and carrying my clean clothes, I tiptoed closer to camp, each step painful as the remaining layers of skin stretched and dried over my bruised hips. Kate was washing dishes at the sink, dropping into dance steps as she sang. Chan was in a porch rocking chair, balancing a bowl on one knee while he read *Charlotte's Web*.

"You gotta hear this," he said, but Kate kept singing and dancing.

I edged closer. Moz sat on the porch floor pressing something brown over my dog's eyes. Pock's face looked normal-sized and his tail twitched with pleasure. I sagged with relief and swiped tears away with my clean clothes.

Moz didn't look up as I stood in the dark, but he said, "Perhaps you should dress. There are children in here."

"Huh?" said Chan. "I'm dressed."

Moz pointed at the book and Chan bent his head to it. Even though cool water dripped down my neck, I felt a hot blush rush up past the drops until it reached the roots of my hair. I moved to put most of myself behind the nearest tree.

Chan waved the book in the air. "The spider talks. The pig talks. The rat and sheep talk. It's so cool."

"You already know much of the language of animals, Chandler, because you know how to listen." Moz stared into the darkness and my tree. "You know how to listen and you are good at imagining their lives because you feel they are important lives. You may be surrounded with people who cannot hear what you hear, but never mistake their ignorance for the truths you alone may hear. If you feel these animal lives, no matter where you go or what happens to you, I believe you will always be in good company."

I shook my head to clear my ears of water and the surprise of Moz's message. There was only one explanation. He knew about the birds and bats—knew how I'd handled each one multiple times to collect them, bury them, unbury them, and then leave them in contaminated culverts. He knew I'd turned each one into a weapon—knew that aiming their small bodies at Pacific Power & Energy cost me each time I left one on a filthy floor. He knew I was close to giving up.

324

He'd never confess to surveillance if that's what he'd done. How was I going to reconcile my freedom with his game warden need to know hidden things, even though his mystical side had just sent me an encouraging message. I didn't have the strength to sort out which man had spied on me. My legs shook so I wrapped my arms around the tree and leaned into it.

"What's out there?" Chan asked. "What are you looking at?"

"Nothing I am afraid of," Moz said, rising to open the screen door. "You should stay here and hold this poultice to Pock's eyes. I will take these extra ones with me. Please tell Kate that everything she cares about is in good hands if I do not return."


I don't remember much of the drive from Antler Camp to Moz's tent. I do remember sounds and smells. Because the edge of the tent platform hung over a small stream, I heard rippling water under my pillow. I heard more water drip into a basin as he wrung out bandages to place on my thighs. Each piece of cloth smelled like herb tea I'd never drink. His oddly high-pitched voice chanted something about his grandmother—his nokemes. Nokemes repeated over and over sounded like more water running over more rocks.

The bed creaked as he sat next to me and cut pieces of tape and gauze. When our eyes met, we smiled at each other but didn't talk. Something that smelled like Pock's fur when he was clean and dry and at his doggie best got pulled up over me. I heard a sharp, angry bark when all I could see out the tent door was stars.

"Fox," Moz said. "Fox is hunting."

When I woke up, I was alone with the stream. My phone

sat on top of my clothes and I called Kate.

"Where are you?" she asked.

"I'll call back after I get some more sleep. I'm good. I'm good."

When Ken Douglas knocked on the platform to announce his arrival, I pulled on the sweatpants and pajama top and stepped out with bare feet.

"You look dressed for success," laughed Ken. "Moz sends his regrets. He was due to be shipped out for undercover work today. He did try and delay it, but the Montana man we wanted arrived here last night, and his department is owed one of our top people no bad guy could recognize, so ..."

He smiled and shrugged. I shrugged and smiled back.


After loaning me one of his tan uniform shirts, Ken treated me to breakfast at the Road Kill Cantina, but he'd also invited a team of state police and wardens to quiz me and scribble notes. Francoise slapped bills in front of them, muttering, "Pas gratuit. Vous devez payer." As each reached for his wallet, she winked at me, shook her head, and put more croissants on my plate.

Kate carted me off to the Emergency Room for a tetanus shot. Doctors there sent me home with antibiotics and an order to rest. My wolf misadventures had already taught me that dirty rust in open wounds is a microbe invitation.

While I was busy at the hospital, Chan drove Pock to my vet, illegally of course. She wanted to know how my dog had been attacked by a hornets' nest and what the game warden had used to heal Pock's eyes. She thought that together they might make a fortune off it.

At camp, Kate settled me on a porch cot with extra pillows

and put Lily's will on my lap. "Found it in your bloody pants," she said. "And no, I didn't read it. Neither of us have."

I quickly glanced through its many pages, hoping my mouth wasn't gaping like quiz show contestants who can't believe where the spinning wheel has stopped. When I was done, even though parts of me ached, the rest of me felt whole and well and ready to go.

Kate invited Pock to sit on the cot with her, making my small bed even smaller. He was wet and smelled like the lake. I knew Chan was just out of sight, probably leaning on the sill to hear us. Everyone was ready.

I rustled pages. "Lily says she created this will a few weeks ago when she knew her disease was advancing rapidly, but it looks like her attorneys have included something she dictated only a couple of days ago. They're kind of like footnotes. I guess she wanted the last word. That fits. I'll try to simplify the legal stuff.

"She left the Texas ranch to her niece. Twenty-five percent of any profits from anything done on it—cattle or wind leases—will go to a new organization that protects Maine's north woods tourism landscapes and its high-elevation topography from industrial wind." I flipped a page and looked up. "Well, there was no way around using some of that formal language. I'm charged with creating this organization and forming its Board of Directors, but I must hand it off to an executive director I select within one year."

"Big, big money," whispered Kate. "Maybe millions."

I talked a bit louder. "She's created an educational trust fund for anyone I deem–it says deem—worthy of becoming a leader of the next generation's environmental warriors. It funds anything this person wants to learn at any institution, including all living expenses."

Kate called, "You got that Chan? You might as well come out here. I think you'll be my mother's deemed person." She winked at me. "The divorce takes care of my schooling. Mum made sure Dad would pay all that, so you're good to go on this."

Chan, his brown face unusually pale, stepped onto the porch and leaned up against its screens. Behind his glasses, his green eyes were wide.

"I am to appoint Ross Clunie of Clunie's North Woods Camps as board chairman of this new organization and help him arrange a study analyzing the effects of wind development on tourism that is—and I quote—'a million times better than Scots wearing skirts got done.'"

I cleared my throat. It was tight and dry. "She's prepaid my vet for Pock's lifetime, and I can pick up my new phone at her attorney's office. In Bangor, she's arranged for me to have any new Subaru I like. And new tires anytime I want."

Kate bounced up and down on the cot. "Oh, Mum. Oh, Mum. This changes everything. Everything!"

"She's hired a crew to come to the camp and replace all the windows and doors so no one can break in. There's a footnote where she admits to entering my shed and looking through my papers." I groaned. "Is there anyone who hasn't ripped off my work? There's no mention of your apartment, Kate, so I don't think Lily was your thief."

My daughter bent to rub Pock and hide her face behind swinging hair. "I've got news on that, but let's do it later. She leaves you no big trust fund?"

"No, but there's a footnote that sounds like her. It says, 'Cassandra Patton Conover does her best work poor when she can imagine what the average Mainer might lose when big corporations win. However, she needs a good car, a good

328

phone, and a safe house so she worries less and can be free to cause more trouble.'"

Tears blurred my eyes.

"There's more?" asked Kate.

I wiped my cheeks and grinned. "She gave a grant to the Bangor Weekly to fund half the cost of keeping my column on money and the outdoors." I had to chuckle. "Oh, good one, Lily. Well done. She says to get the money the paper has to publish an exposé about the woods delivering more non-timber jobs than timber ones."

Chan moved a chair next to the cot, sat, and lifted Pock onto his lap. "That true?" he asked.

"Yup," I said. "It didn't used to be, but it is now. I'll have to dig up sources people will believe."

Inhaling deep breaths. I reread the last page three times.

The young ones leaned toward me. "What?" they asked.

I blew out air I'd been holding in. "She's instructed her estate executors to make Premier Power & Energy a bid on the Eagle Ridge Wind Project's leases—all of them, the current project and land leased for expansion. If her lawyers are able to buy the leases, she wants them to also buy the land from Great Nations Forests and put the entire ridge, mountain, and surrounding lands into a conservation trust where development and tree harvesting are not allowed."

Kate whistled a long, soft whistle. Chan raised Pock's front paws and clapped them together, his smile growing wide. "I could be an old man by the time there's woods coming back, but I'll be out there. Lots to do."

I lowered the will and used my stern voice. "We can't breathe a word. No one should know the buyer's identity if anything does come up for sale. PP&E might be eager to unload the leases and skip out on further liabilities after it earned bad press for its construction failures. Great Nations Forests might sell if it's offered good value for lands it's already cut hard. Neither of these corporations will want anything to do with Lily Rose Baines Johnson—even if she's dead and gone. So, not a word. These sales, if they happen, will get done by attorneys who know how to manage stealth sales."

I looked out the window at familiar trees that leaned protectively toward my walls. I had a hard time cutting any one of them until I was sure the roof was at risk. "It doesn't seem to matter that barely a tiny chunk of Maine has any no-cut, wilderness lands. If this looks like a conservation purchase to lock up woods away from people who want to cut it down, the outcry could stop it. We should pretend we know nothing."

Kate ran fingers over her lips to mime zipping them and raised her other hand to zip Chan's as well. "I didn't even get to meet her," she said.

I stuffed another pillow under my legs so my hips could be happier. "I had no idea who Lily really was," I said. "I didn't. Not until that last day when she explained how the ranch funded her reasons for being here. Even at the end, her thoughts weren't on herself—only on work she wanted done if she couldn't do it."

Chan lifted his head. "I think she didn't want anyone to know how smart and powerful she was or know she had resources no one would ever think she had. Hiding what she had gave her space to do her thing."

Kate reached over to slap his back. "Smart, smart kid you are. We're going to find you a smart, smart school."

# THIRTY

Two days later I checked my emails and found Lily's angry hornets video. Somehow, she'd found time to send it before we looked for Teddy. Cringing, I could only watch half of what was clearly torture. I planned to give the footage to Lily's new Board of Directors. They could decide its future, but I wasn't going to tell anyone about her unhinged attack. The internal detection systems that first warned me about Lily were reliable, even if she'd broken through to affect me deeply.

I looked for news of Matt Pruitt or Ridge Dumais, but found only confirmation that the Eagle Ridge Wind Power Project was closed for the foreseeable future.

When he wasn't running with Pock, Chan worked on school papers he'd retrieved from his silent mansion, refused to talk about his mother and sisters, and spent hours on my ancient computer. After he was asleep, I tracked his online travels and found he'd posted a video of fish and animals dying in mud.

He must have edited the audio, increasing the sounds of thrashing fish and squeaking creatures and then fading them out so all I heard was buzzing flies. A red banner crawled across the bottom of the screen with contact information for Great Nations Forests and Premier Power and Energy. Chan added a voice-over asking viewers to share it out on the web. I looked and found millions of people all over the world watching Chan's world die.

I sent the mud video to the Department of Environmental Protection, proud to credit Chandler Perkins with reporting a serious erosion discharge to state waters. I was quite sure that any energy company looking for wind permits on steep slopes would find the video center stage at any public hearing.

I also found pictures Avian Haven had emailed to Chan. Even though the eagle was housed in a long, high cage that allowed him to fly, he liked to hang off the fence and bite it. It was a sad sight. I could only imagine how Chan felt because he wasn't sharing his computer travels or his feelings with me.

There was silence from Moz in Montana, but that wasn't unusual when he worked undercover. I printed out a small map of the state and circled the Flathead and Kootenai National Forests—remote places poachers might favor.

It was October before Kate reappeared with someone who couldn't take his eyes off her. Almost a younger version of Moz, he was lean with high cheek bones and night-black hair. "Mum," she said, "This is John Attean Francis. We're bringing you dinner."

John grabbed both of my hands and held them as he asked the location of my cooking fire. I looked at Kate. She pointed him toward the fire pit by the dock. "He's got moose steak and loads of tomatoes and potatoes from his dad's garden, and he's a great cook."

We settled into porch rocking chairs. "All this John activity is so we can talk, right?" I asked.

"So you can meet John, *and* we can talk."

"For starters," I said, "where have you been? I've left messages and not much comes back."

Tears came quickly. "I needed time to cool down," she said.

"Something I did?"

She shook her head, and it all came tumbling out. John was a forester for the Natural Resource Office of the Penobscot Nation, but he moonlighted for Moz's security company. Hired to watch over Kate without her knowing she had protection, he'd been busted after only two nights. "I mean no one's on the street in Orono after midnight on a weeknight," she said. "I told him he might as well park himself in the lobby of my apartment building and make himself comfortable. Then I invited him up for coffee."

"Then he got moved upstairs," I said.

She laughed her wind chime laugh. "Right. He got moved upstairs. Actually, he got tired of hearing me sob behind a closed door when he made his nightly rounds."

Leaning forward so our knees were touching, she shared a familiar story. Her university advisor had published a ground-breaking article about how Maine's carbon-storing trees would be a better climate change solution that any amount of wind power built in the state. "He stole my work, Mum, and an international forestry journal—a very prestigious journal—ate it up." Her lips quivered. "Under his name. Didn't even give me a chance to have a byline on it."

"How'd he get your notes and research? Didn't he have to ask you for them?"

It turned out that John Attean Francis was good at detective work whether it was tree theft on reservation lands or theft of tree research. "He traced the date of my break-in to my advisor appearing with research that wasn't on any university computer. It had to be easy to slip my apartment keys out of my coat and steal what he needed."

"I don't get it," I said. "Why would he do that?"

"Because he saw his chance to become famous. Last summer there was huge news about a Swiss study that proved how growing more trees could solve almost a quarter of the planet's warming crisis. Researchers said it could be the top climate change solution and the cheapest to execute. They used satellite imagery to map trees and forests around the globe and then did the math based on how each species ate up carbon."

So?" I asked.

Kate stopped rocking and bounced angrily in her chair. "Apparently, I jumped up and down in the office too much and he connected the dots. I'd found a way to show how trees outperformed wind—at least in Maine—and forests had the official global nod to save us from burning up. I think he wanted to be the first one to show how he could make the Swiss study's theories real on a real piece of ground. I set it up. I proved the Swiss study was the real deal. I just wasn't thinking fame and fortune. Silly me. Head in the trees."

She jumped up and stalked around the porch. "You know that thing about how bats die 'cause all the air somehow gets sucked out and they crash? Of course you do. Air's been sucked away from you for forever. It's men! They suck out all the air. They take it all! We can't even live. We just crash."

I thought the bat comparison was stretching it, but I understood her anger.

"John Attean looks like a man," I said. "A really nice one."

Kate dropped back into her chair and pointed angry fingers at me. "You know what I mean. Don't make me manage what I feel into something logical."

I rocked for a while, thinking how the official hearing transcript contained Kate's testimony. There might even be video. "Kate, may I use my get-even skills on thinking up a way to get you credit? In ways no one can connect back to you or to me?"

She lifted her shirt and wiped her eyes on it. "Only if you check everything with me first."

"Done," I said.

"OK, Mum. Go get 'em."

John appeared at the porch door with a platter of everything that was not cereal. Drawn by the smell of real food, Chan and Pock materialized from an endless run. We sat and ate steak and tomatoes and potatoes until the loons and stars came out.

A few days later, Ross Clunie dropped by to see Lily's will. He cut a big slab of banana bread. "I know her attorneys will send me an official copy, but I thought I owed you some Lily history." He lifted the bread to look under it. "This is interesting. How'd you get it to taste like trout? May I take a slice to my chef?"

I wrapped him up the rest of the loaf and tossed in all the remaining bananas in the freezer while I listened. A few decades ago, he'd found Lily at the end of his dirt road, sleeping in a school bus shelter he'd built for his kids. She asked if she was as far from Texas as she could get without a passport.

Lily was about the same age as his daughter, so he told her she'd gone far enough, took her home, bunked her with the rest of his girl children, and let her use his last name to finish school. "I'm sure she lied about her age, but to me she acted seventeen, and she was on the run from a boarding school she said was trying to—," he smiled, "Texify her with table setting classes and lectures on how to make men feel special."

"I'd bolt," I said.

Ross made her send a letter home saying she was fine, working on a farm, and very happy. No one came after her. Then he welcomed her into his family operation and she spent her teen years doing what his kids did: bailing boats and fixing motors, cutting wood, making blueberry muffins, shoveling roofs in winter, and preparing whatever guests caught or killed for dinner or transport.

When she left for college in California, everyone cried on the dock as Ross taxied her away in his floatplane and flew her to Portland Harbor. "She hugged me hard and told me she'd inherited enough money to be free, but not quite enough to fix all the broken stuff we had. Later I found the check she'd stuffed in my back pocket. It bought me a whole new dock system, but I'd have stuck with the rot just to have her back." He wiped his eyes. I had to wipe mine.

He showed me a letter confirming his appointment to the Maine Tourism Commission. Its other members wanted him to introduce legislation to redraw the map of potential wind sites—this time with the Tourism Commission at the table. I hoped Ross would call on his Scots kinsmen to march down state house corridors blaring bagpipes if he needed reinforcement.

When Ken came by to ask why I wasn't getting back to his wife about a dinner date, I just stared at him. "Right," he said. "Millie thinks *you think* she's gone and corrupted herself so she sent this letter. We'll expect you at six, earlier if you want an insider update on the bad boys in your life." He handed me an envelope and agreed to a tug-of-war with Pock that lasted until his truck.

Millie's letter wasn't really to me. It was a copy of a letter she'd sent to her fellow select board members and every news outlet in the state. It had an interesting heading where she'd superimposed a copy of a twenty-thousand-dollar PP&E check made out to her campaign. Over it in big black letters she'd scrawled, *VOID. I am not this stupid.*

Below the check, she'd listed the town's proposed Community Benefits Package, something every developer offered up every community to win permit approval. For fifteen years  and for supporting the Eagle Ridge expansion, Piscataquis County would get two hundred thousand a year, the town of Greenwood, forty thousand dollars a year, twenty thousand a year to the Maine Trout Coalition for stream restoration at the project site, and thirty thousand each year to

Conservation Maine to buy and protect land somewhere else in Maine.

Pennies compared to what they'd haul away as profit.

In italics at the bottom of the letter, she'd added red meat for reporters. "Five Greenwood board members enjoyed PP&E sponsored trips valued from five to eight thousand dollars. Destinations included guided Idaho fly fishing on the Snake River and guided elk hunting in Alberta, Canada."

I was at Ken and Millie's house by five o'clock, turning Pock loose in their fenced yard so their massive Newfoundland Rocky could roll him over and over until they both collapsed. I sat at their table and folded my hands. "Millie, I'm here because your note about free PP&E trips was snarky and brilliant. And I do want the bad boy news Ken's offering, and I love you both."

Millie poured wine into a flower vase larger than any glass she had. "Pace yourself," she said. "Took them long enough to get around to the story." She handed me a copy of the Portland Press Herald with two front page stories and one page folded over deep in the paper.

The larger headline featured an old photo of Ridge Dumais holding up a frozen lake trout during an ice fishing derby. "Tried to Bury Them Alive" was the lurid headline. Ridge had been charged with aggravated attempted murder for using a Premier Power & Energy bulldozer to try and smother two women he'd lured into a culvert on the company's wind power site. Since neither he nor his lawyer were talking, the article was short and thankfully did not include our names.

"Whom do I thank for keeping Lily's and my name out of this?" I asked. "I know the press hounds will find out eventually, but right now I'm so grateful."

They lifted glasses in a toast and I joined them. "I see. He may be in Montana, but he's kind of here, too."

The smaller front-page item, "Man Dismembers Hermit to Save Job," featured Matt Pruitt pleading guilty to a misdemeanor for abuse of a corpse. When the judge sentenced him to fifty days in jail, a two thousand dollar fine, and seventy-five days of community service, he wanted to know why Matt had violated someone's dignity in such a brutal manner. Matt explained that he'd done it to save his job and apologized to Alvin Erikson's family.

The story inside was about Erikson. Black lung disease caught up with him in a porta potty on a wind power site in Maine. While it took searchers days to find all his body parts, his black hands revealed both his identity and a lifetime spent in West Virginia's coal mines. Game wardens who found his tent site were amazed at all the clothing and household items he'd accumulated from camps as far away as Greenwood and Millinocket.

"That explains my underwear and stolen papers," I said.

Ken turned red. He had to know about my underwear and Alvin Erikson.

"Oh, let him off the hook, honey," Millie said. "We all know about the panties Moz found." She opened the oven door. I wanted to lean into the lasagna and garlic bread perfume. "Alvin seemed to be writing up the story of his life on the backside of what he took from your shed. Looks like he thought the best way to end his days was far away from coal country. He wrote that sleeping near wind turbines gave him peace he never had, and he wished his kids and neighbors' kids could come work in Maine."

She turned back to Ken. "Any way you could make the

insider news she's come for quick?" she asked. "Food's ready."

"Can do," Ken said. "Should we wait for eagle boy?"

I shook my head. "Haven't seen him today."

"Good, clever kid," Ken said. "Too bad he's so in love with that bird. I won't make that kind of mistake again. I'm too old to go head over heels with something that's not my wife." He cracked his knuckles and rearranged the salt and pepper shakers.

"First, at my request the Department of the Interior has a forensic team combing a dump site at PP&E's Eagle Ridge site. Yellow tape everywhere. Unfortunately, the person who apparently sent me feathers and a map to a bird slaughterhouse is no longer alive to give the feds essential details."

He stared at me for a full minute, but I just smiled serenely so he continued. "The birds were clearly killed by turbine activity. PP&E went to great lengths to hide that level of mortality as well as toxic waste that should have been properly handled. It is very likely that company will never get another license to operate another facility."

I continued to smile helpfully, but under the table my hiking boots wiggled in a happy dance. Ken pointed his finger at me, shook his head, and continued.

"When Matt Pruitt pleaded guilty without a trial, lots of details got buried—except to investigators who took his statement. Here goes. He found a dead man with no identification in one of the porta potties just after he found out that cement poured into many of the turbine pads was substandard."

He chuckled. "Not that it was a surprise if a tower leans so far over that blades fall off. Pruitt knew he had to close the site down and figure out a repair if he wanted to save his job. He thought if he created a crime scene and dispersed body parts in the woods, not only would anti-wind protestors get blamed for it, the project might get shut down long enough for him to figure out a fix without regulators descending on him."

Millie waved us into seats. "Well, it's the stuff of a movie, but it also makes some kind of grim sense."

Ken passed me garlic bread and I filled my mouth with it. There was no reason to share Matt's and my history.

"Ridge was a surprise to me," he said. "I've known the man for years. If it's any consolation, I don't think you made him snap, Patton. Lily and all she represented was an alien life form to him. She was coming for his job, just like he was sure previous environmental saviors had come for the jobs of his father and grandfather." He raised his hands. "I know. Nothing is that simple, but somehow it got very simple for Ridge."

I used wine to wash down a chunk of bread. "He had us trapped in the culvert. Why'd he stop?"

"Thank your life for technology, Ms. Conover, even if you have deep scorn for it." Ken handed me a plate so full of lasagna, noodles flopped over the side. "Ridge was angling to leave his forestry career and get hired as PP&E's head of security. He'd already installed cameras everywhere—motion sensitive units that pinged a warning when large life forms activated the recording feature."

Millie snorted. "That'd get old. Who wants to be pinged every time a moose walks by?"

"Not me," Ken said. "When the crime lab analyzed the video footage found in his ATV, they saw Chandler Perkins dashing all over the project site as he searched for his eagle. He must have set off multiple alarms on Ridge's watch that was too smart for its own good. We think Ridge left off burying you so he could shoo the boy offsite and collect his cameras in case they might incriminate him. He probably planned on returning to the dump, but the eagle, trained to Chan's red gloves, decided Ridge's red hat was also a good landing spot. Too bad everyone involved panicked, but there you have it."

My head hurt, and I didn't have an eagle on it. "OK, Ken," I said. "That's probably enough."

"Almost," said Ken. "At Ridge's house, investigators found footage of Matt moving the bulldozer into place over something lying in the parking lot. No real images of the deed, but the dozer's shovel is clearly moving up and down. If he needed it, Ridge was probably saving the footage to implicate Matt in another heavy machinery crime at the dump site."

Millie balled up a napkin and threw it at her husband. "I'll lose my appetite if you keep this up. Patton, please say the grace. Doesn't matter that you already ate bread. We like grateful stuff."

I was not a grace type of person, but one leaped onto my tongue. "I'm feeling grateful the Bible's Old Testament is so unforgiving." I bowed my head and said, "'For they have sown the wind, and they shall reap the whirlwind.'"

"Good Christ," said Millie, green glitter on her glasses' frames sparkling as she laughed. "Not expecting anything like that. Pass the salt."

After I got home that night, I untied the bent fender from the roof of my car and threw logs in the lake for Pock until all of Rocky's Newfoundland drool was washed from his coat. In the kitchen Chan's note was taped to a pile of dishes he'd washed. I immediately recognized it as both a goodbye and a thank you, and as I read it, I executed a few celebratory dance steps. Pock watched from a safe kitchen corner.

*My mom and sisters get home tonight. I'm driving to Boston to get them. Ha ha. Don't worry. You should know MY plan worked. My mom used divorce papers to get my father to his mosque. She signed them outside the separate women's prayer room where he made my sisters pray all the time. He was so happy to be free of her he didn't look at surroundings he wasn't used to. The American embassy was 4 blocks away from the back-door women have to use. Please visit us soon. Bring Pock, please.*

Apparently, a cubby to funnel someone toward something tantalizing worked in Saudi Arabia as well as it did in Maine. I looked carefully at an empty cereal box where black magic marker obliterated the health claims I liked to read. Chan had copied a line from *Charlotte's Web*.

"'You have been my friend,' replied Charlotte, 'That in itself is a tremendous thing.'"

I hugged the box.

# THIRTY-ONE

A s September slid toward October, I knew my ski area job would start as soon as the snow did. Anita Stockdale sent me a clipping describing an experimental program using dogs at wind sites to enhance "mortality research." She'd scrawled margin messages. "We were so ahead of the curve. Bring Pock to my spring job and I don't think they'll care who you are. Disease and gawd knows what (but we know) have lowered Maine's bat population by 97%. Lots to do. A."

One morning, along with bits of frost, I found a message from Moz in my mailbox. I bent and touched the frost with my lips just to make sure we'd finally moved on from heat. I carefully opened the envelope in case he'd sent me animal parts that would come out in pieces.

On the back of his return plane ticket from Montana he'd written an invitation. *In three days, please meet me at noon on Fifth St. John Pond. Bring Ken's spotting scope and bandages that will stick to dog hair. I will bring much more.*

I thumped around the camp complaining about cryptic communications until I realized I liked deciphering them. I decided I liked trying to decipher Moz, too, and I should stop whining about it.

Three days and three hours of pitted dirt roads later I was just south of the Canadian border headed toward a remote campsite on Fifth St John Pond. Fishing season was over, so the only vehicles I passed were speeding log trucks and bear hunters with dog cages crowded into their trucks. Above the pond at the top of the last hill where I knew I'd soon lose a signal, I filed my flight plans with Kate and surveyed the endless woods ahead of me. Real woods.

I sent a silent thank you to The Nature Conservancy and the state's public lands office for buying up territory whenever they could. This was where the real work of saving Maine for our grandkids was most visible. Then I drove to a rutted parking lot, rigged a sling for the spotting scope so it could hang off my back, shouldered my pack, and started hiking.

When I could smell a wet breeze off the water, I started looking for Moz. He sat on part of a crumbling dam where the pond trickled into the river below. Pock had leaped into his lap. I arrived at the dam wall just in time to see the flick of a knife blade and a brief spurt of blood.

"Bandages, please," Moz said.

I sat and handed him mounds of sticky webbing he wrapped around Pock's head. My dog looked like he'd been suited up to resist chemical warfare, but he seemed happy to explore blueberry bushes looking for fruit the birds had missed.

I was too speechless to ask about the ceremony I'd just witnessed. Moz reached for my hand and pressed a tiny, silver sliver into it. It was the best gift ever.

"Quite a while ago Chan texted me to pass along a message from your vet who had discovered that the swelling around Pock's head had relocated his microchip close to the surface of his skin," he said. "Ordinarily, it would be dangerous to extract an identification chip that has been inserted into an animal, but in this case the doctor was offering to remove it. Chan and I thought we might create a surprise for you."

I lifted the chip into the wind where it blew away toward Canada and put my hand over my heart, thumping it up and down slowly. "Best gift ever, Moz. Thank you. Cousin Liz will be so pleased. We had to use bolt cutters to free him, and he was so weak we had to carry him to her car. This is so good. Now our vet doesn't have to keep a secret about a patient that's been dognapped, and I won't worry about someone making a claim on him."

I gave his arm a playful punch. "What's next?"

His grin got so close that his lips touched my lips or maybe he was just leaning in to pull the spotting scope off my back.

"More gifts of freedom," he said, standing and reaching for a tripod leaning on the dam.

He attached the spotting scope, aimed its massive lens up the pond, and adjusted its focus. "Out there," he said, waving me over and bending my head to the eyepiece.

A bright blue canoe drifted slowly toward us. Even in a pond, the St John River's current always leaned downstream toward the ocean. In the stern of the canoe, Ken Douglas raised his paddle in the air. Chan and Teddy occupied the bow seat, the eagle fluttering his wings even though his eyes were covered.

When Moz raised his arm, Chan lifted the eagle and with his free hand, pulled the hood off the bird's head. The wind ruffled feathers up around his startled yellow eyes. The scope was so powerful I could see tears on Chan's cheek as he rubbed his face against his best friend's chest.

I stayed bent into the scope. "Do you think he'll go?"

Behind me, Moz was ready with an answer. "Tall white pines for nests and perching. Abundant fish and abundant wildlife. He may catch food or he may steal it from others. Two hundred thousand thirty acres of protected woods that will never see a wind turbine. Most likely female eagles are plentiful. Why wouldn't Teddy want to relocate here?"

I saw the bird lift off the glove. He rose up over the canoe, circling and circling. First higher, then lower to buzz Chan's head. "He's trying to make up his mind," I said. "What happens if he lands again?"

"Ken will add him to his department's educational program where he will help school children learn about birds of prey."

"Oh god, Teddy," I said. "Not to disparage the kids, but go for it. Get free."

Ducking into the bottom of the canoe, Chan slipped from sight. Teddy swooped low over the boat, maybe looking for him, maybe saying goodbye. His enormous wings filled my vision as he beat the air and then I lost him until I found his shadow skimming over the pond. I tilted the lens up and found him again when he was only a small speck in the sky. Then he was gone.

My chest hurt from leaning too long on the tripod or maybe it hurt from Chan's tears. "You missed it," I said to Moz. "I didn't share the scope."

He wrapped one arm around my shoulders. "Today is your day and Chandler's day. Ken and I are merely assisting."

I turned to see the boy and the biologist lift the canoe around the far side of the dam and paddle away down river. It was so shallow, they had to climb out and walk the boat around rocks, but they were paddling when they disappeared—paddling, laughing, and shouting commands at each other.

"Two wildlife professionals," Moz said. "One current and one who will be."

We sat on the dam wall until the sun sank and cool air dropped down on us. I tried to remember the endless heat so I could savor goose bumps crawling up my arms, but nothing mattered except the pond and the coming night. We watched late-season stoneflies hatch and skim over the water, ripples

DEADLY TURN

following each burst of insect life as fish rose to feed. We watched Pock drag sunken branches out of the water and chew them into pieces.

"Those bandages won't last," I said.

Moz tilted his head and looked at me. "What are you thinking?" he asked. "What is important right now?"

I couldn't help myself. "You're asking me instead of telling me what *you* think *you* know?"

I expected a scowl, but he threw his head back and laughed a rare, deep laugh. "Amazing as it seems," he said.

"I've got such a long list."

He lifted the hand I had nearest him and pulled it into his lap. "Proceed," he said.

I pointed at the bulging backpack leaned up against a birch tree. "I hope you're prepared and there's chocolate bars."

He waited.

"First, I want to know, Mr. Long Eyes, if with a spotting scope, you watched me frame Premier Power & Energy with birds they'd killed—birds I placed at their dump site."

His eyes, when he swung them toward me, were bright, shining, wet stones in a river eyes. Penobscot eyes. I knew the answer.

"Well then, I want the best dinner over a fire that you can concoct. I want to hear coyotes howl so near the tent Pock's and my hair will stand on end. I want to get up early and watch moose wade out to dip their heads under water to eat a plant breakfast. If there's sun tomorrow, even if it's a cold sun, I want to lie in it and do absolutely nothing while I listen to the pond and trees."

I dropped my voice to a whisper, not sure if I could get all the words out. "And ... and ... I want to do that with you."

Head down, Moz waited to see if I'd reached the end of my

list. He squeezed my hand and dropped it to go unpack a frying pan and whittle wood shavings into kindling. Behind us in the trees, Hermit Thrushes sang delicate notes that descended into faint bits of musical air. I imagined them fluffing their feathers in dark branches as they settled for the night.

I thought about what else I wanted. I wanted Kate to get credit for her work and her scummy advisor to get exposed. I wanted to meet Chan's family. I wanted the summer's loon babies to get better at flying so they'd leave my cove before it got too cold and too late. I wanted more dinners with Ken and Millie.

I wanted a long ski season so I could beef up my bank account. If she needed a partner, I wanted to help Cousin Liz rescue more starving dogs. I wanted Lily Rose Baines Johnson's lawyers to buy all of Eagle Ridge so it could recover and Chan could wander up and down helping the woods and its wild ones return. I wanted to join Ross Clunie on his porch and watch the dark night sky with his guests.

I could have kept going, but one thought kept crowding out all the others.

Perhaps I wanted to adjust my hibernation agenda. If I really was part of some misfit, underground grapevine that aimed people like Lily at me—people seeking misfit assistance to salvage one corner of a disappearing world—maybe I wouldn't fight the invitation quite so much. There'd be no money in it, but if I could work alongside chickadees, pine martens, moose, coyotes, wolves, and wild ones of all sizes and shapes and then rest on Antler Camp's porch, I'd feel rich anyway.

I watched my dog chew on the bone Moz had brought for him.

I also wanted two impossible things. I wanted Pock to live

forever, and I wanted the night at Fifth St. John Pond to never end.

# Author Notes

Avian Haven is a real place. It was incorporated as a nonprofit by Marc Payne and Diane Winn in 1999. Its team of volunteers and staff handle over 2,500 birds from more than 100 species. "We care for wild birds that are orphaned, sick, and/or injured, with a goal of releasing them back to their natural roles in the wild." (Please find them on line and donate!)

Wildlife Services is a federal agency under the U.S. Department of Agriculture. With our tax dollars, it specializes in killing wild animals that threaten agriculture—especially predators such as coyotes, wolves, and cougars. This slaughter contributes to a loss of biodiversity and ultimately Big Agriculture's takeover of wild places that are often our public lands. In 2018 it slaughtered 1.5 million native wild creatures and 1.1 million invasive animals — everything from armadillos to hawks to wolves. (Write your congress-person.)

Carbon and Forest Research: The (real) Swiss study I mention in the story explains that restoring degraded forests all over the world could capture about 205 billion tons of carbon. (Global carbon emissions in 2020 were around 10 billion tons per year.) Clearly, restoring forests and preventing inappropriate harvesting are powerful climate change prevention tools. (Does your state have a carbon-reducing, forest enhancement plan that prevents forest fragmentation and loss?)

New Wind Technologies: This novel is not intended to be anti-wind power. It does, however, speak against ill-considered, forest-fragmenting development where it does not belong. Newer technologies being developed may reduce the need to place turbines or transmission technology in remote, wild settings, but wildlife research and science must lead and drive this process, not arrive late in the permit and building process. Wind power or energy transmission projects should

351

SANDRA NEILY

not displace or degrade regional tourism. Accurate mapping of landscapes that support multi-billion-dollar tourism economies and protection for these assets is essential.

# Deadly Turn Book Club and Reader Questions

What do the story's first words (where the narrator "clutches a dying bat," wondering what they have in common) tell us about Cassandra Patton Conover?

Patton tells her dog that the bat is "family." What larger themes and messages are already appearing here?

Pock (the dog) is clearly an important character. How would you describe him if he were human?

How does Maine's northern forest landscape shape various characters' behaviors and motives?

Why does Patton try to avoid her past as a "famous green do-gooder." If you could drop your past and start over, what choices would you make?

The teenager Chan is eager, impulsive, and idealistic. Why do you think the author paired him (and his eagle) so closely with Patton?

The author says she's crafted Moz from "many different Maine Game Wardens" she's known. What did you know about game wardens before you read the novel? And afterwards?

How does Patton compare with other central female characters you've met? (It's OK to go all the way back to Little Women.) What seemed familiar about the forest and its wildlife? What surprised you about this landscape and its wildlife as you read the novel?

Before reading *Deadly Turn*, what did you know about wind power and its development and uses?

The author used energy experts to help her develop the story's "Trees Beat Turbines" messages. Has the novel expanded or changed your views in any way?

In the first *Mystery in Maine* (*Deadly Trespass*) and in this novel, Patton is not an eager law-breaker, but when she'd pushed, she's good at it. If you have a threatened special place, what might you do to protect it?

Lily Rose Baines Johnson is a pivotal character whose will creates practical gifts and opportunities for Patton, her daughter Kate, and Chan. If you could craft a will where someone also leaves you and the people you love practical gifts, would it look like?

WWW.AUTHORSANDRANEILY.COM

# Acknowledgements

Thank you to Dr. Julia Moukharskaya and the entire Harold Alfond Center for Cancer Care team. I wrote half of this novel in 2015 before I was diagnosed with an energetic form of breast cancer. That I could finish the novel, welcome my grandchildren, fish rivers with husband Bob and ski across the lake with Raven running beside me, is down to their expertise, care, optimism, and compassion. I am eternally grateful.

Thank you to all my readers who have pestered me, asking, "When's the next book coming out? I can't wait." On days when I didn't think it would, one of you would pop up to ask that and send me back to the keyboard with renewed hope and energy.

Special appreciation to Tom Holbrook of the RiverRun Bookstore and Piscataqua Press and also his insightful co-editor, Kellsey. They are both brilliant "fixers" of mangled punctuation and phrasing, but also respectful partners of an author's intent, voice, and unique characters.

Thank you to my original editing and feedback team; they gave full honesty and support at the same time. Equipped with a background as a north woods sporting camp owner, then as an editor many state publications, and always a lifelong friend, Kyle McCaskill caught the grammar, the spelling, and anything that didn't make 'woods sense.' Or any kind of sense.

Linda Koski (retired canoe outfitter), Gretchen Tobin (graduate school friend, consultant to multinational corporations, accomplished outdoors woman), and Dr. Sally Stockwell (long-time Maine Audubon wildlife biologist, friend, ski partner) encouraged me to rethink anything that felt out of character, slowed the narrative, or felt 'off' about Patton's relationship with the natural world. Thank you all!

SANDRA NEILY

A special thank you to Michael Good (Down East Nature Tours in Bar Harbor, Maine). He proofed the manuscript for bird behavior and habitat accuracy. Michael knows so well the carnage turbines cause in our Maine flyways; the loss causes him great personal pain.

I appreciated the help of several carbon sequestration experts who also wanted to remain anonymous to create professional distance for the organizations they serve. Their feedback allowed me to write accurate accounts of how "trees might beat turbines."

Endless thanks to sister Liz for her demented cards, supportive calls, and treats that allowed me massages just when I needed support. (In the novel, cousin Liz is a 'nod' to her.)

I am indebted to two books that share intimate relationships with birds of prey: *H is for Hawk* by Helen Macdonald and *Peregrine Spring, A Master Falconers Extraordinary Life with Birds of Prey* by Nancy Cowan.

This acknowledgment might have the same kind of "snark" as my narrator, Patton. Without the Forces of Darkness relentless assault on our remaining forests, I might not have spent hours indoors, typing. FOD's, you know who you are. Not enough people know what you do. That's why I write.

And finally. How could I have managed any of this: the lows of cancer treatment, the effort to restart and rewrite the rest of a suspended novel, and the loss of our two loved dogs when we needed them most—without the steadfast, never wavering love and kindness of my husband Bob. Bob who never stopped believing in me and what is not just a book, but a mission. (And Bob, who also gets apoplectic whenever we drive by an endless, as-far-as-the-eye-can-see stump field that used to be the Maine woods.) I even dearly love your grumbling. Thank You!

Made in the USA
Las Vegas, NV
12 December 2024

13911023R00215